THE GIRL ON THE RED CARPET

Phil Mews

Hafen Publishing

For Martin,
The love of my life

In loving memory of
Diane Brown
(1972 – 2023)
Your warmth, kindness and friendship brought us
home. Thank you
X

ALSO BY PHIL MEWS

Orphan Boys

CHAPTER 1

The Phone Call

I had all the makings of a perfect Sunday evening right there in front of me. The flat to myself, a hot bath mixed with copious amounts of Dead Sea bath salts and lavender oil, a glass of red wine and the book that I'd barely been able to put down all weekend. It was a blissful close to two days of peace and quiet. Having emerged from my relaxing soak and blown out the tea lights that I had diligently placed along the windowsill, I wrapped my wet hair in a clean white fluffy towel and completed the "spa" look by slipping into a sumptuous toweling robe. It was a Christmas gift from my parents the previous year after I had successfully steered my mother away from the dressing gown that she had originally intended to buy me. Having seen the hideous item that she had had her eye on, it came as no surprise that she had already picked up an identical one for Granny. I remember thinking that this was what my life had amounted to, getting the same dressing gown as my grandmother.

"Hardly living the dream, Lizzie," I said to

myself. After a minute, I unwrapped the towel around my head and dried the excess water from my hair, wiping the steam off the large wall-mounted mirror, I took a moment for a little self-assessment. At thirty-one years old, I wasn't looking too bad. I had a slim figure although reluctant to show it off so I often found myself buying a size twelve or fourteen in the clothes shops settling for a looser fit that provided comfort and drew less attention to me. My shoulder-length chestnut hair had a natural look despite the slightly greying roots which were now over two centimetres long and as I brushed it back off my face, I promised myself to book myself in to get my colour done once pay day had arrived and my dwindling bank account had been replenished. I didn't really have any hang-ups about my looks and I wasn't like some girls who spent two hours every morning perfecting their make-up and hair. I was more of a 'scrape it back and clip it' girl where my locks were concerned and make-up was always just the bare minimum, often applied in a hurry. I always seemed to prioritise everything else rather than allow myself enough time to get ready but I'd been the same all my adult life and that was unlikely to change now.

I took my empty wine glass through to the kitchen, pausing for a moment to look at my mobile that was plugged in on the wooden kitchen worktop. I opened the Facebook app and saw that my post with the photo of the hot bath, glass of wine and book illustrating the calm relaxing Sunday night I was having at home had now received twenty-three 'likes'. I felt unashamedly smug as I topped up my glass of wine. Once I was in my bedroom I laid back on my bed, thankful that I had taken the time to wash the bedlinen that morning and remake the bed with fresh white sheets that smelled of M&S fabric softener. My mother would be proud as my room normally resembled a teenager's bedroom after a birthday sleepover and it usually didn't smell much better.

"Perfect," I said, as I picked up the book. Only fifty pages left of the Trisha Ashley novel that I'd only bought yesterday morning from the bookshop across the street on Chiswick High Road. I'd lived here in this leafy west London suburb for the past twelve months renting a small two bedroom flat above a bookmakers. Although the flat wasn't much to look at with its woodchip wallpaper and swirly carpets, my flatmate James and I had made it homely and the place had a relaxing shabby chic feel to it, with the emphasis very much on the shabby rather than the chic. My peace was shattered by the ringtone of my phone in the kitchen. I'd toyed earlier with switching it off but that would cause me untold anxiety. Apart from being on flights, I couldn't remember the last time that I'd turned off my phone. I couldn't even turn it off in the cinema.

Sod it. Nobody could be calling with anything important on a Sunday evening. I had planned to call Dad as I did every Sunday night but I'd decided to wait until Monday evening instead and texted him to let him know. It would most likely be my mother and I really didn't want the ambience of my perfect evening ruined. Even if I did want to talk to her, I didn't have the energy, so relaxed was I right now. I waited for the phone to stop ringing. If it was important, they would leave a voicemail and as I waited for the "ping" that told me that I had received a message, the phone started ringing again. Whoever it was, they were persistent. The phone stopped again but just as I reached over to pick it up, it started ringing a third time and the name flashed up on the screen. Serena Goldman. What on earth was my boss doing calling me on a Sunday evening?

"Serena, hi," I said, catching sight of my own forced smile in the reflection in the kitchen window.

"Oh Lizzie, hi. Listen, I'll get straight to the point," said Serena.

"Why not? You usually do," I muttered under my breath, perhaps a little too loudly.

"Sorry? I didn't hear you Lizzie, bad signal."

"Nothing. What can I do for you Serena?"

"I need you to work the night shift tonight, Lizzie. We're a man down and I need you to do tomorrow morning's show," she said, emphasising the urgency.

I had been working as a producer for the last six months on *UK Today* which was, until a year ago, the country's highest rating breakfast TV show. Serena Goldman was the show's executive producer and co-owner of Sabre Productions, the production company that made the show for the channel.

"Is there nobody else that can do it? It's not really convenient. I had planned to..." I said, my heart sinking as Serena interrupted.

"I know it's not ideal Lizzie, but poor Bianca isn't well and she said that she had seen on your Facebook status that you were planning an early night. It wouldn't hurt you to take one for the team now, would it?"

"Yes, I'll do it," I replied resignedly.

"Thank you darling. I've already taken the liberty of asking production to order a cab for you. It will be outside your flat in five minutes."

"Of course, you did Serena," I muttered sarcastically, aware that she now was no longer listening to me.

I pressed the red button on the screen to end the call but Serena had already hung up. Sitting on the bed I glanced over at the glass of red wine and paperback that sat on the bedside table, almost pleading with me for my attention.

"Bugger," I cursed. Bloody Facebook. I'd forgotten that Bianca had sent me a friend request on my first day in the office and always wary of the need to play the game, I accepted the invitation. Working in television was like no other industry. The lines between professional colleagues and personal friendships would always be blurred and it was expected, in this age of social media, that you acquired as many friends in the industry as possible. After all, it was the best way to get more work and as a freelancer on short-term contracts in London, it paid to have all the help that you could get.

I left the wine on the kitchen bench with a note for James, my flatmate, telling him I had been called into work. He was still out and hadn't been home since yesterday evening which wasn't out of the ordinary. I had long since ceased to second guess his whereabouts when he didn't return home after a night out. He's probably with some guy he met in a club last night. I dressed hurriedly and did my best to dry my hair that was still damp from the bath. There was no time to style it, so I brushed the damp tresses quickly and pulled them back with an elastic hair band. Grabbing my coat and bag, I closed the flat door behind me and hurried down the communal staircase with its musty smell and grubby mustard-coloured carpet. The taxi was waiting outside on the road and as I climbed in, I looked back at the betting shop that sat below our flat, its windows reflecting my image as I steeled myself for an all-nighter in the office. This wasn't how I had planned to end my quiet weekend.

By 3:30am in the almost empty production office that faced onto the South Bank of the River Thames, I looked up from my computer monitor, my head heavy with having been awake all night. It normally wasn't a problem for me as I always factored in some sleep before doing a night shift but of course, thanks to Bianca, I had found myself here under duress. I stretched my arms out and yawned whilst considering pouring myself another coffee from the Nespresso machine in the office kitchen. The programme's script didn't actually need too much doing to it as the presenters normally made most of it up as they went along. I looked across at the large whiteboard on the wall that listed the presenters for each day. Alex and Lydia. It could be worse I thought. Lydia Black had been presenting the show for years and was a pro who got on with the job with the minimum of drama. Sadly, the same could not be said for her co-presenter.

Alex Garner had been a stalwart of British daytime telly in the eighties and nineties, but his career path had taken several downward turns to the point where he had ended up doing corporate videos and the occasional presenting gig on a cable channel that was so far down the list it sat somewhere between the music channels and the soft porn. Having eluded the shopping channels for as long as his bank manager would allow, Alex's fortunes took a turn for the better when he was booked for Britain's latest hit reality TV show. The producers had told Alex to be himself. Alex's agent, who knew him better than anyone, told him to be anything but himself. The real Alex was an over-confident, greedy and misogynistic oaf with a whole plateful of chips on his shoulder. He had been bitter for many years blaming his career failures on everyone but himself. He could never bring himself to acknowledge the atrocious reputation that he had created for himself and having treated everyone in his path like something he had scraped off his shoe, he had come to reap the rewards of his bad behaviour. He had been notoriously vile towards the runners in particular. These poor young individuals who were starting out in the TV industry and whose job it was to fetch and carry for every member of the production team, especially the presenters, had had to put up with a lot from Alex back in the day. What Alex had failed to realise was that the production runner whose life he made a misery, six years down the line would be the producer choosing a new presenter for a prime time show on one of Britain's premier channels. Alex had made plenty of enemies on his way to the top and he soon found he had very few friends on the way down. It had been almost a year since he had done the reality show and was back to sitting in front of the nation's viewers as they ate their breakfast. Lydia Black, on the other hand, was far more relaxed. She had been popular with the viewers for many years but at forty-nine, she was all too aware of the continuing trend of current affairs and magazine programmes being presented by a silver-haired older man with a much younger glamourous female co-presenter. She had accepted the possibility that her time left on the show could well be limited.

At my desk, I was a million miles away and came back to my senses with a thud. On the table next to my desk Stuey, the production runner had dropped a large bundle of newspapers.

"There you go Lizzie. Isn't Bianca supposed to be doing today's show?"

"Don't ask." I rolled my eyes dramatically, my way of letting Stuey know that I was on his side. He laughed as he knew Bianca well enough to know that she had pulled a sickie. Bianca was only ever ill on a Monday morning.

"I'll just split the papers and give you yours, the rest will need to go into the dressing rooms, the Green Room and on the set. Looks like it's a slow news day."

"Thanks Stuey."

He smiled sympathetically at me, "Can I get you a coffee or anything?"

"I'm fine cheers. I've had enough caffeine to keep an entire battalion awake. Anyway, you'd better get the Green Room set up before any celebs arrive."

Although we wouldn't be on-air for at least a couple of hours yet, experience had taught us to get everything ready down at the studio nice and early. Most celebrity guests were ok and demanded very little but if we had a group such as a popular boy band in the studio, they would inevitably arrive with a huge entourage of management, record company people and their own hair and make-up team. There were no extra runners to help out in these situations and it would be down to Stuey to ensure that they all had breakfast. If it was simply a case of administering tea, coffee, toast and cereal it would have been ok but it was never like that. De-caff soya lattes, quinoa porridge and egg-white omelettes would often be demanded. Only last week they had had the latest British teen heartthrob singing sensation on the show who, when he let his guard down, dropped his urban street twang and reverted back to his Buckinghamshire private school accent. This morning there were no singers or bands as guests on the show thankfully.

I ploughed on going through the papers, picking out stories for the presenters to discuss. As the entertainment and sports team started to trickle in for the early shift, the office soon filled with chattering voices. I looked around for Stuey as I needed him to photocopy some scripts for me while I typed up the news stories but he was nowhere to be found. He was probably setting up the Green Room and the dressing rooms.

"Why don't they get someone in to help him?" I asked myself.

I walked over to the photocopier and looked out of the window. It was still dark. A vintage-cream coloured little van pulled up outside the studio and the driver was being questioned by security. The sign on the van read "The Bearded Bakers" and a handsome guy with a beard and a man-bun leaned out of the window to sign the visitor ledger. I knew what this was. Serena's latest obsession was with all things Shoreditch and hipster. She spent ridiculous amounts of money on having croissants and pastries delivered by these guys every morning only for them to sit on the coffee table on set in the studio. By the time that the show came off-air at nine, the once tasty and moist pastries were as dry as a bone having sat under the studio lights for three hours. If only our executive producer could put in as much effort with the actual content of the show as she did with the pastries, then perhaps our dwindling ratings might improve.

I grabbed the running orders and scripts from

the photocopier and went down to the studio floor. The lights were on and there were already a couple of technicians on stepladders fiddling about with the studio lights when a loud booming voice suddenly filled the room.

"Good morning you lovely lot! How are we all this morning?" The voice was followed by a rotund man with a beaming smile wearing an ankle length waxed coat which looked as if it had a built-in cape draping across the shoulders. Michael De Vere, our studio director, was a huge personality and despite having the voice of a Shakespeare stage actor, he was a warm and generous soul. I was always surprised that for such a camp loud gay man, he gelled brilliantly with the gruff, straight and occasionally grumpy studio technicians.

"Morning Lizzie my darling! Got some lovely D-listers in for us today?" he joked as he air-kissed both of my cheeks.

"Just the usual, an actress from *City Police,* the police drama that never seems to end, an MP and Jake doing the celeb news."

"Oh well, never mind. As they say, you can't polish a turd but you can roll it in glitter. The only thing is, with Alex presenting this, there's never enough glitter available when you need it," he joked mischievously and with that he swept up the metal stairs that led to the gallery control room.

Out through the studio door, I moved to the backstage area where the guests had started to arrive in the Green Room and Stuey was running around like a headless chicken looking stressed.

"You ok Stu?" I asked.

"How the fuck am I supposed to do scrambled egg whites on toasted rye bread at this time in the fucking morning?" All I have is a toaster, two white loaves and a jar of effing marmite," he said exasperatedly.

"That's celebs for you Stuey," I replied sympathetically.

"Oh, it's not for the celebs, it's for...."

"Oh Stuey," said Serena who had just appeared behind him. "If you could get me a double skinny macchiato as well that would be lovely."

Stuey forced a smile and nodded. Serena Goldman was a dark-haired woman of diminutive stature in her early forties and visually she was somewhat unremarkable. Her slightly scruffy casual appearance was not to be judged lightly because even though she looked as if she had just thrown on some clothes from her bedroom floor, the sum total cost of her outfit would exceed an entire week's salary for me.

I rolled my eyes at Serena's breakfast demands from Stuey, perhaps too obviously but I couldn't help it. That was just typical of our executive producer. The team could be running around trying to get the show on-air and she would swan in and order breakfast and some poncey coffee knowing fine well that the only tools that he had to work with were a kettle, cafetiere and a toaster. With the studio crew briefed and the gallery crew finished their meeting, we had fifteen minutes until we went on-air. I sat myself in the producer's seat in the gallery and tested the talkback which enabled us producers in the gallery to talk directly to the presenters. Alex was now on the studio floor flicking through the running order and swearing to himself, forgetting yet again that he was wearing a radio mic and that all of us in the gallery could hear every word that he was saying.

I felt my phone vibrate in the pocket of my jeans. At ten to six, who could be phoning at this time? I pulled out the phone as it continued to vibrate.

"Mum" was all that was on the call display. "Christ!" I muttered.

That's all I needed right now. After more than thirty years on this earth, one thing that I knew for sure was that there was no such thing as a brief conversation where my mother Joyce was concerned. I rejected the call. Mum would have to wait. The last thing that I wanted was to talk to her before going on-air and allow myself to become distracted. Leaning over my computer in the gallery, I clicked the mouse over the screen to check through the first fifteen minutes of the script once more.

Ten minutes until we were on-air. The phone vibrated again. I glanced across at it. It was my mother, again. It will be a dead celebrity. She was accustomed to calling and texting me at all hours as the voice of doom, namely announcing another celebrity death. I remember when I was younger and she woke me up at four in the morning on a Sunday to tell me that Princess Diana had been seriously injured in a car crash in Paris. I recall that I wasn't really interested and immediately went back to sleep only to be awoken at fifteen-minute intervals by her giving me updates straight from the BBC News channel. When Diana's death was finally announced by Martin Lewis an hour later, Mum didn't come back upstairs. She let out a piercing scream from the living room which was then followed by an hour of wailing that had the neighbours calling round to see if she was ok.

I checked the news feed coming through to the gallery expecting to see the news of another celebrity death but there was none. Why else would she be ringing?

"Five minutes to air," the director's PA called. My phone vibrated for a third time. What could she be after? I grabbed my talkback headset and radioed through to Sally the Researcher who was down in the Green Room.

"Everything ok Sal?"

"Yeah, I think so. That actress from *City Police* is a nightmare though. I didn't realise that she's big pals with Serena. They've had poor Stuey run ragged with their demands since they arrived," she whispered. "She's awfully high and mighty for someone who is best known for advertising instant coffee."

"Ahh so that's what she's doing in this early. I wondered what was going on. Serena normally doesn't show her face until after eight," I replied. "Buzz me if you need me but I'm staying up here this morning."

Looking across to the row of seats in the gallery in front of me, I could see John the director was still gossiping through the talkback with our presenter Lydia who was in place on the sofa on the studio floor.

"Four minutes to air," the PA shouted.

My phone vibrated again and *"Mum"* flashed up on the screen once more, the fourth time in the last quarter of an hour. It was no good I thought, I was going to have to answer it.

"Mum, I can't talk, we're about to go on-air in a minute. What's going…"

I stopped talking. All I could hear was crying.

"Mum, what's wrong? Are you crying?"

"Oh Lizzie, I've been trying to call you. Where are you?"

"I'm at work, I told you. What's happened? I know the Queen hasn't died cos we'd be the first to know here."

"Oh Lizzie, it's your father…." her voice trailed off.

"Dad? What's wrong with him? I spoke to him last week. He was driving down to Leeds Bradford Airport to meet Clive his boss yesterday for some conference in Lisbon. He'll be on the flight right now so I thought I'd call him tonight."

"He's dead Lizzie," Mum said, unable to hold back the devastating news any longer.

"Two minutes to air," the PA announced.

I felt sick. Had I misheard her?

"Sorry Mum, for a second there I thought you said that…"

"Yes, your father is dead."

I hadn't heard incorrectly. My stomach twisted into a knot. I could see the people in front of me taking their seats as we were about to go on-air.

"Lizzie?" she repeated down the line. As much as I tried, I found myself unable to speak.

"Lizzie? Lizzie!" I suddenly snapped to my senses aware that Alex the presenter was looking directly at the camera and shouting my name.

"Lizzie, am I leading the interview with the Shadow Culture Secretary?" said Alex.

"Lizzie? Did you hear what I said about your father? Lizzie? Speak to me darling!" said Mum, raising her voice .

My stomach knotted even more tightly and in one sudden movement, it unraveled itself and I was sick in the bin next to my feet.

"Counting down to air. Ten, nine, eight…."

"I'll do the bloody interview then shall I?" Alex shouted petulantly.

"Lizzie! Did you hear what I said? Your poor father!"

It was as if I was suddenly aware that I hadn't responded to my mother yet. "Mum, I can't talk. I'll call you back in five."

I was shell-shocked. Serena stormed into the gallery and made a beeline for me, her face looking far from happy.

"Lizzie, I'm not happy about the set this morning. Can you see what the problem is?"

I lifted my head up from the wastepaper bin in which I had just been sick. I looked at Serena and then glanced across at the bank of screens at the front of the gallery. The set looked fine. What was she on about?

"Do I need to spell it out Lizzie? Croissants. There's no croissants on set. It's a fucking breakfast show and there's no fucking croissants on set. That runner is your responsibility and he's forgotten to put out the pastries on the studio floor. It's all in the detail Lizzie. How can you expect to make it in this business if you can't master the basics and learn about attention to detail?"

Serena was ranting now whilst clutching her takeaway coffee cup. I had stopped listening. Of course, Serena hadn't been privy to the telephone call that I had just received but we had literally just gone on-air. My vision blurred a little as I sat back in the chair. I could still hear Serena's voice ranting in the background but I had now given up listening to her. Whatever my mind wanted to do, my body had taken over. I screwed my eyes tightly shut as if this was some awful dream but I could still hear the muffled sound. I felt something sharp in my arm. Opening my eyes, I could see that Serena was now poking me with one of her manicured talons. My hearing returned and suddenly I was back in the room. The director was trying to keep one eye on the monitors whilst turning back to see what was going on between myself and Serena.

Serena was still talking. "Lizzie if you think that you are going to climb the ladder in my company you've got another thing coming." She took another breath and was about to continue her tirade when I suddenly jumped out of my seat.

"Fuck off Serena!"

Now everyone in the gallery had turned to face me. One or two people were literally open-mouthed.

"Serena, you march in here and start spouting about the fucking croissants and not realising that the only reason that there are no fucking pastries on that set is because you've had poor Stuey running around after you and your talentless actress friend as if he is some Notting Hill waiter. The world isn't going to cave in just because your stupid fucking hipster pastries aren't on telly. That's not going to get this steaming turd of a show any more viewers. Take your fucking pastries and stick them up your arse and if you don't know where that is, ask Bianca seeing as though she spends most days kissing it."

Serena stood open mouthed. The rest of the gallery didn't know where to put themselves. John couldn't help smiling as he turned back to the screens and spoke to the presenters on the talkback system.

I took a deep breath and said calmly to Sally on the talkback radio.

"Sally can you cover the rest of the show up here for me, I need to go home. Thanks."

"You can't go home. We've only just gone on-air."

Serena said quietly, shaking with rage.

"Serena, let me tell you something. I'm going home, now. I've just been told that my father is dead and I'm going home to see my family."

"Oh well, I'm sorry I didn't think…"

I simply glared at her and removed my headset.

"Well, if you must go…" Serena was now aware that almost everyone in the gallery was still staring at her.

"Yes Serena, I must go, now," I replied forcefully.

"If you could mention the croissants to Stuey on your way down…" she said before realising from the look on my face that she had again crossed a line. "Don't worry about the croissants," she added.

"I won't. You can be assured of that." I said coldly.

We were now into the first commercial break. John, the director jumped out of his seat and wrapped his arms around me.

"So sorry darling. You go, I'll get one of the team to get a car for you to take you home."

"Thanks," I said. I didn't cry. I'm not sure why but the tears didn't come. Maybe I was numb. This was all too much, I had to get out of here straight away and get some air.

Five minutes later, I sat on the low wall outside the studio entrance. I'd asked Geordie the security guard for a cigarette. I've never been a proper smoker but I'd seen people in films smoke when times were tough and perhaps I thought that it would help. I didn't give it much thought, nor anything else for that matter. It was like some surreal dream where I was watching myself from outside my body. Twelve hours ago, I'd been lying in the bath without any cares in the world and now here I was living some sort of nightmare.

Ten minutes later I was in the back of a people carrier as it made its way along the Albert embankment towards Chiswick. The Houses of Parliament and Big Ben were still illuminated across the river as the first stream of commuters headed into the city to face the dark gloomy Monday morning. As they prepared themselves to start a new week, it dawned on me in the back of the car that my life had now changed forever.

CHAPTER 2

Heading Home

During the ride home, I called Mum back and managed to get a little more information from her regarding the circumstances of my father's sudden death. She wasn't particularly coherent and the details were still sketchy. She said that Dad had been found in his hotel room earlier this morning but there wasn't much more to go on at this stage. I did my best to reassure her and told her that as soon as I had packed some clothes, I'd get the first train out of King's Cross up north to Durham. Once the taxi had dropped me off outside my flat in Chiswick, I slowly climbed the stairs, my legs feeling almost as exhausted as my brain. Despite feeling as if I was in a trance, I finally managed to get the key into the door on the third attempt. In the kitchen, there were now two empty wine glasses alongside the note that I had left for James last night and the empty bottle in the small recycling bin on the floor. In my bedroom, I lifted my suitcase down from the top of the wardrobe and throwing it on the bed, a small puff of dust bounced up in my face in the process. Wrapped around the handle was a paper luggage tag with the letters LHR printed on in bold. My holiday to Thailand was the last time that I had been abroad earlier the previous year. I had gone away with my former flatmates Rhona and Moira before they had moved out and gone their separate ways and I had found this flat with my gay best friend James.

I removed a number of random items of clothes from the wardrobe and threw them into the open case without any thought to folding them or whether they would be suitable for the trip home. Looking at the shiny red party dress in amongst them, I remembered why I was packing but couldn't be bothered removing it. I sat down on the bed pushing the case along to give me more room.

"I can't do this," I shouted out loud in disbelief. "This can't be happening."

I looked across at my disorganized bookcase and sitting on top was a framed photo of me on the finish line of the Great North Run a few years ago. Sweating and grinning with my medal around my neck, I was flanked on either side by my proud parents, smiles beaming out at the camera. Staring at the picture, my eyes rested on the image of Dad's smiling face. I was conscious that I still hadn't cried since my mother's phone call earlier this morning. Not a tear. Not wanting to feel emotionally inept, I moaned in an effort to bring on the tears, desperate for the release but nothing came. A quiet knock on the bedroom door was followed by the appearance of James, my flatmate, looking deeply concerned.

At six foot four with perfectly coiffed dark hair and a neatly trimmed beard, James cast a striking figure. He was wearing a pair of rugby shorts and nothing else which was pretty much his normal attire at home. I regularly teased him about it especially considering the last time James was anywhere near a rugby ball was when he was at school. James was more into rugby players than rugby balls.

"What's happened Hun?" he asked, thinking that maybe something had occurred at work. He moved towards me and shifted the suitcase right over to the far side of the bed against the wall before sitting down and stretching a comforting arm across my shoulders.

"It's my Dad, he's dead." I had no energy to offer anything more than that.

"When? What's happened?" he said, trying to make sense of the situation. I'm sure the fact that I wasn't crying had thrown him off balance a little.

"A hotel at Leeds Bradford Airport. Last night, I think. I don't know. Michael is on his way down there now with Elaine to speak with the police."

James had met my brother and his wife on two occasions in the past, most recently when he had accompanied me to my cousin's wedding as my 'plus one'.

"Are you going home just now?" he asked, looking back over at the suitcase. I nodded. "I'll come with you. I'll just throw some stuff in a bag and make a phone call."

"No, you have to go to work. It's past eight and...."

I stopped mid-sentence as I saw the figure of a tall blonde man appear at the bedroom door wearing nothing but a pair of white briefs with the word Aussiebum printed across the waist band.

"Hi," said the stranger.

"Oh, Lizzie this is... Sven?" James interjected hurriedly, trying to remember the guy's name.

"Anders," the stranger corrected him.

"Yes... Anders," James said in agreement, with only the smallest trace of embarrassment. "We met at the Vauxhall Tavern last night and it was easier for Anders to come back here. I'm afraid we polished off your red wine."

"That's fine, I wasn't going to drink it at work. I'm sorry to have disturbed you both."

There was a moment's silence where none of us were quite sure what to say next.

"Where do you live Anders?" I asked, not wanting

to discuss my dad in front of a complete stranger.

"Brixton," the blonde replied.

"Well, it's good job you came all the way over to Chiswick then. Brixton's a long way from Vauxhall," I said jokingly, knowing that they're almost bordering neighbourhoods in South London. Aware that I was wiping away non-existent tears and looking a wreck, I changed the subject as I had to get a move on.

"I need to catch a train," I said to James.

"I'll come with you," he replied. "You can't go home on your own."

"I'll be fine. Mum is going to pick me up at Durham I think. I need to be on my own and see to her when I get there."

"If you're sure," James replied reluctantly. "At least let me go with you to King's Cross."

"Haven't you got work this morning?" I asked.

"No, I'm working from home." He bent his fingers in the air making those quote signs that I hated so much. "Sven, I mean Anders, can come along."

"I need to get back home but I can come with you as far as Green Park but then I'll go south on the Victoria line from there," the handsome Swedish stranger said before going back into James's room.

"Bloody hell James," I whispered. "You're punching above your weight with that one."

"Cheeky fucker. You're right though, he is fit," James agreed before suddenly remembering that I was grieving my dead father and perhaps feeling that the comment was inappropriate. "Are you sure you don't want me to come up to the North East with you?"

"No, it's fine thanks. I'm going to need all my energy to deal with Mum and to be honest, I need to spend some time with Jayne. I haven't seen her since Christmas or spoken to her for that matter. It will be good to catch up with her."

Jayne was my best friend back home and we had been friends for as long as any of us could remember. She and her Australian husband Brian lived on their sheep farm on a remote hillside high above my home village of Branthwaite in County Durham.

"I'll pack some stuff and we'll get going," I said, not wanting to hang about in the flat.

In the kitchen I emptied the contents of the tumble dryer into a basket before carrying them through to my room and tipping them directly into my suitcase. Twenty minutes later, the three of us were walking down Turnham Green Terrace, James gallantly pulling my case along behind him with one hand whilst pulling his new Swedish friend with the other.

We managed to make it to King's Cross Station without being too harassed. James had said goodbye to Anders as our tube pulled into Green Park station. I had urged James to go with him but it was Anders who insisted in the end that he return to Brixton alone. At King's Cross, I couldn't be bothered with self-service ticket machines so I decided to buy my ticket from the kiosk. As the cashier was about to print the tickets, James interjected from behind me.

"Can you make that a First-Class please?" he asked the cashier.

"James I can't afford...." He reached across and inserted his credit card into the card machine.

"This is on me. I had a win at the Casino on Friday night." I was going to remonstrate further but I didn't have the energy and any protest would have been futile.

James paid for the ticket and with a protective arm around me, he scanned around for the lounge. It had been about a year since I had last been here but in that time the multi-million pound development of the station had been completed. The whole place had been modernised and upgraded, and in some parts, completely rebuilt. Through the throngs of people staring up at the electronic noticeboard, I spied the entrance to the First-Class Lounge and made my way towards it through the crowds with James in tow.

"Are you sure that you don't want me to come up to Durham with you?" James asked me one more time.

"No, I'll be fine but if you could come up for the funeral, it would be nice to have you there."

"No problem. Keep me posted as to your plans. Call me if you need to, especially if your mother goes off on one," he joked, doing his best to lighten a dreadful situation.

I knew that I wouldn't be able to get through the funeral without him. He gave me the tightest of hugs and patted me gently on the back. Walking away, he continued to look back and wave until he had stepped on the escalator and descended into the bowels of the tube station below.

Outside the entrance to the lounge, a sizeable crowd of people were waiting to have their photo taken holding onto the Harry Potter luggage trolley underneath a sign saying Platform 9 ¾. I felt like a bit of a fraud as I waited for the lift next to a couple who were clearly dressed from head to toe from shops on Bond Street whereas I my clothes were more from the sales racks at the opposite end of Oxford Street. As the woman wearing a tweed jacket politely smiled and looked me up and down, I felt all the more self-conscious of my battered suitcase which was stuffed to the gunnels with clothes and had clearly seen better days. I looked at my watch and realized that I only had half an hour until my train departed so I turned around and made my way to the almost empty coffee shop opposite thinking it might be a quieter place to wait.

Fifteen minutes before the train was due to depart, a voice on the Tannoy system announced that all seat reservations on the train to Edinburgh had been suspended. Edinburgh? That was the train that I needed to get to go to Durham.

"Oh shit" I thought, "it's going to be a free-for-all on the seats." When the platform number eventually came up on the electronic noticeboard, it was as if someone had fired the starting pistol at the beginning of a race. People who I had thought might be elderly and infirm were now almost at a sprint with their suitcases to get to the train first and grab their desired seat. "Fuck it," I muttered to myself as I slipped into first gear and sped ahead weaving my way around slower moving people all the time dragging my monstrous suitcase behind me, selfishly not caring that I might take out anyone who got themselves caught up in my path.

Clambering onto the next First-Class carriage along the line, I swiftly dumped my case into the rack by the door before edging my way along the aisle to grab the first available seat. There was a table of four seats sitting free as I threw my handbag across the table sending it spinning and finally sliding off the edge of the surface and landing in the corner seat just as a fierce looking grey-haired woman went to place her copy of the Daily Mail on it. Realising that she had been beaten to the window seat, the woman looked me in the eye and scowled. I simply gave her a warm kindly smile in return and immediately extinguished any fire that may have been about to start. I placed my coat on the overhead rack as quickly as I could only too aware that other people were desperately trying to get past me to proceed further down the carriage and claim the Holy Grail that was an available First-Class seat. I squeezed into my seat in front of the grey-haired woman who was still looking at me with daggers.

"You *do* realise that this is First-Class?" the woman said nastily, as if suggesting that I couldn't afford the ticket. I didn't bother to reply, I didn't have the energy.

"It would have been nice for us both to have had a window seat Gerry," the woman muttered in a passive aggressive manner to her husband sitting next to her. Her husband mumbled with his finger in his mouth as if he was trying to remove something that had caught underneath his dentures as he leaned forward and placed a carrier bag on the seat opposite him, the one next to me.

"That'll stop someone sitting there and I can stretch my legs out," he said selfishly. As his wife spent the next two minutes fussing about, trying to get herself organised and settled in for the journey, I did my best to zone her out which actually didn't take any great effort. I was numb and heart-broken and having got off on the wrong foot with the couple opposite, I was secretly relieved that I wouldn't have to spend the next three hours engaging in polite conversation.

As more people walked down the carriage in the vain search for available seats, a young girl in her mid-twenties that I vaguely recognized, hands covered in tattoos and her face adorned with numerous piercings, stopped in front of me and smiled.

"Is that seat free?" she asked, looking at the vacant seat next to me which was currently occupied by the elderly man's bag. I did my best to smile back and nodded. That was hard, smiling.

"Excuse me but this *is* First-Class," spat the woman with the Daily Mail looking the girl up and down.

"Good job that I've bought a First-Class ticket

then, isn't it?" replied the girl politely. The elderly man across from me sighed at the inconvenience of having to get up and remove his bag to give up the seat. His wife looked over the top of her Daily Mail tutting once and then a second time just in case she had not been heard first time around. As the girl sat down next to me, she gave me a smile as if in solidarity. I knew where I'd seen her before. We'd had her on *UK Today* last year after she won a tv cookery series and already she had written a best-selling cookery book that had stormed the Christmas book charts.

The train slowly pulled out of the station as the girl unpacked her laptop and she was soon engrossed in typing on her keyboard. I sat back and my thoughts turned again to Dad.

As the train sped northwards, we arrived at the first station along the route which was Peterborough. A large man with a bushy ginger beard moved along the carriage and stopped at our table. Looking down at the ticket that he held in his hand and then up at the seat number on the window frame above my seat.

"Excuse me, you're sitting in my seat" he gruffly announced looking directly at me.

"I'm sorry," I replied, breaking my train of thought for the first time since London. "They've cancelled all reservations. It's a case of grabbing any available seat I'm afraid."

"But you're in my seat, I reserved it!" he was now shouting. "You need to move, now!" he continued as his face reddened.

"I'm sorry but I'm sitting..." but before I could say any more, my neighbour leaned forward and stood up to face the aggressive man.

"She's told you, there are no seat reservations on this train. Your reservation is not valid on this journey. Everybody here is in the same boat so you need to move along, find an available seat and stop hassling this woman."

Defeated, the man with the beard began his retreat along the carriage to find somewhere else to sit. The old woman tutted once more from behind her Daily Mail while I was actually trembling somewhat at the altercation.

"Thank you," I said.

"Hey, it's no problem," the girl replied. "Are you travelling on business?" she asked.

"Er... no," I replied quietly. "Bit of a family emergency." I left it at that. I didn't want to go into the details with a stranger and certainly not in front of the rude elderly couple sitting opposite. I hoped that she wouldn't question me further on the matter as the last thing I wanted to do was start crying. Thankfully she didn't press me and simply offered a soothing smile that made me feel that I was amongst friends. I slipped back into deep thought about my dear Dad and how I was going to handle my mother on my arrival in Durham. Dad had always been the buffer between me and Mum, cushioning the direct and often, over-bearing brusque manner that she had. My mother was high maintenance at the best of times and I had often thought of her as the rose and my father as the long-suffering, patient gardener tending to his bloom with love and affection. He was the calm to Mum's storm and he neutralized her behaviour much of the time. Without his calming influence, she would be tricky to handle over the coming days and weeks.

I was staring out of the window until I suddenly realised that the train was approaching Durham station, having seen the road from Langley Moor pass beneath me as the carriages trundled over the bridge. I excused myself from my seat as the girl next to me stood up to allow me out. The older woman sitting across couldn't resist one final scowl and hurriedly pushed her rubbish across the table onto my free newspaper. I hadn't intended to take the paper with me but, indignant at the old woman's rudeness, I grabbed the paper from the table sending the various sandwich wrappers and napkins scattering back towards her and her equally rude husband. He gave me his best neighbourhood watch look of disapproval while his wife tutted again, louder this time. I reached up to the overhead rack to retrieve my coat and scarf as I thanked the tattooed chef who had been sitting next to me.

"Take it easy, I hope things work out for your family," she offered, by way of being kind.

"Thank you. Enjoy the rest of your journey." I motioned my eyes to her travel companions. By way of reply, she smiled and then rolled her eyes comically.

Waiting by the door with my case, I stooped to look out of the window as the train slowed down on its approach to the station. The old doors with the sliding windows were a thing of the past and now replaced with ones made of super thick toughened glass that could have been from an aircraft. As the train moved across the viaduct, the familiar sight of Durham Cathedral sprang into view, like an old friend greeting me. The sight of this beautiful, majestic building made the hairs on the back of my neck stand on end. It never failed to have that effect. Thirteen years ago, when I returned from working in Australia, I'd never been so relieved to see the cathedral and on seeing it's familiar outline across the city again today, I knew that I was home.

CHAPTER 3

Sinking In

I tied my scarf around my neck tucking it into my thick winter coat and bent my finger so that my knuckle hovered over the button on the train door that was still illuminated red. I had done that for years. It was when I was working in a bar in Sydney years before with a girl who was a germ freak and who told me some scary statistic about how many different traces of urine and faecal matter could be found on the button at pedestrian crossings. This revelation had made me sick at the time and aware of my embarrassing habit of biting my fingernails, I started using my knuckle to press lift buttons and operate traffic signals and have continued to do so ever since.

The train finally ground to a halt and the light turned to green ready for my knuckle to spring into action. I took a deep breath, knowing that my mother would be on the other side.

"Here goes," I muttered with an overwhelming sense of dread.

The cold Durham air blasted straight into the carriage as the door opened. It was always so much colder here than London. I scanned the platform for sight of my mother who was coming to meet me. I hadn't wanted her to and would have preferred anyone else but despite my misgivings and protestations, she had insisted. There was no sign of her. I stepped down from the carriage and placed the case on the platform next to me as I paused to check my phone for any messages. Before I had even finished typing in my six-digit PIN number, I heard a familiar voice.

"Hello stranger."

I looked up to see my best friend Jayne standing in front of me, her eyes full of tears and love. I was gone. I could be brave and stoic no longer. My own tears erupted as my friend threw her arms around me and drew me in to the tightest of hugs. Neither of us were aware of anyone else on the platform at that moment or how long we ended up standing there like that. Some things can't be rushed nor is there any need to rush them. It's a measure of friendship when one person feels their friend's pain to such a degree that it hurts themselves almost as much and I knew that Jayne was feeling my grief right now. Despite having had three hours on the train from London to be alone with my thoughts, I became aware of the overwhelming reality of Dad's death right there on the station platform.

As the cold air swirled around us, I pulled myself slowly from Jayne who, taking my lead, followed suit. Stepping back, she was a sharp contrast to the Londoners that I'd been living amongst down south. Wearing a wax jacket, jeans and ankle riding boots, I knew she had taken time out from work on her farm to come down to Durham to meet me. Her dark blonde hair pulled back in a ponytail revealing a face reddened by the chilly winds that regularly battered the hillside farm where she lived and worked.

"Oh Lizzie, I'm so sorry. I don't know what to say," she said sympathetically. I took a fresh tissue from the packet in my pocket and wiped Jayne's eyes and cheeks. It was soaked. "It should be me giving *you* tissues."

"Don't be daft," I replied distractedly. Once again, I looked around the platform for any sign of my mother. "Mum... my mum was coming to meet me..."

"She called me and asked me to come down to get you. She's waiting at home for news as your Michael and Elaine have gone to Yorkshire."

"Yeah, Mum said when she called me this morning. Have you seen her yet?"

"No, to be honest, I called my Mam to go and sit with her while I drove down here to come and meet you. It only took me half an hour," Jayne said. Jayne's mother Muriel was a close friend to my mother and they had both lived in the same village for the past forty years. It was lovely to hear Jayne refer to her mother as 'Mam' as did most people in the north-east of England. As a small child, I was chided by my mother for calling her 'Mam' as she stupidly thought it to be common and she insisted on being referred to as

'Mummy' and in later years, 'Mum'. My mother could be a complete snob, even about the smallest of things.

"Did my mum tell you what had happened to my dad?"

"A little bit," said Jayne hesitating for a moment whether to reveal more details to me right now. "She mentioned something about your dad being found early this morning by hotel staff. Apparently, his boss, Clive, was staying at the same hotel and they were getting an early flight out to Lisbon for a conference. Clive was waiting in the foyer for your dad and when he didn't show up or answer his mobile, Clive tried knocking on the door and still no response. The hotel staff called the police immediately after the duty manager went in his room and found him. There was nothing that could be done."

I couldn't respond with words. This was more detail than my mother had told me on the phone several hours earlier. Jayne had managed to park her four-wheel drive jeep near to the entrance and as I climbed in the front seat, the old familiar smell of the farm hit my senses, that combination of smells.... dogs, horses, dirt and that familiar country scent that I associated so closely with my Dales upbringing.

As relieved as I was to be greeted by my best friend at the station, I didn't feel much like talking at all. The car pulled out of the station and wound its way up the hill out of the city heading west towards the North Pennines. It would have been the perfect opportunity to fall asleep but instead I found my thoughts going back over the years, visiting long-forgotten memories of day trips with my parents to Durham, driving back home along this road. More often than not I'd be clutching a CD or book in the back seat, having spent my pocket money that I used to save for such trips to the city. After all, there wasn't much to spend it on in our village other than sweets. The city of Durham faded behind us as we drove through several villages on the outskirts, each one of them a shadow of the glory days of their coal-mining past. Rows of quaint red brick terraced houses, many with "For Sale" signs outside looking sad and somewhat neglected. I couldn't help but think that had the same houses been for sale in the East End of London, they would be ten times the value. The villages too were soon left behind and the landscape gave way to fields, abundant at this time of year with sheep nursing their new offspring. I could still feel some of the tears on my cheek as I leaned into the passenger window making out my own reflection in the glass. At that very moment as we slowed on our approach into Brancepeth village, I saw two little lambs jumping as they played with each other. I smiled for the first time today and it served as a reminder that life is indeed a circle and that Elton John was right. The sign at the junction told us that my home village of Branthwaite was now only fourteen miles away, not that I needed a sign to tell me that. Jayne looked over and smiled at me but didn't attempt to make conversation. She knew me well enough that I was content in the silence just now. Fifteen more minutes passed along with countless more memories in my train of thought that was all over the place with no sense of direction.

"Welcome home." Jayne's voice pulled me right back into the present as we passed the sign telling us that we had arrived in my home village.

"Oh Christ, we're in Branthwaite already. Can we pull in outside the newsagent? I need a cold drink and to gather myself before I see my mother."

"Do you want me to come in with you?"

"No thanks, I'll be fine. I'll only be a couple of minutes,"

No sooner had I got out of the car and started to walk across the road to the shop, a familiar figure hobbled towards me with one of those walking aids on wheels. Norah Whittles, the village gossip, was still going strong despite her advanced years and limited mobility. I watched with dread as she made a beeline for me.

"I thought that was you. I'm so sorry to hear the news about your Dad. Yorkshire wasn't it? Leeds? Someone in the butchers said it was Leeds but then Mary in the paper shop said it was Sheffield. Have they found out what happened to him? Was it his heart? I remember a while back he'd been bad with his nerves but..." she said, without coming up for air.

"Norah, can I just stop you there?" I couldn't cope with her right now. Norah looked at me with wide eager eyes, waiting for some nugget of the details of Dad's death but she would have to wait. Her tongue was now protruding from her mouth, the way it would when she filled in her lottery slip in the paper shop.

"Thank you, Norah," was all I uttered before leaving her standing there alone. In the shop I pulled a bottle of fizzy water out of the fridge and left £1.50 on the counter, before walking straight back out without acknowledging anyone. Such an action felt very American where they leave dollar bills for food without waiting for someone to confirm that they had paid the correct amount. Norah was still standing outside the shop and her tongue was still hanging out as I walked straight past her and across the road to Jayne's jeep.

Minutes later we pulled up outside my childhood home, a red brick 1930s semi-detached house that, like my mother, alluded to a grander setting. Opening the unlocked front door, I braced myself to see Mum in a state of utter devastation. What I didn't expect was to see her at the top of a stepladder wearing a pair of yellow marigolds and scrubbing the top of the kitchen wall units.

"Mum" I had prepared myself to embrace my grief-stricken parent and was knocked off kilter at the sight of her in full domestic overdrive.

"Oh hello darling, you made it here ok then?" she said, a little too casually. I was lost for words. "How was the journey dear?" She continued scrubbing.

"Fine," I said distractedly as she carried on cleaning, giving the task in hand her full concentration. "Where's Muriel?" I asked as to the whereabouts of Jayne's mother who had gone to visit Mum earlier.

"Oh, we had a cup of coffee and a quick natter but I sent her on to the shops as I had lots to be getting on with here," said Mum, not pausing for a second from her cleaning task. Jayne had kindly brought in my case from the car and placed it in the hallway at the bottom of the stairs as I turned to her.

"She's scrubbing the cupboards!" I whispered in disbelief to my best friend.

"Is she ok?" I shrugged my shoulders in response.

"Listen love, I need to get back to Brian as he's in the middle of lambing. I'll ring you later?" Jayne said, swinging a large bunch of keys. She hugged me tightly. "It's just shock. I'll phone my Mam and see if she is coming down later. Give me a shout if you need anything," and with that, she left me to it.

I wandered into the living room and noticed the marks in the deep piled carpet indicating that it had been recently hoovered. On the windowsill sat three sympathy cards. "Good news certainly travels fast" I thought. The polished upright piano stood in the corner of the room behind the door, the top of it covered with the familiar framed photographs. As I looked at each of them, my eyes came to rest on a picture of my parents dressed in evening wear on one of the many cruises that they had been on in recent years. Dad's familiar features boasted an uncomfortable smile, one of his traits. If it had been up to Dad, their holidays would have been spent in a farmhouse in the south of France where he could wear shorts and a crumpled linen shirt all day long. The formal dress was Mum's thing, always keen to put on a show and impress others. I stared into Dad's eyes on the photo as I sat down on the voluminous sofa and leaned back, popping my feet up on the coffee table and immediately thinking better of it and retracting them back onto the carpet. I could hear the noise of the scrubbing pad and the creak of the aluminium step ladders coming from the kitchen. Stretching my arm across the cushions I felt a clump of woollen material under my hand. Dad's bottle green cardigan. Lifting it towards me, I followed my instincts and held it to my nose. Inhaling the smell managed to release something from within me and before I knew it, I was silently sobbing. It was only the second time so far today and it certainly wouldn't be the last. No sound came from my mouth as I clutched it close to my chest. I felt my upper body begin to rock with the rhythm of my grief. I opened my mouth wide as if yawning but it was to allow my body to project the full capacity of my despair. I hadn't noticed that the scrubbing in the kitchen had stopped and that my mother was now standing at the door. She looked in and it must have been the sight of her youngest child breaking her heart that let her own emotions loose on the world. She sat down next to me, slowly taking the corner of the cardigan sleeve that I was hugging and rubbed it gently between her gloved thumb and forefinger. She was careful not to intrude on my grief as she knew that Dad and I had a special bond. Of course, it was common for fathers to be close to their daughters and mothers to be closer to their sons, but Dad had been unique in that he had enjoyed a special relationship with both me and my brother Michael. It was something that niggled my mother over the years and I actually think that it chipped away at her confidence, not that anyone ever noticed, such was the exuberance of her personality.

I turned to Mum. She was still holding the pan scrubber, caked in a layer of Cillit Bang foam, small droplets of which were dripping onto the oatmeal carpet. She placed it on a ceramic coaster and slowly peeled off her marigolds before cuddling me into her. We sat together like that for what seemed like an age with nothing further needing to be said.

My phone vibrated in my pocket telling me that I had received a text. I was still held in my mother's tight embrace and as I opened my eyes, my vision of the room was blurred due to the tears.

"I'm going to wash my face, Mum. I'm shattered."

Upstairs in the bathroom, I sluiced myself with the chilled cold water. I scooped a handful of it from the tap and drank it, something that I would never have dreamed of doing in London but up here the water rolled in from the nearby fells and into the reservoir high above the village. Drying my face with a fluffy peach hand towel, I held it against my nose. That familiar smell of my mother's fabric softener. She had used the same one for years and had even taken to decanting the regular stuff that she bought from Tesco into an empty Marks & Spencer bottle. She made me laugh as if any of my mother's friends would care and secondly, as if any of them were going to look in the cupboard under the kitchen sink. All that mattered was that she cared. She was a woman who ironed tea towels and stacked them in colour order in the kitchen drawer. Mum had tea towels for different seasons of the year, red ones for Christmas and once May beckoned, the duck egg ones made an appearance on the rail along the front of the range cooker. More fool the person who might have thought that anything in her house was there by chance or accident. She had spent an inordinate amount of time over the years buying household items that tied in perfectly with her vision of a perfect home. Even the acquisition of a butter dish would be given as much consideration as the purchase of a new car.

Placing the towel carefully back on the rail, I straightened it to make sure that the embroidered peach flowers on the corner faced the front neatly. It would save Mum from tutting and fixing it herself, as she was accustomed to doing. I crossed the landing to my old bedroom. I'd seen films where grown-ups go back to their childhood homes only to find that their parents had kept everything as it was, with their old posters on the walls. Not with my mother. As soon as I had gone off to university twelve years ago, she was unable to resist the temptation to give the room a makeover. Pushing open the door, I looked around. It had been changed yet again. My old bed had now been replaced by a white wooden New England-style day bed that was covered in cushions decorated with butterflies and bird cages. The temptation to swing my tired legs up onto the bed was too great and soon I was carried into a long overdue deep sleep.

CHAPTER 4

News From Yorkshire

It was how I imagined an out of body experience to be. I was in my bed at home in London and my whole body was paralysed. Looking towards the bedroom door, it opened slowly and I could see Dad wearing his cardigan and carrying a chandelier. It didn't make sense at all. Why would he be carrying a chandelier? The crystal pendants chinked together as he approached me, that old familiar smile on his face. I screwed up my eyes and on opening them, my Dad had gone and I was no longer in London. I was back in Branthwaite and in front of me Mum was standing, holding a tray.

"I thought you could do with something to eat darling," she said in an uncharacteristically quiet voice. "Heaven knows when you last had a meal."

Her instincts were right as the last thing I'd eaten was the sandwich that Stuey had given me in the studio early that morning. Leaning forward, I pushed my hands down to heave myself up the bed, aware that the duvet was now over me and the array of cushions had been moved over to the window seat. Mum must have come upstairs and covered me while I was asleep.

"What time is it?" I asked.

"It's not long after four. Michael is back from Yorkshire."

On hearing of my brother's return, I wanted to get out of bed and speak to him, to find out precisely what had happened to Dad.

"Just stay there, Lizzie. He stopped by an hour ago, but he had to go and pick the children up from school. He's taking Amy to a friend's birthday party and Josh is going to cubs. He'll call back shortly to see you and Elaine can pick up the children from their activities later," she said reassuringly.

I was a little perturbed at her calm attitude. I wasn't used to her being so relaxed and it was certainly a contrast from the woman on top of the stepladder in the middle of a cleaning frenzy that had greeted me little more than three hours ago.

I had decided that over the next week I would submit to my mother's requests and opinions as frankly, I didn't have the willpower to disagree with her. Sitting up in the bed as she placed a sandwich in front of me, it felt as if I had taken my hands off the steering wheel as I relinquished control of my life, for now.

"Eat up dear, it's coronation chicken, your favourite. It's from Marksies." Mum added. I chuckled to myself. Despite having just lost her husband, she was still able to name-drop when it came to making a sandwich as if I would care whether the food came from Marks and Spencer or Greggs. Normally she would reserve the M&S food for when "her ladies" came to visit but clearly, she felt the need to pamper me right now.

"I'll pop downstairs and potter on dear. You eat that up and wash your face and comb that hair before your brother arrives," she asserted, with a tone of parental authority which on another occasion I might have taken for bossiness.

I rolled my eyes and tucked into my sandwich. Twenty minutes later I was downstairs in the kitchen, taken aback to see the room covered in clothes. My clothes to be precise.

"Oh Christ, she's been through my case," I thought. Not that I had anything to hide but after many years of living away from home, I was used to having my bags treated as private property. Mum had taken the liberty of emptying my entire suitcase of its contents and now each item was either hanging from the handles of the kitchen cupboards having been ironed or was in a pile on the shiny white wooden kitchen table. She had one of those ironing boards with all the pop out shelves underneath and the iron sat on a huge plastic contraption that looked more like something from Star Trek than in a domestic kitchen. Of course, she could never just buy a regular iron for fifty quid, she had to have the Mercedes of irons and my poor dad had long since given up suggesting that she do otherwise. Resistance was futile and we, as her family, had learned this many years ago.

"I'm ironing your clothes darling. They looked as if they had just been thrown into the case in the middle of an air raid." I was about to respond and then, taking a deep breath, once again I decided that there was no point in questioning the status quo. "There's nothing suitable for you to wear at your father's funeral dear. You'll need to run through to Nancy's shop at Streatlam to get something." I shuddered at the thought. Nancy was my mother's friend who owned a boutique in a nearby village and as much as the clothes at Nancy's shop were lovely and very stylish, they were very much aimed at an over-70s clientele. I felt that I had enough going against me in life without dressing like my mother.

"I'm fine Mum. I'll go over to Newcastle with Jayne and buy something."

"Only if you're sure darling." I didn't reply.

Ten minutes later, the front door opened and Michael came through the hall into the living room. Although I had only last seen him at Christmas, I was still always taken aback by his height and despite looking so tired, at six foot five he still cut a handsome silhouette. He was carrying a holdall and suit carrier that I didn't recognize but intuitively knew they belonged to Dad. His face looked rugged not having shaved for a couple of days and his eyes were puffy, I presumed, from crying.

"Hey Sis," he said, placing the bags down on the armchair by the fireplace. I stood up and embraced him. Holding each other tight, neither of us said anything. Mum was standing by the living room door, tea towel in hand, and wiping a tear away stoically before retreating to the kitchen. She didn't want to be in the way.

"When did you get back?"

"A few hours ago. I had a few errands to do, dropping the kids off at their activities. Elaine's picking them up later," he replied.

"Are those Dad's?" I said, acknowledging the bags on the armchair. He nodded somberly. "Are you ok?" Stupid question I know but it's an automatic response.

"Yeah. The hotel manager was so kind as were the rest of the staff. Clive, Dad's boss was there waiting for us."

"Us?" Mum asked. She was back standing in the doorway.

"Elaine came down with me for moral support. Worked out better because I ended up driving Dad's car back."

"Your father's car? It's at your house?"

"No, it's outside. I thought I'd leave it here. Elaine will pick me up in the next half an hour,"

"So, what happened down at the hotel?" I asked, sitting down on the large sofa and encouraging my brother and mother to do the same.

"Clive was waiting for me in reception. We had a couple of minutes chat before the hotel manager joined us. She was very kind and offered her condolences. Dad had been moved by the ambulance staff to the mortuary and now that the police had finished with the room, we were able to go up to it. The hotel staff had left it exactly as it was, they do that in these cases to allow the family to retrieve their loved one's belongings and spend time in there should they wish."

"You poor darling, having to pack up his things," Mum said, rubbing her hand repeatedly across Michael's knee.

"It's fine Mum. To be honest, most of his stuff was still in the bags because he had an early flight this morning. There were just a few things to go into his briefcase and his toiletries from the bathroom. They're all in the bag there. The briefcase is still in the car."

"So, what else did the hotel manager say?"

"She asked if we wanted to keep the room for the rest of the day in case any other family members wanted to see it but I took the liberty of telling her that it wasn't necessary."

"Absolutely, you did the right thing darling," she agreed.

"Clive then took Elaine and I to the hospital to meet with the police and make the formal identification." Mum looked shell-shocked.

"You mean, they took you to see him?"

Michael took a deep breath. "Yeah. They had a special viewing room with a glass window. We weren't allowed in the actual room with him as they hadn't done the post-mortem yet. That was to take place later this afternoon."

"How was he?" I asked, then as if I felt that

the question was ridiculous. "It was *him*, wasn't it?" I realised that I was clutching at the remote possibility that this was all some awful case of mistaken identity, some dreadful error and Dad would walk through the door at any moment.

"It was him, Sis," he confirmed, tears now running down his cheeks. "It was definitely him." Michael's words tore at my heart. This was now our reality. Dad was gone and there was no return to our life before.

"How... how did he look?" I asked, wondering if it was perhaps appropriate to ask such a question and found myself immediately doubting whether I ought to have asked him such a thing. I asked more out of concern for Dad than some morbid fascination.

Michael smiled gently as if to reassure me. "Peaceful, just really peaceful Sis. The police are getting in touch with me tomorrow once the post-mortem results have filtered through to their office. The policeman at the hospital said that the doctor who attended the scene at the hotel thought that it may have been a heart attack in his sleep as he was still under the bed covers when they found him. They didn't suspect anything untoward."

"I should hope not," Mum interjected.

"So, what do we do now?" I asked.

"We need to instruct a funeral director and they will liaise with the police and the hospital," said Michael. "Sis, do you want to come with me to get the briefcase out of the car?"

"I can do that darling," offered Mum standing up, still clutching her tea towel.

"No, it's fine, I just wanted a moment with Lizzie," said Michael, doing his best to force a smile. Nodding his head to one side, he motioned to me to follow him out to the gravel drive where he had parked Dad's car.

"Are you sure that you're ok?" I was a little confused as to why he needed me to go out to the car with him.

"I need to talk to you. There's something you need to see," he said, leading me towards the front passenger door. He clicked on the remote key fob and the lights came on. Opening the door, he lifted a purple woollen scarf from the front passenger seat whilst glancing to the house as if to make sure that our mother wasn't looking out. "I found this in the glove compartment."

"It will be Mum's," I replied, not quite sure what my brother was insinuating.

"Well, I've never seen it before, but here, smell it." He held the scarf out for me. It definitely didn't smell of her. Mum had worn the same perfume for thirty years and had never once deviated from her chosen brand.

"That's definitely not Mum's perfume. Jesus Michael, where has this come from?" I was trying to get my head around it. "If it isn't her's…. and it definitely isn't Granny's?"

"I don't know Sis. All I do know is that Mum can't know about this. The briefcase is here. Dad's mobile is inside it along with his laptop," said

Michael, reaching into the back seat of the car to retrieve it. "I haven't had the opportunity to go through anything yet. Can you take a look at it discreetly when she isn't around?"

I nodded in agreement and was about to add words to my response when I was interrupted.

"Have you got your father's briefcase, Michael?" came a voice behind us. Our mother had come out to see what was going on. I jumped and thinking on my feet, I stuffed the scarf under my jumper.

"Yes Mum," said Michael, lifting the case out of the car. "Lizzie will look after this for now, you have enough to cope with. It's freezing out here, go back inside into the warmth."

Back in the house, I put the briefcase at the bottom of the stairs to remind myself to take it up to my room when Michael had left.

"So, what do we do now?" I asked my brother.

"We will need a Medical Certificate of Cause of Death from the authorities. Dad was only sixty-nine so once the post-mortem results are in, depending on whether there is an inquest, we will be able to register the death and instruct the funeral directors to bring Dad back to Branthwaite," Michael replied confidently. He pulled some folded sheets of paper from his pocket and looked over them. "I've got the contact details for the police down there. It's probably better if just one of us is their point of contact, are you ok for me to deal with this Mum?"

"Yes dear, that's probably best. I've already phoned Mr Gurney at Hutchinsons the undertakers, he's coming over on Wednesday afternoon, I'm picking up Granny tomorrow."

"I can pick up Granny," I offered, trying to be useful.

"I would do it but I need to get back to work tomorrow." My brother was an office manager at a local quarry a few miles away and had worked there since he had left school.

"Are you sure you should be going back to work already dear? Surely you can take some time off?" Mum asked him.

"There's no knowing how long these things can take Mum, especially if they decide to hold an inquest. It could take weeks and to be honest, it's not easy to get cover at work at such short notice."

"They shouldn't need to have an inquest should they Michael? There wasn't anything untoward was there?" Mum looked worried.

I could see that Michael immediately regretted mentioning the possibility. "No Mum, it's highly unlikely but they have procedures that they have to follow. It's definitely worth you having a chat with the funeral directors on Wednesday to see what you want to do and then once we have an idea as to when the paperwork will come through, you can instruct them to go ahead." At that moment a car horn pipped outside the house. Michael looked at his watch. "That's Elaine with the kids, I'd better go."

"Oh Michael, bring them in, I haven't seen them since last week," Mum protested.

"I can't, they don't know about Dad yet. We're going to sit them down and tell them when we get home," Michael explained, the look on his face showing he was dreading the prospect, as any parent would in such a situation.

"Of course, dear, you must do that. Whatever you think is right," she replied in agreement.

Michael folded the paperwork and put it back in his pocket and after giving me a hug and Mum a kiss on the cheek, he left.

"Would you like a cup of tea dear?"

"No thanks. I'm going to go upstairs for half an hour if you don't need me down here," I answered.

"No dear, you go up and rest. I'm going to give the fridge shelves a wipe down if Granny is coming to stay. We'll have a little something for supper in an hour if you're hungry."

"That'd be lovely, thanks." As I left the room, I discreetly picked up Dad's briefcase from the bottom of the stairs on the way up. With the bedroom door closed behind me, I sat the briefcase down on the bed. Only then did I remember that I still had the mysterious scarf concealed underneath my jumper. I reached in and removed it, pausing to hold it close to my nose once more. The perfume definitely wasn't Mum's. It was a fresher more citrus-like scent, a bit like Issey Miyake and very different to our mother's favourite, Coco Chanel.

Who could it belong to? Dad didn't have any female colleagues that I knew about. It was then that the possibility that my father could have been seeing another woman hit me. I felt sick at the thought. He couldn't surely? They had been married for almost thirty-four years and despite Mum being far from the easiest person to live with, Dad had been devoted to her. I dismissed such a thought of his infidelity as an absurd notion and hid the scarf under the mattress. I didn't want to go through the briefcase just now but I couldn't stop thinking about the scarf. Who did it belong to? Why had he gone down to Yorkshire yesterday morning if he wasn't meeting his boss until the evening? It wasn't more than a two-hour drive away so he must have been up to something. Not my Dad. Not my darling Daddy.

CHAPTER 5

The Messages

I woke up the following morning to a quiet house and wandered downstairs still wearing my pyjamas, wondering if my mother would admonish me for not being fully dressed at the breakfast table. I needn't have worried as there was no sign of her and the only clue that she had been up was a note on the shiny kitchen worktop.

Lizzie,
Gone to collect Granny. Popping to M&S on the way.
The vicar is coming after lunch so please, no jeans!
Love
Mum x

I chuckled to myself. My mother might be in the throes of mourning her dead husband, but she still insisted on going to Marks and Spencer for cakes if the vicar was calling round. As for the jeans, she had always been on at my brother Michael and I not to wear them on particular occasions, such as Sundays, family birthdays, shopping trips. Normally I would be inclined to ignore her request but at a time like this, I understood the value of doing things for a quiet life.

I toasted a cinnamon bagel and went to make myself a coffee with Mum's sexy new coffee machine. Looking through the boxes of pods, I was unable to find one that didn't contain sickly caramel syrup or vanilla flavouring. She obviously wasn't a fan of plain coffee without any gimmicks, so I settled on a cup of tea instead. Taking my breakfast through to the living room, I flicked on the television where *UK Today* sprang to life. Alex, our presenter, was in the middle of some rant about women's rights whilst Lydia looked awkwardly at the camera, either embarrassed or bemused. Alex had taken to such rantings in recent months and the sharp increase in social media comments, both good and bad, led the executive producers to encourage him in the hope that it would boost the ratings. Meanwhile, Lydia would quietly play the role of the long-suffering co-host. It felt very surreal to me to be watching my colleagues at work whilst sitting in the surroundings of my parents' living room. For the first time, as I glanced around the room and then back at the TV, my two worlds collided gently and quietly. London and Branthwaite were the polar opposites of each other, yet strangely I felt equally at home in both places.

After ten minutes, I could no longer watch Alex who was now interviewing some orange-faced reality TV star about the relevance of beauty pageants. During the five-minute interview, he constantly derided and patronized the woman who was probably not the most competent of people to argue the points, a veritable lamb to the slaughter. I thought that at one point I saw Alex run his tongue across his bottom lip and his eyeline was more directed at the low-cut top the girl was wearing than her face. Switching the TV off and sending Alex's face into an abyss of darkness gave me a brief jolt of pleasure.

After a long hot soak in the bath, I changed into a shirt, sweater and a skirt that were all hanging neatly in my wardrobe and smelling strongly of Mum's fabric freshener. I decided that I had at least another half an hour before she would return home with Granny, so this was the perfect time to go back through Dad's stuff. I pulled the briefcase out from underneath the bed. The lock was easy to open, my birthday was the combination, further reminding me that I was always in Dad's thoughts. There was an opened packet of Extra Strong Mints, Dad's favourite. I saw the mobile phone there but as a way of putting it off for another minute, I picked up the mints instead and held the packet under my nose, inhaling the familiar smell. My brain didn't register "mint", but rather "Dad" instead. The smell had been there all my life and it took me back to being a young girl when I would reach into his open briefcase in his study and steal a sweet. He always knew when I was doing it and would make a joke of berating me for pinching them whilst giving me a sly smile. Putting off looking at the phone for another minute, I lifted out his black leather-bound desk diary and opened it to Sunday.

'8pm – Clive' but above it there was another entry....

'2pm – Carol'

I stared at the page. "Who was Carol?"

I took the smartphone from the pouch in the briefcase and switched it on. It soon sprang to life and asked me for a six-digit passcode. As with the briefcase, I tried my birthdate but, on this occasion, it didn't grant me access. I racked my brains to remember my brother's birthday and on the second attempt, the screen yielded and once it had lit up the home screen with a picture of Dad's grandchildren Josh and Amy, the handset beeped with numerous notifications. I could see that there were new text and Whatsapp messages as well as a voicemail waiting to be heard. I dealt with the voicemail first thinking it was probably just Dad's boss Clive, ringing to see where he was that morning in the hotel. The automated voice told me that there were four new messages and indeed the first three were from Clive, his tone changing from one of impatience to that of concern by the time he had left his third and final message. The fourth message started to play and this time it was a woman's voice.

"Hi David, it's Carol. I just wanted to say I had a lovely afternoon with you and I'm sorry for putting pressure on you to tell Joyce about us. I understand you need to do it in your own time and I'm sorry for snapping at you about it. Have a safe trip and contact me when you're back. Love you."

I was reeling. My initial fears brought on by the scarf were now confirmed, as much as I didn't want to believe a word of it. I wasn't devastated, I was angry. Who was this woman? My adrenaline was pumping as I saved the message to play to my brother later. I took a deep breath and opened up the text message folder, ignoring the numerous messages from Clive and Mum. There were no new messages from anyone else. I scrolled down the message list and soon I saw several labelled under "Carol".

I was trembling, not just because I was afraid of the truth that awaited but I also felt guilty for snooping on Dad's phone. Some things were better left in the dark and not meddled with but as I'd already heard this woman's confident posh voice, it didn't take me long to decide that the not knowing would eat away at me. I had to bite the bullet and open up the conversation with this 'Carol'.

The first message was sent on the previous Thursday morning:

Carol – *David, I need to talk to you. Can we meet this weekend?*
David – *I'm travelling to Bradford on Sunday, flying out early Monday. I can call in and see you. Will you have the kids?*
Carol – *No they're at Jim's this weekend. I'll come to Bradford if that makes it easier.*
David – *Better not. Clive, my boss, will be at same hotel and don't want him asking awkward questions.*
Carol – *Hate this sneaking around. Wish you'd tell Joyce about me. When are you going to do it?*
David – *Now isn't a good time. I know I need to tell her. We can't go on like this. I'll see you Sunday, I'll call in at your place if the kids are away and we can go for lunch.*
Carol – *OK. Sorry to go on about telling Joyce. Sick of living like this.*
David – *What time Sunday? Is 2pm ok for you?*
Carol – *Great. See you then. Love you. Xxx*

I was reeling. An affair? My father was having an affair. I couldn't have been more shocked.

Granted, he had the patience of a saint as far as Mum was concerned but an affair? He had recently turned sixty-nine and had been long overdue for retirement but some issue with the pension investments meant that he had to carry on working for a few more years. I never actually believed that story and was sure that he was actually afraid of retiring and the possibility of spending every day with Mum. So, the scarf must have belonged to this woman. Who was she? How old was she? Young enough to have kids living with her. It sounded like she was divorced or separated, and the kids are living with her but have time with their father. How long had this been going on for? So many questions, but how long would it take me to get the answers?

I could call the number that she texted from, but I didn't want to speak to this woman. I couldn't face that right now and more to the point, I really didn't know what I would say to her if presented with the opportunity. In a moment of madness, I clicked the reply box on the text messages and typed:

"This is Lizzie, David's daughter. I don't know who you are, but I ought to tell you that my father died yesterday."

I didn't have time to regret sending the message because at that moment, I heard a car pull into the drive. I panicked like a guilty teenager, jumped off the bed and quickly switched the phone off before stuffing it and the diary back into the briefcase. Downstairs, the front door opened and I could hear the faint sound of Mum twittering away out loud the way that she does when she is stressed. Pushing the briefcase back under the bed, I checked myself in the mirror, took a deep breath and went downstairs where I greeted my grandmother in the living room.

"Granny," I said, giving her the tightest of hugs. My grandmother, Gladys Constance was an eighty-nine-year-old woman of diminutive stature. Her once-grey hair had recently been coloured a burnished chestnut shade that made her look all the more remarkable given her age. Granny wept gently in my arms and refused to let go of the embrace.

"Oh Lizzie, it should be me in that mortuary, not your dad, not my David. It must have been his heart, your grandad was the same, and your Uncle Derek. Come to think of it, his cousin Clement did as well. Forty-one he was. Dropped down dead at the bacon counter in Asda in the middle of a big shop one Friday. That was a lovely funeral that was. Proper cooked ham he had. The roasted stuff not that awful boiled slimy rubbish we had at Enid's funeral last Friday. Mind you, that was a cremation and I'll tell you this, the ham is never as good at a cremation. I hardly go to them anymore, unless I've got one of them windows in me diary," she said, without seemingly coming up for air.

I was well accustomed to my grandmother's commentary on the funerals of South Durham. Gladys had been to that many, she had proved herself a critic and a connoisseur. If a mobile phone app had been invented to rate funerals the way people did hotels and restaurants, then she would surely be its biggest contributor.

Now she was looking through the sympathy cards on the mantelpiece.

"I see you've only got six cards Joyce, I've got seventeen already, with only two doubles," she shouted proudly.

"That's quick of your friends Granny," I observed.

"Well, they drop like flies round our way what with us all being in sheltered housing bungalows. The nice Indian man in our corner shop, Mr Khan, he sells the sympathy cards in packs of ten. Works out cheaper that way and I can tell you, during that cold snap last winter, I went through a whole packet of them in six weeks."

I wanted to laugh but didn't feel it was appropriate given the circumstances.

"What time is the minister coming Joyce?" Gladys shouted through to her daughter-in-law who was in the kitchen taking Marks and Spencer cakes out of their boxes and placing them carefully on a two-tier cake stand. Mum came through to the living room looking most annoyed.

"It's not a minister, it's a vicar, Gladys. We're not Methodists you know," said Mum, as if Methodism was some kind of social slur.

"Lizzie, please can you pass me one of my good tea towels out of the sideboard."

I rummaged in the drawer and lifted out a perfectly ironed tea towel and shook it open to reveal a picture of Prince William and Kate Middleton. Mum took one look at the tea towel and her eyes widened in horror.

"Not that one, that's a wedding one! I can't have a wedding one out when the vicar comes to discuss your father's funeral. Here.." she said, moving me out of the way and started flicking through a pile of linen in the drawer herself.

"Here, I've found one I bought when I went to London for the Queen Mother's funeral, that's far more appropriate."

I gently shook my head in disbelief. Mum had an obsession with the Royal Family that went back decades. It had been a mild interest for many years until the day that Prince Charles announced his engagement to Lady Diana Spencer back in 1981 and as far as my mother was concerned, Diana might as well have been the new Messiah. She had gone into full mourning on that fateful day in August 1997 when the world was reeling with shock at the death of The People's Princess. She dressed in black for two weeks, her friends sent her sympathy cards and she even laid on a buffet for her "lady friends" from the Women's Institute as they gathered together to watch the funeral. Mum recorded the BBC's coverage of the event (ITV was considered too common of course) on her video recorder and proceeded to watch the video every year on the anniversary of Diana's death.

"Lizzie, would you take your Granny upstairs to her room and put her things away?" Mum suggested.

Upstairs, Granny wasn't really in the mood to start unpacking but she took advantage of the rare moment alone with me to have a quiet word. She turned to me and gently placed her hand on my arm as she was putting the case on the floral bedspread.

"Are you alright poppet?" she asked, concerned. "You mustn't let your mother boss you about. You know what she's like."

"I'm fine Granny. To be honest I still can't believe he's gone. I've cried a lot but it doesn't seem to be sinking in. As for Mum, she's gone into domestic overdrive."

"Well, we knew that would happen. She will face it in her own way dear. If she can cry over Lady Diana, I'm sure she will be shedding tears over your dear father."

Sitting down on the bed next to her case, Granny took a deep breath. "It's all wrong this you know," she said as she began to weep. I crouched down in front of her, taking her weathered hands in mine. "He was a lovely little boy, your dad. Always so particular about his appearance," she reminisced. "He used to carry a little plastic comb with him everywhere he went. Always doing his hair he was."

I hugged her, unsure if I was actually providing any comfort.

"He was so proud of you Lizzie, making your television programmes down in London. He watched all of them and would often rewind it just see your name go up at the end again."

We could hear my mother shouting instructions to me manically from downstairs in the kitchen.

"You'd better go and see what your mother wants Lizzie. I'll take my book down into the living room and keep myself out of the way until the minister gets here."

"Vicar! Not minister!" I said, mocking my mother's voice causing Granny to smile mischievously.

Downstairs, Mum was a hive of activity opening up packets of sandwiches and cutting them into smaller quarters.

"Is the vicar coming for lunch?" I asked her.

"Well, he said he was calling in at Jean Denholm's on the way here to drop off the song sheets for the cub scout jamboree and if it's down to her to give him his lunch, it'd be some potted meat smeared on some cheap white sliced that's seen better days. That's the extent of her catering so he'll be glad of a proper sandwich here. Don't take the salmon or the prawn ones Lizzie, leave them for the vicar, take an egg and tomato one instead."

"Perhaps the vicar might like an egg and tomato sandwich mother."

"Of course, he won't, not when I've got prawn ones for him. His wife, Mrs Barnabas, came to my lunchtime Royal Wedding finger buffet and even four years on, she still talks about my prawn ring."

It took me all my effort not to smile. My mother, as always, was oblivious to the double-entendre she had just uttered.

"They're very popular, prawn rings these days I see," offered Granny who had now appeared at the kitchen door. "We had one at the old folks Christmas Party at the community centre last year."

"Well, I very much doubt it would have been from Marksies," snapped Mum.

"I don't know where she got it, she made it, I think. The lassie who did the buffet went to college and now she does all the funerals round our way. She's very busy."

"You can't be too careful with prawns I find and at least Marksies have the decency to arrange all their prawns facing the centre so you're not having to look them in the eye before eating their ring," said Mum innocently.

I spat out my water at this and started coughing. Granny reached over for a printed paper napkin with some dogs on it.

"Don't use the royal corgis to mop up the water! Here's some quilted towel," she screeched, tearing a length off a roll that was mounted on the tiled splashback.

Do you want a mug for your tea Granny?" I reached into the kitchen cupboard and removed two mugs decorated with faded pictures of Prince Andrew and Sarah Ferguson.

"Lizzie! Not those ones! Not when the vicar is coming! You can't give Prince Andrew to the vicar! I keep them for the workmen. There's a couple of Diamond Jubilee china ones that you can use," said Mum getting herself in a right old fluster.

A moment later, the doorbell rang and Mum answered it.

"Reverend Barnabas, how good of you to call. Let me take your coat and we'll go through to the drawing room."

I mouthed silently to myself "drawing room?"

When did my mother ever refer to it as the drawing room?

In the lounge, the vicar greeted Granny "My sincere condolences Mrs Button. God's blessings be with you," he said, shaking her hand in both of his.

"Actually Reverend, I'm Mrs Constance."

The vicar gave her a confused look. "I'm sorry, I thought you were David's mother?"

"Oh, I am but I married again after my first husband died."

"She didn't wait long," Mum muttered under her breath disapprovingly as she popped back through to the kitchen.

"Oh, I see," said the vicar, a little embarrassed at his assumption.

A minute later, Mum returned carrying a large tray containing a china Princess Diana teapot and an elaborate cake stand which was delicately covered in an assortment of sandwiches and cakes. Setting it down on the coffee table, her eyes widened in horror. In the middle of the coffee table was a paperback book, clearly left there by her Granny. It wasn't any old book, but a copy of *Fifty Shades of Grey*. Unsure if the vicar had already noticed the book, Mum then attempted to place the tray over the top of the offending item and using the edge of the tray nearest to her, pulled the book across the table towards her until it dropped onto the freshly hoovered carpet.

The vicar looked over to see what had dropped and immediately my mother picked up the cake stand and held it in front of his eyes by means of distraction before kicking the dropped paperback across the carpet and under the armchair in one swift movement.

Reverend Barnabas proceeded to talk through the choices of hymns and prayers for the service, making notes in his small leather-bound notebook. Mum however had ideas of her own.

"I'd like 'I Vow to Thee My Country' as that was Diana's favourite."

"Diana? Was she a relative?" the vicar asked my mother.

"Princess," she said, tapping her finger on top of the teapot. She reached down to the magazine rack that was on the floor next to the sofa and pulled out a large book that was bulging with bits of paper sticking out haphazardly.

I looked at my mother wide-eyed. "Mum, what on earth is that?"

"Just my notebook darling, it will come in more useful tomorrow when the funeral director is here. Actually, I've also done a mood-board. I've seen it on the television."

"Yes Mum, when they're decorating a bathroom." I was mortified. Was my mother for real?

She proceeded to discuss potential plans for the funeral which still didn't have an actual date confirmed yet. That could only be done once they had the results of the post-mortem in from the coroner's office. Granny kept interjecting with stories of what hymn some random woman in her village had had at their funeral recently but Mum did her best to ignore her. The vicar, on the other hand did his best to acknowledge Granny as the mother of the deceased and include her in the discussions, much to the detriment of the smooth running of the proceedings. Almost an hour had passed by and the vicar appeared keen to wrap things up.

"Would you like me to say a prayer for David while we are all sat here?" he suggested.

"Well, that would be lovely Vicar," said Mum, who then clasped her hands together and nodded to me to do the same. We closed our eyes and prayed. After a minute, we opened them to see Granny reading the television listings in the newspaper. The vicar smiled and pretended not to notice while Mum threw Granny an accusatory stare. As the Reverend Barnabas was seen to the door, I thought it would be best to make myself useful and clear the tea tray away and do the dishes in the kitchen before my mother pulled the Dyson out of the cupboard under the stairs and gave the living room the once over, yet again.

With the kitchen all tidy, I decided to go upstairs under the guise of needing a lie down, which raised no opposition from my mother. A couple of hours peace and quiet in my old bedroom would give me some space from the passive bickering of the women downstairs whilst allowing me the opportunity to take a another look at Dad's phone and to try to figure out what the hell had been going on.

CHAPTER 6

A Welcome Distraction

The text messages and voicemail that I had discovered on Dad's phone only served to interrupt my sleep throughout the night and by the time that the alarm on my phone went off at eight o'clock the following morning, I felt neither rested nor reassured. When I checked his phone again last night, I could see that my message to the mysterious Carol had been read but she had not sent a reply.

I had to be ready by nine as Jayne was coming to pick me up and we were driving over to Newcastle so that I could buy something to wear for Dad's funeral. We hadn't been notified as to when his body could be released to us so there was no knowing as to when the funeral would be. Despite that, I still welcomed a morning away from this house and my mother's fussing. At least once I had something appropriate and black to wear, that would be one less thing for her to nag me about.

The fifty-minute drive over the fells towards Newcastle presented me with the perfect opportunity to update Jayne about the messages to and from this woman Carol on Dad's phone. My friend listened patiently to me as she drove us, nodding and playing close attention as I rambled on. She was very good at reassuring me although I suspected that she was none the wiser as to what had been going on than I myself had been.

That Wednesday morning, Newcastle city centre wasn't particularly busy and by arriving at ten o'clock, we had avoided the morning rush hour traffic. When I left the house earlier, my mother had pushed two hundred pounds in folded notes into my hand and despite my protests, she insisted that I accept it.

"Buy something nice that you can wear at one of your TV things afterwards, not just the funeral. Nothing too revealing mind you."

I laughed off the comment, good old Mum, always had to get the last word in. As we walked from the car park towards the imposing Greys Monument in the city centre, I said to Jayne "We might as well have a lunch somewhere after the shopping, if you don't have to rush back."

"I'm in no rush, that sounds good to me," Jayne replied.

"Sushi?"

"Sorry, best not risk it."

"Risk what?"

"Nothing, I've just had a dodgy tummy the last few days. Don't worry, there's that little Italian café near the Tyneside Cinema that we used to love going to, if you fancy that."

"It's a deal. You must be glad to have a change of scenery too," I said, to which Jayne readily agreed.

Unlike many women, I've never been a great one for shopping. I usually only venture out when I absolutely need something to wear and even then, I usually make a quick purchase and follow it up with a boozy lunch with friends. They're the best kind of shopping trips.

On this fresh spring morning in Newcastle, it took us less than an hour to find me something to wear for Dad's funeral. Jayne took the opportunity of a rare visit to the city to pick up some shirts for Brian and a gift for her mother's upcoming seventieth birthday. By the time that we had enjoyed a lunch of chicken salad and coffee, we decided to head back over to Branthwaite. As we approached the car park, I felt my phone vibrating in my pocket. Dreading the thought of a call from my mother checking in, I was initially reluctant to answer it. Thankfully, the name on the screen was *Maggie,* my friend and colleague on *UK Today*. I showed Jayne the phone and said, "do you mind if I take this?"

Jayne signalled for me to go ahead as I answered

the call while sitting myself down on a nearby bench.

"Maggie, hi,"

"Hi Lizzie darling, how are you doing?"

"I'm ok, I'm doing ok. It's been a lot to take in and there's still a lot that we don't know but I'm doing fine."

"That's good, I just wanted to check in with you and make sure that you are ok."

"Thanks Maggie, that's so kind of you. How are things at work?"

"Don't you be worrying about work. Everything is fine and everyone is asking after you."

"Everyone? Dare I ask, how is Serena? You know, after...." I said, cringing at the memory of my outburst in the studio gallery the morning that I'd received the phone call about Dad's death.

"Oh, don't you worry about her, she'll get over it, although I think you have commanded a whole new level of respect amongst the team," she added with a cheeky giggle.

"I'm sorry but she triggered me at the worst possible moment," I said, as if I needed to justify my actions.

"Listen, don't worry about it at all. Can you let me have your Mum's address as I'd like to send her something and for you too."

I told her that there was no need to send anything but I complied and gave her the address. It was a relief to know that I still had a job to go back to, not that I'd really given it a second thought considering everything else that was going on around me right now. I said my goodbyes to Maggie and resumed my walk to the car park with Jayne.

Almost an hour later, as we crossed the last of the fells and were soon to descend the steep road into Branthwaite, Jayne pulled the car over into a layby and switched off the radio. Before I had a chance to ask what was wrong, she spoke.

"I was going to tell you over lunch after you suggested the sushi but there were too many people around. The thing is...." Jayne paused to take a deep breath. "The thing is... I'm pregnant." I jumped in my seat giving a small squeal of delight while Jayne reached across with her hands which I grabbed. "Calm down. I wouldn't normally have told anyone but it's early days and I'm only eight weeks so we can't tell anyone, especially after..." her voice tailed off as she turned to look out of the window. I could see my friend's eyes well up.
"What's wrong?"
Jayne took another deep breath.
"I feel bad that I haven't told you what's been going on. I'm sorry. We haven't told anyone to be honest."
"You don't have to tell me if you don't want to. If it something private between you and Brian, I don't

need to know."

"I want to tell you. God knows I've kept it to myself and I would have told you before now, but I didn't want to do it over the phone. I was going to say something the last time that you were home, but it was Christmas and we didn't get any time when there was just the two of us."

"In your own time," I said, reaching across and taking her hands in my own.

"The fact is," Jayne said taking a deep breath, "that we have been trying for a couple of years now, ever since we came back from Australia and Brian got his UK residency status. We didn't think too much about it at first but after the first year, nothing happened and we started to worry that there might be something wrong. We've had all sorts of tests and it's not something that can be pinpointed. So, we are now on our second run of IVF."

She paused and breathed slowly, tears now trickling. I leaned forward and took her hands in mine, rubbing my thumbs across her knuckles with a gentle rhythm in the hope that it might comfort her.

"Jayne, I had no idea." I felt guilty that my friend had been going through this difficult ordeal and I had done nothing to support her. Come to think of it, it also explains why she wasn't drinking when I last saw her at Christmas.

"I'm fine, it's just meant that we have both been

through a tremendous amount of pressure. We've only been married a couple of years but people start asking 'when are we going to hear the patter of tiny feet?'"

"Folk can be so insensitive."

"They don't mean to be. It's just a natural instinct when a couple have been together for a while, to ask them if they are getting married, or when they have been married, to ask them if they are planning on having children. It's just the way people's brains are wired. They don't mean anything by it." I didn't really know what to say so I gave her another half-hug given the confines of the car.

"I'm so pleased for you, for you both and you know my lips are sealed. I was going to ask you to come to the pub one night as I'll need to get away from Mum and Granny, but if you're not drinking..."

"I will go to the pub once we tell everyone but if I was to sit in there nursing an orange juice, people will suss the truth straight away and like I said, it's still early days."

"Fair enough," I replied and with that we were back on the road and dropping slowly down into the village. "As long as you're ok."

"I'm fine. It's not great timing with Brian lambing on the farm as normally I would be up there in the big lambing shed helping him but I'm having to stay away in the house in case I catch anything from the pregnant ewes and it affects my pregnancy," said Jayne. Having grown up in Branthwaite, I was aware of the risks of pregnant women being around sheep giving birth and the possibility of a human foetus miscarrying in such circumstances.

Five minutes later Jayne dropped me off outside my parents' house before hurrying back home to get dinner organised for Brian and the two lads that he had helping him. I dropped my shopping bags at the bottom of the stairs before popping my head through the living room door to see who was about. Granny was sitting quietly on the sofa reading her book and looked up with a smile.

"Had a nice morning at the shops dear?"

"Yes, it was good, thanks Granny and I managed to get something to wear."

"That's good dear. I'm staying in here out of the way as I don't think your mother is very happy at the moment."

"Has the funeral director been?"

"Yes, but I'll let you talk to your mother about that," Granny replied looking very sheepish indeed.

In the kitchen, my mother was loading the dish washer with what only can be described as a concentrated fervour and the atmosphere was frosty to say the least.

"Hi Mum, everything ok?"

You know when you wish you hadn't asked someone a question before you've even finished asking it? Yeah, it was like that.

"That woman.... Your grandmother.... She's gone too far this time Elizabeth, too far."

'Shit', I thought, she's using my Sunday name. This was not going to be good but the opportunity for me to beat a hasty retreat upstairs had passed, if it had ever existed at all. I pulled up a chair at the shiny white kitchen table as Mum took the seat next to me.

"What's she done now?" I asked, trying my best to be sympathetic but not wishing to take sides and thus get caught in any crossfire.

"What's she done? Only gone and made a complete show of me during the meeting with the Mr Gurney, the funeral director. She always has to be centre-stage, your grandmother," she said as I nodded sympathetically, trying not to smile at the huge glaring irony in that last statement. "Not only did she still insist on referring to the vicar as the minister, she started banging on about what she wanted in the funeral buffet for her own funeral, something about prawn vol au vents. She insisted that your father wear his school tie when he is laid out which I can tell you is NOT happening. He's a sixty-nine-year-old man, not a schoolboy."

"Mum, just ignore it and let it go. You have enough to deal with right now," I said, stroking her back reassuringly but doubtful that any input from me would help to calm her down.

"On a positive note darling, Mr Gurney was most impressed by my mood board for the funeral. He said that he'd never seen anything like it and it rendered him quite speechless. I told him that it pays to be organised and that my inspiration came from Princess Diana with a little bit of Operation Tay Bridge thrown in."

"Operation Tay Bridge? What's that when it's at home?"

"It was the code name for the Queen Mother's funeral." I could only wonder how she knew this useless fact of information. Still, best to say nothing, especially where the Royal family are concerned so I decided to try and steer her off the negatives.

"So, did you get everything sorted?" I asked her.

"As much as anyone can without post-mortem results and a death certificate. I've picked out a coffin and given them your father's best suit to bury him in along with his Rotary Club tie," she said, nodding her head in the direction of the living room where Granny was still reading. "Thankfully, I managed to hide that awful 50 Shades of Whatever book of your grandmother's before he arrived earlier." She stood up and moved to the dishwasher where she pressed a button and shut the door, setting it away to do its thing.

"Lizzie, would you come with me later to speak

to the manager at Branthwaite Hall to discuss availability for tea after your father's funeral?" I noticed that she was now looking rather tired.

"Yes of course but don't you want it in the village hall next to the cemetery?" I thought that my suggestion would be easier for everyone on the day of the funeral.

"What? And have the entire WI including Norah Whittles slapping margarine on cheap white sliced? I should think not."

She couldn't have been more assertive and I knew better than to take the discussion any further.

"Did you get something nice to wear in Newcastle?" she asked, changing the subject, much to my relief. "Please tell me you didn't buy trousers?"

"No Mum, I bought a dress. A black one."

"Nothing too showy I hope darling. Remember it is a funeral and not a nightclub that you are going to."

"It's conservative enough even for the Queen," I said mockingly, the joke going right over my mother's head.

After storing my new dress on its hanger in my room, I came back downstairs to collect my handbag and head out to the car with Mum who was waiting by the front door.

"Hurry up, I don't want your grandmother tagging along." I could see that she was anxious to get going.

"Lizzie and I are just nipping out Gladys," she called out before hastily shutting the front door behind us.

Branthwaite Hall Hotel was little more than a five-minute drive outside the village and as we approached the stone lodge that flanked the left side of the entrance to the drive, Mum sighed loudly, crossing herself.

"Sir Richard Featherstone, God rest his soul. He only passed away eight months ago. He was on his sit-on lawnmower and just went. I said to the funeral director that I wanted a double plot next to his at the north end of the cemetery, but he said it might be difficult as there was little space left up that end. I told him that I'm not having your father buried down the other end with the likes of Norah Wittles' husband and all those Labour voters."

I shook my head. Only my mother could be snobbish about a burial plot. Even in the midst of her grief, she still found the urge to be a social climber.

"Did Sir Richard always live in the Lodge?" I asked.

"Oh no, he moved out of the big house about thirty years ago and turned it into a hotel. It used to be a large sprawling estate at one time they say but after generations of death duties, they had to sell off pockets of land here and there to local farmers to pay their way. The Lodge is still a sizeable house and it would be a lot cheaper to heat than the Hall." The drive wound its way up to the main house, flanked on either side with carefully manicured lawns, an orchard of soft fruit bushes and at the top, a grass tennis court and a croquet lawn. As the car crunched across the gravel to a halt, my mother turned the ignition off and pulled down the sun visor to check her make-up in the little mirror. She may be the grieving widow, but she still had to maintain appearances.

An hour later we emerged outside into the spring sunshine, Mum having gone into the smallest details what she wanted for the buffet for Dad's funeral. Marcus, the events manager remained incredibly patient and professional as she listed the specifications required. I was just thankful that she had made a discreet list on a sheet of writing paper and had not brought that godawful 'mood board' with her.

"What a lovely young man he was Lizzie. You could do a lot worse," she said as she clicked the fob on the car key to unlock the doors. Was I hearing her right?

"Mum, please tell me you are kidding. This is hardly the time..."

"Yes dear but you're not getting any younger and you need to cast your net out a little more often.

Be nice to him next week when we are all here and see if you can strike up a conversation with him. That reminds me, best not have any wine at the funeral dear, I know what your friends can get like and you are so easily encouraged."

"I hardly think that my father's funeral is the appropriate place or time to be looking for a future husband, do you?"

"I just thought he was lovely. Nice white teeth, so immaculately turned out and lovely olive skin."

"I think you are mistaking his fake tan for a Mediterranean glow. Anyway, I don't think I'm his type."

"Why on earth wouldn't you be his type?" She couldn't grasp at what I was getting at.

"I'm not his type. I think that he would be more attracted to..." How was I going to put this without shocking her? "He might be more attracted to my brother."

"Don't be ridiculous darling. What on earth makes you think that?"

"Call it intuition," I said, smiling to myself. "You pick these things up when you share a flat with a gay guy."

"Well, I think you're wrong darling. He doesn't look the sort at all."

Keen to drop the subject, I simply stared out of the window on the short drive home. That evening, after dinner, I left Mum and Granny downstairs watching the telly and I went up and had a bath, taking my book with me that I'd been so desperate to finish the previous weekend. I'd been tempted to check Dad's phone again, but the battery had died and even though the charger was in the briefcase, I thought it best to leave it until tomorrow. Tonight, I just needed sleep and lots of it.

CHAPTER 7

Circle Of Friends

Looking at the time on my phone on waking up, I hadn't intended to sleep in until ten o'clock but I knew that my body must have needed the rest. There's something special about letting your body wake up naturally as opposed to the beeping of an alarm. I didn't go straight down to breakfast after showering as I'd heard my mother's raised voice from upstairs so I could only presume that she was already getting exasperated with Granny and the last thing I wanted to do was start the day in the middle of the crossfire between them both. I had just finished drying my hair when I heard the front door go.

Michael was waiting downstairs and without smiling, motioned for me to go into the living room and followed through shortly afterwards with Mum who went straight over to the television and switched it off.

"Joyce, I was watching that. They were just about to show the house after the man had done it up," said Granny, not quite sensing why we had all gathered in the room with her.

Michael interjected.

"I've had the police in Yorkshire on the phone and they have the results of the post-mortem for Dad," he stated, doing his best to remain calm and composed.

"What did it say darling?" Mum asked quietly.

"A simple heart attack. No trace of anything else. They are going to email the paperwork across to me shortly and I'll need to go down later to collect the original copies of the death certificate. It means that we can now go ahead and organise the funeral."

"A heart attack?" I said, with only the smallest degree of relief.

"They think it happened in his sleep and it was likely to have been quite quick," said Michael.

Granny started crying quietly.

"My little boy, my little David," she cried tenderly. Mum moved over to her and sat down on the sofa slipping a comforting arm around her mother-in-law. They might have always been at odds with each other but right now they were united in their grief.

"I'll get on the phone to the funeral director in a moment and see if we can get Monday as the date," said Mum, all the while her hand stroking

Granny's shoulder in comfort, a rare display of solidarity between them.

Twenty minutes later, the funeral was finalised for Monday which only gave us another four days. Michael agreed to put a notice on Facebook letting people know the details and the funeral director said that he would put an announcement in the local paper for the following day. Such was the speed that bad news and gossip travelled in the dale, I thought that a newspaper ad would be surplus to requirements but that seems to be the way that these things are done and who am I to question that, particularly right now. Mum then phoned Marcus at Branthwaite Hall to confirm the booking for the wake afterwards so now there was little else to do.

"Lizzie darling, would you like to come to the florists with me to choose the flowers?" Mum ignored my brother who was standing next to me, presumably because she did not think to ask a man.

"Actually Mum, I think I'm going to go for a walk for a few hours. Why don't you take Granny with you?" I suggested looking over at my grandmother who was sitting on the sofa looking rather lost in the midst of her grief.

"Very well," she conceded.

"Michael, do you fancy coming with me for a walk? I've hardly seen you since I got back," I said, concerned at how tired and stressed my brother was looking.

"Thanks, but I need to get back to work. I'll give you a call later if that's ok?" He looked around to check that Mum had left the room before he continued. "Did you have any more thoughts about that scarf?" he whispered.

"Not really but there was a voicemail. I also had a look at the messages on Dad's phone and replied to one of them. I can't talk about it here but perhaps we can meet up when you finish work?"

"Yeah, that sounds like a good idea. Why don't you give me a call later when you have ten minutes free? I'd ask you over to our place but Amy has taken Dad's death particularly badly and I don't want to discuss anything about the scarf or the messages near her or Josh."

I agreed with him and suggested that it would be better for *him* to call *me* when he was on his way home in the car.

"If you're going for a walk, would you call by our house and take Archie with you? He hasn't had a good run out since the weekend. Archie was Michael and Elaine's Jack Russell terrier that they had rehomed from a local stray charity the previous summer.

"No problem, it will be lovely to see the little fella," I said delighted at the prospect of some company on the walk, even if the conversation wouldn't be flowing with my four-legged companion.

"Mum has a spare key so you can let yourself in. There are some poop bags and treats next to his lead near the back door. Don't let him go off the lead if you're heading near the old quarry as there's too many rabbits up there and he almost got wedged in a rabbit hole a couple of weeks ago," he said smiling. It was the first time I'd seen his face light up a little in the past few days.

Half an hour later, Archie and I were walking happily up the steep hill towards the old limestone quarries that overlooked our pretty village. The spoil heaps had merged into the landscape and now provided grazing for sheep on their steep grassy banks. I'd had a brief chat with James my flatmate on the phone as I'd left the house. He was going to travel up on the train the following afternoon ahead of the Friday rush and I'd agreed to pick him up from Durham station. The thought of him being here for a few days brought me a tremendous sense of comfort, not just in the midst of my bereavement but as a buffer and escape from the madness in the house where Mum and Granny did nothing but wind each other up. Despite the morning having started off a little bit cooler, the temperature had risen and already I was sweating with the steep uphill walk. I removed my jacket and tied it around my waist and for a brief moment, a breeze whisked along to cool me. Along the flat tarmac road that ran past the old quarries, there were frogs everywhere and at first, I was concerned that Archie would try and eat one but as it was, he wasn't bothered by them. The sun bounced off the ponds at the bottom of the quarry face while along the left-hand side of the road, the verge dropped to a steep ravine which lay shaded amongst the trees, the sound of running water giving away the existence of the burn running through the middle. On a beautiful spring day like today, there was no shortage of walkers out, many of them with dogs. I did sometimes miss this place and today I certainly felt like I'd never been away. The surroundings evoked all sorts of wonderful memories of walking along here with Dad and Michael. There was many a Sunday morning when Mum would be busy cooking lunch and she would insist on using the separate dining room with its large oak table and heavy high-backed chairs. From ten o'clock, the potatoes and the rest of the veg would be on a rolling boil with the pan lids rattling away on the stove, the kitchen windows steamed up and Mum, ready to snap with the stress of cooking this one perfect meal every week. Inevitably, the rest of us would be shoo-ed out from under her feet and so began the tradition of the Sunday morning walk with Dad. We would vary on a number of routes depending on the time of year but this walk up alongside the old quarries was my favourite. Dad was always so gentle and calm, quite the opposite of Mum and us kids always enjoyed our walks out with him. As the road curved round to cross the burn that was now level with it, I tried to remember the last time that I came up here with Dad. I think it was when I came back early from Australia about thirteen years ago after I split with my ex-boyfriend Paolo. At the time, I was a wreck and he brought me up here for some peace and quiet and to avoid the thousand and one questions that Mum was firing at me. He was great like that. He always knew exactly what I needed.

It had been sunny all morning but looking up at the clouds coming over from the fells, the sky was turning a light shade of graphite. Rather than go any further along the route which would take us up through the forest, I thought it best to turn around and walk back the way we had just come if we were to beat the rain. Once we reached the main road it was downhill from there and it wasn't long before I once again let myself into Michael's house, giving little Archie a rub down with the towel and leaving him in his bed contentedly gnawing on a chewy treat.

Back at the house, I went upstairs and immediately plugged in Dad's mobile to charge it up. I used the double socket that sat behind the bed so that I could conceal the phone down behind the headboard. Mum hadn't mentioned his phone since Michael brought it back from Yorkshire with the rest of his belongings but as she was in and out of my room each day, I needed to protect her from the messages to and from the mysterious Carol. This evening, I would look back through them and decide what to do next, if anything. After all, she hadn't replied to my message telling her that my father was dead.

Downstairs Granny was still in the living room engrossed in her book.

"Did you have a nice walk out dear?" she asked me without diverting her eyes from the page.

"Yes, Granny, it was lovely and Archie certainly enjoyed himself."

"Archie? Is that a gentleman friend of yours?"

"No, it's Michael's dog."

"So you don't have a young man at the moment?" Her voice was unable to conceal her disappointment.

"Not at the moment Granny."

"You want to find yourself a rich man Lizzie. This Mr Grey in the book seems to know what he's about. Are you out tonight dear? It's just I was hoping that you could put a colour through me hair so it's ready for the funeral on Monday. If you could go down to the shops and pick one up, nothing too dark mind you. I don't want to be mistaken for Joan Collins, *again*." I couldn't help but laugh. As much as she managed to wind up Mum, Granny was adorable and very funny without realising it. Finally looking up from her book, she smiled at me. "Would you pop the kettle on dear? I'd love a cup of tea but I've been staying out of your mother's way."

"No problem, Granny."

"And Lizzie? For heaven's sake, don't use the wrong mug," she said mischievously.

"Do you want a Harry and Meghan one or a Princess Margaret?" I asked her, joining in on the joke.

"Better do a Princess Meghan one, dear. If you give me the Princess Margaret one, you'll need to fill it with gin." At least we had made each other laugh, even if it was at my mother's expense.

Five minutes later, I carried in a small tray with two mugs of tea. My mother wasn't joining us as she was busy on the phone in the dining room to one of her friends.

"I found some chocolate biscuits in the tin, Granny. I think we're allowed to eat these ones," I said, referring to Mum's rules about what food is to be kept for visitors and guests.

"I asked your mother if she could get me some fig rolls when she gets the big shop in. I've been bunged up for almost two days and can't seem to get anything shifted."

Granny's unexpected reference to her bowel movements, or lack of, put me off my biscuit before I'd even removed the foil wrapper. What was it with elderly people and their toilet habits? They always feel the need to tell the world about them.

"I'd blame all that fancy bread your mother buys from Marksies but I've never been right down there since I started going through the change last year."

I would have spat out my tea, but I thought I'd initially misheard her.

"Granny, did you say you started going through the change *last year*?"

"Yes, it came on after the harvest festival in September and I've never been right since."

"But Granny, you're eighty-nine," I served to remind her.

"Some women go through it a little bit later than others," she replied as a matter of fact.

There was no more that I could add to that, so I decided to change the subject once more.

"You do know that it's Mum's birthday tomorrow?" I said.

"Oh, I did remember. I have something wrapped up in my case for her."

"To be honest Granny, I'd forgotten what with everything that's happened this week. I'll ring Michael and see if he has remembered and has any bright ideas. She might not actually want to acknowledge it this year with us losing Dad."

A quick phone call to my brother revealed that he

too had forgotten the birthday. We agreed that he would pick up a card from himself, Elaine and the kids and that we would club together to get her a gift. Normally I would have bought her some beautiful flowers but the house was already full of them and she had already filled every single vase that she owned plus a few that she had borrowed. I thought it would be better to give her something that perhaps she could use at a later date and we agreed that a voucher for a Spa Day at Branthwaite Hall would be perfect for her.

The following morning was a lazy one and I didn't want to make a fuss around Mum for her birthday as she had mentioned the night before that she wasn't in the mood for celebrations, which was as I suspected. She was pleased with a discreet card and the joint present of the Spa Day.

"Do you mind awfully if I don't put my birthday cards up darling? It doesn't feel right somehow displaying them amongst your father's sympathy cards."

"Of course, that's fine Mum," I said and as I reached in to hug her, we were interrupted by the doorbell.

I let her answer the door assuming it was someone for her and she returned with a huge bouquet of white roses. Rather than looking gratified, she was shell-shocked.

"What's wrong? You look like you've seen a

ghost," I said, immediately regretting my choice of language.

"Perhaps you're right, darling. They're from your father."

I took the bouquet from her and placed it on the sideboard in the small space that was left amongst three other vases full of blooms. I removed the card from the plastic stem and handed it to her.

"To my darling Joyce, Happy Birthday my love, David" she read out. "A single kiss. He always put a single kiss, never more. He always said that one kiss matters more than a dozen," and with that, she erupted into tears. This was the first time that I had really seen her cry since I returned home at the start of the week. Not just a few tears but full on proper crying. I hugged her but offered no words of comfort, conscious that that nothing I could say would help at this moment.

By noon, I had headed out in Dad's car armed with a shopping list from Mum to go Marks & Spencer and the big supermarket. The delivery of the bouquet had really knocked the wind out of her sails and as a result, she didn't feel like going shopping. I'd called Jayne's mother Muriel who had the bright idea of taking Mum to get her hair done over in Hexham, a beautiful historic market town just over the border into Northumberland but still only a thirty-minute drive away. My mother normally got her hair done at the small local salon but she had said she couldn't face being sat with people offering sympathy today. She needed to be anonymous and with that, Muriel had managed to successfully get a cancellation appointment at a big fancy salon in the town.

Two hours later, with the boot loaded up with shopping, I left the supermarket car park and made my way up the steep winding road that led to the entrance of Durham railway station. James's train was on time and I'd told him to come straight out to the car park as there was nowhere for me to leave the car, with it being a usual busy Friday afternoon. My spirits lifted the moment that I saw him and as he wrapped me in one of his trademark hugs, I could smell the distinct whiff of beer on his breath. I stepped back and looked into his eyes.

"Jesus James, you're pissed already and it's only half past two in the afternoon. How much have you had to drink?"

"Well, I only bought myself a couple of cans from the buffet carriage as I couldn't get a First-Class ticket but then I ended up sitting across from these four lads from Durham who are working down in London on the Crossrail tunnel. They had loads of beer and asked me to join them. Lovely lads, especially one of them," he said, followed by a small cheeky hiccup.

"Oh God James, please tell me you didn't..." I said, worried that it might be someone I knew.

"No, don't be silly, just a bit of harmless flirting," he laughed. I opened the back door of Dad's car for him to put his bag on the seat and he jumped in the front. I reached into the side pocket of the door and extracted another tube of Extra Strong Mints that he must have had stashed there.

"Here, get some of these down you. I can't have you going into Mum's stinking like a brewery." I was unable to hide my pleasure at one of my best friends being here with me.

During the drive back to Branthwaite, I updated James on all that had been going on, in particular, the messages on Dad's phone from the mysterious woman and the scarf that Michael had found in the car. We called in at Granny's bungalow on the way home to check that everything was ok and to pick up the post for her. There was quite a pile of cards lying on the vestibule floor so I thought it would be best to bring them up to Mum's for her to open. When we arrived back home, my mother was sat on the bottom two stairs on the phone while wiping the skirting board with a duster in her free hand. With her hair blow-dried into a more voluminous style than normal, she was quite chipper and clearly the run out with Muriel had done her good. Granny was nowhere to be seen so I presumed that she had been banished to her bedroom.

"Hello darling, I'm just finishing this call. Yes Marjorie, be sure to tell Lady Featherstone if you see her in Waitrose later on. Bye for now," and with that she replaced the receiver down on the phone.

"Lizzie darling, you are never going to believe what has happened. The most wonderful thing..." she said only noticing James afterwards. "Oh hello dear, I'm Elizabeth's mother, you can call me Joyce." She shook James's outstretched hand distractedly.

"Hello Mrs Button. I'm James, Lizzie's flatmate. I'm so very sorry for your loss."

"Thank you dear, that's very kind of you."

"So, what happened Mum?" I asked, curious for her to continue the story.

"The doorbell rang an hour ago and it was a florist with the biggest bouquet. You'll never guess who they are from," she said, but before I could even reply, she took me by the hand and practically dragged me into the living room. There on the sideboard now taking centre stage was an enormous bouquet of bright tropical flowers topped with half a dozen orange Birds of Paradise. She proudly held up the card from the flowers and read aloud, *"To Mrs Button and family. We were so sorry to hear of your loss. With sympathy, Lydia Black, Alex Garner and all the team at UK Today,"* she ended on a triumphant note. "Can you believe it Lizzie? Celebrities paying tribute to your father," she said, somewhat inaccurately.

I knew that the flowers would have been arranged by Maggie as she was so thoughtful like that, but by adding Alex and Lydia's names to the card, Mum would now be even more insufferable over the next few days.

As Mum basked in the glory of her 'celebrity flowers', I showed James his room upstairs and as he hung up his suit on the back of the door, we made the decision to beat a hasty retreat to the pub. Downstairs, as we were leaving, my mother was already making another phone call to a friend to tell them about the flowers and I instantly knew that going out for a drink was the right decision.

The Grey Bull had been my local of choice since I was fourteen when I used to sit through in the back pool room with my friends and sip half pints of cider and blackcurrant, well out of the way of the local police. The pub itself had changed very little over the years, still owned by the same family although the landlady Diane hailed from Yorkshire as she had married the landlord Stuart a few years ago and taken up residence in the village. Diane's friendly personality coupled with her no-nonsense approach soon made her popular with the locals and it felt like not only was she was one of us, but that she had been here for years. As it was now after four o'clock on a Friday afternoon, the pub was already filling up with workmen who tended to finish earlier on a Friday after a long week on building sites and quarries that were some of the biggest local employers. The sight of so many young lads in their late teens and early twenties had James's eyes popping out of his head before we had even reached the bar.

"You just calm yourself Casanova, remember, you're not in Soho now," I teased. "You see all those guys?"

"Oh yeah," he answered unable to take his eyes off the array of lads in dirty jeans, boots, t-shirts, and Hi-Viz vests.

"All of them are off limits."

"All of them?" James sounded like a disappointed schoolboy.

"Every. Single. One."

"I'll try my best," he replied mischievously.

"You better had."

Diane approached us with a smile. At five foot seven with a slim figure, Diane looked radiant as she wore a long silky black and white jumpsuit and with her shiny blonde hair nestling over her shoulders, she put the rest of us scruffs to shame.

"Hey you," she said coming out from behind the bar to give me a hug and a kiss. "Long time no see," she continued, probably forgetting that it was only Christmas when I was last here.

"I'm so sorry to hear about your dad. You know where Stuart and I are if you need anything at all," she said generously. I thanked her for her kindness and ordered some drinks as she told us to grab the table that had just been vacated next to the log burner over in the corner of the bar. Lots of the locals smiled at me sympathetically, knowing that I was back home because of my father's death. The jukebox was playing some AC/DC through in the poolroom and it was only when the song came to an end could the click of the pool cue against the balls on the table be heard. Diane brought my gin and tonic over and placed it next to James's pint of Italian beer. She put his change on the table in front of him and he immediately said to her,

"I think you've forgotten to charge us for one of the drinks,"

"I haven't forgotten," Diane replied. "You're not in London now sunshine."

Looking around at the group of lads standing at the bar drinking and then down at his change on the table, James announced to Diane and myself, "that's it, I'm moving to the North!"

Diane laughed and turned to me, "Another convert. He definitely will be when you tell him that you can buy a three-bedroom house in the village for less than a hundred thousand pounds."

James's jaw dropped and his mouth gaped open.

"You have got to be kidding me! A hundred

thousand? You couldn't buy a garage lock-up in London for that."

As we settled by the fire with our drinks, I updated James a bit more on what had been going on but I was careful as to what I said out in public given that in this village, like every other, everyone knows everybody. I had been hoping that Jayne would pop in as I had texted her earlier, but she had got caught up with making dinner for Brian and her brother who were both busy with lambing. I also remembered that she'd said in the car on Wednesday that she didn't want to go to the pub until she had publicly announced her pregnancy. James and I stayed at the Grey Bull for a few more hours and both of us put away our fair share of alcohol. James was happy being in a relaxed environment and even returned from the toilets on one occasion surprised that the locals made conversation with him at the urinal.

"You definitely wouldn't get that in London," is what he kept saying.

By the time that we got home, it was after eleven and the house was in darkness. We had ordered fish and chips at the pub for dinner after messaging Mum to tell her not to bother cooking for us. I poured James a glass of cold tap water for him to take upstairs, something which he eyed with suspicion and held it out at arm's length as if it were some animal that was about to bite him.

"A glass of good clean northern water to take to bed," I said to him as he swayed with his drink in the kitchen doorway.

"I'd have rather brought something home from the pub to take to bed," he replied smiling. I laughed, not quite sure whether he was referring to a drink or one of the local workmen. Knowing James, he probably meant both.

CHAPTER 8

Killing Time

James and I emerged from our respective bedrooms at the same time the following morning, our hangovers clearly in sync with each other. I'd really enjoyed the evening in the pub and it had done me good to get out of the house and have a few drinks to relax. The locals, along with Stuart and Diane behind the bar, were fantastic and did their best to keep my spirits lifted. James couldn't resist flirting with some of the lads in the bar over the course of the night and the banter level was raised at one point when one of them suggested to his girlfriend that he might "switch sides". This didn't go down well with the young lady, even though it was very much said in jest.

Downstairs, I could see that Granny was busying herself in the dining room as I passed the door on the way to the kitchen. James had nipped out to the corner shop to buy a paper as he always did in London every Saturday morning and returned shortly afterwards with a small bundle of today's tabloids.

"I need to keep on top of my showbiz gossip. Well, that and the need to see which of my clients have been making a tit of themselves," he said, winking at me.

As a celebrity agent, James's client list had been boosted in recent years by a host of reality TV stars and Instagram "Influencers", a term which I always found amusing as I always think of "influenza" rather than "influencer" and the reality was that influenza was probably more entertaining. We'd decided in the pub last night that we would go for a long walk today and stay well out of my mother's way, especially as the vicar was coming round again to iron out the final details for Dad's funeral on Monday.

In the dining room, I could see that Granny was arranging sympathy cards along the windowsill.

"Hello dear, I'm just putting my cards out. Your mother won't let me have them up in the living room because she's jealous."

"Jealous?" I enquired.

"Yes, because she only has thirty-seven cards and I've got fifty-four," she boasted triumphantly.

"It's not a competition, Granny."

"Try telling your mother that dear."

I left her to it and at that moment Mum came in

through the front door looking harassed.

"Morning Lizzie darling. *That* woman is infuriating," she said putting her handbag and car keys on the console table in the hall.

"Which woman is that?" I wasn't sure if I should dare ask.

"Valerie whatshername, the church warden," she replied sounding exasperated. "I've been to the church to check on the flowers for Monday and the path leading up to the front door is all overgrown with bushes and God-knows-what. I told her that it will need cutting back by Monday and all she could say was that 'we're keeping it wild to attract the bees'," she said, mimicking a pathetic voice which I presumed to be that of Valerie.

"I told her that the bloody bees can find somewhere else to feed. I'm not having the mourners skirting around the bushes behind the coffin like some wretched conga line on a Benidorm hen weekend."

Knowing that we had made the right decision to go out for a long walk, James and I didn't hang about any longer. Outside it was another sunny April day although there was quite a chill in the air, so we were relieved that we had been cautious and taken our thicker coats with us. Across the road, stood the once majestic Brampton House which served as a nursing home for as long as I could remember. I could actually recall Dad telling me that it had once been a luxurious spa hotel for wealthy Edwardians before serving as a convalescence home during the war. As we were both curious to explore the grounds in their abandoned dilapidated state, we didn't hesitate to push the rusted gate open and as it offered little resistance, we took that as an open invitation to proceed. The once manicured lawns were now overgrown and mossy underfoot whist providing a playground for the dozens of rabbits that scattered in every direction on our approach. Several long greenhouses where plants had once been nurtured and cultivated, were now mere shells with very few panes of glass still intact. The whole place was eery and in my current mood, I didn't feel like hanging about, so we left the greenhouses behind and made our way round to the more formal ornate gardens at the front of the house that led down to the river. Looking up at the windows with their art deco stained-glass designs, I half expected to see Mrs Danvers staring back at me. As beautiful as this house was, Manderley it was not. The lawns rolled down from the front of the house to the riverbank where the stone urns that once stood proudly were now solemnly sat as if embarrassed by their current state of neglect. There was a little latch gate at the bottom of the garden that led directly onto the earthy footpath that ran alongside the riverbank. It wasn't particularly well maintained and at various points it dropped away into the river itself, probably as a result of the flooding that had occurred here a couple of months back. I'd been in London, but I'd seen a number of videos on friends' Facebook feeds showing the torrents of water flowing at speed downstream carrying anything it could with it. The footpath took us right along to the far end of the village, not once leaving the riverbank until we finally reached a large back iron railway bridge that crossed over the river at an angle. At this point the footpath took us up away from the river and we stepped onto the railway line.

"Is it safe to be walking on here?" James asked as he lurched from one concrete sleeper to the next in an effort to establish a rhythm of walking for the next couple of miles.

"Yeah, it's fine. Although the line is still functioning it hasn't been used for a couple of years. They've had a shed load of lottery money to do it up and turn it into a tourist attraction."

"Like the Harry Potter train?"

"That sort of thing, I guess. I know there's quite a few locals who think it's a money pit and we'd be better off ripping up the tracks and turning the line into a cycle path and walking route."

"There's no going back once you do that though," replied James. I had to agree with him. It was lovely to walk along the railway line on this cool sunny day. It would be such a shame to see it torn up. Forty-five minutes later we reached the next village where the old railway station had recently been converted into a pub. Along the platform were a number of tables and chairs, several of which were already taken by people who, like us, had stopped for an early lunch.

"Are you hungry?" I asked James.

"Seeing as though you made me skip breakfast, I'm starving now," he replied, not without a hint of good humour.

"I'm evil I know," I said, playing up to the part. "Fancy sitting outside?" I suggested, motioning to a free table at the end of the platform that was nestled beside a pile of old trunks and suitcases that had been meticulously placed there to add to the period feel.

"It's very Downton Abbey. Maggie Smith could walk along here any minute."

"Excuse me, that's *Dame* Maggie Smith to you, you oik," I joked giving James my best period drama voice.

"All the best ones are dames. Dame Maggie, Dame Judy. Dame Edna."

"Dame Edna isn't a real dame you ninny."

"Wash your mouth out," shouted James whilst crossing himself as if he were in church. Perhaps he had said this a little too loudly as several people at neighbouring tables turned and looked in our direction.

"Ignore them, James. You don't have an audience," I warned him, well aware that once he has people watching him, my flatmate could never resist the opportunity to play up to the crowd. A young girl brought two hand-written menus over to us and informed us that the Soup of the Day was parsnip and carrot with cumin and the Pie of the Day was turkey, red onion and cranberry.

"I love that you have a Pie of the Day. Proper Northern food. But, having said that..." he continued perusing the menu, I'm going to go for the chicken Caesar salad."

"Quelle surprise!" I said in the most godawful French accent. "You always go for Chicken Caesar Salad."

"What can I say? I'm a creature of habit."

"Oh, trust me, I know!" I replied giving him a knowing grin. "Well, I need some comfort food. I'm going to have the fish finger sandwich with a side order of skinny fries," I announced placing the menu face down and signalling to the young waitress that we were ready to order. I had intended on ordering a coffee but when James asked the waitress for a bottle of Sauvignon Blanc with two glasses, I didn't object. It was just after twelve and therefore acceptable to have a drink. Plus, it was the weekend.

James did a sterling job of keeping the

conversation away from death, funerals and mourning so instead we gossiped about his latest client who was an 'influencer' and was already making a name for herself as being 'difficult'.

"So did she really call you to ask if you could phone Harvey Nichols and ask them for three pairs of Jimmy Choo heels in an assortment of colours, for free?" I asked him, still in slight disbelief at the brass neck of his client.

"Oh yeah. I told her to get stuffed but not using such polite language." James replied whilst rolling his eyes. "As if a high-end department store would want to publicly associate themselves with her. She'll learn the hard way. If she spent less money on lip fillers and Botox, then she'd be able to buy her own shoes."

"I know I work in telly, but I still don't really get this thing about these so-called 'influencers'."

"It's all smoke and mirrors. They create the image of living an amazing life but most of it is faked and a lot of them don't have two beans to their name."

"Really?"

"Oh God yeah. It's quite worrying the level of delusion that some of them live with, particularly with those that approach our agency wanting us to represent them. Obviously, we are there to make money but the last thing that we want is to have a large number of reality stars on the books. It puts off the people with real talent, the ones who make it onto the prime-time weekend chat shows. They're the ones who bring in the real money and kudos. They're generally much nicer people too."

The food arrived and was soon devoured. The three mile walk to get there had certainly worked up our appetites and it wasn't long before we were sat with empty plates and contemplating having "one more for the road" which we inevitably did.

"We can't go back to the house pissed," I warned James, trying for once to be the sensible one. "Remember the vicar could still be there when we get back and I think that we ought to stay in tonight. Mum wouldn't appreciate us going to the pub two nights in a row and leaving her alone with Granny. Come to think of it, Granny wouldn't appreciate being left alone with my mother!" I said giggling.

"Why don't I cook for us all this evening? Nothing fancy, just some carbonara," James suggested generously.

"That's a nice idea and really kind of you James. Not a boozy one though. Mum is going to the chapel of rest tomorrow with Granny and Michael to see Dad." I was aware that we would need to talk about the funeral at some point this afternoon and we had done very well to avoid the subject up until now.

"And what about you?" James asked, reaching

across the table taking my hand in his.

"What about me?" I tried to play the innocent.

"Aren't you going to the Chapel of Rest?" he asked, looking me right in the eyes. Mine started to well up.

"I'm not sure to be honest. One part of me wants to go and say goodbye... my heart wants that, but my head is telling me that I should remember my father just how he was with his warm loving affectionate smile. The truth is, I don't honestly know James."

I was determined not to cry. We had had a lovely lunch so I urged James to drink his glass of wine that had only been brought to the table a few minutes ago so that we could pay the bill and head back on the three mile walk to Branthwaite.

"Drink up," I ordered him. "We can talk about this more on the walk back home." I asked for the bill and nipped to the loo. By the time that I had returned a few minutes later, James's wine glass was empty but still cold, condensation dripping down the side of it. He was smiling and had that familiar look on the face that I always recognised when he had had a few drinks.

"I'll just pay the bill and we'll head off," I announced.

"It's ok, I've taken care of it." James replied, smiling and folding the receipt before sliding it into his wallet.

"There was no need. Thank you."

We decided that as we had had several large glasses of wine between us, that it might be a better idea to walk the quiet back road to Branthwaite rather than trying to negotiate the railway line's concrete sleepers and risking us both spraining our ankles ahead of the funeral.

An hour later we rocked up outside my parents' house to find a black Mercedes parked outside.

"It will be the funeral director. Better have one of these," I said, offering him an extra strong mint before taking one myself.

Inside, a voice hollered through from the lounge, "Lizzie darling, is that you? We're in the drawing room." I momentarily sniggered at Mum referring to the lounge as the drawing room yet again.

My mother was on the sofa alongside Granny and a man in his late forties was sitting on the armchair opposite them holding a black leather folio case in which he was making notes on a pad. Strewn across the table was mother's "mood board" notebook surrounded by magazine cuttings of photos of what appeared to be Princess Diana's funeral. James slipped quietly up to his room not wanting to intrude on the meeting, so I sat myself on the other free armchair. I noticed that the television was on which seemed strange, then I realised as I squinted through the sunbeam shining directly onto the screen that it was showing a recording of

Princess Diana's funeral. The box sitting on top of the video recorder had the label "Princess Diana Funeral – 1997". "Why date it?" I thought, she only had one funeral.

As much as I was used to my mother, I felt sorry for the funeral director who in his career, I would imagine, had never experienced a funeral planning meeting quite like this.

"Lizzie, this is Mr Gurney who is arranging your father's funeral on Monday," announced Mum. The man gave a sympathetic smile as he leaned forward to gently shake my hand.

"I've just been ironing out the finer details with your mother," said Mr Gurney who did his best to hide the weary look on his face, albeit unsuccessfully.

"Lizzie. I've added an additional funeral car to the cortege. I don't want your Auntie Barbara following us in your Uncle Derek's car. I saw them in Sainsburys car park last week and it must have been at least six years old as well as needing a good run through the car wash." Just when I thought that my mother couldn't be more of a snob, she comes out with a corker like this. "We've looked at the plots on the cemetery as well. I had a walk up there earlier and made some notes. Sir William Featherstone has a plot free just across from him. It would be nice for him and your father to be near each other," she said.

You would be forgiven for thinking that she was talking about two children having their first day at school.

"If it would be comforting for you to know he will be buried near a friend, we can try our best to arrange that," Mr Gurney said, trying to be helpful.

"They didn't really know each other well between you and me, Mr Gurney but it would be lovely if Lady Caroline would see my husband's headstone when she goes to visit Sir William." Mum said with a triumphant tone, which was somewhat inappropriate for the current situation. She had been desperate to move in the same social circle as Sir William and Lady Caroline Featherstone for years and it now looked as if she would finally achieve her dream, albeit it in the local cemetery.

"Are we having vol au vents Joyce?" piped up Granny who had been sitting silently up until now, occasionally flicking through a magazine. Without waiting for an answer, she turned to me, "She took my book off me Lizzie." I smiled sympathetically.

"As I said to you earlier Gladys, they're taking care of the catering up at Branthwaite Hall and no, we won't be having vol au vents."

"Well, if there's nothing more to arrange, I'll be on my way Mrs Button," said Mr Gurney, zipping up his folio case as he rose from his chair. "Thank you for the tea and delicious cake."

"I always say, you can't go wrong with Marks and Spencer, Mr Gurney," replied Mum in a posher than usual accent. "Did you see my flowers Mr Gurney? They're from Alex and Lydia on that *UK Today* programme. They're good friends of the family you know." Mr Gurney smiled once more. I could see that the poor man must have thought he was in some bizarre alternate universe where life was one permanent sitcom setting.

Once the front door had shut and we were on our own, Mum dropped her stoic façade and her forced smile vanished.

"Lizzie, can you give me a hand in the kitchen for five minutes please? Oh, and give your grandmother that wretched book. I've hidden it behind Nigella and Delia," she said, indicating the wall mounted bookcase in the kitchen. I retrieved the forbidden volume of Fifty Shades and took it through to the lounge. Now that Granny was occupied with her book, Mum shut the kitchen door.

"That woman really is the limit." Mum was looking particularly exasperated. "I must be a saint to be so patient with her. Well, I can tell you Lizzie, my patience is rapidly running out. Did you know she had been drinking? She's been at my cooking brandy this morning. I tell you, if I need to make an emergency tiramisu, I won't have any to soak the sponge fingers."

"Are you sure it's brandy?" I was doing my best to be the voice of reason.

"Yes. I found my Princess Margaret mug in the airing cupboard earlier and she hadn't been drinking tea from it."

I tried my best not to smirk at the irony of Granny's choice of mug for her secret tipple.

"Did you and James have a nice walk?" she asked, and I was relieved for the change of subject.

"Yes, it was lovely thanks. We walked down the railway line to the station at Harehope. It's been converted into a pub you know. We had a lovely lunch."

"That's nice dear," Mum replied absentmindedly as she washed the dishes.

"James has offered to cook dinner for us this evening, if that's ok with you?"

"That's kind of him dear. I hadn't thought about what we were going to do for supper. Perhaps you could help him? I need to pop out to see Muriel as she has kindly offered to do the flowers in the church for your father's funeral and I want to give her the money for them before I forget. She's been to the nursery today to get the bulk of them and she picked up an order of lilies from the florist in the village." I looked at her for a moment, noticing for the first time just how tired she looked. Behind the bright stoic façade, she was struggling.

"Mum you look done in. You need some rest. Have you been sleeping?" I asked what I knew to be a futile question.

"Not really, darling. My mind is in overdrive with funeral arrangements during the day and when I get to bed, I find myself lying there on my own. Oh Lizzie," and with that the tears came. I hugged her so tightly as she sobbed, her torso shaking gently to the rhythm of grief. "I miss him so much Lizzie. I know I rabbit on a bit, but we had a good marriage. We were happy." At that moment, I couldn't help but think of the scarf in the car and the text messages, perhaps somewhat inappropriately. I couldn't say anything to her about it. I didn't even know what to think about it myself.

It was a quiet uneventful evening. James cooked a delicious dinner of penne carbonara followed by a pear and chocolate tart that he whipped up in no time using a defrosted packet of puff pastry, a jar of Nutella and a tin of pears. After we had eaten, Granny retired to her room to finish her book while my mother watched some Saturday night telly. James and I joined her once the washing-up was done and by ten o'clock we collectively decided it was time for bed. A long day lay ahead of us tomorrow with the visit to the chapel of rest where Dad was to spend his final night.

Hours later, I turned over in bed and looked at my

phone that was charging on the bedside table, if only to check the time in the absence of any clocks in the bedroom. Quarter to two. I must have lain awake for the last half an hour and avoided looking at my phone, determined to get straight back to sleep. Alas, that was not to be the case. I couldn't stop thinking about Dad and the visit to the chapel of rest later today. Yesterday afternoon I was very much veering on the side of not going but now I was worried that I wouldn't get to say a proper goodbye. I tiptoed through to the small bedroom across the landing that had once belonged to my brother. James was fast asleep, that was, until I sat down on the side of his bed.

"I think I've decided to go and see Dad tomorrow," I said to him, looking for assurance that I'd made the right decision.

"If you're sure," he replied sleepily. "I think it's a good idea but when you get there you can always change your mind if you want. Don't let anybody force your hand." I nodded in agreement and returned to my bed where sleep finally came and enveloped me.

CHAPTER 9

The Mystery Woman

By eleven o'clock on Sunday morning, Michael had arrived and we were all assembled in the living room with our coats on, ready to go to the chapel of rest. James had offered to stay behind and cook lunch for us all on our return and Mum had pointed out where everything was in the kitchen. It had been arranged the previous evening that once we were back from the chapel of rest tomorrow, that Michael's wife Elaine would bring the children down and join us for lunch. What with all the arrangements for the funeral and Michael insisting that they didn't miss school, this would be Mum's first opportunity to see her grandchildren since Dad died at the start of the week.

Michael had two drawings that Josh and Amy had done for their Grandad which he handed to our mother.

"I thought that we could put them in the coffin

with Dad," Michael said nervously to her, not wanting to set her off crying.

"That's a lovely thought darling," said Mum, trying her best to remain composed. She studied the pictures for a moment and handed them back to Michael before turning to me.

"Didn't you have something that you wanted to put in with your father Lizzie?" she asked.

"Yes, I have some photos that I have printed out, ones from us growing up and a couple from that lovely family holiday in France that we had a few years ago. With that, we climbed into Michael's car and set off on the six-mile journey to the funeral director in the neighbouring village.

I still wasn't sure until the last minute that I wanted to go into the chapel to see Dad. In the end, I felt a momentum that carried me into the funeral director's office although I held back and let Mum go in first on her own. The rest of us sat on the large comfortable corner sofa in the reception area, my brother and I flanking Granny on both sides. Ten minutes later Mum came out, wiping her eyes which were now red and shiny.

"Would you like to go in and see your father now dear?" Not being keen to go in there on my own, I suggested that Michael and Granny join me and that we all go in together. I'm not sure why I was nervous as it was just my father in there but if the truth be told, this was my first time seeing a dead body. To say that I felt uneasy was somewhat of an understatement and that only led me to feeling pangs of guilt.

It was a mere thirty minutes later that I was in the car with the window down to allow the cool breeze onto my face. Dad had looked peaceful but it certainly didn't feel like it was him and I decided not to hang around. I put the photos down the side inside the coffin, told him I loved him and left the chapel. I didn't pause in the reception area but instead, headed straight out onto the street where people were going about their normal Sunday morning lives. Michael followed me out to check that I was ok which I reassured him that I was and that he could go back inside and take all the time that he needed. I was relieved to have had that brief moment with Dad and by doing that, I could finally start to process my grief which had been on pause all week. Outside on the street, I closed my eyes and I could feel him with me. In my heart, I knew that he would be with me wherever I go and that gave me comfort that I would be able to rely on in the coming weeks and months.

Back at the house, James had done an impressive job of laying the table in the dining room for lunch. He had found a box of green candles in the sideboard along with a crisp white tablecloth and set eight places around the large table.

Mum greatly appreciated his efforts and once the children had arrived with Elaine, we seated ourselves at the table. She had been the first to get in there and ensconced herself in a chair facing the window, muttering something about not wanting to sit looking at Granny's mass of sympathy cards covering the sideboard and the large wooden bookcase.

James served up a leg of lamb on a large platter surrounded by an abundance of roast potatoes, crisp and golden roasted to perfection before removing the lids of the remaining tureens of vegetables that sent small clouds of steam rising up from the table. Granny was on her best behaviour and tucked into a generous plateful of dinner with gusto. For an elderly lady of diminutive stature, she could certainly put away a generous portion. Elaine and Michael didn't have very much to say for themselves and if I didn't know any better, I'd say that there was a frostiness between them which was odd for today of all days. I didn't give it any more thought and once the main courses were finished, I helped James to take the dirty plates and leftover food through to the kitchen.

Josh and Amy were getting restless, so Michael suggested that they go out to play in the garden. Around the table, the conversation was a little muted with Michael and Elaine not looking directly at each other. I wasn't sure what was going on with them. Michael hadn't been himself since I returned home last Monday but given the week's events, that wasn't surprising. An hour passed and James's sticky toffee pudding had been devoured along with a large tub of creamy vanilla ice cream. Michael and Elaine made their excuses and left although the children were keen to stay. Granny retired upstairs as she wanted to finish the final four chapters of her book and thought it wise to be out of Mum's way while she read. It was an early night for everyone with a long day ahead tomorrow. James had said that he would be going back to London after the funeral and that Jayne had agreed to drive him to the station in Durham afterwards. I didn't want him to go but I knew that I had to help sort out some of Dad's things for a few days before returning to London myself.

The morning of the funeral saw the house become a hive of activity. Thankfully Granny had decided to remain upstairs out of the way once she had had her breakfast which gave me a sigh of relief knowing that at least she and Mum wouldn't be bickering this morning. I tidied the kitchen and filled the dishwasher with the breakfast things and just as I'd finished wiping the surfaces, the florist arrived at the front door with the funeral flowers which I laid on the large coffee table in the living room. She handed me a handful of small cards which were to be written out by us all and placed on the corresponding floral arrangements. I went upstairs to take my mother a card, but she wasn't in her bedroom and on further searching, I discovered that she wasn't actually in the house. Two minutes later, the mystery was solved as she came in through the front door.

"Mum, where have you been?"

"Just up to Branthwaite Hall darling, a couple of last-minute things to check," she said, taking her coat off.

"The flowers have arrived. Here's a card for you to write out for your arrangement." I told her.

"Thank you. I'll go upstairs to get changed and write it up there." Michael had asked me to write the card from us both and to include Elaine and the children. Sitting in the living room, I racked my brain for the most appropriate thing to say but I couldn't focus. My mind kept drifting off to the text messages on Dad's phone from the mysterious Carol and the scarf that Michael had found in the car. I told myself that this wasn't the time or the place to be going over that in my head. In the end, I could come up with nothing more than "The best Dad in the world, Love Always, Lizzie, Michael, Elaine, Josh and Amy xxx".

An hour later everyone assembled downstairs in the living room while Granny was sitting flicking through the TV guide magazine.

"Oooh, that Michael Balls is on *Loose Women* today. I like him, Michael Balls. Shame I'm going to miss it."

None of us knew quite how to respond to the inappropriate comment from the mad old woman in the corner so we said nothing. Mum came in and immediately straightened Michael's tie and checked my dress, picking up bits of non-existent fluff off my shoulders. As I glanced around the room, I noticed that the huge bouquet from Lydia, Alex and the team at *UK Today* had been moved to somewhere else in the house which I thought was strange. James came into the living room and quietly said "they're here," We couldn't see the road from the living room as the window looked out onto the back garden and across the field to the burn. Out through the front door and across the short gravel drive to the road, the hearse had parked followed by three black Mercedes funeral cars, each gleaming so clean and served to add to the air of formality for the occasion.

Looking at the hearse containing Dad's coffin, my first reaction was to crack a joke at my brother.

"I'm surprised she didn't have a horse-drawn gun carriage."

"Oh, I did ask darling, but they didn't have one." I was startled by the sound of my mother's voice behind me. Not having realised that she was within earshot I immediately regretted my cheeky quip but then I ascertained that she thought that I was deadly serious. Michael and James carried out the three floral arrangements to go on top of the coffin and handed them to two of the drivers who took them. A small spray of white roses at the top from Mum, a large spray of cala lilies, my favourite flowers, in the middle from myself, Michael, Elaine and the children. At the foot of the coffin was the most beautiful arrangement of white and yellow marguerite daisies from Granny.

"Beautiful, aren't they?" said Granny who had sidled up next to me. Your mother didn't want daisies, she thought they're too common but I said to her, 'I want daisies'. We always had a garden full of them when we lived at Oakenshaw Terrace when your dad was a young lad."

"They're beautiful Granny. More than that, they're perfect."

"This is all wrong you know, our Lizzie. That should be me in the hearse, not my son. Not my David. I never thought I'd ever be burying my only bairn." Poor Granny was unable to hold it together any longer. James approached us and kindly offered to escort Granny back into the house where he seated her in the chair in the living room as we weren't due to leave just yet.

It was another fifteen minutes before the funeral

director indicated that we should be ready to go. My mother had a list of who was to travel in each car and directed the other mourners accordingly.

"Gladys?" she said, standing out in the front garden. "Lizzie, where on earth is your grandmother?" she added exasperatedly.

"James had taken her back inside to have a seat. I'll go and get her."

In the house, I headed to the living room checking in the kitchen and dining room en route for my wayward grandmother. There she was in the middle of the living room kneeling on the floor in front of the television.

"Granny, we have to get going."

"How do I go on with this blessed thing?" she replied as I took a step forward to see she was holding the remote control for the TV up to her eyes.

"Granny, you can't watch telly, we have to go to the church."

"I'm not watching it. I'm trying to set it to tape *Loose Women* because that Michael Balls is going to be on it," she said, still trying to figure out how to work the remote.

"We haven't got time for that, Granny. Come on!"

"Just show me how to do it darling. I really don't want to miss him."

I told myself that it was the grief talking and concluded that it would be far easier to set *Loose Women* to record on the TV planner than continue to argue with her. Once she was reassured that it was set, she allowed me to help her up off her knees, loudly passing wind as she did so and joined me outside at the hearse. Mum was annoyed but said nothing as I eased Granny into the seat next to her. Once we were all in and the doors were shut, Granny let out another fart, this time much louder than the previous one and sadly for the rest of us including the poor driver, far more pungent.

"Can we ask the driver to stop at the shop on the way? I need a packet of mints," said Granny. Mum was about to say something but I took her hand and said,

"Granny, we're not passing a shop. We're going straight to the church, following the hearse."

"But I always like a mint to suck on at a funeral." At that moment, one of the pall bearers who was sat in the front passenger seat reached back and handed her half a tube of polo mints.

"Thank you, Son," Granny replied appreciatively. I could hear my mother taking a deep breath in an effort to maintain her stoic composure.

As the cortege moved slowly through the village behind the hearse, people stopped on the roadside to bow their heads in respect. I was glad to be in the car for the short journey to the village church having initially and swiftly shot down my mother's suggestion that Michael and I walk the route behind the hearse just like Princes William and Harry had done for Diana.

There was quite a crowd waiting for us as we pulled up outside the church gates which was a lovely surprise and strangely comforting. The funeral service was lovely and as I'd let Mum do her thing with organising it all, there were certainly one or two surprises. As we were finishing *The Lord's Prayer,* I had noticed one of the church wardens wheel a large flat screen TV across next to the coffin. I thought perhaps that they might play a slideshow of photos from Dad's life. What I hadn't expected however, was for a fuzzy image of Elton John on pause to appear on the screen and spring to life to belt out *Candle In The Wind.* Not just the ordinary version either but the one performed at Princess Diana's funeral at Westminster Abbey. I was mortified and wished for the song to be over, let alone the entire service. Just before the proceedings concluded, the vicar announced that while only the immediate family would attend the burial in the village cemetery, the remaining mourners were invited for refreshments at Branthwaite Hall. I'd remained fairly stoic throughout the service apart from the tears during the eulogy, but it was at the end when they played a recording of Louis Armstrong singing *We Have All The Time In The World* and the four pallbearers lifted Dad's coffin up onto their shoulders did my tears flow once more. I followed behind holding up Mum and at that moment, I saw for the first time face-on just how many people had turned up to the church to say goodbye to my father. At the end of the aisle, as we turned left towards the entrance porch of the church, I spied a woman sitting in the front pew of the bell tower, tears flooding down her face, racked with grief. She had short cropped dark hair and wore a thick black coat that looked very expensive. I didn't recognise her and it was only the sheer level of her grief that made her stand out from the crowd and brought her to my attention. Who was she? I didn't have time to dwell as we were soon back in the funeral cars and following the hearse up the winding tarmac drive to the cemetery. The vicar had kept the burial committal brief as the rain started when we arrived at the graveside. Mum had got her wish to have Dad buried just across from Sir William Featherstone. With the coffin lowered gently into the ground, I blew Dad a kiss goodbye and threw a white rose on top of the coffin.

Granny, eager to throw some dirt into the grave grabbed a handful and using me to steady herself at the graveside with her other hand, she enthusiastically chucked the soil into the grave. She did it with such force that her handbag slipped straight off her arm and fell into the open grave. There was a collective gasp from all of us present at that moment. Unfortunately, the handbag had hit the side of the grave on its way down and the loose fastening clasp had come undone so not only was the handbag lying down there on the coffin lid but a variety of contents including a half bottle of brandy, various bottles of tablets, a tv remote control and a mobile phone were scattered across the wooden lid. Just when I thought that nothing else could go wrong, Granny's mobile started ringing and vibrating on the coffin.

There we were, standing around the graveside as *Roll Out The Barrels* echoed from the grave. Thankfully, the young lad who had dug the grave had been quick on his feet and had brought a litter picking stick from the truck and after several attempts lying on the ground and stretching his arm down, he retrieved first, the offending phone followed by the other items. The phone ringing had stopped momentarily before starting up again. By now I could see that my mother was seething with anger and Granny didn't help because instead of promptly switching off the phone, she answered it there and then.

"Oh, hello Maureen. Yes, it went well thank you. No, we've not had the buffet yet."

"Granny, not now," I said, almost dumbstruck in disbelief that she had taken a call at the graveside. "Yes, I did record it. Are you watching it now?" Granny continued.

"Gladys!" snapped Mum, at which point Granny

looked up and realised that everyone was staring at her, many of us with open mouths.

"Maureen, I'm going to have to go. I'll call you later and tell you about the buffet."

With that she ended the call and put the phone back into her handbag. She then turned as if to apologise, but my mother had already walked away in disgust and was striding towards the waiting cars. To my surprise, I found that I myself was now being hurried to the cars by Granny who had latched herself on to me, looping her arm through mine.

"Come on Lizzie, I want to make sure I get there before they start the buffet dear."

"Don't worry Granny, Mum has made sure that we've catered for plenty of people."

"That's all well and good dear but if it's like the funerals down our way, the second they take the cling film off the platters, it's like firing the starting pistol for the one hundred yards dash."

As the car left the cemetery and went through the large wrought iron gates, a solitary figure was standing on the grass holding a large black umbrella with one hand and a bunch of red roses in the other. It was the woman from the church, the one with the short hair that I'd seen crying. Now she appeared far more composed as she solemnly looked straight at me as the car drove past her. Nobody else in the car seemed to notice her or said anything. I turned around to look at her once more out of the rear window as she walked through the gates and up the drive to the cemetery. Whoever she was, she had been close to Dad and she knew exactly who I was.

During the short drive up to Branthwaite Hall, I could think of nothing else but the mystery woman. Could she be the mysterious Carol? On our arrival at the hotel, I didn't get the chance to dwell on the matter any further as I was soon consumed by well-wishers offering their condolences. Granny made straight for the buffet and out the corner of my eye I spied Norah Whittles empty a tray of chicken satay skewers into a carrier bag whilst looking around checking that the coast was clear.

James made a beeline for me and handed me a gin and tonic in the large glass goblet.

"Here you go, get that down you," he said winking at me. I wish I had asked him to accompany me to the cemetery, but he had gone with Jayne and Brian in their car to pick up his bag from the house as they would be taking him to Durham station shortly to get the London train. When I told him about Granny tossing her handbag into the grave and the ringing phone he couldn't resist doubling over in laughter, despite then getting one or two disapproving looks from some of the older mourners in the room. Perhaps it was a good job he wasn't with us at the grave as I don't think he could have contained himself.

There was a small crowd hovering around a table next to where Mum had placed a Book of Condolence. I couldn't make out quite what was grabbing their attention until I moved in closer and saw for myself.

"Oh Christ, she hasn't," I found myself saying. On closer inspection, I said, "She bloody well has." There on a table, was the bouquet of flowers that had been sent by Alex, Lydia and the team at *UK Today*. James was now beside me sniggering mischievously.

"So that's where she had got to first thing this morning." My mother had trumped all expectations this time and here she was, greeting funeral guests and directing them over to the table to look at her 'celebrity flowers'.

"You have to hand it to her," said James. "On a local level, she's a walking masterclass in PR."

"She's bloody showing off, that's what she's doing." I found myself drinking down the gin swiftly before the empty glass was removed from my hand and immediately replaced with a replenished one. Granny had set herself up on the table nearest the buffet table along with a number of old ladies who could have been friends of the family that I didn't know but I suspected that they were more likely to be professional mourners. The ones who scour the local papers for the death announcements and then fill their diaries with funerals. According to Granny, it was less to do with a morbid fascination and more about getting their lunch or tea for free each day. Granny was deep in conversation and with a plate of funeral food in front of her and a number of brandies lined up, she appeared content in her natural habitat.

A group of my old friends had set themselves up at two large tables in the corner of the room and judging by the number of empty glasses, they were making a day of it. As I went around the room thanking people for coming whilst simultaneously avoiding questions about my relationship status, I took ten minutes out in the corner at what had soon become the rowdy table. Stuart and Diane from the pub carried another round of drinks over including a gin for myself which Diane referred to as a "Branthwaite measure". On tasting it, I realised that she wasn't kidding and reached across the table for one of the bottles of tonic to dilute it a little. I told them that this was going to be my limit for this afternoon but I did promise to join them all back at The Grey Bull later.

In the bustling function room, I had a good chat with Clive, Dad's boss who promised to stay in touch and that Mum needn't worry about finances as there would be a lump sum payment made for "death in service" as well as Dad's life insurance policy. In addition, his private pension would kick in so she would be more than financially comfortable in the coming years, I hadn't realised that Dad had planned to retire later this year and now tragically he had been robbed of his quiet retirement time. Clive and his wife Dorothy had kindly offered to take Mum and Granny back to the house while Michael and I decided to go back to the cemetery to check that the flowers had been put back neatly over the grave once it had been filled in. It had never occurred to them to check until Granny had piped up at the hotel after her umpteenth brandy.

"You want to check that they've put them flowers on the grave. There was a fella in Sunderland, turns out that when he had filled the grave in, he would put the flowers in the truck and take them back to the florist. They would give him cash and then reuse the flowers for another funeral."

"Oh, don't be silly Gladys, people don't do that sort of thing, certainly not in the country," Mum replied, now getting very irritated after spending a full day with my grandmother.

"You want to check, people do all sorts when there's a credit crunch," Granny responded.

My mother took me aside and asked me to go to the cemetery on the way home and check, even if just to stop Granny banging on about it.

Michael had decided not to drink at the wake as he wanted to keep a clear head. Elaine had picked up her car on the way back from the cemetery so that she could collect Josh and Amy from her sister's house where they had been playing with their cousins. It had been decided that being only seven and eight years old, they would not attend their Grandad's funeral, but they could come along to the hotel and see everyone afterwards. Michael dropped me at the cemetery gates before returning to the hotel to collect his wife and children. I was more than happy to be on my own and to walk up to the grave alone. As I climbed up the drive, I looked up at the hills that rose above the village and already there was a profusion of new spring lambs scattered across the grassy spoil heaps of the old limestone quarry.

"New life," I said to myself. How appropriate for this place of death to be surrounded by new life. The grave had indeed been filled in quickly and efficiently by the young lad who had stood back from the graveside as we said goodbye only a couple of hours earlier. The three main displays of white flowers that had sat on the coffin had been delicately arranged in the correct order down the middle of the grave but now there was the glaring addition of a bouquet of red roses that I'd seen that woman carrying earlier. There was a card attached to the cellophane wrapping and on closer inspection, I could read the message written in a neat hand:

'With all my love. Carol xxx'

Considering the brief message I spent the next five minutes staring at the card, re-reading it time and time again, my anger building with every moment that passed. At first, I was angry at this woman's intrusion... her intrusion into my father's affections, her intrusion into my parents' marriage and our lives and now her intrusion into my own grief. This was the time when I ought to have been having a quiet moment to talk to Dad, my own private time with him and I was angry with her for leading me to focus on her. She was nothing to me and how dare she muscle in on my emotions as I was dealing with the first major loss in my life.

I couldn't take any more and left the graveside, walking home along the riverbank. When I reached the house, Mum was in the kitchen putting leftover buffet food into an assortment of Tupperware containers while Granny was fast asleep in the living room, mouth gaping wide open.

"She's had a long day bless her," I said.

"She's had a lot of brandy you mean," Mum replied curtly but adding nothing more. She looked tired herself.

"Mum, why don't you leave that and go and have a

lie down upstairs? I can finish that for you."

"It'll only take me a minute darling, I'm almost done. Why don't you go up to the pub? I heard some of your friends say that they were going on there for a drink afterwards. You don't want to be stuck in the house with two old women."

"Yeah, I think I will, but I'll get changed first."

When I returned downstairs ten minutes later wearing jeans and a sweater, my mother opened her mouth as if to admonish me for my choice of attire, but then she thought better of it.

I must have stayed at the pub less than two hours as tiredness overcame me and as I walked the five-minute stroll back home, Jayne called me to check in. She confirmed that James had made it to the station ok and that they were at home with their feet up waiting on the last of the ewes to lamb up in the cow shed. Back home, the house was silent. The hoover was stood abandoned in the living room so Mum must have been cleaning yet again. Her 'celebrity flowers' had been reinstated in their prime position on the sideboard surrounded by more vases and an array of sympathy cards. It was time for bed and given everything that had happened today, I decided not to look at Dad's mobile again until the morning.

CHAPTER 10

Affairs In Order

It must have been the first night in the last seven days that my dreams had not been filled with images of my father, mystery texts or the scarf so I can only put it down to the cumulative exhaustion assisted by the numerous gins that I had consumed in the pub after the funeral yesterday. Downstairs on the kitchen table, Mum was sitting looking through a small pile of bank statements and paperwork.

"Good morning darling, did you sleep ok?" but before I could answer she continued, "I'm just looking through the bank paperwork, but I can't make head or tail of it, your father always took care of the finances," she said, looking unusually vulnerable.

"Can I help with anything?" I offered.

"Thank you darling but you're going back to London in a couple of days. I spoke to Michael briefly on the phone just now and he's going to go through it all. He has the number for your father's financial advisor and together they are going to process the probate paperwork."

"Do you have enough money?" I asked unsure that I had spare to lend her, even if she didn't.

"Yes darling. There's a few thousand in my current account that will last me until it is sorted. The funeral director said that he had already been paid by Clive who insisted picking up the bill for your father's funeral."

"That was incredibly kind of him."

"Yes, I offered to reimburse him but he wouldn't hear of it. Branthwaite Hall said that they would hold off sending their bill for a couple of months because we have spent so much there in the past what with meals, wedding anniversary parties and what not."

"Wow, you wouldn't get that in the city."

"You *can* help me this morning though. I thought that we could go through your father's clothes and bag them up for the charity shop in the village," she said tentatively.

"*Your* charity shop?" I asked, referring to the only one in Branthwaite and the same one that my mother was a volunteer at. "I mean, do you want to see Dad's clothes for sale in the shop where you work? We can always take them to the one down the road in Harehope," I said, doing my best to be pragmatic.

"Absolutely not Lizzie. Your father's clothes were

all from Marksies or Frasers and THAT shop in Harehope just sells market stall and supermarket tat. Are you able to help me?"

"Of course, I can. Are you sure that you're ready to do it?"

"There's never a good time for these things darling and if you're going back to London on Thursday, there's no time like the present. If I'm being honest, I don't much fancy doing it on my own. We can leave your grandmother here. She will be content watching the television. I thought we'd treat her to lunch before taking her home tomorrow."

"So, you're speaking to her again, after what happened yesterday?"

"I'd rather pretend that hadn't occurred and I have to remind myself that as much as she annoys me, at the end of the day she is a mother grieving for her son. I don't envy her that and if I'm still to consider myself to be a Christian, I must learn to let it go and do what I can to support her."

Upstairs we bagged up Dad's clothes into bin liners, a task which felt cold and detached. My mother made sure that I kept shirts and jumpers separate from trousers as it made them easier to sort in the shop. Once we had loaded the bags of clothes into the car, we did one last sweep round for any remaining items.

"Oh, that's your father's cardigan hanging in the

cupboard under the stairs. Grab it will you and I'll add it to the others."

I retrieved the green cardigan from the hook, the one that I had bought him and holding close to me, I took one last sniff. It still smelled of him.

"Actually Mum, I'd like to keep this one if that's ok. I only bought it for him last Christmas," I admitted.

"Are you going to wear it?" she said, looking slightly puzzled at my request.

"Only in the house but I'd feel comforted to know that I have it."

"Very well dear, pop it in your room so it doesn't get left behind when you leave on Wednesday."

I hadn't expected the charity shop to be shut when we arrived, but Mum said that they were closed for a whole week as the manager was on holiday and they didn't have enough volunteers on some days. Inside, the shop didn't smell musty as most charity shops are inclined to do and although it had been a couple of years since I'd been in here, I could see that my mother had definitely made her mark.

"Mum, how come the clothes rails have celebrity faces taped to the top of them?" I asked, bewildered at the life-size cut out faces of actors and presenters that lined the top of the rails.

"Oh, it's my new system, do you like it?" she said proudly as she walked towards the nearest rail. "These are items for a more senior lady. We have the Gloria Hunniford section here for glam daytime wear and over here we have the Dame Judi Dench rail for the older lady's evening wear. Something one might wear on a chat show."

"Do many of your customers appear on chat shows then?" I asked trying to maintain a straight face.

"Don't be facetious darling. You know what I mean." Without waiting for a reply, she continued.

"These are for a younger lady about town." She pointed to a rail adorned by a face I didn't recognise.

"Who is this?"

"Darling, I thought you worked with celebrities on that television show. It's Wincey Willis," she said, as if that should have been glaringly obvious to me.

"What about the men's section?"

"Oh, they're all just filed under Alan Titchmarsh and Michael Gove. We take most men's clothes although I won't accept ripped jeans. We send *them* on to our Sunderland branch."

"Why is this rack separate?" I asked pointing to the rack of trousers.

"Oh, they're ladies' slacks more geared to a woman that wouldn't wear a skirt. It used to have Victoria Wood on it but since she passed I've changed it to Sandi Toksvig."

I shook my head in disbelief.

"Well, we have to remain upmarket dear and I love that Sandi Toksvig. Very clever lady she is."

"I know, I've actually worked with her and she's lovely. So, do people instinctively know which rack they should be looking at?" I was trying hard to get my head around the logic of her bizarre layout system.

"Most of the time it's fine although sometimes I have to give the odd customer a prod and steer them away from Carol Vorderman when they're clearly more of an Ann Widdicombe."

There wasn't anything I could add to that. My mother was certainly a one-off and I wouldn't have her any other way.

"Actually, while we are here, once we have brought your father's things in from the car would you give me a hand to re-do the window as I'd like it done before Raymond, the manager returns from his holiday and there's some boxes that need moving out of the office for the Sunderland branch."

I wasn't going anywhere and if it helped my mother out, then I was happy to assist. In the office on one of the desks was a box full of paperback books. On closer inspection it was actually full of copies of the same books.

"Mum, this box here. It's full of copies of Fifty Shades of Grey."

Her smile vanished.

"You can't put those out in the shop darling, the vicar's wife Mrs Barnabas sometimes comes in. I don't want her or the rest of the village thinking that we're some sort of back street pornographer. It was bad enough your grandmother having that wretched book out on the table when the vicar called in last week."

"How do you actually know what this book is like? You seem very well informed," I replied mischievously.

"Well, I did read it," she whispered as if anyone might hear her. "I read it so that I knew what all the fuss was about and I can tell you Lizzie, it was filth, pure filth and the two sequels were just as bad."

"You read all three?"

"I skimmed them," she replied, desperately backpedalling. "This is a family shop and I'm not having that sort of smut in it."

Before I had a chance to comment further, she handed me another box from the office and instructed me to load that and the rest of the boxes by the back door while she went through to the front of the shop to dress a mannequin for the window.

Ten minutes later I went through to see how she was getting on shouting through as I went.

"Nearly done dear although I'm not sure if I've put this on the right way round."

When I saw what she had done, I stopped dead in my tracks and if my jaw could have hit the floor, it would have. There was my mother stood next to a mannequin that she had just dressed from head to toe in leather bondage gear.

"What do you think dear? It must have come from someone's fancy dress box. It looks a bit like some sort of gladiator outfit don't you think?"

I physically couldn't speak.

"Someone might buy it for Comic Relief or Children in Need. We'll just get this into the window if you would give me a hand dear."

I could have said something. I could have stopped her, but some mischievous force took over me and I helped her lift the bondage-clad mannequin into the centre of the shop window.

"Someone might use it as a Batman costume. It will need some tights and a cape. That's all the rage now you know, men dressing as superheroes."

"Really?"

"Oh yes. Derek Green who lives next to the antiques shop, split up from his wife and had a very messy divorce. She won't let him see the children, so he dressed up as Superman and chained himself to the Tyne Bridge. Perhaps he might like this for his next demonstration?"

"I don't think that it would help his cause to be honest."

"Well, he can have it for a small donation. I like to

think we provide a community service."

We left the bondage gear in the window and locked up the shop before returning home for lunch.

Back at the house, I took myself off to my room for an hour while I called Maggie at work and updated her on the funeral and informed her that I would be back in the office next Monday, exactly two weeks to the day since Dad died. Afterwards I reached behind the bed for Dad's phone and switching it on, I wondered if there were any messages from this Carol woman. As it was, there weren't any and I was tempted to send one to her asking if she was the woman at the church and the cemetery yesterday. As I was about to start tapping the keys, I thought better of it and switched the handset off again. I called Jayne and arranged to pop up to the farm to see her for an hour and catch up as this would be the last opportunity I would have before returning to London.

The following morning, I carried Granny's suitcase downstairs and put it in the boot of Mum's car while my grandmother took down the dozens of sympathy cards in the dining room. I'm sure that I heard her counting as she lifted each one and deposited them in a carrier bag as my mother came through from the garden with a large carrier bag full of clinking glass.

"Put these empty bottles in the boot dear."

"Don't you have glass recycling here?" I asked, puzzled at her request.

"Yes, but your grandmother has managed to work her way through quite an amount of alcohol during her stay and I don't want the neighbours or the bin men to see my box full of brandy and stout bottles on collection day. That sort of thing sticks to your reputation you know. We'll dispose of them discretely at the supermarket car park when we get to Durham this afternoon."

Once we had eventually got Granny and her luggage into the car, not forgetting her empty brandy and stout bottles, Mum drove us up to the cemetery so that Granny could see Dad's grave before she went home to Durham. Walking along the path to the far end where Dad had been buried, Granny soon became distracted by the different gravestones we passed.

"Eeeeh, look at this one Joyce. Died aged eighty years old. That's tragic, no age to go," said Granny not realising how ridiculous that sounded. It was then that I remembered the bouquet of red roses that the mysterious Carol had left on Dad's grave two days ago would still be there. As they were the last thing that I wanted Mum or Granny to see, I walked ahead quickly. When I reached the grave, I discreetly moved Carol's flowers to another grave two rows away, taking care to ensure that neither Mum nor Granny saw me do it. Granny had a few tears at her son's graveside whereas Mum and I remained stoically silent which wasn't unexpected given the amount of crying done in the last nine or ten days. As we walked away, Granny stopped in her tracks.

"Hang on, I forgot something," Granny said, before shuffling back along the towards Dad's grave. My mother and I followed at a short distance, both of us thinking that Granny wanted one quiet moment alone at the graveside. I think that both of us were astounded standing there on the path as we watched my grandmother delve into her handbag and take out a disposable camera and proceed to take photos of the grave and the flowers. Mercifully, she stopped short of asking me to take one of her posing next to the grave. Moments later a slightly breathless Granny caught up with us putting the camera back into her handbag.

"I wanted to get some snaps to show Renee and Marjorie in the sheltered housing," she said, as if taking photos of graves was the most natural thing in the world. Mum remained silent and was clearly counting down the hours before we dropped Granny off at her home. It was on the car journey to Durham that I remembered I hadn't returned the bouquet of red roses back to Dad's grave. My first thought was to leave them where they were but as the half hour journey wore on, guilt overcame me. "What if the family of the grave that now had Carol's flowers on saw them and were wondering what the hell was going on? What would Dad think of me?" I would need to go back up there later this afternoon and move the roses back across to his grave and as reluctant as I was to do so, it was the right thing to do.

We took Granny for a pub lunch before going to the supermarket and ensuring that she was stocked up for the week. At her home, even more cards were waiting on the doormat and once we were sure that she was settled in, we left her to open her post before returning to Branthwaite. I'd asked Mum to drop me off at the cemetery after telling her that I wanted a private moment alone with Dad before I returned to London the next day. It wasn't quite a white lie as I'd wanted a little bit of quiet time up there to be alone with my thoughts and at the same time it gave me the opportunity to put the mystery woman's flowers back on Dad's grave. Walking home half an hour later I fiddled with the card that I'd removed from the red roses in case my mother or anyone else should go to the cemetery in the next week or two. I'd tried many times in the past week to rationalise this woman's messages and her actions, this woman Carol, but no matter how many reasoned arguments I formed in my head, nothing could mask the fact that my father had being having an affair. If his diary was correct, then he would have met her on his way to the hotel the day before he died and therefore, his last day on this earth was one filled with deceit.

CHAPTER 11

Return To London

There was no chance of my sleeping in this morning what with my mother clattering about downstairs amongst the cacophony of noise provided by the vacuum cleaner, coffee machine and washing machine's spin cycle. I descended the stairs having been showered and dressed and once Mum was satisfied that I was presentable, she ushered me out of the kitchen and into the living room. The smell of spray furniture polish filled my nostrils as I looked around the bare surfaces. She had taken down the dozens of sympathy cards that had adorned the room for the past ten days and now lay in a pile on the coffee table ready for the recycle bin. The only one to escape this fate was the small card that had come with the flowers from Alex, Lydia and the team at *UK Today*.

"She's going to milk that one for years to come," I muttered.

"Do you want milk darling?" she said, standing at the door, causing me to momentarily jump out of my skin.

"No thanks," I replied, quickly assuming that she hadn't heard my comment in full. "I was just thinking it looks bare now that all the cards are down, a bit like after Christmas."

"I know Lizzie dear, but it doesn't do to hold on to all these things. I'll bring us a nice cup of tea through and we can have ten minutes to look through them all together before I throw them out."

Sitting next to me on the sofa with the pile of cards on the coffee table, my mother picked each one up and after reading it she turned it over to see on the back of the card where it had been bought from.

"Oh, look Lizzie, there's a card here from Elaine's mother *and* it's from Marksies," she said, her face lighting up at the sight of a M&S logo on the back of the card. "She does surprise me. I always had her down as a Morrisons shopper, or one of those awful foreign supermarkets that everyone seems to go to nowadays," she added snobbishly.

Good old Mum, she even finds room for snobbery when reading sympathy cards. At least she's consistent I suppose. Looking at my watch, I saw that I only had a couple of hours before my train departed from Durham so after toasting myself a couple of crumpets in the kitchen, I took them upstairs to eat while I packed the last of my stuff. I opened Dad's briefcase and removed his diary along with his mobile and charger. I took the Thailand keyring off his car keys as I didn't trust my mother to remove it before selling the car. She had asked Michael and I if either of us wanted the car but Michael had recently bought a fancy four wheel drive and I certainly didn't have a need for one in London, let alone anywhere to park one.

A couple of hours later the train pulled out of Durham station and my heart was filled with a mixture of sadness and relief. It had been an intense time being at home as well as coming to terms with losing Dad but as I gazed out across the city, I blew a silent kiss to Durham Cathedral, the beacon that will always signify home to me. I texted James to let him know that I was safely on the train. I'd spoken with him last night and he had promised to meet me at King's Cross as he had a lunch meeting and nothing else scheduled in for the day. I hoped that he wasn't going to get in trouble for not being in the office but he does seem to be able to make his own hours as he goes along. I managed to read a few chapters of my Trisha Ashley novel that I'd been reading the night before I received the news about Dad. I'd brought it up from London with me with the intention of finishing it but with everything going on, I hadn't had much energy for bedtime reading and even during the day, I found it incredibly difficult to focus my brain on anything.

James was waiting outside Marks and Spencer at King's Cross Station with a couple of carrier bags of groceries and his work bag neatly slung across his chest.

"Hi babes," he said, enveloping me in the tightest of hugs as if he hadn't seen me for months as opposed to a couple of days since the funeral.

"Thanks for coming to meet me. I know I told you that you didn't need to, but I'm glad you did."

"No worries. I've got one of those 'dine in for a tenner' meals and extra wine. I say 'dine in for a tenner but they've gone up to fifteen quid now. I know you get a bottle with the deal but when is one bottle of wine ever enough?"

"Never," I replied, leaning into him as he put his free arm around me. Descending down into the tube station on the escalator, I momentarily forgot to stand on the right when James suddenly pulled me in out of the way of a guy in a suit who was behind me trying to walk down the left.

"I don't know Lizzie. You leave the Big Smoke for ten days and you forget the laws of the city."

"At least nobody is going to come up to me and ask how I'm doing," I said, thankful of another golden rule of the city which forbids people to make conversation with strangers.

Back in the flat, I dumped my case on my bed and as I went into the living room removing my coat, James handed me a large glass of red wine.
"Don't forget your medicine. Fancy some comedy or a rom-com?"
"Perfect."
We barely spoke a word for the next couple of hours as I lost myself in the film, a nineties British romantic comedy that I'd first seen at uni. James looked after me, topping up my glass, handing me a plate of steaming hot seafood linguine and administering foot rubs at intervals. "Every girl should have a James," I said to myself when he nipped out to bring two dishes of tiramisu for pudding.
The next morning, I woke late from a long and peaceful sleep. The flat was quiet, James having gone off to work. A note on the draining board in the kitchen read

Gone to the gym & work… I've left you the dishes to keep you busy lol. Text me if you want to meet later for a drink when I finish work. J xx

A burst of energy led to me having a shower and clearing the dishes in record time. I was conscious of being in the flat alone and as much as I love my own company, I knew that if I was to stay in the flat all day by myself, I'd get maudlin so I headed out into the world. The sun was shining bright and the daffodils on Turnham Green swayed gently in the breeze. The tube station platform was quiet and I took the time to sit on one of the brown slatted benches and take in my surroundings. I love this station and the fact that it's above ground. The District Line train heading eastbound takes you past another two stations above ground before it descends below at Hammersmith. Changing onto the Jubilee Line, I emerged back into the daylight at London Bridge. I hadn't been here for a while, but I knew the area well from a few years back when I'd shared a small flat in Southwark. I made my way towards Borough Market and as it was Friday morning, I knew it would be easier to navigate than on a busy Saturday when it would be swarming with a mix of yummy mummies and tourists. When I first moved to London, a friend brought me here one Saturday morning and I instantly fell in love with the place. The bustling market stalls selling all kinds of food for you to take home and cook. Back then there was very little in the way of takeaway food, it was more about ingredients but as I turned the corner into the market, I could see that it had changed dramatically since the last time that I was here. Gone were the rough and ready fruit and veg stalls and in their place were sleek units selling everything from Japanese street food to wheatgrass smoothies. It was still wonderful, but I couldn't help feeling that its soul had been ripped out during the refurbishments and wondered where the old school greengrocers had moved on to.

I found a little stall that had a few tables and chairs alongside it so after ordering some "smashed avocado" on toast, I picked up a coffee from the neighbouring van and sat myself down. A slim man in his forties and wearing a flat cap and horn-rimmed glasses sitting at the next table smiled behind his large beard and offered me his newspaper. I thanked him but politely declined. I hadn't seen the news since Dad died and I wanted just one more day of shutting out the woes of the world before I immersed myself back fully into the twenty-first century. The avocado on toast was delicious but at £8 I felt as if I was paying tourist prices. I was content for a while sitting, people-watching but I was aware that fresh customers were milling around looking for somewhere to sit so I gave up my table and took the remains of my Café Americano with me to sip as I meandered around the other stalls.

I did come across my favourite stall of years ago run by an artisan bakery in Shoreditch selling the most delicious slabs of chocolate brownie that just melted in the mouth. I recognised the bearded guy serving the loaves of astronomically-priced sourdough. He was one of the Bearded Bakers that deliver the posh pastries to our TV studio. I refrained from buying the brownie as I was stuffed and as I was planning on being out all day, I didn't really want to carry it around with me. I replenished my coffee at another stall advertising it's special 'artisan roast' and noted that everything here is 'artisan' now and it all comes with 'artisan' price.

Clutching my takeaway coffee, I exited the market area and onto the cobbled street that took me west along past the old Clink Prison and out onto the paved walkway that ran alongside the River Thames. The sun had brought out its share of visitors and joggers who weaved in and out of the groups of people. I never could understand why people chose to go jogging along the South Bank, particularly when it was so busy when there were plenty of quiet back streets running parallel to the river. The cynic in me told myself that they were there to be seen but today I was determined not to be cynical. As I walked closer to the Millennium footbridge, the crowds of tourists thickened so for respite, I ducked into the Tate Modern. There was a Picasso exhibition on at the moment which had people queuing out of the door for tickets, but I chose to just wander around the free areas which was actually most of the building. I wasn't there to see anything in particular, but rather just use the place to distract myself. I did come across a small free exhibition by, what I was informed on the sign, as an exciting new artist from East London. The 'exhibition' consisted of a series of ten large, framed colour photographs where the artist had stripped naked, bandaged up his own genitals crudely before daubing them with pig's blood and proceeding to take a series of self-portraits. I couldn't help but think that he had probably received a fifty-thousand-pound arts grant to take them. I stared at them, incredulous that this was considered as art, conscious again of that cynicism seeping in. I had a moment of self-doubt that there was something about the photos that went completely over my head and that everyone else seemed to get. I caught sight of a couple to my right staring intently at the same photo, both stroking their chins before one of them said "Well, I suppose it highlights the juxtaposition between the idea of genital mutilation and social conformity."

"Bollocks," I muttered a little too loudly which prompted the couple to both turn and stare at me. Making a sharp exit, I moved on to the next room smiling to myself as it had reminded me of a story that James once told me. He said that a few years back, a small group of students went into the Tate Modern with a bag of small flatpack cardboard boxes where, in one of the galleries, they folded them into shape and stacked them in a random pile on the floor before leaving a printed sign with some pretentious description. They then stepped back to the edge of the room, discreetly took out their mobile phones and proceeded to film as visitors gathered to stare at the pile of boxes and spout some pseudo-intellectual crap, thinking that they were giving the boxes a genuine critique. The joke was on them but I'm sure that someone would consider that the entire prank was a work of art in itself.

Back outside, I decided to give the Millennium Footbridge a miss largely due to the fact I could see it bouncing up and down due to the crowds of people crossing over it and as I was already feeling slightly bilious from the images of bandaged genitals, I opted for terra firma. I continued further along the South Bank, heading west under Blackfriars Bridge where a handsome young guy was playing the Spanish guitar. He looked up and smiled at me. I could do nothing other than stare back at him and for a moment it felt as if he had looked directly into my soul, so piercing were his eyes. Aware that I was gawping at him, I fished into my purse for some change to give him. I only had a tenner and a few coppers so I thought "Fuck it", pulled out the note and dropped it into his guitar case alongside the mixture of coins already there. He looked at me wide-eyed as his playing faltered a little.

"Thank you," he said in a beautiful accent. The look he gave me lasted a lot longer and if I didn't know any better, I'm sure that I saw a tear in his eye. I smiled and left him playing as I walked past the Oxo Tower towards the entrance to Gabriel's Wharf. Here, a large courtyard surrounded by an array of small independent cafes, restaurants and shops drew people away from the riverside with the promise of tasty treats. My eyes were drawn upwards to the neighbouring building which was the TV studios where *UK Today* amongst other shows was based. The bright studio lights of the first-floor studio were visible through the large windows which I knew would be the live mid-morning show that had been filmed here for the best part of twenty years. Suddenly my mind flashed back to work. Yes, the real world had been carrying on in my absence and it would be waiting there for me on Monday morning. It had now been almost two weeks since I'd been to work when I received the news of Dad's death and although I knew that I would be ready to return on Monday morning, now was still my grieving time. In an effort not to bump into any work colleagues, I decided to give Gabriel's Wharf a miss and stride onwards in the direction of Westminster. Passing the BFI, the British Film Institute, I was reminded of one of my favourite films *Truly Madly Deeply* where Juliet Stevenson played the part of a woman grieving for her recently deceased partner and imagines that she sees him playing the cello outside the BFI on the pavement. I looked over at the spot and decided that if I shut my eyes tightly, I might see Dad on opening them. There was no logic or reasoning to this, but I would have given the world at that moment to see him just one more time, to tell him how much I loved him. I took the leap of faith and opened them. He was not there. This was my reality and I had to get used to living in a world where my father would not be present.

Further along the river, lengthy queues of tourists waited for the London Eye. I had already been on it about six times myself as it was always the go-to tourist attraction whenever I had friends or family visit the capital. On Westminster Bridge, I walked towards Big Ben. Despite it being almost noon, the footpath was now crowded with tourists clutching selfie sticks and I couldn't help but smile at them, not just because they were visitors to our city, but it was lovely to see them so thrilled with seeing this place for the very first time. I remember how I felt the first time I came to London with the school when I was thirteen. Seeing these famous landmarks in real life filled me with such excitement and despite having lived in London for several years now, I made a conscious effort not to take these iconic surroundings for granted even on the most mundane of days. Most Londoners that I knew resented the tourists, especially my flatmate

James. The endless tutting as they stood on the wrong side of the escalators or stopped suddenly to get their bearings on crowded tube station platforms.

Having reached the corner of Whitehall and Parliament Square, I was tempted to carry on walking up towards Trafalgar Square passing Downing Street and the Cenotaph, but I felt my legs starting to tire. Instead, I nipped into the supermarket on the corner, picked up some glossy celebrity magazines and walked down into Westminster tube station, the vast cavernous concrete walls echoing the announcements made over the Tannoy. With many of the passengers disembarking here, there were plenty of seats to choose from on the Westbound train and I settled myself in for the journey home. The magazines, most of which were decidedly trashy, weren't my reading of choice but I would be back at work in two days and with my role on the Entertainment Team, I'd have to 'gen up' on my celebrity news and gossip.

For the remainder of the weekend, I didn't venture out more than two hundred metres from the flat. My former flatmates Rhona and Moira called round on Saturday night and we ordered in a Thai takeaway while James was out at a bar in Ealing watching some drag show. I messaged him to say that we had ordered too much food and that he was welcome to join us after the show but when he didn't return home that night, I could only presume that he had received a better offer. Sunday was simply a cosy day of lounging around the flat. James eventually made it home by noon but after a croaky hello from the door, he hibernated into his room and was not to be seen for the rest of the day. I settled in for my Sunday evening with a hot bath making sure that this time, I didn't put any smug posts on Facebook. A new week lay ahead and I hoped that it wouldn't be as eventful as the last two. What I didn't know at that moment is that the rollercoaster ride was only just about to begin.

CHAPTER 12

The Red Carpet Incident

I'd taken a book with me for the early morning tube journey as I did every time that I travelled on the `London Underground, although this morning I must have stayed on the same page from Turnham Green station all the way to Embankment, unable to focus my brain.

Once I was back in the *UK Today* production office, lots of people made a point of saying hello, one or two of them tilting their heads to one side providing extra sympathy. It was nice to know that they cared and I appreciated their kindness. In the office, my desk looked much as I'd left it two weeks ago apart from the addition of a handful of envelopes which I presumed to be sympathy cards. Downstairs I walked into the studio gallery where Maggie was flicking through the running order sheet on her desk while scrolling through the script on the computer at the same time. She looked up and smiled, winking at me and mouthing the words "catch you in a minute" and seconds later the programme's theme sprang to life on the bank of screens in front of the director. "That's us into the break. Three minutes to air," the director's PA shouted and with that, John the director stood up and made a beeline straight for me with his arms outstretched.

"Lizzie darling, how are you?"

"I'm fine," I said before repeating the words in case I wasn't quite sure the first time around.

"You caused quite a kerfuffle last time you were in here."

"Oh shit." I was dreading the worst kind of fall-out from my tirade at Serena, my boss and co-owner of the production company.

"Don't worry about her Lizzie, you know what she's like. That morning she actually left the building the minute her actress friend had been on-air and nobody saw her for the rest of the day." I didn't know quite what to make of this although I soon had that impending sense of dread that perhaps, despite the extenuating circumstances, my card had been marked by Serena and my future on *UK Today* was not so secure. I didn't have time to dwell as Maggie had now rushed over to me and gave me the tightest of hugs. We only had time to have a few words before the gallery PA advised everyone that there was thirty seconds before we were back on-air. I made myself scarce and went down to the kitchen next to the studio's green room, where Stuey the runner was looking harassed again, apparently with a large coffee and tea order for the studio guests.

"I'll make the drinks and you take them through Stuey," I told him. He was appreciative of the helping hand. I did the washing up and tidied the kitchen while Stuey cleared up the Green Room. While the production team had the post-show debrief meeting, which I didn't need to attend, I scooted back up to the office to make a start on tackling my email inbox. There were no direct messages from Serena or Jeremy which I wasn't sure was a good sign or not. The rest of the morning was fine. I had a meeting with Maggie where she informed me that while I had been off, there had been a bit of a reshuffle of the team as the channel had decided to increase the emphasis on showbiz and entertainment stories after 8am while the previous two hours of airtime would be focussed on news and current affairs. The upshot of the change was that I was to be moved onto the Showbiz Desk with immediate effect. Despite the decision having been made without my consultation, I was more than happy as this was far more my forte rather than hard news and politics. After all, I was a television producer and not a journalist. The only downside to this move would be that I'd have more direct contact with Jake, our so-called "Showbiz Editor," but I'd decided that the best way to deal with him was to always smile and kill him with kindness.

At lunch time, Maggie suggested that the two of us go for a walk along the South Bank. Sitting down on a bench overlooking the Thames, we ate our sandwiches and caught up on the last couple of weeks. Maggie was eager to find out how I was really doing which I reassured her was fine, although I couldn't resist telling her about the mystery woman at the church and cemetery and the messages that she had left on Dad's phone.

Back in the office that afternoon, Jeremy, our other executive producer and Serena's business partner, made an appearance. He asked me how I was doing but as I answered him, his eyes were distracted across the room at a new guy who had just joined the team. Handing me a card, he turned his attention back to me.

"Party at my house this Saturday, we'll be watching the Boat Race from the lawn," and he wandered off before I had chance to say thank you. It felt strange being invited to the boss's house as Jeremy was not the sort of person who would usually mix with us plebs in the lower ranks of production.

The following morning, I was up and out early as I had to be at the studio for eight so that I could be around for the last hour of the show being on-air. The only point to any of us going in at that time was to ensure that we were around the second that the show ended at nine and so that we could catch the presenters before they left the building for the day. They always had cars waiting for them that were booked by the production and they were never in the mood for hanging around. Today I would be leaving the studio with Jake, our Showbiz Editor and there would be a car waiting to take us to a small private cinema in Soho to watch a press screening of a film. It was my job to accompany Jake to the screening and afterwards, write the questions for him to ask the film's stars and director. It was a tight turnaround for this one as this afternoon we were to attend the press junket at the Dorchester hotel. The idea of a press junket is to get all the actors, the director and producer together in a swish hotel, then the press come along and each person has a fifteen minute time slot with the star to ask them questions on camera. The film company already have the cameras and crew set up in each room and they simply give you a memory stick with the footage when you leave which we take back to the studio and edit it for our entertainment report the following day. The film's premiere was taking place that evening with the red carpet rolled out in Leicester Square, and as always, we had a place 'behind the rope' along the red carpet. It's a lot of effort for just one film but as this was one of the biggest releases of the year, we had to cover it for the programme.

I sat alongside Jake in the cinema and we were surrounded by at least a dozen journalists including our rivals from the other channels. The film "Tango Master" was a dance-filled musical featuring Jet Shield, arguably Hollywood's biggest star of the last ten years and because this was a huge departure from his usual tough guy superhero and spy roles, the film was garnering quite the buzz in the media. That and the fact that Jet had just paid out one of the largest divorce settlements in Hollywood history. Despite the huge interest in the film and that our access to interview Jet was a big deal, Jake seemed disinterested and spent most of the film on his phone. As I glanced across at him, I could tell by the orange blobs that shone from his mobile into the darkness of the cinema that he was chatting to someone on well-known gay dating app. I didn't want to say anything at that moment considering how many other journalists were sitting around us, but I was concerned that by taking no notice of the film, he would screw up the interview that we had lined up with Jet this afternoon. There would be no danger of that happening if I had anything to do with it as I'd be writing up the questions for him as soon as we got out of here. Two hours later the film ended triumphantly and although I was on a high as I stood up in the cinema, my mood was instantly dampened when I looked down to see Jake still on his dating app, oblivious to what was going on around him. After another ten seconds he looked up from his phone and barked,

"Is my car outside?'"

"I don't know," I replied sharply, "and I won't know until I get out into the foyer." I was annoyed at his rudeness.

"Just make sure it is there. I don't want to be hanging around and have to chat with this lot," he responded sharply. "I have places to go."

"Remember we have to be at The Dorchester in less than two hours," I reminded him, trying my best not to sound like a parent dealing with a petulant child despite that not being too far from the truth.

"I know that you stupid girl. I have been working in this business long enough to know what I'm doing without having to take instructions from some two-bit northerner with bad hair and cheap shoes," he spat cruelly. Like the rest of the team at *UK Today*, I was used to Jake's erratic behaviour and venomous outbursts. Putting up with such nastiness from some presenters (and producers) was all part of working in TV. It shouldn't be like that but sadly it was. A woman standing across from us making notes into her phone looked across and smiled at me, as much in solidarity as in sympathy. I decided that the best way forward was not to engage in any further conversation with Jake and leave him to his chat on his dating app. I made a discreet call to the office to get an ETA on his car, heaven forbid that he would ever have to do anything for himself. Once it was confirmed that the car was a couple of minutes away, I asked to speak to Maggie in the office to let her know that I was going to plonk myself in the nearest coffee shop to spend the next hour writing up questions, ready for Jake to interview Jet Shield this afternoon. I would then make my way to The Dorchester and meet Jake there. Jake had already requested that his car take him to a restaurant in Old Compton Street where he was apparently meeting a friend for lunch. I'd refrained from pointing out to him that it was little more than a five minute walk from the cinema. I thought it best not to put him in a bad mood, especially when we had the interview this afternoon and he would need to be on top form for dealing with Hollywood's biggest name.

A couple of hours passed in a Soho coffee shop and I'd managed to get a decent set of questions together for Jake to ask Jet. As we were only allocated a fifteen-minute slot, it didn't need to be an extensive list. I made sure that I arrived at The Dorchester in plenty of time, in order to run through the questions with Jake so that he wasn't reading them for the first time in front of our star. "Prior planning prevents piss-poor performance" my Dad used to say to me back when I was doing my A Levels. Whilst I didn't expect Jake to be at the hotel waiting for me, I had hoped that he would at least arrive at the agreed time but as the next twenty minutes ticked by, my heart sank and I had a terrible feeling in the pit of my stomach. I called through to the production office to see if they could locate his driver who it turned out, was driving from Stockwell which was a couple of miles south of the river. "What the hell is he doing in Stockwell? He said he was meeting a friend for lunch in Soho. Never mind, if he's ten minutes away, at least I know he'll be here shortly." A woman with a clipboard came out of the lift and approached me, asking to see my press pass which I duly showed her.

"Where's your presenter?" she asked.

"He's on his way. He got delayed in traffic after…. a meeting." Christ. He had me lying for him now.

"It's quite a tight schedule that we have as it's the premiere in Leicester Square this evening. Seeing as though it's *UK Today*, I'll swap you round with one of the online shows to allow your guy more time to get here," the woman said helpfully, forcing a half smile as she returned to the lift. Ten minutes later, Jake's car pulled up outside and he got out looking harassed and quite dishevelled compared to when he'd left me earlier. It was obvious that wherever he had been and whoever he had been with, had had something to do with the fact that he had spent the entire morning on that dating app. Seeing that I was holding the questions that I'd glued onto a set of *UK Today* cue cards (I'm the consummate professional), Jake snatched them out of my hand without a word and marched off towards the lift. Once we were up on the floor outside the interview room, I took Jake gently by the elbow.

"There's a mirror over here if you want to check yourself before we go in," I said trying to be helpful which, given the state of him, was most definitely warranted.

"I'm perfectly capable of finding a mirror myself, you silly cow!" he hissed back at me and at that point his face dropped when he realised that Jet Shield himself had emerged from the room and had witnessed Jake's rudeness first hand. With a raised eyebrow, Jet looked over at us as I blushed with embarrassment at our presenter's behaviour. Jet held out his hand as Jake blurted out

"Jet, so lovely to see.."

Jet walked straight past Jake and towards me.

"Hi, I'm Jet." He smiled at me, making direct eye contact. I was shaking and held out my limp hand which he shook.

"Lizzie, Lizzie Button," I replied, my voice trembling almost as much as my hand.

"I take it you're interviewing me next," he said, still smiling and still ignoring Jake who by now was looking dumbfounded.

"Er, no not me. I'm just a producer. Jake will be interviewing you." I said, stumbling and nodding to my dishevelled colleague.

"OK, I thought you would be the one appearing on screen. Pity," he said before turning to Jake who was smiling nervously. "Right, let's get to it," and with that, he swept back into the room. Jake was now sweating profusely and muttering erratically to himself. He sat himself down in the chair opposite Jet but not before dropping his pile of question cards on the floor. I had taken the time to number each of them so that Jake didn't get them in the wrong order but as usual, he wasn't paying attention. The cameraman gave the signal that he was ready.

"Right, shall we get to it?" said Jet professionally.

It was awful. It couldn't have gone any worse. Jake was all over the place, stuttering, losing his place and stumbling over the simplest of sentences. It didn't help that Jet was doing his best to retain a smile but after fifteen minutes, everyone in the room including the crew were relieved that it was over.

"Well, thank you Jet, it was lovely to meet you again," Jake said nervously, still sweating. If we had thought it couldn't get any worse, Jet looked at him and replied, "Have we actually met before?" He didn't give Jake time to respond before adding,

"Can I tell you something my friend?" Jet was now looking directly at Jake whilst towering over him. "On all the movies that I work on, I ask one thing, that every person on set is treated with respect. It doesn't matter how famous you are. Respect. Never forget that my friend."

He smiled at me and shook my hand.

"Thank you, Lizzie. Are you coming to the premiere later?"

Gobsmacked that he had remembered my name, I replied "Yes, we will both be there in the press pen on the red carpet."

"Good luck," he said, motioning to Jake but not taking his eyes off me. "Hopefully I'll see you later."

Jake remained silent in the lift on the way down and didn't once look up from his phone, where he was typing on that dating app again.

"OK Jake, I'll see you back at the office at 5pm and we'll head to Leicester Square with the crew together." Jake didn't look up but muttered in agreement. His driver was waiting outside the hotel. He got in the car, reading out a street name directly from his dating app to the driver.

The Dorchester's concierge hailed me a black cab and once I was heading back to the office, I called Maggie to update her on the disastrous interview with Jet Shield and forewarning her that the footage might not be usable for tomorrow's show.

Half an hour later, sitting in an edit suite with Maggie, we watched back the interview footage.

"Jesus wept," said Maggie. "What's with the sweating and rapid eye movement. Is he on something?" she asked in reference to Jake.

"I don't know but he was behaving very strangely from the moment that he arrived at The Dorchester." I'd numbered his cue cards for him, but he dropped them at the start of the interview and got them all in the wrong order.

"I'm going to have to show this to Jeremy and Serena. It's a mess. One of the biggest films of the year and he's screwed it up. We'll get him in this afternoon for a meeting to sort this out. Hopefully we can get some decent footage on the red carpet tonight that we can use instead. Lizzie, you have a break just now as you're working at the premiere later. I'll see you back here at quarter to five."

Only an hour later at four o'clock, my phone rang. "Lizzie, it's Maggie. We can't find Jake anywhere. We contacted the driver who said he'd dropped him off at some block of flats in Stockwell again after the interview, but he doesn't know which flat. Jake told him to come back at quarter to four but he's not there, he's not answering his phone. The guy's a bloody nightmare."

"OK, can we get another presenter to do the red carpet? What about Chloe who stands in when

Jake's away?" I suggested.

"She's in Dubai. It's no good, you'll have to do it Lizzie."

"Me? I can't do it, I'm not a TV presenter." I was astounded by her suggestion.

"Lizzie, you're articulate, you're good looking and most importantly, you've seen the film. You will know what to ask him about."

"But there must be someone else. What about Bianca?"

"Nah, she's too up her own arse and she's not experienced like you."

By now, I was standing in a shop doorway, my legs shaking, petrified at the thought of going on camera for the premiere.

"Lizzie, we'll use the questions that you wrote for Jake this afternoon, so you don't need to worry about that. Where are you just now?"

"I'm up in Covent Garden."

"Great, jump into a shop and pick up something else to wear and some make up if you don't have any on you. Keep the receipt and we'll pay you back. Get a cab and be back here for an hour's time. Is that ok?"

I didn't have the chance to argue as Maggie had hung up and I was left holding my phone. I hate clothes shopping at the best of times, so I picked up a long ankle-length white gypsy skirt and a blue top. I was already wearing heels that would go with the outfit so after quickly grabbing a lipstick and some mascara from a pharmacy, I jumped in a cab and headed back across the river towards the South Bank studios. When I arrived back at the production office, I was ushered into a small meeting room by Maggie who looked stressed and exasperated.

"Did you manage to get something to wear?" she asked and I held up the paper carrier bags in response. "Good. Listen Lizzie, I've not managed to get hold of Jeremy or Serena all afternoon. Apparently, Jeremy is meeting the party planner that's overseeing this Boat Race thing he's having at the weekend and Serena's gone off for a bloody facial or something."

This came as no surprise and neither of our executive producers were ever on hand when we really needed their advice or some issue needed resolving. They would be the first to complain if something went wrong and neither of them had been consulted.

"I've had to phone Jenny who's the head of daytime for the channel and although she's pissed off with Jake, she's said it's ok for you to do the red carpet tonight," Maggie said, reassuring me.

"How can she be ok with me doing it? She's never met me before."

"She trusts my judgement."

I really didn't know what to say. The thought of

interviewing celebrities on the red carpet didn't exactly fill me with dread as I was more than used to dealing with them in the years that I'd already spent working in TV. It might have been imposter syndrome, me masquerading on the red carpet as a TV presenter. I didn't have time to think about it right now as the cameraman would be here in a minute, so I nipped into the toilets and got changed in a cubicle, resting my bag on top of the cistern. Who said TV was glamourous?

When we arrived at Leicester Square in the taxi, we lugged the basic camera kit out and I took a moment on the pavement to get my breath. We'd had to get out at the corner of Leicester Square and Charing Cross Road as the traffic ahead of us had ceased to move towards Trafalgar Square. Already, Leicester Square was heaving with crowds, many of them tourists not quite believing their luck at stumbling across one of the biggest film premieres of the year whilst on their holiday to London. Everyone was eager to catch a glimpse of Jet Shield, so it made it even more difficult to fight our way towards the direction of the press pen alongside the red carpet. Finally, security let us through after checking our passes and while Keith our cameraman set up his camera and tripod, I checked my outfit, relieved that the long ankle-length skirt was comfortably cool on this balmy April evening. Not having had time to do much with my hair, I tied it up with a single clip in a classic style and applied one final brush of lipstick. I had my question cards in my hand and now did my best to memorise the questions which was easy because at these events, you were lucky to get two questions with each celebrity. As this film was all about ballroom dancing, I'd come up with my sure-fire question, "Who would be your ultimate dance partner?"

It wasn't long before the celebrities started arriving and soon I felt a lot more confident as my question about the dancing was going down a treat. Some people named big stars while others said that their ideal dance partner would be their Gran or their Mum, which was sweet. A huge cheer erupted as a limousine pulled up at the far end of the red carpet and Jet emerged smiling and waving as he always did. For the last ten years, he'd consistently been a huge draw for cinemagoers but this time there was an even bigger buzz about him. Another twenty minutes passed before Jet approached our section of the red carpet and I could see that he was wearing a tailored black suit with a white shirt and a black tie. The barriers alongside the red carpet had changed from metal sections for the public and autograph hunters, to simple classic red rope and polished brass bollards. As he got closer, Jet looked over and seeing me with the cameraman, he walked straight towards me.

"Hey, Lizzie," he said smiling at me. I was completely taken aback that he had yet again remembered my name. I did my best to keep my cool and look professional.

"Hi Jet, you're on *UK Today*. Can you tell me, apart from your co-star in this movie, who would your ideal dance partner be?"

He looked me in the eye and said, "You Lizzie." Before I had a chance to react, he'd taken my microphone out of my hand and handed it to his assistant who was standing to the side out of camera shot. He took my hand and with the other, he pulled the rope barrier to one side. I didn't know what was happening but aware that I was on camera, I played along.

Jet led me into the middle of the red carpet and promptly twirled me around like a ballroom dancer before turning me around over his arm so that my back arched right over. He held me there for about ten seconds which felt more like ten minutes and not once did he take his eyes off me. I was aware of the cheering from the crowds and the cacophony of noise that was added to by the clicking of cameras and the shouting of paparazzi photographers. Eventually he pulled me back upright and I felt a little dizzy but managed to maintain my composure. He was still looking at me when I broke my gaze, his arm still around my waist. Still dazed, I was trying my best to take the whole scenario in when I became aware that the photographers had not stopped taking photos of us.

"Thank you." My words stumbled out. "I'd better get back," and with that I returned to my spot behind the rope cordon. One or two photographers did their best to reach round to take more pics of me and a journalist came over and asked me who I was. I explained that I was a producer on *UK Today* and that I was merely standing in for Jake.

I'd decided that we probably had enough interview footage to do us for tomorrow's show and that perhaps it would be a good idea if we packed up and got back to the office. Keith, the cameraman, said that he would take the footage back to the production office and one of the showbiz team on the night shift would edit it for tomorrow's show. As we were packing up, a woman tapped me on the shoulder.

"Hi Lizzie, I'm Madeleine, Jet's PA for the promotion tour. He's asked me to ask if he can have your phone number?"

I recognised the woman from this afternoon's interview at The Dorchester Hotel and she'd been the one who had taken my microphone from Jet on the red carpet. I didn't know what he would want my number for, but I complied with the request and gave it to her. Normally I would have taken the tube home, but I needed to call Maggie and tell her what had happened, so I took a taxi back to Chiswick.

My telephone conversation with Maggie had lasted the thirty minute journey home. She said that I needed to come in for half past four in the morning so that we could have a briefing about tonight's event on the red carpet as inevitably, it would be a talking point on the show. This left me feeling embarrassed to say the least. Back in the flat, James was eating some pasta while watching the TV. I chose not to say anything about this evening's events for no other reason than I was exhausted.

"Nice skirt," he said. "bo-ho chic meets Mamma Mia?"

"Something like that. I'm off to bed, it's been a long day."

"Fancy a glass of vino?" he said, holding up a white wine bottle.

I'd better not, I'm in early tomorrow and they're sending a car for me at half four in the morning. Goodnight."

In my bedroom, I picked out an outfit out that I could wear tomorrow as Maggie had dropped the bombshell that I might be required to go on camera in the studio. It would be purely to link to the film premiere due to Jake going AWOL. I plumped for a pair of smart jeans, plain top and a short jacket. My head was buzzing with the events of the last ten hours. This was crazy, all too crazy to believe. I'd like to say I lay in bed with images of Jet twirling me around the red carpet but as it was, sleep enveloped me almost as soon as my head touched the pillow.

CHAPTER 13

Overnight Sensation

When my alarm went off at quarter to four, I felt like I'd only slept for mere minutes. My head was fuzzy and I didn't have the energy to lift the heavy duvet off me. Glancing over at my phone, I could see that quite a few notifications had come in overnight.

"Oh Christ, the red carpet," I said. Suddenly it all came back to me as if I'd had some crazy night out involving lots of vodka shots. I didn't dare look at my phone as I had to get ready and the car would arrive soon. I put my outfit that I'd chosen last night into a suit carrier and at the last moment I added a couple of spare options, something I'd always told studio guests to do when I've booked them to appear on our show. After all, you don't want to clash with the person sitting next to you as a legendary British actress told me when I first started working in TV.

Out on the street, the car was waiting with the lights on and the muffled sound of the radio coming from within. The driver climbed out and walked round to open the door for me as I approached.

"Good morning. To go to the South Bank Studios?" he said, with a hint of an Essex accent.

This felt weird as I rarely got taxis, let alone have the driver opening the door for me. As we pulled onto Chiswick High Road, I asked him to stop at the newsagents on the corner as I wanted to pick up some papers to brief myself en route to the studio. Inside the shop, the papers were displayed on wall-mounted racks and that's when it hit me, like a train. I, Lizzie Button, was on the front page of almost all the papers with Jet Shield twirling me around like some Hollywood starlet. I must have stood there for a moment with my mouth gaping wide open as I was brought crashing into the present. Hurriedly, I grabbed a copy of each of the national tabloids, and the broadsheets too. Mr Khan behind the counter smiled at me as I paid,

"Hello my dear, I know *you*. You are now my second most famous customer." He gave me a wide smile revealing several missing teeth. I didn't know what to say and as I searched my purse for change, I realised I was going to have to pay by card. So much for quickly nipping in and out. I looked around the shop as Mr Khan put my card in the machine.

"Oh, just do contactless," I said in a hurry to get away quickly.

"Contactless no working," replied Mr Khan.

Two lads in high-vis vests and work gear were now behind me in the queue, one of them holding a copy of The Sun, his mate holding a copy of The Mirror. Both of them were now grinning inanely at me, somehow having managed to recognise me even with my back to them. I tapped my number into the card machine, grabbed the papers off the counter and went to leave before Mr Khan stopped me to hand me my card. As I left the shop, Mr Khan shouted to me,

"Hey lady! Don't forget to invite me to the wedding." He wasn't the only one laughing right now, as the two workmen had also joined in. In the car, I asked the driver to put the light on for me in the back so that I could read the papers.

"Jet Keeps It Strictly Professional" one of the front pages read, while the Sun had run with the headline "Jet Sweeps Mystery Girl Off Her Feet."

I felt a bit sick. A combination of nerves and seeing myself splashed across Britain's national newspapers. I couldn't read anymore. I asked the driver to switch off the light and I sat back in the darkness as we turned off at Hammersmith and drove swiftly towards central London. Crossing the Thames opposite the South Bank, I steeled myself for the onslaught of questions and more likely, the piss-take from my colleagues. I studied my phone scrolling through the list of missed calls, text messages et cetera. I didn't even dare check my social media. The car came to a halt outside the studio entrance and I could see at least a dozen paparazzi photographers waiting. "Who is on the show today?" I wondered. We normally only ever had paparazzi outside when we had a big star or a controversial politician in the studio. Balancing the newspapers over my arm, the driver opened the door for me as I was bombarded with an onslaught of camera flashes and people shouting at me

"Lizzie! Lizzie! Are you dating Jet?"

The driver stepped in front of me, looked me in the eye and smiled.

"Don't worry Miss, I've got your bag."

Stuey was already on the pavement waiting for me but to be honest I could barely see him for all the flashlights of the cameras.

"Lizzie, over here!" one photographer shouted.

"Lizzie is it true you went to Jet's hotel last night?" said another. By now, all the photographers were pressing forward aggressively, all of them desperate for a shot.

"Morning twinkle toes," said Stuey with a mischievous smile having managed to push his way through the small throng. "A good night was it?" The driver handed Stuey my bag and we hurried up the steps and through the revolving doors into the building.

Instead of walking up to the production office, Stuey lead the way directly towards studio dressing rooms where Maggie was waiting for me outside the make-up room, sporting the biggest grin on her face.

"Here she is, Posh Spice! Your dressing room is ready and we've re-decorated it overnight as per your wishes. Chinese silk wallpaper and there's a hundred Indonesian cala lilies. We've counted them. Four times."

Both Maggie and Stuey were now in fits of laughter.

"Fucking hell. I need a coffee."

"Would that be a double skinny decaf macchiato with extra foam?" Stuey asked mockingly.

"Ha ha, very funny, you cheeky beggar."

"Lizzie, I need to get you into make-up," said Maggie tapping her watch.

"Do I need it?"

"Come on, you know the score. Stuey will get you a coffee and some toast and we'll chat once you're in there."

Now I really felt like a bona fide presenter as we often brief them in the make-up room when time was short on the morning. Mandy our head make-up artist and stalwart of the show greeted me with a big hug before guiding me into the chair in front of the mirror.

"Someone's been a busy girl," she joked, smiling revealing her perfectly white teeth. With a single sweep, she threw a make-up gown around my neck, fastened it at the back and then proceeded to tie my hair back.

"Now, what are we going for today? Smoky eyes?" she teased.

Looking in the mirror, I could see her smiling cheekily behind me. I also saw Maggie enter the room.

"Serena and Jeremy are coming in, so is Jenny." Maggie said.

"Head of daytime Jenny?" Now I was curious.

"Yep, you've managed to get the show and the channel a whole lot of publicity."

I replied with no more than a nervous laugh. "You might laugh Lizzie, but even a Kardashian couldn't get this sort of publicity. You're on the Meghan Markle scale. You're all over the news, not just the newspapers, but across the Internet. The word is that you have even been on American TV this morning. This is the biggest showbiz red carpet story since Liz Hurley decided to wear that safety pin dress."

"Fuck" was all I could say in reply.

"It will get even more interesting in a few hours when New York wakes up. It's the number-one story trending on Twitter."

"Really? Number one in Britain? Wow!" I said, not quite believing what she was telling me but trying to take it all in at the same time.

"Not Britain, Lizzie. It's number one trending across the world," she announced with just the tiniest air of fanfare. My stomach lurched. This was too much to take in. I could hear lots of voices and movement in the corridor outside. "Everyone in the production team is buzzing with the story. Well, almost everyone," said Maggie, her voice tailing off.

"Bianca?" Now I was questioning the obvious.

"Yep, predictable as ever," said Maggie. "Her face is tripping her this morning," she continued with a mischievous smile. "I need to go back up to the office. See you shortly," and with that she swept out of the room clutching her clipboard.

Mandy and I spent the next fifteen minutes chatting about last night's events on the red carpet as my face was transformed into someone far more glamorous than the real Lizzie Button.

The peaceful atmosphere of the make-up room didn't last much longer. I heard his voice before I saw him and for a fleeting moment, I wished myself to be in a different place. Anywhere other than here.

"Lizzie! My dressing room! Two minutes!" Jake screeched angrily, a tone that we had heard on this corridor many times before. I didn't get a chance to reply before he turned on his heels and stormed off in the direction of his dressing room. This didn't bode well. My natural reaction was one of nerves, not being the best at confrontations but my newfound confidence told me that I needn't worry and that I didn't have to answer to him. Mandy applied one final brush to my cheekbones and told me that I was good to go. I thanked her and as I stepped out of the make-up room, I could overhear Jake arguing with Maggie further along the corridor.

"What the fuck was *she* doing there last night?" Jake shouted. "Since when does she go onto the red fucking carpet and interview celebs?"

"Jake, we called you ten times in the space of half an hour, the car was waiting outside those flats in Stockwell as you had arranged with the driver and there was no answer at the door. What were we supposed to do? It was the premiere of one of the biggest films of the year," Maggie responded confidently. "And don't think I've not seen the footage from your interview with Jet Shield at The Dorchester yesterday, the entire thing was a car crash from start to finish."

He didn't reply. I could now see that he was pacing in circles, rubbing his hands across the back of his neck, something he always did when he was stressed or angry. As senior producer, Maggie was not going to let this go.

"Where the hell were you anyway? You had your schedule, and you knew exactly what time the car was picking you up," she continued.

"I lost track of time. I met some friends after I left the Dorchester and we went to a party..." his voice stumbling and tailing off. He must have realised that perhaps he had said too much.

"A party? Who goes to a party on a Wednesday afternoon?" said Maggie. Before Jake had a chance to respond to the question, I seized the opportunity and walked confidently towards them, aware that I stood a better chance of Jake being more civil if his defences were down and Maggie was there for back up.

"Hi Jake," I said, looking at his dishevelled appearance and his blood shot eyes. I thought it best not to bring up the fact that he was still wearing the same clothes as when I'd left him yesterday afternoon. Jake twiddled his fingers and looked at his feet like a schoolboy who had been summoned to the headmaster's office. I noticed that his facial muscles were twitching. He appeared very agitated so I decided at this point that the best course of action would be to say nothing. For the first time in the last two minutes, he looked me in the eye.

"Right then, you'd better give me all the details of last night's premiere!" he snapped.

"No problem, give me a moment." I thought that the best tactic at this moment would be to comply with him.

"Actually Jake," said Maggie, turning into him,

"Can it wait till later? Lizzie is going on-air, but someone will be along to see you shortly. Probably best if you get yourself cleaned up and stay away from the studio floor for now." Jake opened his mouth as if to answer but Maggie had already started guiding me along the corridor away from him.

"Maggie, have you got two minutes?" I said, eager to speak with her in private.

"Yep, No problem. There is a spare dressing room we can use."

If I was going to discuss anything about last night, the last thing that I wanted was for little ears to be listening in, particularly Jake's. Maggie turned on the bright fluorescent strip lights in the large empty dressing room.

"So, how did it go? Has he called you yet?" said Maggie, unable to hide her eager anticipation.

"No, not yet. Maggie, I don't want Jake and the team to know about Jet asking me for my number. Have you told anyone?"

"Not a soul."

"Good, I'd like to keep it to just what happened on the red carpet."

"To be honest Lizzie, your being twirled around on the red carpet by Hollywood's biggest star will give us more than enough to talk about. That's the moment that's splashed across the papers and on the Internet."

"Jake doesn't look too happy," I said, trying my

best to keep a straight face.

"Of course, he isn't happy. He's probably angrier with himself than he is with you. That will teach him to piss off to an afternoon chem-sex party with someone he's just met on a dating app."

"Really? I thought his behaviour was erratic to say the least. Do you think that's actually what happened?"

"I know it's exactly what's happened. It was discussed at an executive meeting last week with Jeremy and Serena. There have been several comments on Twitter in recent weeks about his blood shot eyes and shaking hands. Half an hour in the studio make-up chair can only cover up so much. I know the Jeremy and Serena can fairly hoover up the coke themselves but when it's affecting what's on the screen, then we have a problem. A major problem."

"Jesus, it's another world to me," I replied honestly. Apart from the occasional joint I'd smoked at university, the nearest that I had come to being near any drugs in recent years had been my flatmate's poppers that he annoyingly chose to keep in the fridge at home.

"So, what am I to do this morning?" I was aware that time was ticking on.

"I've spoken with the powers that be and I think that we should tell the story as it is. You are our producer who bravely stepped in at the eleventh hour to keep the show going and do the interviews on the red carpet. Then Prince Charming came along and whisked you off your feet. Does that sound ok to you Cinders?" Maggie teased, unable to suppress a laugh. "The channel are happy to play it out that way, that's why Jenny who's head of daytime has come into the gallery for this morning's show."

"I'm still trying to take it all in," I said, which wasn't a lie.

"Yeah, Jeremy's had to get out of bed uncharacteristically early and Serena is flapping around, apparently trying to find a coffee grinder as she brought in some artisan roast beans for Jenny's coffee."

"Does Jenny like special artisan roast beans?" I asked her, with a huge dollop of sarcasm.

"Trust me, Jenny's happiest with a mug of builders tea and two sugars," said Maggie as she looked at her watch. "Well, I'd better go and speak with the bosses about Jake. It might be a good opportunity for you to go and find our presenters Lydia and Alex. They will be keen to hear all about your red carpet experience."

Outside in the corridor, Stuey was running about looking very stressed as usual.

"Are you okay Stuey?" asked Maggie.

"You don't know where I can find a slate do you?" Stuey replied in a state of flux.

"A slate?"

"Yeah, it's for the artisan pastries for the woman

from the channel. Serena wants them taken up to the gallery and said that they must be served on a slate."

Maggie and I both rolled our eyes in unison.

"Don't bother with the slate Stuey. A plate will do, you've got far too much to be getting on without worrying about bloody slates."

"But Serena says……"

"You leave Serena to me."

With that, Stuey reached into the kitchen cupboard and removed a large white square plate, transferring the Danish pastries onto it.

"Oh Stuey? Don't forget the fresh strawberry garnish."

For a moment, I could see his face freeze as he must've been thinking, "where am I going to get fresh strawberries at this time of the morning?"

"Maggie don't tease the poor lad," I said, nudging her gently in the ribs. Stuey's face, still frozen like a rabbit in the headlights, only gave way once Maggie started laughing.

I popped my head into make-up where Lydia was now having the final touches to her hair done by Mandy.

"Hey Ginger Rogers," she said teasingly. "Did you get up to anything yesterday evening?"

I blushed. "No nothing special," I answered, mockingly feigning innocence.

"Seriously though Lizzie, how amazing is this? It

could be the start of something very wonderful for you," said Lydia generously.

"With Jet? He's only met me twice," There was no way that I was able to consider the thought of romance or even friendship with an A-List Hollywood star.

"If not with Jet, then certainly with your career. Something tells me you won't be an producer this time next week."

"What? Do you think they're going to sack me?" I said, not quite getting the gist of her last comment.

"No silly, this will be amazing for your profile and your career."

I'd never ever considered having a 'profile' as I was always content to remain behind the camera.

With a little time to spare after I had popped into Alex's dressing room to say hello, I decided to head up the stairs to the gallery which was the control room for the studio. By the time I reached the door, I could see through the windows that it was already busy. It only took two seconds after me walking in for the entire team there burst into a round of applause and cheers while I looked around the room embarrassed. I could see every single person clapping and cheering. Everyone that is, except Bianca who was staring at me, clutching on a clipboard, and sporting a face like thunder before stomping out the door on the other side of the gallery. John, the studio director approached me before stopping to curtsy and pretend to doff his cap mockingly.

"Oh Lizzie, I'm so sorry." His face suddenly looking very serious.

"What for?" I asked, wondering what on earth was wrong.

"About the carpet. We didn't have time to roll out the red one for you," he said with a burst of laughter before wrapping me in a tight hug. "Enjoy your moment, Lizzie. Go with it as you never know where it may lead to," he whispered into my ear. Pulling back, he held both of my arms in reassurance.

"It's a slow news day I'm afraid, so we will probably have you on screen quite a lot during the the show. Is that okay?" I simply nodded in response, my head trying to grasp the reality of the situation.

The show went to plan. Well, almost. They invited viewers to phone in at one point so you can imagine my horror when Alex the presenter said, "Lizzie, the next caller on the line is your mother, Joyce." I was frozen to the spot on the sofa.

"So, Joyce how do you feel seeing your daughter dancing on the red carpet with the big Hollywood star?" Alex said mischievously.

"Well Alex, may I call you Alex? Well Alex, I've begun to give up hope of Elizabeth ever meeting someone. She was never going to find Mr Right working on all those silly property programmes you know. I only hope that this Mr Shield's intentions are honourable," said Mum down the phone line for everyone in the studio and the viewers across the country to hear.

I wanted the sofa to swallow me up. I was about to cut in with a response and laugh it off, but my mother swiftly continued.

"Elizabeth has never had much luck with men, there was this one chap in Australia, but she caught him with another woman."

I must have looked mortified as Lydia cut in and tried to save me any further embarrassment.

"Joyce, has Lizzie inherited her dancing feet from you?" Lydia asked, attempting to lighten things up a little.

"If only Lydia. Oh, thank you for the beautiful flowers you sent me when Elizabeth's father passed away. I've got the little card framed now, next to a photo of Princess Diana and Mother Theresa on my Laura Ashley console table in the drawing room."

I knew my mother had always put on airs and graces but now she had taken it to a whole new level.

"Would you like to see your daughter on the red carpet again?" Lydia asked.

"If she wears a nice dress and not those silly jeans, then yes, of course," my mother replied only serving to embarrass me even further, if that was remotely possible.

"Joyce, you should come and be our fashion commentator for the Oscars," added Alex, gleefully stirring up the pot with his wooden spoon. On the phone, Mum giggled like a schoolgirl.

"Of course Alex, will I get my own dressing room?" she replied. I think she actually thought he was being serious.

"Joyce, we will have a star on the door with your name written in gold sparkly letters," said Alex.

For fuck's sake Mum, can't you see that he is taking the piss? I thought.

"Elizabeth, darling. Please will you call me after the show? You didn't answer my calls earlier." Mum had obviously forgotten that she was live on-air. The rest of the programme was embarrassing but thankfully, nothing reached the excruciating heights of my mother phoning in.

When we came off-air at the end of the show, Serena was waiting for me behind the cameras.

"Lizzie, can you hang around please? I'd like to have a word if I may." I nodded in compliance. I switched on my phone and as the screen came to life, I could see that the voicemail icon was flashing, I had a text messages and countless more on the messaging apps. They would have to wait. Lydia, scrolling on her phone as she walked towards me, looked up and smiled,

"Well done this morning. You were great. Your mum sounds like a handful if you don't mind my saying."

"She's lovely but she is also a bloody nightmare," I replied, trying to laugh off the embarrassment of the last two hours.

"Listen Lizzie," said Lydia. "I've just had a message from my agent, Melanie. She was watching this morning's show and she would like me to introduce you to her. Is there any chance that you could meet for lunch today?"

"Well... I suppose I can." I wasn't quite sure how to respond.

"Don't worry, she won't bite. I'll call you in an hour or so. I have to go, as I have a personal trainer appointment at 10."

Why did her agent want to see me? It seemed like such a strange request. Zig-zagging my way towards the studio exit, I tried my best not to get in the way of the technicians who were busy packing up for the day. On *UK Today*, we had the luxury of having the studio to ourselves so the programme's set could stay in place day after day, week after week. I popped into make-up where Mandy handed me some cream and wipes. I never wore much make up normally and after the heat of the studio lights, I was keen to get it off my face. I also knew that make-up would be a safe haven away from Jake. It was common knowledge on the team that once his 'tangerine sheen' has been applied at studio each morning, he kept it on all day. With my face now clean, I made my way back to my dressing room but slowed down as I walked past Jake's door, from which I could hear raised voices.

"If you think that I can be replaced by some common Northern slapper, then you are seriously mistaken!" Jake screeched. With that, Serena and Maggie appeared at the door.

"Lizzie my dear, can we meet in the Brain Storming Bar in five?" said Serena in a tone that was much softer and kinder than she normally used for speaking to me.

The Brain Storming Bar was actually just an ordinary meeting room with a coffee machine and fridge full of expensive French bottled water. Serena had given it a stupid name to make the production team feel like proper telly wankers. I had only been waiting in the room for a minute before Serena walked in, closely followed by Jenny the head of daytime and Maggie.

"Lizzie, you've met Jenny before," said Serena, introducing me. I nodded nervously. Serena was being nice to me and as lovely as it was, it really unnerved me.

"Hi Lizzie, well done today, you were great," said Jenny, readjusting her seated position on the sofa opposite me. "Lizzie, I have something we'd like to put to you. Jake is going to be taking a few weeks off."

"Oh, I didn't realise he was going on holiday."

"Well, he's not exactly going on holiday. He's having some time off to deal with a few matters...... and you will see later today that there is a story about him at a..... party, if you could call it that. The thing is Lizzie, we're a daytime show with the family audience. Like I said, he's taking a few weeks out which puts us in a tricky spot."

"What about Chloe who normally covers for him?" I asked, still not grasping where this conversation was heading.

"She is currently in Dubai recording a millionaire property show and will be there for the next two weeks. Anyway, I was thinking what with you being such a natural on the red carpet last night, the viewers really like you Lizzie and we have had great feedback on Twitter and Facebook during this morning's show."

I stared at Jenny before looking at the others. Serena's face was dead pan, giving nothing away while Maggie, my friend, emitted a beaming smile.

"So you're asking me to....." my voice tailed off, not daring to say aloud what I think they were trying to tell me.

"Lizzie, we want you to be the new showbiz reporter for the show. You'll be brilliant. We would need you to start straightaway. Maggie mentioned that we have a place on the red carpet for something tonight."

"It's a charity thing at the Tate Modern gallery," said Maggie.

"Er yes…" I replied, not quite believing it.

"Super," said Jenny clapping her hands together excitedly. "Maggie will give you more details and I'm sure Serena will compensate you at the going rate."

Serena momentarily rolled her eyes before switching to a smile before she got up and left with Jenny.

"Break a leg Lizzie!" shouted Jenny from the corridor.

I turned to Maggie, about to burst with excitement.

"Oh my God. My flatmate James is never going to believe this."

"Neither is your mother."

CHAPTER 14

A Face In The Crowd

My phone didn't stop ringing all morning and that included my mother calling several times. I'd received a call from Lydia to confirm lunch with her and her agent Melanie at a little bistro close to Borough Market. In addition, I'd had a missed call from James. I was going to call him back when my phone rang with an unusual number beginning 001.

"Hello?"

"Hey Lizzie. It's Jet, Jet Shield."

"Oh hi," I replied, my heart pounding.

"How are you doing?"

"Yeah, fine thanks. It's been… it's all been a bit mad since last night on the red carpet."

"Sorry about that, I seem to have caused a stir, particularly with the press."

"Yeah, that's a bit of an understatement," I said and then immediately regretted saying it, worrying that I sounded sarcastic or annoyed.

"Are you ok? Have you been getting harassed?"

"No, I'm fine. They've made me a presenter on the show." I was trying my hardest to sound cool about it.

"Wow, that's great. What about the other guy?"

"Jake? Long story." I let out an exasperated sigh.

"Well how about you tell me all about it over dinner?"

"Tonight?" My legs were shaking.

"I can't tonight, I'm on the way to the airport as we're heading to Berlin for a premiere over there. I was going to fly straight back afterwards but I need to do some stuff for TV there tomorrow morning. Would tomorrow evening be ok?"

"Yeah, that would be fantastic. Where should I meet you?"

"I was thinking my suite in Claridges Hotel. If I go to a restaurant with you right now, we won't get any peace and quiet. Are you ok with that?"

"Sure, that sounds lovely. What time should I meet you?"

"If you come for seven and I'll have Madeleine meet you in the foyer and bring you up."

"Great, thanks. See you tomorrow," I said, no longer able to contain the excitement in my voice.

"Looking forward to it Lizzie."

I was reeling. Here I was, Lizzie Button from Branthwaite in County Durham going for dinner with Jet Shield, one of the biggest film stars in the world. This was all happening so fast, how much had my life changed in twenty-four hours? I called James to let him know I was ok. He admonished me for not having said a word last night when I arrived home about what had happened on the red carpet. I explained that had I have told him, we would have been up for hours, we'd have got stuck into the red wine and I had to have a clear head for my early start this morning. I chose not to tell him about my dinner date tomorrow night, but I did update him about my impending lunch meeting with Melanie, Lydia's agent.

"She's a big major agent with really good connections. I worked for her briefly a few years ago before she set up her own agency. Bit of a ball breaker when it comes to contracts but that's a good thing."

"It won't put you in an awkward position at work if I don't go with someone in your office?" I asked, worried that he might be feeling snubbed, albeit professionally.

"Not at all. To be honest things are rocky here. The two partners are always fighting so it's only a matter of time before they go their separate ways. You could do a lot worse than Melanie."

James told me the percentages that the presenters' agents all charge and gave me a couple of questions to put to Melanie to get the right answers to. I called my mother back briefly, but I didn't have the heart to tell her off for embarrassing me this morning. To be honest, I didn't really get the chance to speak as she barely stopped for breath during the entire four-minute call.

With my phone calls done, I walked back up to the *UK Today* production office and over to Maggie's desk where she was looking through the script notes for tomorrow's show.

"Can we have a chat?" I asked her.

"Sure, wanna get out of here and go for a coffee at the little place across the road?" I loved Maggie, she could read me like a book.

In the café, Maggie put the coffees down on the table and took a seat, while ensuring that her phone was switched to silent signalling to me that I had her undivided attention.

"Are you ok? Your brain must be turning to mush right now, trying to make sense of all this." I sat staring at my coffee trying not to give the game away.

"Just a little. I am meeting Lydia and her agent Melanie for lunch today. I think she wants to take me on as a client."

"You'd be in good hands. I'm pleased we've got the chance to chat. If she can, Serena will try to get you to do this showbiz role for little more money that you're already getting. That's what she does. She promotes people but tells them that the status of the job title makes up for the low pay. She's well known for it in the industry and it's a pretty disgusting tactic to be honest."

"Really? I wouldn't know where to begin."

"That's what an agent is for. Let her earn her commission," said Maggie, her knowledge offering me reassurance.

"But what about my office work? My normal job? Don't I need to come in and do that too?"

"No, certainly not while you're presenting. You know it's a busy job Lizzie. You'll have plenty to keep you occupied. You might need to start bringing a change of clothes in with you for now as we don't have much of a wardrobe budget. Remember you're back on the red carpet tonight. After your lunch, go home and chill, get changed and I'll have a car pick you up at five to take you to the Tate Modern."

"There's no need, I have my Oyster card so I can travel on the tube no problem. I can't be bothered travelling all the way back to Chiswick anyway. I'll come here to the office for five and will go from there."

"OK, only if you're sure."

"Maggie, I have got one more thing to tell you, but you have to promise that you won't tell a soul."

"Of course, what's up?"

"Jet called this morning, about half an hour ago."

"Jet..." Maggie said, not quite registering who I

was talking about. I looked at her with my eyes wide open and the penny dropped. "Jet Shield? Oh Christ."

"Shhh" I whispered, grabbing her hands across the table and looking around the café to see if anyone had heard her.

"Yes, I'm having dinner with him tomorrow night."

"You're kidding me, that's fantastic."

"I know. I'm nervous as hell already and it's not for another thirty hours or so. What should I wear?"

"Where is he taking you?"

"I'm going to his suite at Claridges," I replied. Maggie smiled and raised an eyebrow. "It's just dinner. I think he feels bad that I've been splashed across the front of the papers."

"My best advice is to go with the flow. Have no expectations. Fate has dealt you a good hand this week Lizzie, so just embrace the opportunities that come your way and most importantly, enjoy them." With our coffees finished, we went back to the office and I smartened myself up for lunch with the woman who could potentially become my agent.

I met Lydia and her agent Melanie for lunch and immediately struck up a rapport, despite the fact that I felt a little intimidated in the presence of these two formidable women. After an hour of discussion over delicious food, I agreed to be represented by Melanie who in turn, agreed that she would call Serena to negotiate a contract and money for my new presenting role. I couldn't believe that this was happening to me, aware that in the back of my mind, the imposter syndrome was kicking in again. I nipped up to Oxford Street on the Jubilee line to get a couple of items of clothes, in particular something suitable to wear on camera tonight. Something with no brand logos. You're not really supposed to wear logos on screen, it's all to do with advertising and product placement.

A couple of hours later, I was back in the office sitting at my desk when a figure sidled up to me, only just visible in my peripheral vision.

"Oh, I didn't realise that the presenters are now slumming it up in the office. We don't have a runner to fetch you a coffee." It was Bianca. A very sour faced Bianca and those comments were typical of her jealous, venomous nature.

"Don't you worry Bianca. I'm perfectly capable of grabbing myself a mug of instant if I want one," I said, determined not to rise to the bait.

"Sorry, I shouldn't have spoken to you like that." For a moment I thought she was about to apologise. "I should have gone through your agent," Bianca continued, hoping that her comment was enough to sting me. Thankfully after the last twenty-four hours I would soon learn to develop a thicker skin but for now, Bianca was on a roll, and she wasn't about to stop. "I'm not sure it's worth you actually having an agent, if you're only going to be covering Jake for a week or so," she added jealously.

I ignored her. I wasn't about to waste my energy arguing with the office bitch. We had never got on particularly well and I felt it a shame that my own good fortune had caused my colleague to be so enraged with jealousy. Bianca only had herself to blame for her own shortcomings so with that, I left her to stew in her bitterness.

The cameraman was waiting in the car outside the office, all ready to go to the Tate Modern gallery for tonight's red carpet event. This time he was accompanied by a runner and an assistant producer. I nipped out and told them to go ahead without me and that I'd see them along there shortly. It would only take me ten minutes to walk along the Thames riverbank and this would allow them to get a decent place alongside the red carpet and I would also give me time in the office to go through a quick briefing of tonight's event with the entertainment producer. A short while later, in a cramped toilet cubicle, I changed into the new outfit that I bought earlier and with a spring in my step I walked along to the Tate Modern along the Thames footpath.

By the time that I arrived at the Tate Modern gallery, it was already busy in the press pen with numerous paparazzi photographers jostling for position, several of them standing aloft on small folding steps. I'd already had some experience of working in the press pen and despite changing attitudes towards women, this was still very much a male-dominated environment. As I stood patiently while the cameraman clipped on my radio mic, I could hear group of photographers nearby talking about me.

"She's quite fit but more of a face for radio," one of them joked.

"If she gets another date with Jet Shield, he'll give her enough cash for a new face," his colleague commented cruelly.

If I hadn't been about to go on camera, I would've taken such comments to heart, but already I was growing a thicker skin. I knew I had to put this to one side, get my head down and concentrate on the job in hand. I switched my phone to silent, checked my make-up and then I did a test piece to camera. It felt so strange standing there holding the microphone, talking directly at the lens. This didn't feel like me and it didn't feel like my life. If I'd told myself forty-eight hours ago that this is what I'd be doing, I wouldn't have believed it, not in a million years.

On the red carpet, one of the organisers

approached me. He was an energetic and efficient lad dressed in a bright blue tailored suit and sporting a French pompadour hairstyle.

"Hi, you're Lizzie Button, right?"

"It was the last time I checked," I said and seeing his earnest facial expression remain fixed, I immediately regretted my feeble attempt at a joke.

"Great, we were wondering if you could come and step into the middle of the red carpet for some paparazzi shots. It would give us some amazing publicity for tonight's charity event."

Unsure if this was a good idea, I complied and wandered up to the centre of the red carpet. To keep my bosses on the show happy, I held my microphone which was clearly emblazoned with the *UK Today* logo, firmly in front of me. This would ensure that the *UK Today* branding would appear in any photos of me. The paparazzi in the press pen went crazy with their cameras and I was immediately conscious that I would come across as publicity hungry. I appeared somewhat reluctant and ignored the questions about Jet that they were shouting at me before ducking back to the safe confines of my colleagues at the side of the press pen. This evening, I was conscious more than ever of the rising tide of imposter syndrome that was haunting me from within.

One by one, the cars pulled up on the roadside

at the rear of the Tate Modern, the sun blocked out by the shadow cast from the looming edifice of this former power station. It's fair to say that this event, in contrast to the one last night in Leicester Square didn't have the draw of A-Listers, so amongst the occasional TV chef, presenter etc there were all the usual suspects. The ones who had briefly been in a soap ten years ago but were now more famous for their chaotic personal lives. The ones who could be guaranteed turn up to anything, even the opening of an envelope. The same ones whose tired, weary agents reluctantly made the routine calls around the TV companies and channels saying "if you have anything for _____, he would be extremely grateful." The same agents who were forced to collar producers at industry events and tout their clients' qualities. The ones that the British public appear to have little or no appetite for. Alex Garner, the presenter of our show had once reached this point in his career not that many years ago. The point that you get to when the shopping and gambling channels look appealing. Luckily for him, fate had dealt him a hand which eventually revitalised his flagging career.

It was in the middle of interviewing one such celebrity, that a face in the crowd on the other side of the carpet in the public enclosure caught my eye. I wasn't quite sure at first and I was genuinely listening to the person I was interviewing. I thanked my interviewee and wished her a pleasant evening before concentrating my gaze across the carpet once more. I struggled to re-focus. It couldn't be, could it? The face was there, the same face that I last saw, crying at the back of the church at Dad's funeral and again at the cemetery gates. It was her. I blinked in the hope that I was mistaken and that she was just a random face in the crowd. I wasn't mistaken. This time I shut my eyes for a couple of seconds and on opening them, the woman looked directly at me. My knees began to tremble, this was no coincidence. This woman, Carol, she was here because I was here, pure and simple. I felt sick and very quickly remembered that I was still on camera. I leant forward and took a deep breath whilst trying to stop my legs from wobbling.

The next celebrity waiting to be interviewed was almost in front of me and there was no time to waste. I introduced myself to my next interviewee, a young pop star who had recently wowed audiences as an actor in a TV drama. I pretended to look at my notes for a second and as I looked back up, the woman in the crowd was gone. I had no time to react. My cute pop star stood in front of me smiling, waiting patiently for my question.

Two hours later, I was back at the office and given that I was still on the front of today's papers, I decided to take the advantage of the presenter's perk of a car home to avoid anyone wanting to take pictures of me on the tube. Once back at the flat, I set my alarm for 4:30 in case I forgot. James was nowhere to be seen, so I wrote him a note and stuck it on his door telling him I'd phone him tomorrow. In my room, I delved into my case which was sitting on the floor, still half unpacked from my trip up north. I retrieved Dad's mobile, plugged it into a charger and waited a minute for it to come to life. I went straight into the messages to see if there were any new ones but there weren't. I took a deep breath and began to type a message to the mysterious "Carol".

'I saw you tonight, in the crowd at the Tate Modern. Coincidence? I would ask who the hell are you, but I don't want to know. My dad has gone and whatever was going on between you both is over too. Leave me alone!'

I was going to sign my name at the end of the text, but I was sure she would know who had sent it. I pressed send without any delay and felt relieved for having done so. Despite being exhausted, I had hoped that sleep would come instantly, however it rarely does when you want it to. Instead, images of the woman in the crowd danced through my head and continued to haunt me in my dreams well into my sleep and beyond into the night.

CHAPTER 15

Dinner Date

I struggled to heave my exhausted body into the car that was waiting for me at 4:30am. I hadn't had the best night's sleep despite having gone to bed as soon as I had got home and sent the text to the mysterious 'Carol'. The woman, who I had now come to accept as having a clandestine relationship with my father, now repeatedly intruded into my dreams throughout the night. With Dad now gone, I wished that she was too. The past couple of weeks had been difficult enough without dealing with this. I flitted back and forth between despair and anger on the vast spectrum that is grief. I missed Dad so much, but I couldn't believe that he had been deceptive enough to have an affair behind Mum's back. As a result, I began to question how well I actually knew him which, in turn, made me angry again.

Outside in the street, the smiling driver opened

the door for me and wished me a good morning. It was the same guy who had picked me up yesterday and already I had taken some small comfort in the familiarity. It's not easy in a huge city like London to meet people you know outside of work and home. This morning, someone in the office had already requested that the driver have some of the today's newspapers waiting for me on the back seat. I knew that they did this for the regular presenters to allow them to browse the front pages on their way to studio. I settled into my seat and scrolled through my messages and emails on my phone when the front cover of The Sun on the seat next to me caught my eye.

"You've got to be fucking kidding," I said to myself.

They'd put me on the front cover again. A photo of me standing on the red carpet at last night's fundraising event filled half of the page, the other half consumed by the headline "Jet's Girl Goes Solo". Most of the other papers, at least the tabloids, had had a similar idea and that morning I'd made the front page across seven different publications for doing nothing more than standing on a red carpet, the only difference being this time was that they all now knew who I was. To be on the receiving end of media attention like this only served to remind me what a fickle shallow business it was that I worked in.

I presented two entertainment reports on *UK Today* that morning and although Lydia was lovely towards me on set, Alex was quite the opposite. He couldn't help himself making remarks to me across the morning, most of them patronising and many of them while we were live on-air. As a presenter, he clearly thought that he was untouchable and could get away with saying anything. When we came off-air, Jeremy came up to me on the studio floor and congratulated me with a warm embrace, certainly something that he had never done while I was a humble producer. "Lizzie, I just wanted to check that you *are* coming to my Boat Race Party this Saturday?"

"Yes, that would be lovely, thank you. Is it ok if I bring my friend James?"

"Yes, and if Jet happens to be still in town..." he said, the true nature behind his invitation rearing its ugly head.

"I don't know what his plans are," I replied, walking out of the studio and purposely ending the discussion right there without giving Jeremy the opportunity to engage further. He had a cheek trying to use me to get A-List actors to his party, but it certainly came as no surprise. The invitation for Jeremy's party to watch the Oxford and Cambridge Boat Race had been circulated around the production office a couple of days ago and initially, I wasn't keen to attend having just returned from Dad's funeral. Within an hour of the invitations landing on the desks, the office was buzzing with chat about who was going, what they would be wearing (this coming as much from the guys as it did from the ladies) and most importantly, which celebs would be there. There was no denying that Jeremy was incredibly well-connected and he counted many famous faces amongst his circle of friends. Bianca had declared that she would be attending and it was obvious that her presence would be as much to climb that greasy social pole, as well trying to improve her career prospects at the same time. With the likes of Bianca there, I knew that I needed back-up and so I'd asked James to come along and be my wingman. With his confidence in such situations, James would prove to be a valuable asset and a bit of gay arm candy never did a girl any harm. I had nothing to prepare or research for tomorrow's show, so I decided to go straight home and prepare myself for an evening with Jet Shield, once more taking advantage of a taxi to take me across town to Chiswick.

As the evening sun flickered across the streets of London's West End, I climbed out of the taxi at the entrance to Claridges and made my way into the foyer. On Maggie's advice I'd worn sunglasses but as I lifted them back to rest on my head, nothing could dissipate the overwhelming sense of imposter syndrome that I was feeling. People like me don't belong in places like this. I had actually been here once before about six months ago for drinks with my old flatmates Moira and Rhona. It had been a special occasion for Rhona's birthday and because we were taken aback by the exorbitant prices, we left after our first two G&Ts and moved on to somewhere a lot cheaper. In the foyer, the woman behind the reception desk looked across at me enquiringly, perhaps as if she had seen me somewhere before and given the front pages of the papers in the last two days, I could take an educated guess as to where. I quite wasn't sure how to ask the way to Jet's suite without sounding like a stalker, given the level of protection that such hotels provide for the rich and famous. I was about to ring Jet's number when I saw Madeleine, his PA walking over towards me smiling.

"Hi Lizzie, good to see you. Jet wanted me to double check that you're ok to have dinner in his suite?"

"No problem. He did say on the phone yesterday that we would get more peace and quiet there, away from camera phones," I said. Saying that felt so alien to me and I could sense the imposter syndrome looming again. I shut it out and ignored it, determined to enjoy this once in a lifetime experience. In the lift, there were just the two of us.

"Are you ok?" Madeleine asked kindly, obviously sensing my nerves.

"Yeah, fine. Just trying to take it all in," I replied, forcing a smile in an attempt to appear more confident.

"You'll be fine. I've worked with a lot of big stars and I have to say that Jet is definitely one of the most down-to-earth actors I've known."

The door opened and a moment later Madeleine led me into the suite.

"He's just on the phone wrapping up an interview and then he'll be with you. I'm just across the hall if you need anything," she said, indicating the room on the opposite of side of the passage.

"Thank you," I replied gratefully, as I wandered into the sitting room of the suite, immediately I was able to hear Jet's voice through the adjoining door. I spied a bottle of champagne on ice and two glasses on a large round table that had been laid out for two for dinner. A moment later, Jet came into the room wearing navy jeans, a crisp white shirt and polished tan brogues that looked very expensive. I had always had a thing about men and shoes. If I saw a man wearing bad shoes, it would put me right off him, but there was certainly no danger of that happening here tonight.

The evening went well. Jet was very well read

which shouldn't have come as a surprise to me. It turned out that he was fascinated by English literature, particularly E.M. Forster.

"Would you like to do a film adaptation of one of his novels?" I asked him.

"I'm afraid that I've missed the boat on that one. They've already been done in the eighties and nineties. Emma Thompson won the Oscar for Best Actress for her role in Howard's End. Those Merchant Ivory films are masterpieces so you couldn't top that," he conceded.

"So, what sort of films would you like to do next?" I asked, genuinely curious to know.

"I've got two that I made last year but I've decided to take some time off this year after promoting Tango Master and shooting my next movie. It's been a tough six months what with the divorce and all." His smile withered for a brief moment as he gazed across the other side of the room and I could see that he was still very raw from the experience. "I'm sorry, you don't want to hear about all that."

"No, it's fine, but you don't have to talk about it. Whatever is said here tonight, is between the two of us," I told him, aware that his guard would be up, what with me working on a news and entertainment programme and us only having met in the last two days.

"There's actually not a lot to tell. We were really happy at one time but we both have high profile careers. We spent less time together as the years passed and we drifted apart. Classic Hollywood story. It only turned nasty when the lawyers got involved."

The melancholic look on his face lasted a few more seconds and aware that the mood had come down, he changed the subject. "So how are you dealing with the last forty-eight hours being in the spotlight? I feel guilty for dragging you onto the dance floor, well, just a little. If I hadn't have done it, then I suppose that I wouldn't have had the pleasure of your company this evening."

"It's been ok. I suppose that I'm lucky that I already work in the media so I know how all this works and with people that I know. I have connections to people who can help me navigate my way through it and now I've got an agent," I said, laughing a little in embarrassment and more so at the surreal nature of the last few days.

The dinner was delicious although I don't remember much about eating it. Jet was the perfect gentleman and when I suggested that perhaps it was time for me to head home, he said that he understood as I would have an early start in the studio the following morning. He went through to Madeleine's room to ask her to arrange a car to take me home.

"It's all sorted," Jet said, as he returned smiling. He was always smiling and I wondered if he had always been that way or if it was his actor training. "I'd like to see you again Lizzie, if that's possible. No pressure," he added sincerely.

"That would be nice," I replied, taken aback that he was suggesting another meet up as I'd assumed that this was a one-off.

"I'm afraid that I'm flying to New York in the morning to do some promo stuff for the movie and then we are off to Sydney for the Australian premiere."

"No worries," I said, unsure what to suggest. "You have my number so call me and let me know when you're next back in town."

"I will," he replied, as helped me on with my jacket. A true gentleman. "Thank you Lizzie. I've had a lovely evening."

"Thank you for dinner and for having me as your guest." Standing in front of each other once more, he towered over me and as I expected him to kiss me on the cheek, he reached down and brushed his lips against mine and kissed me.

I could still feel the tingling sensation on my lips minutes later as the lift pinged telling me that I was down on the ground floor. I might have been on the ground floor but my head was in the clouds. Despite Madeleine's kind offer to escort me to the entrance, I told her I was happy to make my own way downstairs and out to the waiting car. As I approached the door, I regretted not taking her up on her suggestion. The cacophony of shouting, flashing and clicking hit me like some rogue orchestra playing the notes randomly in any order. Six paparazzi photographers were waiting for me down on the pavement. The hotel concierge along with the driver who had opened the car door, both chivalrously acted as a makeshift barrier to keep the photographers at some sort of distance and soon I was in the car, safely hidden behind the blacked-out windows. As we drove in the direction of Knightsbridge, the driver looked at me in his rear-view mirror and asked me if I was ok. I reassured him that I was as I smiled weakly. My happiness after a lovely evening was now overshadowed by a sense of dread, surely the papers couldn't want any more photos of me. I thought it might be best to put in a call to Maggie, but I decided to wait until I was back home in the privacy of my flat. It wasn't the sort of conversation that I wanted to have in front of the driver, no matter how lovely he was.

At home, there was no sign of James. I poured myself a glass of red wine resolving to just have the one, knowing that I was back in early tomorrow morning. I called Maggie and it sounded as if she was up to her eyes in it at home with her two boys, so I kept it brief and simply told her that all was well and I was now back home. I updated her on the situation with the paparazzi outside the hotel and she reassured me that despite it being likely that I'd be in the papers tomorrow morning, the story would soon lose traction. She said that between my agent and the team at *UK Today*, a ring of support and protection would be thrown around me and that I wasn't to worry.

As I was climbing into bed, my phone pinged once more, it was a message from Jet.
"Thank you for a lovely evening. I've heard that you were bombarded on your departure. Sorry about that. Hope you're ok. J xx"
I must have re-read his message about five times before I eventually went to sleep and as I drifted off, I went over that kiss in my mind, time and time again convinced that I could still feel the tingle on my lips.

In the studio the following morning as we came off-air, Maggie walked in wearing her coat having just arrived from dropping her sons off at school. Walking back with me to my dressing room, she began her earnest questioning.

"So last night you told me about the paparazzi, but you didn't tell me about the dinner with him."
"It was delicious, I had guinea fowl," I replied, knowing that wasn't the information she was after.
"Not the meal you ninny, how was things with

243

you and Jet?"

"It was lovely, he was the perfect gentleman. He asked me lots of questions about myself and was genuinely interested in me. He wasn't starry at all. I did feel like a bit of an idiot as I shed a few tears talking about my dad, but he was lovely and genuine. I couldn't stay late as I knew I had to be in here early this morning, so his assistant arranged for a car to take me home."

"Was she there the whole time?"

"No, she was in her room across the hall."

"So, it was a good night?" Maggie was not ready to accept that there wasn't any more juicy gossip.

"Yeah, it was...... lovely."

"Have you made any plans to......?"

"See him again? No, he did text me though, thanking me for having dinner with him. He's off to New York today but he does want to see me, he said."

"So, I'm not to go shopping for a hat just yet?"

"Don't you dare."

CHAPTER 16

Showbiz Party

It was Saturday morning and the sun was shining. As I lay in bed, I did my best to take in the enormity of this week's events. Even just seven days ago, my life was very different and as I remained snuggled under the heavy duvet, my mind raced through the last ninety hours. It was all very well me lying in bed, but the thought of a busy day ahead dwelled on my conscience. It was no good, I needed to get up. I pulled back the nautical blue striped curtains of my bedroom and craned my neck to see out of the high window. With the sun streaming through the dirty panes of glass I could see the bright blue sky above the rooftops across the street.

Pulling open the doors of my wardrobe, I scoured the stuffed contents for something to wear to Jeremy's Boat Race Party this afternoon. I couldn't select anything that I normally wore to work but then again, I didn't want to be seen to be making too much of an effort. Dressing for such events had to be carefully considered and be made to look effortless. With that in mind, I selected the smart jacket that I'd worn on the show the other morning and teamed it up with a plain white shirt and blue jeans. It wasn't yet weather for sandals so a pair of brown ankle boots seemed appropriate enough, given that we would be standing around on Jeremy's lawn. My caffeine-addicted body told me that I needed coffee. With the kitchen being so tiny, the fridge was just outside the door in the hall along with a microwave and kettle. As I bent down to retrieve the ground coffee from the fridge, I glanced up and looked at the charred blackened door of the microwave. "Fucking hell, James," I muttered under my breath. My flatmate was supposed to have replaced the microwave in the last two weeks since he inadvertently blew it up. Plenty of people cook baked potatoes in a microwave but I didn't ever expect to have to explain to my dizzy friend that you don't cover baked potatoes in tin foil before placing them in there.

Sitting in the living room sipping coffee and looking at my phone, I could see that I had quite a few notifications. At any other time, I'd eagerly click on them, but I didn't have a lot of time for distractions this morning. I wanted a day of being just plain old Lizzie and not acknowledge my sudden ascent to the echelons of celebrity and all that came with it. I drained the last of my coffee and set about running the bath for myself. Saturday mornings were usually spent with James and I lazing around the flat as he would normally make an effort to sleep in his own bed on a Friday night, albeit rarely alone. This morning was no exception and I heard him seeing his overnight guest to the door and mumbling vague directions to Turnham Green tube station. We met in the hall, him with a trademark cheeky grin.

"Croissants or fry up?" he offered.

"Ooh, a fry up would be good, but we don't have the stuff in for it. I could nip over to M&S across the road," I replied.

"Not to worry. Get some slacks on and I'll treat you to breakfast at the caff," he said enthusiastically. "You can be my celebrity date, so you'd better bring your shades."

"Aren't you going to wash first?" I said, only too aware that his guest had just left and his hair was a mess.

"Nah, I'll do it when I get back. I need food first." He was already pulling on his coat and dipped into his room to grab his wallet and keys. I put off my bath until afterwards and clipping my hair back, I quickly checked my unmade face in the mirror. Indifferent to my appearance right now, we headed down onto Chiswick High Road.

The little greasy spoon café halfway along

Turnham Green Terrace was a favourite weekend haunt of ours. It was a no-frills establishment with its 1970s teak panelled walls, plastic chairs and Formica-topped tables. In the evening they served up the most delicious Thai food at well-below London prices. To top it off, it didn't have an alcohol license so you could take along your own booze. No booze for breakfast though as both myself and James knew that we would likely drink our fair share later on at the party. After a breakfast of bacon, poached eggs and huge amount of bubble and squeak, I linked arms with James as we wandered back to the flat. I did get the odd second look from a few people that we passed on the way but nothing on the scale of being in central London with the paparazzi pestering me. James said that he was going to call in at the newsagents to pick up the day's papers, this time not only out of his professional interest but to see if there were any more stories attempting to link me to Jet. I said that I'd catch him back at the flat as I wanted a soak in the bath before we walked along to Jeremy's.

I was crossing the road at the zebra crossing just outside Waterstones when I caught a glimpse of a woman across the road looking directly at me. At first, I thought it might have just been some random member of the public who had recognised me from the TV or the papers but on closer inspection, it wasn't. It was her, the mystery woman from the cemetery. It was Carol, Dad's former mistress. As much as I hated the thought of describing her as his mistress, there was no getting away from the fact that was who she was. There was no more than a handful of seconds when we were both standing on opposite sides of the road, staring at each other. A driver in a double decker bus beeped his horn which snapped me out of my hypnotic state and reminded me that the vehicles were waiting for me to cross the road. I was about to cross, but the bus drove through the crossing impatiently and the minute it was past, I legged it across to confront this woman once and for all. By the time that I'd reached the other side, she had boarded that very same bus and it was now heading in the direction of Brentford. I ran over to our flat and once I was upstairs in my room, I took dad's phone off the white painted mantlepiece and dialled her number. She answered but all I could hear at the other end was her breathing and the noise of the bus's engine. She hung up on me, so I dialled the number again and this time it went straight to voicemail. I toyed with the idea of not leaving a message, but I was far too angry.

"What the fuck! What the hell do you think you're playing at? If you've got something to say then for Christ's sake, say it to my face. Stop fucking stalking me and have the balls to speak to my face!" I pressed the red button to end the call, the beat of my heart pulsing through my body. I was incensed and I was shaking. What the hell was she doing? I asked myself as I paced about the flat. A moment later James came in clutching an armful of newspapers and he could see that I was shaken. I told him what had just happened, and he did his best to calm me down.

"We're not going to dwell on that mad stalker woman or stalker paparazzi today," he said assertively. "We're going to a party and we're going to have some fun." I compliantly agreed to get ready for the party and put the latest appearance by Dad's bit on the side out of my mind. I decided to have a shower instead of a bath to ensure that there was enough hot water for James to do the same. Once we were ready and James had popped back to his room for another blast of his Jean-Paul Gaultier, he emerged stuffing what looked like a packet of condoms into his jacket pocket.

"Condoms? Really James? It's a Boat Race Party on my boss's lawn, not a gay club we're going to."

"Hey, I was a cub scout. Be prepared," he said, doing the Scout symbol with his fingers and looking less like Akala and more like Benny Hill.

We called in at the little branch of Sainsbury's on Chiswick High Road and were delighted to discover that they had Moet on a discount deal. I normally wouldn't have taken champagne to a party, but this was no ordinary party. This was a TV party, with real TV people and if there was some sort of device that could measure levels of pretension, it would go off the scale at such an event. With the chilled booze in hand, we set off for Jeremy's flat.

Jeremy lived in Barnes and as it was a lovely sunny spring day, James and I chose to walk down to the river and along the Thames, cooing as we walked past the multi-million-pound river-fronted properties. The Oxford and Cambridge University Boat Race is traditionally held on this stretch of the River Thames on a Saturday afternoon in March or April. It starts in Putney and heads upstream past Hammersmith and finishes just before Chiswick Bridge further west. All along the riverbank of the Thames, crowds were starting to gather, a mixture of families and groups of young people some of whom had already started drinking. There was a lovely buzz in the air and to me, it felt like just another busy weekend in London. It was after the fourth or fifth occurrence that I realised that people were staring at me as I walked along with James. Some of them gave me nothing more than a secondary glance, others went further to nudge their companion and whisper indiscreetly whilst blatantly pointing at me. We're often not the most subtle folk us Brits, are we? I did my best to pretend that I hadn't seen them and continue to chat to James who was in the throes of relaying to me the details of the guy that he had brought home last night.

As we crossed over at Hammersmith Bridge, I looked up the address once more on my phone and the little pointer on the map told me that we were just around the corner, as music boomed in the distance. The further we got along the bridge, the louder the music became and as we looked over onto the riverbank below, we could see that the party was already in full swing with at least thirty people gathered next to a series of white gazebos on the lawn. At the ground floor of the most stunning red brick Victorian mansion block, I rang the buzzer and Jeremy came to the door, greeting us with an uncharacteristic enthusiasm.

"Lizzie, lovely to see you and who is this you've brought with you? Jet's stunt double?" he said mischievously, not taking his eyes off James who was equally flirty in return. I was sceptical at Jeremy treating me like his best friend whereas prior to last Tuesday, he had barely acknowledged my existence. He led us through to a large kitchen with a granite-topped island taking centre stage. On top were two huge copper ice buckets the size of bin lids, each holding half a dozen bottles of champagne. These were promptly lifted by two handsome waiters dressed in black and carried out to the garden. Jeremy took the bottles from us and scrutinised the carrier bags.

"Some champagne for you Jeremy."

"Oh Bollinger, lovely," he replied, presumptuous of the brand that we had selected and on opening the bags, he discovered that it was the much cheaper Moet & Chandon. He forced a smile ungratefully and put them to one side in a manner that suggested he'd more likely use it for cooking rather than drinking.

As the kitchen was buzzing with a catering team that had taken it over, Jeremy escorted us out to the garden whilst not taking his hand off the small of James's back. Alex and Lydia were there along with most of the production team, although Jake was noticeably absent. I knew that Maggie couldn't make it as her eldest boy was playing rugby for his school and wild horses and A-Listers couldn't keep her away from her family commitments. Over on the lawn underneath one of the gazebos, stood Serena along with a group of women who were all wearing designer outfits and sunglasses. They all looked as if they were dressed for the Henley Regatta, rather than an informal house party. Serena, on seeing me walk over, immediately left her friends and made a beeline for me.

"Lizzie, darling. So lovely to see you," she said and then looking over my shoulder, "Is Jet not with you?"

"No, I'm afraid he had to fly to New York yesterday and then he's travelling straight to Sydney for the Australian premiere," I replied, confident that I wasn't divulging any of Jet's plans that weren't already out in the public arena. She was unable to hide her disappointment.

"Well, not to worry. You must come and meet some people." Taking me by the elbow, Serena led me over to her group of socialite friends. Everyone was very polite and did that whole air kissing thing when they met me. Once I had been introduced to Arabella, Camilla, Portia and India, I felt rather out of place, primarily for not having a first name that finished with the letter 'A'. These women came from a world of au pairs, ski holidays and socialite parties whereas my world was more off-licenses, takeaways and the village pub. After ten minutes of intense questioning about Jet and my dalliance with him on the red carpet, I looked around for an escape route. Sadly I wasn't quick enough because Serena had already summoned the professional photographer that Jeremy's party planner had hired. As our group stood ready to pose for a picture, myself reluctantly, Bianca appeared beside us and attempted to join the line-up for the photographer.

"Oh Bianca," Serena said acidly, "Would you mind waiting over there while we have this taken? He'll be along to take some of you and the office team soon, I'm sure."

As Bianca walked away embarrassed and with her tail somewhat between her legs, she turned back and gave me an icy stare. Once the photo was done, I made my excuses saying that I needed to find the bathroom and as I walked towards the kitchen, I scanned the groups of guests in earnest, trying to locate James. Unable to find him, I went up to the bathroom and as the door opened, James came out followed by a girl who I'd seen on a reality tv show last summer. They were both grinning and as she was rubbing her nose, I didn't need to ask what they had been doing in there together.

Five minutes later I was back outside where Jeremy gathered all of his guests together and looking at his watch, he addressed everyone, thanking them for coming. He made special mention of Lydia and Alex, the latter now very drunk and struggling to stand still and just as I thought that he was going to finish, I heard my name.

"And not forgetting our rising star, the darling of the red carpet, Lizzie Button," he said as all eyes on the lawn turned to me and a round of applause broke out. "So, fill your glasses, enjoy the party and let's give these rowers a damn good cheer."

We didn't have to wait long for the Oxford and Cambridge boats to glide swiftly past us and in less than a minute, the excitement and cheering was over. As the afternoon wore on, everyone was getting quite drunk, especially Bianca who cornered me as I stepped out onto the patio after getting myself a glass of iced tonic water from the kitchen bar.

"Oh, look who it is, the darling of the fucking red carpet, Lizzie fucking Button," said Bianca slurring her words loudly. "You really think you're all that, don't you?"

"Bianca, you're drunk, and I don't think that this is the time or the place," I reasoned, in an effort to placate her.

"I'm not drunk, you silly cow. So where is your oh so famous film star boyfriend now? Gone back to his ex-wife?" she spat, staggering across the patio. "I don't know why the fuck they want you on the show. As if our viewers want to watch some thick as pig shit northerner when they're having their Rice Krispies."

"Bianca, I'm going to leave you to it. You've had more than enough champagne," I said, trying to remain diplomatic and also aware that she had garnered quite the audience of onlookers.

Bianca poured her full glass of champagne down her throat and dropped the glass, smashing it on the stone patio. Serena stormed towards us and turning to Bianca she said, "what the hell are you playing at Bianca?"

"Here's my friend Serena. You see Lizzie? You'll never be part of our circle of friends," Bianca hissed.

"I already have enough friends Bianca. You're my employee, not a friend. I gave you a job on the show because your mother knows my husband," said Serena, in an effort to clear up any confusion over Bianca's desires to climb the greasy social pole. Bianca went to reply to Serena, and I would have expected some sort of apology. What I didn't expect and as it turns out, neither did Serena, was for Bianca to vomit. As she lurched forward, Serena took the brunt of the sick emitted from Bianca's mouth. By now, every single person at the party was staring at Bianca, including the party planner and the catering staff. Stuey gallantly came over and removed Bianca from the patio taking her to the bathroom as Serena, now caked in vomit, stormed off through the house and out of the front door onto the street.

By six o'clock, almost all the party guests were drunk but thankfully, I'd restricted myself to only three glasses of champagne since I arrived, as I wanted to keep my wits about me, especially given the past week's events. Bianca's drunken display which led to the sudden departure of Serena from the party, was the sole topic of conversation among the remaining guests. I asked James if he was ready to head off home, to which he agreed and offered to go up to the spare bedroom to collect his jacket from the makeshift cloakroom. He didn't return for ten minutes, and I'd now become cornered by Alex who was incredibly drunk, leaning into my space leeringly whilst offering slurred titbits of advice on how to make it as a celebrity. James eventually came back downstairs, grinning and noticeably flushed and when Jeremy followed a moment later, my suspicions were confirmed.

"Forgotten anything?" I asked him.

"I don't think so," he said, looking down at his empty hands. "Shit, jackets! Back in a sec," as he ran upstairs. Thankfully this time, Jeremy didn't follow him. We said our goodbyes to our host and thanked him for his hospitality. I wanted to avoid getting caught up in lots of hugs and kisses, so I popped my head outside and shouted goodbye to the remaining guests without lingering. It was a slow relaxing walk back across Hammersmith Bridge and as I chatted, I was aware that I only had fifty percent of James's attention. I could see that he was immersed in looking at his phone, clearly messaging someone and grinning in the process.

"Why were you so long up in the bedroom getting the coats?"

"Was I long time? I was just looking for my jacket

in the enormous pile on the bed?" His efforts to be coy weren't fooling anyone.

"Yet you came down without it and when you went back up, you found it in a matter of seconds," I teased.

"Well, Jeremy was up there and we happened to get chatting."

"He has a boyfriend you know."

"Yeah, Jeremy said he's back in Australia right now, but they've got this open relationship thing going on," he said, looking up from his phone and smiling like the cat who'd tasted the cream. My boss and my flatmate. I felt a little bit sick but didn't show it.

As we approached the first pub on the riverside path over on the north bank, I suggested to James that perhaps we should have one more for the road as the night was young. He looked at the busy heaving pub and back at his phone. He was about to speak when we were interrupted.

"Lizzie!" a voice shouted ahead of us. It was Rhona, my old flat mate standing outside the pub smoking in the company of two guys.

"Rhona, so lovely to see you," I replied, genuinely pleased to see an old friend even though I had only seen her last Sunday evening when she came round for a takeaway after my arrival home from Dad's funeral.

Rhona introduced us to her two friends, Simon and Guy, the latter of which offered to get us some drinks in at the bar. James, who had still been texting on his phone, looked up and smiled.

"Actually, I'm going to split if that's ok. I'm on a promise."

"Oh James, not Jeremy," I said, laughing knowing my protest was falling on deaf ears. "Seriously though James, have you really been with every gay man in London that you now need to shag my boss?" He merely laughed back at me and after saying his goodbyes, he ran back in the direction of Jeremy's flat across the river.

Rhona and I had a lot to talk about as it was our first opportunity to catch up since the incident on the red carpet and my much-publicised dinner date with Jet Shield. Simon and Guy returned with a round of drinks and after a few minutes of polite chit chat, they left Rhona and I to catch up in private. After an hour, Rhona had to leave as she was going off to meet Moira, our other ex-flatmate for drinks down the road. Not wanting to walk the remainder of the route along the river on my own, I walked around to the taxi rank two streets away with Rhona and after saying our goodbyes, I took a cab home to the flat.

I'd only been in the door two minutes and my mobile rang with a foreign number coming up on the screen.

"Hello stranger," the voice on the phone said. It

took me almost ten seconds to respond because although I knew the voice instantly, it had been thirteen years since I had last heard it.

"Paolo, is that you?"

"Sure is. How the hell are you?" he replied. I then proceeded to question my ex-boyfriend, the same one who had done the dirty on me in Australia all those years ago, as to exactly why he was calling me and, more to the point, how the hell had he got my mobile number?

"I still had the phone number for your mum and dad written down from years ago so I thought I would give it a try."

"Well, she shouldn't have given my number to you and as for my dad, he died last week."

"Yeah, your mum said. Sorry about that," he said insincerely. It was then that something occurred to me.

"Paolo, are you still in Australia?"

"Yeah, I'm in Sydney."

"Then it must be about seven o'clock on Sunday morning over there," I said, attempting to work out the time difference in my head.

"Yeah, I suppose it is."

"So, you took it upon yourself to call my mother, who you have never spoken to before, from Australia where it's early on a Sunday morning?" It was time to get to the crux of the matter. "Paolo, what exactly is it that you want?"

"Lizzie, I just wanted to talk to you. I saw you

in the papers over here and.." his voice tailed off. Bingo! It suddenly all became clear.

"Paolo, you have had thirteen years to call me. Thirteen years and yet, thankfully, you have never once picked up the phone. I can only now presume that in the light of recent events here in London, you're after money."

"Lizzie, you've become very cynical with age. Why would I call you to ask for money?" Paolo replied, unable to disguise his smarmy tone.

"So, you don't want money? That's ok then." My patience was already wearing thin.

"Well, I didn't say that. Actually, now that you mention money, I've got myself into a bit of a financial pickle over here Lizzie so if you could see your way to helping me out...."

"Paolo, given the way that you treated me all those years ago, the way that you cheated on me left me broken. I had no-one out there Paolo. I had to return to England alone. It took me years to fix myself and put behind me everything that happened with you. I still hate you Paolo, so don't be disappointed when I tell you to fuck off and don't call me ever again!"

I ended the call right there and hoped that he wouldn't call back. I probably ought have blocked his number, but I didn't get a chance as my phone started ringing again, this time with Jet's number flashing up on my screen.

"Hi Jet," I said doing my best to sound upbeat and pretend that the call from Paolo had never happened.

"Hey Lizzie, how are you doing?"

"I'm ok," I replied, my voice faltering a little.

"Are you sure? You don't sound ok."

"No, I'm fine. Just a little tired. It's been a long day and I only got home ten minutes ago. Where are you? Australia?"

"Yeah, I got here a few hours ago and I'm just going to bed even though it's early morning here." The coincidence of receiving two phone calls from Sydney in five minutes didn't pass me by.

"Lizzie, I've got Madeleine here with me. I've had an idea and I wanted to run it by you," he said.

"That sounds intriguing," I replied, wondering what this idea of his could be.

"I wanted to invite you to come out to Sydney for the Tango Master premiere on Tuesday night. After that we can have a couple of days in the city exploring together. How does that sound?" I certainly wasn't expecting that.

"Jet, that sounds amazing, but I can't just up sticks here and jet across to the other side of the world for a mini-break. Besides the fact that I have to work, there's the cost of the flight, hotel and everything."

"Lizzie, I would pay for the flight. Madeleine is here and ready to book it if you agree. There's a flight from Heathrow early tomorrow morning which means you would get here for Monday evening, Australian time. You can stay here at my hotel, in your own room of course and I will cover it. It won't cost you anything," he said generously. "Jet, I'll need to speak to work. Give me twenty minutes and I'll call you back."

I called Maggie who was in the middle of cooking pizzas for her boys and their friends. She thought it an amazing opportunity and assured me that they could cover the showbiz reports for the next few days as my attending the Sydney premiere with Jet would inadvertently bring in more publicity for *UK Today*. She also said that she would check with Serena and Jeremy. I told her that she probably wouldn't get hold of Jeremy as I knew he would be otherwise engaged right now but I did remember to tell her about the incident at the party with Bianca throwing up over Serena. It took less than five minutes for Maggie to call back to say that Serena had agreed to me going to Australia but perhaps I could do a live segment from Sydney for the show one morning. Within forty-five minutes I had hastily packed my suitcase and set my alarm, having left my passport and keys by the flat door so I wouldn't forget them. Thirteen years had been a long time and despite everything that had gone wrong for me back then, I yearned to return to Sydney and now unexpectedly, I had the chance. Life does indeed move in mysterious ways.

CHAPTER 17

Chance Of A Lifetime

By the time that I arrived at London Heathrow Airport at 530am that Sunday morning, I'd only had about four hours sleep. The phone call from Jet had taken me by surprise, more so the invitation to join him for the premiere of Tango Master in Sydney. The other call that I'd received, the one from Paolo, I did my best to ignore. I approached the Emirates desk with my reference number for the booking along with my passport, expecting to be directed to the regular check-in desk for the flight.

"Hello Madam, we will check you in over here," the airline's check-in supervisor said, leading me straight to the First-Class check-in. Imposter Syndrome had well and truly kicked in before we had even reached the desk which didn't take long as there was nobody waiting to check-in on First-Class. There *was* a lengthy queue however, for the economy class and one or two people nudged each other in reference to me standing at the First-Class desk. I assumed it was because they thought I didn't look smart enough to be travelling First-Class rather than them recognising me from the papers this last week, but when one lady shouted over "Is Jet not with you?" I realised what was going on. The girl on the check-in said, "Hello Miss Button," before her colleague had even had chance to hand her my passport and booking reference. I gather that she too must have recognised me from the same source as my fellow passenger.

As soon as I had checked in, I was assigned a special escort that are, apparently, normally reserved for royalty and VIP travellers such as Jet Shield. Once I was through security, she offered to act as a personal shopper but, there wasn't anything that I needed other than a couple of newspapers and magazines. Once I had my reading material for the flight, I was taken directly to the First-Class Lounge where they had an array of breakfast options available as well as a fully stocked bar complete with huge bowls full of iced champagne bottles. The last thing that I wanted right now was alcohol and so I thanked my escort as I settled into a discreet seat in the corner of the lounge with a coffee, an almond croissant and the first of the Sunday papers, dreading what I might find on opening it.

Despite it being ridiculously early to phone my brother Michael to update him briefly on my trip, I gave his number a try. I apologised for waking him and Elaine, but he said not to worry as she was sleeping in a different room. That certainly struck me as a little odd. I asked him to tell Mum that I was going to Sydney for a few days along with the addendum that, under no circumstances, was she to pass my number on to a single other person. I gave him the contact details for Melanie's agency to pass on to her. If they were going to take fifteen percent of my earnings, then they could jolly well earn it. I might sound ungrateful at this point, but in time I would come to learn that as an agent, Melanie and her team were worth every penny that they were paid. Now that I think back to my all too brief conversation with Michael, there was something about the tone of his voice that told me that all was not well with him and coupled with the fact that he was sleeping in the spare room, domestic life at my brother's was clearly far from rosy. I promised myself that as soon as I had a moment in Sydney, I'd call him to check that he was ok.

No matter how much I tried to put it out of my mind, I was still reeling from Paolo's phone call last night. I'd managed to get through the last thirteen years or so without him, so I don't know what the hell he was playing at. That's a lie, I knew only too well what he was after and that was money, as he blatantly admitted. Paolo was never the sharpest knife in the drawer, and he obviously thought that my bank balance would be loaded overnight since I'd stepped onto the red carpet with Jet. Looking around me at the splendour of my plush surroundings, I was determined to enjoy this once in a lifetime opportunity and given what I'd been through in the past month, I told myself that I deserved it. The time seemed to fly by. Once I'd gathered my things together, ensuring that I had my passport and boarding pass to hand, I made my move to leave the lounge, at which moment a smartly dressed man in an Emirates uniform approached me.

"Miss Button? Hello I'm Francis. I'm here to escort you to your cabin on board the plane."
At first, I thought he was joking but he wasn't.
"Oh, thank you," I said, feeling rather flattered and a little embarrassed. More so, once that I became aware that other passengers in the lounge were staring at me. I smiled graciously and accepted his kind offer. As I tried to keep my head down and my eyes in front of me, I noticed that some people were taking photos with their phones.
"Does Beyonce go through this?" I asked him jokingly.

"I think that she does Miss Button," Francis replied, giving me a reassuring smile.

"Please call me Lizzie," I told him.   As we reached the desk at the gate, he introduced me to another of his colleagues, a beautiful woman with flawless make-up that put my own to shame. She checked my passport and relieved me of my boarding pass as together we boarded the plane which was a huge Boeing 777-300 and from someone who knows nothing about aircraft, this was in a different league to any other plane that I had travelled on before. I was given my own cabin. Yes, these planes had individual first class cabins which had a seat that converted into a luxurious bed. The cabin was the length of three of the aeroplane's windows and not only did it have a fridge and a selection of drinks and snacks, but there was a little tray that opened out and contained noise-cancelling headphones, a notepad and pens and some very posh toiletries. The bed was topped with a sheepskin quilt and from it, you could control your own lighting to a more ambient setting if you preferred. I thought that it couldn't get any better when I found a pair of binoculars for me to use during the flight.

It was just over a seven-hour flight to Dubai, and I'd planned to sleep for half of it so that I wasn't exhausted by the time that we landed for our two-hour stopover. The cabin crew were attentive but not in your face, so I had the opportunity to get my head down for a while and catch up on some much-needed sleep. Once we had landed in Dubai, I was again personally escorted to the Emirates First Class Lounge where this time, I just had a coffee and some water as I sat and phoned my brother. I'd been worried about him since I last spoke to him at Heathrow earlier and although he did his best to assure me that he was fine, I could tell by his voice that he was far from okay. That boy wasn't going to win any prizes for acting. I suspected that all was not well at home and that his marriage to Elaine was on very rocky ground right now, that much was obvious. I told him that I would call him from Sydney at some point when I had free time and when it wouldn't be the middle of the night back in the UK.

When I re-boarded the same aeroplane, now bound for Sydney, I braced myself for the thirteen-and-a-half-hour flight ahead of me and by this time, I had long given up trying to figure out what time it was back in the UK or in Australia. On this much longer flight I allowed myself a couple of glasses of red wine with my dinner. Once I'd exhausted the newspapers and magazines that I had brought with me, I watched a couple of Jet's films that were available on the built-in TV in my cabin. It was hard to think that the same guy who was jumping off buildings while shooting gangsters, was the same man that I had had dinner with and opened my heart to. The same man who had kissed me so tenderly. Those horrible feelings of self-doubt began creeping in again. What would he want with a plain Northern girl like me? Girls like me don't date film stars. In my head, I could hear Maggie shouting at me to stop these negative thoughts and with that, I snapped out of it and ordered one more glass of wine.

After a good long sleep, ably assisted by the red wine, I woke and was served a breakfast of bacon, scrambled eggs and mushrooms along with more coffee and that posh orange juice with the bits floating around in it. I'd had time to have a wash and make myself more presentable for my arrival in Sydney. When the captain announced that we were due to land in thirty minutes, I took the opportunity to use the binoculars that had been thoughtfully provided with the cabin. Out of the window I could see the Blue Mountains. Sitting on the outskirts of Sydney, they are arguably one of the most picturesque mountain ranges in the world. It had been my intention to visit them the last time that I was here, but I had found myself getting caught up in that cycle of working, socialising and sleeping, always assuming that I would have the opportunity to do it another day. Given the circumstances of my sudden departure from Australia all those years ago, it wasn't something that I wanted to drag up now, let alone dwell on. The past was consigned to the past I told myself. Down below with no clouds to hamper us, the view as we approached Sydney Harbour was nothing short of breath-taking. I scoured the ground below me with the binoculars in search of the famous Sydney Opera House, one of the world's most iconic buildings and for me, my favourite (after Durham Cathedral of course). The moment I caught sight of the Sydney Harbour Bridge spanning the water in this most beautiful of settings, there was a glimpse of a white building tucked behind it and a few seconds later as the plane moved round, I saw it in all its glory. In the years since I left Australia, I had often dreamt that I was back here in Sydney only to be cruelly awakened and thrust back into my reality. I stared through the binoculars and reached down to pinch myself. Could I really be here? The sun was already low and starting to set behind us, as the lights of the city sprung to life down below. By now, I had manoeuvred my bed back into the sitting position and obediently fastened my seat belt in preparation for landing. As we turned southwards away from the harbour towards Sydney Airport, I sat back and closed my eyes to mentally prepare myself for the week ahead. I was going to be spending the next six days with arguably one of the most famous men on the planet, but at least here in Australia, I could be low profile and avoid the attention that I'd received in London in the past week or so. At this moment, I had forgotten that Paolo, my ex, had apparently seen me in the Australian papers. Add to that the fact that I was about to attend a film premiere where the eyes of the press would be on us, I really did have no idea as to what lay ahead over the coming days. As the wheels of the aircraft touched the runway, I took a deep breath and said to myself out loud, "Here you are Lizzie Button. Relax and enjoy it."

Once I'd been through customs and security, it was out into the open space of the Arrivals Hall. I had presumed that I would get myself a cab to the hotel but there in the crowd was Madeleine, Jet's PA, waiting for me with a welcoming smile.

She reached out and gave me a hug as if we were old friends and I could have loved her for that. In that moment, despite being across the other side of the world, I felt as if I wasn't alone.

"Good flight?"

"The best," I replied gratefully, knowing that it had been she who had arranged my trip on Jet's behalf. "Those cabins are a revelation. I'll never settle for Economy again," I joked.

"They are pretty special, and Jet insisted that I have one for this trip even though the film company objected on grounds of cost."

"So, he persuaded them otherwise?" I said presumptively.

"No, he just paid the difference out of his own pocket."

"Lizzie, over here" a man's voice shouted over to my right, I turned and right in front of me was a paparazzi photographer who clicked his camera a dozen times in my face. I must have looked startled, but I didn't have time to take it in.

"Are you here to see Jet Shield, Lizzie?" he shouted across the crowd of people waiting in the arrivals hall.

Instinctively, I pulled down the sunglasses that were sitting on my forehead as Madeleine put a protective arm across my back and guided me hurriedly towards the exit.

"How could he know I was here?" I said to her, knowing full well that it wouldn't have been leaked by anyone in Jet's team. She led me to a waiting car where a smartly dressed driver took my case and put it in the boot. Inside the plush interior of the car, Madeleine set about updating me as to the plans for the next few days, not making a single reference to the incident with the photographer that had just occurred.

Jet was currently at the hotel and had some press to do in the next couple of hours, but she assured me that he would be free then for the rest of the evening. Tomorrow, he had junket interviews, similar to the ones he did when I first met him at The Dorchester Hotel. He would be doing those for the bulk of the day and the premiere would be in the evening, followed by a party. Madeleine went on to say that the following day, Jet would have a few days off so he and I could explore Sydney together. All of this sounded wonderful. I was grinning with excitement as the car sped across the world-famous Sydney Harbour Bridge from where Madeleine pointed out the Opera House.

"The hotel looks straight onto it, although I'm afraid your room doesn't have a view of the Opera House as it's the last available one on our floor."

"Don't worry about that. I'm just glad to be here, you've done so much for me already." Madeleine winked at me, as if to say don't worry about it.

"Thank you for making him smile," she said to me unexpectedly.

"He's always smiling, that's his thing," I replied, trying to make small of the compliment.

"Not in private. He's been pretty shaken up lately what with… everything," she revealed, obviously taking care to avoid the word 'divorce' and ensuring that she remained professional.

We pulled up outside an impressive looking hotel that stretched along the waterside directly across from the Sydney Opera House. The hotel wasn't a tall structure, only four stories high but it was impressive all the same, despite being dwarfed by the majestic Harbour Bridge that ran behind it. The lettering of the sign saying "Park Hyatt Sydney" was uplit in lights that seamlessly faded from one colour of the spectrum to another. Inside, the lobby, with its sleek modern interior design, oozed class from every angle. Madeleine escorted me over to an executive check-in desk where, after producing my passport and signing a couple of forms, I was handed a key card by the helpful reception manager. With little more than a flick of his finger, a member of the staff in a smart uniform appeared next to us and took my luggage as we followed him to the lift. I looked at his name badge which read Carl. I made a mental note of his name as I always try to remember someone's name, no matter how brief our meeting. Upstairs on the second floor , Carl showed me into my room and placed my luggage on the dedicated bench, so it was ready for me to open and unpack. I went to give him a tip as I pulled a twenty-dollar note out of my wallet, unsure what was an acceptable amount to tip. I'd never stayed anywhere where my cases had been taken to my room for me, yet another aspect of my new life that felt so alien. He graciously thanked me and left Madeleine and I alone.

"There's a mini bar over there," she said, pointing to a large well-stocked fridge in the corner of the room's entrance lobby. "There's also an ice box. Don't worry about the bill as Jet will pick that up for you. If you need anything from room service, just go for it." She was so kind and I gathered that she sensed just how much of a fish out of water I felt at this moment. "Jet's finishing up some interview just now," Madeleine said, looking at her watch. "Do you want to come and say 'hi' before he starts the next batch of radio interviews?"

"Yeah, that would be great, just give me a minute." I took the toiletries bag out of my suitcase and nipped into the bathroom to freshen up and check my make-up before Madeleine took me through to Jet's suite.

"We have booked the entire floor for this week, so you don't need to worry about being accosted going between rooms. The elevator is programmed so it will only stop at this floor if someone has access through their room key."

"That's clever, I wouldn't have thought of that."

"We have to be careful. You're always going to get someone who wants to get onto the floor that shouldn't be here." A moment later Madeleine opened the door to Jet's suite and immediately I could hear his voice.

"... yeah it's great to talk to you. Thank you for having me on your show," Jet said as he turned the corner to face me, his face immediately lighting up as he ended the call on his phone.

"Lizzie, you made it." Immediately he embraced

me in a hug and planted a single kiss on my cheek. "It's great to see you too," I said, feeling less nervous than I thought I might. This was, after all only the fourth time that I'd met him and the first time since he kissed me goodbye after our dinner at his hotel in London last Thursday. He'd been to New York since then and here we were, reunited on the other side of the globe. There was so much that I wanted to say to him right there but as Madeleine reached across between us holding another mobile phone, I knew that it would have to wait. Jet smiled and mouthed the words "see you later" before launching into another radio interview. I told Madeleine that I'd head back to my room to unpack and take a shower before leaving her and Jet to finish the day's business.

In my room, I saw that Madeleine had left a printout of Jet's itinerary for the next two days with a note to say, "Just so you know what's going on and help you navigate your way over the next two days," which I thought was really kind of her. I unpacked the clothes that I had hurriedly thrown into my suitcase on Saturday night after the Boat Race Party and decided on a shower rather than a bath, a decision made by nothing more than a fear of falling asleep, although I shouldn't be that tired having slept on the flight. I had a lengthy spell under the shower and made full use of the array of expensive toiletries that had been left in the bathroom for me. As I laid out on the bed, wrapped in one of the expensive white towelling robes provided by the hotel, I could evade sleep no longer and drifted off, hopefully not to a faraway place as I was quite content with where I was right now.

An hour later I woke up to the sound of my mobile pinging. I saw that it was 7pm local time here and opened up the text message. It was from Jet saying *"Interviews finished for today, got couple of calls to make and get changed - I'll call round in an hour and we will head out for dinner if that's ok. Madeleine has made reservations. J xx"*

I slipped on a pair of linen trousers and a top, applied the bare minimum of make-up and taking a small cardigan with me, I walked out onto the street in the balmy Sydney air. My memory kicking in, I immediately got my bearings so I walked across the road in the direction of Circular Quay. As the white edifice in the distance drew closer with every step, I braced myself for my private reunion with my beloved Sydney Opera House. It was just as I remembered it and as long as I didn't look behind me, where dozens of shiny new skyscrapers had sprung up since my last visit, the Opera House looked the same. Just the same, just as I remembered it. In the years that had passed since I was last here, so much had changed in the world. So much had changed in me but as I stared out at the lights bouncing off the white tiled roof, I smiled as I recognised some of the girl that was here back then – she was still here. "Lizzie Button, if you had told yourself all those years ago that you would be here just now and how you came to be here, well, you'd never have believed it."

Aware of the time and that I'd be heading out for dinner with Jet shortly, I took one more look at the Opera House, this time taking a photo with my phone – I'd only just clicked it and the screen lit up with an incoming call. It was Madeleine, Jet's personal assistant.

"Lizzie, hi, are you in your room?"

"No, I'm just across at Circular Quay walking back from the Opera House to the hotel. Is everything ok?"

"Yeah, it's just that the press here have got wind of your arrival in Australia and it's been on the radio. They've guessed that you're probably in the same hotel as Jet," she said cautiously.

"Really? Oh shit," I replied, immediately wondering what the implications of this would be.

"It's fine, I wouldn't worry about it. It's not the way we hoped they would find out, but you can't keep a good thing secret, no matter where you go. I've checked with the desk manager downstairs and there's no paparazzi outside. Might be a good idea to get back here pronto though."

I picked up my pace as I walked the short distance back to the hotel and seeing the entrance clear of photographers, I thought I was home and dry.
"Hello stranger."
That voice froze the length of my spine. I turned around, knowing what was to come.
"Paolo, what the … What are you doing here? How did you know?"
"Good news travels fast," he replied grinning. His face was unmistakeable, despite him now being bald and thirteen years older, coupled with what I presumed to be a healthy drug habit. His features were gnarled and weathered but not like an explorer, just a man who had lived in his own world, anaesthetising himself through the years with one substance or another.
"It's good to see you Lizzie, we should go and get a drink or something," he suggested rather too presumptuously, motioning towards the hotel entrance with the tilt of his head.
"Paolo, I told you on the phone the other night. I want nothing from you or to do with you." I was unable to stop tears welling up and did my best to hold them off. I mustn't show him that I'm upset.
"Lizzie don't be like that," he said laughing off my reaction. "We've a lot to catch up on. I was hoping that you could see your way to helping me out."
There it was. Right there at that moment, it

hadn't taken him long at all to get to the crux of his visit. He wanted money.

"Paolo, I don't know why you think I'm minted now."

"Of course you are. You have a millionaire film star boyfriend and you're rolling in it," he sneered. Nothing that I would say would bring him back to reality. I walked away but at that moment he grabbed my arm forcefully. "Now listen here you little bitch, I want a hundred thousand dollars. I need to get out of this place and move to Cambodia. That would just be pocket change to your boyfriend. You owe me Lizzie," he said, snarling at me. His grip on my arm tightened and as I struggled to break free, two guys in suits appeared out of nowhere and knocked him to the ground, almost taking me down with them. I recognised them as Jet's security team so they must have seen me as they came out of the hotel to check that the car was ready.

"We'll just get the hotel to call the police Miss Button," one of the guards said as his colleague effortlessly pinned Paolo to the ground. Against my better judgement, I asked them to let him go. As much as I hated Paolo, he was doing a good enough job of continuing to screw up his life without me pressing charges against him. I didn't see him as a danger, merely an annoyance. At that point Jet himself appeared at the entrance to the hotel and ran across towards me. Not wanting any further confrontation, I looked back to check where Paolo was, but he was now across the other side of the road, his jacket still twisted around his torso.

"You don't know what you're taking on with that one mate!" he shouted across at Jet who, apart from giving Paolo a look, did not dignify the comments with a response.

"Are you ok?" Jet said, taking my hand and checking my wrist for marks.

"I'm fine, I just need five minutes in my room to sort myself out then I'm all yours," I said, doing my utmost to conceal the fact that I was shaken to the core by the incident.

Hours later, after the most wonderful dinner, Jet walked me to my room and held me as I opened the door.

"I'll come in to say goodnight and then I'll leave you to rest. I'll be doing publicity all day tomorrow but you're coming to the premiere with me, yeah?"

"I wouldn't miss it for the world, but it's going to take a lot to beat the last one," I said, memories of him whisking me off my feet and onto the red carpet. With that, Jet leaned forward and kissed me, wrapping his arms around my body. His embrace felt like the most natural thing in the world but before I could get carried away in the moment, he pulled back, smiled and gave me one more kiss before returning to his room. There was no hurry, and some things are too good to be rushed.

CHAPTER 18

A Night To Remember

As much as I thought that I would sleep in until late, I was awake by half past seven the next morning. My phone lit up with a notification telling me that I had a text message. Opening it up, my heart sank on seeing that it was from Paolo. After that stunt he pulled last night outside the hotel, I wanted rid of him as swiftly as possible.

"Please Lizzie, you need to help me out. Talk to Jet and he will give you money for me."

He wasn't the least concerned as to how I was, or how I was feeling. That's Paolo for you, selfish to the core. Determined to nip this in the bud, I texted a curt two-word reply that ought to send a clear message back to him. I then made sure that I blocked his number on my phone before he had a chance to respond. There was no way that I was going to let him spoil this once in a lifetime trip for me. He'd ruined enough of my past and the past was where I was determined to leave him.

I had the day to myself and here I was in Sydney, Australia, the place that I had longed to return to one day and create new positive memories. Having opted for the luxury of a room service breakfast, I was ready to go out and explore the city. I stepped out of my room and into the lobby where I saw Madeleine.

"Oh Lizzie, I'm glad I've caught you. I've arranged to have some dresses delivered later this morning. There's no hurry but you can pick which one you want when you get back. The hair stylist and make-up artist will be here about 5:00pm if you would like any help getting ready for the premiere," she said checking a sheet on her clipboard.

I didn't know what to say. I wasn't sure that I needed either but I didn't want to appear churlish and decline the kind arrangements on offer to me. "That's very kind of you Madeleine. I really appreciate you looking after me," I said gratefully.

"You're welcome. I'll phone Jet's driver and get them to bring the car around for you just now if you're heading out," she replied, already scrolling on her phone for the driver's number.

"Actually Madeleine, would you mind if I just took a bus? I know where I'm going, and I think it would be more discreet."

"Only if you're sure," Madeleine replied cautiously.

"I'll be fine. Remember I used to live here."

"Of course. Call me if you need anything. Anything at all."

Out in the autumn sunshine, I walked back across to the Opera House, wanting to see it yet again but this time in the daylight. I still had to pinch myself that I was here. Rather than immediately rushing around, I took a leisurely walk along the perimeter with the harbour and the vast span of the Sydney Harbour Bridge on my left and the iconic grandeur of the Opera House on my right. Sitting myself down on a bench wearing a sunhat and shades to protect my identity as much as my skin from the sun, I cast my mind back to the last time that I was here.

It was twelve-and-a-half years ago when I'd flown out to Australia on my own with my backpack, a twelve-month working visa and a belly full of adventure and ambition. I didn't know back then what I was going to do, except I remember being determined not to work in an office. Within three days of my arrival at Sydney Airport as a naïve nineteen-year-old, I'd got myself a job working three shifts a week in an Irish bar in the Rocks area near the Harbour Bridge. A week later I'd added to this by getting four weekly shifts in a vegan café and juice bar in Bondi Junction. I chuckled to myself at the memory of my having lied at the interview at the café when I told them that I was a vegan. That then sparked the memory of how I was given a verbal warning in my first week after I turned up to work with a rough hangover one morning and they found me out the back tucking into a bacon sandwich. Even to this day, a bacon sarnie and a can of Red Bull are still my cure after a heavy night, although hangovers stick around much longer now that I'm past thirty.

I'd only been living in Sydney about three weeks when I first met Paolo. He worked behind the bar with me at the Irish bar, but he told everyone that he met that he was going to be a sports journalist. With his wispy blonde hair and cheeky smile, I soon fell for his charms and it wasn't long before I fell in love with him. After only three months together, we bought a battered old VW campervan and set off on our travels down to Melbourne and Adelaide and then on up into the outback via Coober Pedy and on to the majestic natural wonders of Ulhuru and King's Canyon. We'd spent time up near Townsville on the Great Barrier Reef and had many days out snorkling. Unfortunately, we had spent a lot of money on nights out while we were travelling, so rather than spending the next two months leisurely meandering down through southern Queensland

and the Gold Coast, we headed directly to Sydney and back to work. On our return to the city, Paolo and I moved in together. It was nothing grand, a small room in a basement flat in Bondi sharing with another British couple and their Dutch friend. Coming back to work in Sydney after the holiday of a lifetime was a heavy bump back down to earth and I remember that's when things started to go wrong for Paolo and I.

Looking out across the sparkling water of the harbour just now, I slowly brought myself back into the present as if I'd been hypnotized by the memories of what went before. Right now, I was here in this beautiful special place, at the most incredible time of my life so I wasn't about to let memories of past heartaches cloud my experience of the present.

I had planned to get a regular bus over to Bondi Beach but as I walked around from the other side of the Opera House, one of those hop-on/hop-off tourist buses pulled up ahead of me so after enquiring if it went in the direction of Bondi, I jumped aboard. I hadn't been on the bus five minutes when I received a text message from Maggie back in London telling me that they had got cover for me back home for the next week and that I wouldn't be required for any filming here in Sydney. It came as a relief to know that my time here was my own. Travelling around the corner of Hyde Park, we continued on up through Oxford Street, past some of the gay pubs that I used to frequent with my friend Jeff where we spent many a Sunday evening watching drag shows in the Oxford Hotel in Darlinghurst. I found the familiarity of London street names being replicated here on the other side of the world somewhat comforting. Onwards through the Paddington area, again the scene of many a Sunday afternoon drinking session, we eventually approached Bondi Junction. By now, I was in need of coffee so I disembarked the bus and continued on foot. I walked past several enticing coffee shops but hurried on in search of the vegan café where I had worked all those years ago. I couldn't help but laugh when I stumbled across it only to discover that it was now an independent burger restaurant. After a coffee and a delicious Portugese custard pastry at a neighbouring cafe, I continued on up towards the Waverley Cricket Ground, it's northern perimeter running alongside Bondi Road. As I reached the corner I crossed over and turned into Park Parade, my stomach tensing up as I reached the house in question. The house that contained the basement flat where I'd lived with Paolo thirteen years ago didn't look any different and given the circumstances under which I left this place, I couldn't bear the thought of going back mentally to that moment in my past, especially right now.

I didn't hang about and turned on my heels straight back onto Bondi Road and down towards the beach.

Bondi Beach, obviously iconic the world over, isn't the most picturesque beach in the world. Don't get me wrong, it's beautiful but I've seen far prettier beaches in Scotland, Mallorca and elsewhere in Australia for that matter. Despite that, there is still only one Bondi Beach and as I removed my sandals and let the warm sand push up between my toes, I closed my eyes and listening to the crashing of the ocean waves, I took a moment to appreciate my surroundings. My life had changed in a multitude of ways in the last few weeks and despite the pain of losing Dad, my discovery of his extramarital relationship and Paolo coming out of the woodwork after years of silence, I was in a good place. The universe seemed to be looking after me right now and I had every right to take a moment and enjoy all the positive things in my life.

After half an hour on the beach, I felt exhilarated and exhausted in the same breath and the thought of trekking all the way back to the hotel was too much, so decided I could afford to be extravagant and get a taxi back. I knew that if I called Madeleine, she would send Jet's driver across to collect me, but getting a cab for me was still keeping my feet firmly on the ground. I was determined that much.

Forty minutes later as the taxi pulled up outside the hotel, I spied two photographers waiting and trying not to fear the worst, I momentarily presumed that they were there to get a shot of Jet. I paid the driver and walked straight through the entrance without moving my glance from the focused point straight in front of me. I could hear the clicking of the cameras and them shouting my name, but I was fast becoming rather adept at ignoring paparazzi. Unphased, I went straight up to my room, catching Madeleine in the hall on the way. I briefly told her about my trip down memory lane, the photographers outside and that I was going to try and have a nap for an hour or two before getting ready for this evening's premiere. She informed me that the stylists had delivered a selection of dresses, shoes and accessories for me to choose from for tonight. I thanked her and arranged for the stylist and make-up artist to come to my room in two hours, leaving me enough time to get my head down.

In the room I could see the rail over in the corner with the selection of gowns along with a pile of boxes and expensive looking shopping bags on the floor. Not wanting to allow myself to become distracted, I ignored them and went straight to bed, making sure to set myself an alarm on my phone.

I must have slept for almost the full two hours, but I didn't feel particularly rested for it. I'd had the most vivid dream about moving out of the flat in Bondi all those years ago, the discovery that Paolo had been shagging around behind my back and given the circumstances that had led me being rushed into hospital at that time, my head was a mess. My face felt wet as I woke up and I could only assume that I had been crying at some point in my sleep. A lengthy spell in the shower and blasting Kylie's new album as I dried myself helped to lighten my mood and by the time that I'd opened the curtains and tidied up my room, Madeleine and her small army of girls were knocking at the door, all ready to pamper me for my big night with Jet.

I had secretly hoped that I would have had time to get a spray tan but having written off that idea, I chose a red floor-length dress designed by an up-and-coming Sydney designer that sparkled beautifully when the light caught it. I wondered what my mother would make of me wearing this stunning red gown and so I made a mental note to ask Madeleine to take a photo of Jet and myself before we went down to the car. I chose to wear my hair tied up in a simple style given that it was still warm outside, and I didn't want the heat to frizz it out. Jet came through wearing a traditional dinner suit with black bow tie and looking incredibly handsome, his face lighting up when he saw me in my dress.

"You look sensational Lizzie," he said quietly, smiling but not taking his eyes off me for a second. We posed for photos that Madelcine kindly took with my phone.

"Wait until my mother sees this." Scrolling through my phone, was looking at the images she had just taken.

"Beautiful," said Jet. "Madeleine, could you give us a minute?"

"No problem, the car needs to leave in seven minutes," said Madeleine, walking out into the hall closing the door behind her.

Jet turned to me, smiling.

"You look happy with yourself," I said to him.

"Of course I am, have you seen my date tonight?" We both laughed. "Are you ok?" I nodded. "I'm sorry I've not been around much since you arrived," Jet said apologetically.

"Don't apologise. I've had a lovely day wandering down to the beach. I'm just so pleased to be here."

"I have something for you." Jet took a slim black velvet box out of his jacket pocket and handed it to me. I opened the box and there was the most beautiful silver pendant. Hanging from the chain was a bird, encrusted in what looked like tiny sapphires.

"Jet, it's beautiful. I don't know what to say."

"It's a kookaburra."

"I love it. Thank you," I said. He took the case from me and removing the pendant, he walked around behind me and clipped it gently around my neck. As I turned to face him, he leaned in and kissed me on the cheek.

"Let's go and have a blast, shall we?" he said, smiling as he opened the door for me.

By the time that we stepped outside the hotel, there were at least six or seven paparazzi photographers waiting for us. Jet didn't hang about and guided me straight into the back of the waiting car. "Let them wait until we get to the theatre."

It didn't take long for the car to travel through the streets of Sydney from the hotel to the famous Hayden Orpheus Picture Palace where, according to Madeleine, many of the world's most famous films had held their Australian premieres. There was a huge crowd out there and way above the throng in the distance was a huge picture of Jet in his sparkly suit and the words "Tango Master" spanning the breadth of the building. Other stars had already arrived ahead of us including Jet's co-stars from the film, although his lead co-star Marina Delaney couldn't come to Australia as she was now in her third trimester of pregnancy and couldn't fly. I was conscious that I had received so much press attention over the last week and that the media were talking about my possible relationship with Jet rather than Jet and Marina's performances in the film. I'd said this to Jet last night over dinner and he assured me that despite my concerns being more than admirable, there was nothing that we could do to counter it and that was just the way that the business worked. At the end of the day, it was all good publicity for the film. I reminded myself of the time when Elizabeth Hurley stole the show at the London premiere of Four Weddings and a Funeral. I was just a kid at the time, but I remembered the images of her wearing the safety-pin dress that outshone all the stars who were actually in the film.

I'd already had a discussion with Jet and Madeleine before we left the hotel that I didn't want to speak to any press on the red carpet. I was more than happy to go along and be Jet's date for the event, but the cast and crew were there to promote the movie, the result of all their hard work. All the while, the car edged closer to the end of the red carpet and before I knew it, it was time for us to step out and make our appearance.

"You go first," I said to Jet, who was holding my hand in reassurance. As he stepped out of the limo on my right the crowd erupted in cheers. Through the glass panel in the sunroof above me I could see his arm aloft waving to the throngs of the crowds who had waited patiently for his arrival. I waited as he walked around to my side of the car and when Madeleine had opened the door for me, Jet leaned in and reached out for my hand. He smiled at me.

"They're going to love you, Lizzie. Let your star shine." With a wink of his eye, he took my hand, and I did my best to step out of the limo as gracefully as I could in the floor-length gown. Nothing could have prepared me for the noise. The cheers from the crowd were deafening and overwhelming to say the least.

Madeleine, who herself was wearing a beautiful black dress, had already briefed me that she would walk behind Jet and myself along the red carpet and when Jet had to speak to any press or go to the crowd to sign autographs or take selfies, she would wait with me on the carpet so that I wasn't stood on my own or ambushed by any press. I did end up answering a couple of questions about how I liked Australia or where I had got my dress. I made sure that this wonderful dress designer received the credit that she so richly deserved. This had to be the most surreal experience of my life. Seven days ago, nobody knew who I was and here, a week later, I was being photographed as a celebrity on the other side of the world. I'd worked in television long enough to be mindful that as quickly as a person can become famous, their star can fade at a similar speed. As Jet moved amongst the crowds of fans piled in behind the metal barriers, he kept looking back over at me to check that I was ok. He was conscious that this was not my natural setting and whereas he already had ten years of a blockbuster film career under his belt, I was a bit like a rabbit in the headlights, although I did my best not to appear so. We must have spent about half an hour or more on the red carpet before we finally left the crowds and the clicking cameras behind and entered the theatre. As we met the theatre manager, the mayor of Sydney and other VIPs, Jet whispered into my ear "You got the biggest cheer of the night out there."

"No, they were cheering for you Jet," I said, a little embarrassed.

"You're a sensation. They love you." I noticed that he hadn't stopped smiling since he came into my room at the hotel earlier.

The film was a triumph and I enjoyed it far more the second time around, sitting next to Jet. After we left the theatre, we went to the Sydney Centre Point tower for the party. The lifts took us up eighty-three floors above street level to the bar that gave us a 365-degree panoramic view of the Sydney skyline. The bar was tastefully decorated with a plush red carpet and retro-style furniture. A pianist was playing in the corner and waiting staff moved effortlessly amongst the crowd with trays of canapes and drinks. Jet was busy talking to the Australian head of the studio and for a moment, I found myself looking for Madeleine who I saw was having a very serious-looking conversation. The grave appearance of Madeleine's face didn't offer me any reassurance as she looked across at me. She finished her conversation before she approached me.

"Have you seen Jet?" she asked, somewhat distractedly.

"He's over talking to someone from the studio, I think. Is everything ok?"

"Yes, I was just speaking to the Australian PR manager for the film. It's all fine." Over the years I've become rather adept at reading people and despite Madeleine's assurances that all was fine, I suspected that the truth was quite different. As I turned around, Jet was at my side. "Can I finally tempt you to a glass of champagne?"

I obligingly took the glass from him and sipped it. I'd made a conscious decision to stay off the booze for the evening as I wanted absolute clarity of mind. This was going to be a night like no other I would ever experience, and I wanted to remember every single second of it.

After an hour of mingling with some of Australia's biggest names in entertainment, Jet made a beautiful impromptu speech where he publicly thanked me for accompanying him tonight and "making him look good". I blushed and thanked him graciously. He put his arm around me and said "Would you like to get out of here? We can have a drink on my balcony overlooking the harbour and your beloved Opera House."

That sounded like the perfect ending to the most idyllic of evenings. Jet motioned to Madeleine that we were ready to leave and minutes later we had descended back to ground level to our waiting limo.

Back at the hotel, Jet poured us both a glass of champagne in his suite as we watched the lights glimmer across Sydney Harbour. I felt so comfortable with him and as he held me in his arms, he kissed me and I could do nothing but respond. That night we made love for the first time and as we lay there in our darkened room, the lights of the harbour reflected through the windows and danced across our entwined bodies. At that moment both of us were in a state of absolute bliss, both unaware that tomorrow lay waiting ahead of us with a very different turn of events. Thankfully there were several hours to go before tomorrow came.

CHAPTER 19

Secrets & Lies

I'd slept on and off for the last five hours although we did wake to make love once more before early morning arrived and the sunrise could be seen across Sydney Harbour. I could hear a buzzing noise on my side of the bed and the light emanating from my phone told me that someone was trying to call me. I leaned across and saw that Maggie's name was flashing up. She would know the time difference and that it was only five in the morning here, so for her to call it must have been urgent.

"Maggie, hi. Is everything ok?" I asked, dreading bad news that would spoil my state of bliss.

"Lizzie, I'm sorry to call you. I'm on the late shift here and the newsfeed has a story that's come through from one of the Aussie tabloids about you. Well, they're all about you at the premiere, but this one particular paper has run a very different story." She sounded more than a little troubled. I was perplexed as to what could they have said about me that was so negative. I hadn't led a particularly exciting life in my thirty-three years on the planet and I certainly had no skeletons in the cupboard. I laughed it off.

"Oh Maggie, did they not like my dress or my hair or something?"

"No Lizzie, I'm afraid it's rather more serious than that," Maggie replied gravely.

My immediate reaction was that the mystery woman at Dad's funeral had come forward. Before I could share this thought with Maggie, she continued. "It's your ex-boyfriend in Australia. Paolo?" She paused for a moment to see if the name would bring a note of recognition from me. My heart sank.

"What's he said?" I asked her, not really wanting to hear the answer.

"He's sold his story. He's basically said that you and he lived together in Sydney thirteen years ago and that…"

"Maggie, what did he say?" I asked anxiously, aware that Jet was now awake and propping himself up in bed next to me.

"He's said that you aborted his baby behind his back and then you left him." I felt sick.

"Maggie, I need to go," I said, shaking whilst trying to press the red button to end the call.

"Lizzie what's happened?" Jet asked. I didn't

respond other than to jump out of bed and run into the bathroom where I dropped to my knees and proceeded to vomit into the toilet. I tried getting up but feared that I would pass out. How could he? How could he do this to me? How could he say that I did that to him, to our baby? He knew the truth as much as I did. That wasn't something that any decent human could twist over the years, twist to become something so radically different and sinister. After more wretching and tears, I was pulled round into the sitting position next to the bath tub by Jet who had his arms around me, telling me that everything was going to be ok. How could Jet say that it was going to be fine? He didn't know what was wrong or what had happened.

"Jet, it's the papers. One of them has run a story from my ex. It's not true Jet, I would never have done that, not behind his back," I sobbed. I was immersed in tears as I remained on the floor. Jet stood up and started to run me a bath before heading straight into the bedroom. A minute later I heard him on the phone, probably to Madeleine. He appeared back at the bathroom door with a small bottle of water.

"Have a drink. Whatever this is Lizzie, we can fix it," he said, trying his best to reassure me.

I felt better once I'd had a bath and was sitting on the bed drying my feet. "Do you want to talk about it?"

"Not really, but you deserve to know what's happened and more importantly, the truth." I pulled the bathrobe tight around me as I sat back into Jet's bed, propped up comfortably by several pillows. I told him about my trip here thirteen years ago, how I had met Paolo working in the bar and how we both fell head over in heels in love. By the time that we'd returned from our campervan trip I already had had a sneaky suspicion that I might be pregnant given that my period was late, and back then, I was never late. A trip to the doctor confirmed that I was indeed six weeks pregnant. It certainly wasn't planned and as I'd only just had my twentieth birthday, it wasn't how I had envisaged starting this new decade in my life. We had decided to wait until I was twelve weeks gone before we told anyone, especially my family. That was a call I hadn't been looking forward to making. I'd carried on working in the vegan café although I wasn't able to pick my shifts back up in the Irish bar. I came home from work one afternoon earlier than planned and heard voices in our bedroom. To see Paolo in our bed fucking the landlady was not what I had expected to come home to. I grabbed my bag and throwing the most basic of clothing items into it, I made to leave. Paolo had put some shorts on by now, and had done his best to stop me from leaving. Trying my hardest to open the door to the flat, with Paolo holding it shut with his foot, I gave the door one last yank and twisted around in pain as I crumpled to the floor. I must have blacked out as I didn't recall the paramedics arriving. The next thing that I knew was waking up in a hospital bed feeling incredibly groggy.

The doctor informed me that I'd lost the baby. I'd had what they called, an ectopic pregnancy. At that point in my life, I'd never heard of an ectopic pregnancy. I'd have rather that fate had dealt me a kinder hand and been blissfully unaware for several more years. They referred to my baby as a fertilised egg when explaining it to me. I learned that the egg had implanted itself outside of the womb and in one of my fallopian tubes and that the surgeons had been left with no choice but to remove the foetus through emergency keyhole surgery. I sobbed at the memory of the brief time that I was a mother. It had been all too brief.

Jet held on to me, his hand rubbing my arm by way of comfort. After a couple of minutes, he slowly got up from the bed, reluctant to let go of me.

"I'll be back in five minutes," he said, putting his robe on. It was nearer ten minutes by the time that he had returned.

"I've spoken with Miranda and the press manager. We can take out an injunction on this guy from spreading his lying filth any further. It's up to you."

"I need to make a couple of calls." I was desperately trying to take control of the situation but not sure how to accomplish it. First, I called Maggie back and spent fifteen minutes updating her along with a precis version of the truth about my ectopic pregnancy and how Paolo had demanded a hundred thousand dollars from me on the evening of my arrival in Australia.

"Lizzie, you need to get your side of the story across but first, I'd suggest that you call your agent Melanie straight away. She needs to be fully updated so that she and her team are in a position to handle matters over the next few days," Maggie said helpfully.

"I'll do that right now. Thanks Maggie, you're a star."

"Give me a shout if there's anything that I can do to help at all."

Ten minutes later, I came off the phone having spoken to Melanie who had been very quick to reassure me that she and her team would be there to support me. Jet phoned through to Madeleine's room, asking her to bring the newspapers through in fifteen minutes once we had both had time to dress. He then phoned down to reception and ordered some breakfast for us both on room service. I was amazed at how calm he was and despite me falling to pieces in front of him, he kept his cool and dealt with it in a calm, collected manner.

Madeleine had thoughtfully separated out the offending newspaper when she brought them all through. I had thought that photos of myself and Jet might have featured in one or two of the editions, but I wasn't prepared for us both to be splashed across the front pages of nearly all the Australian dailies. My dress had clearly impressed the newspaper editors and had the desired effect of gaining invaluable publicity for the Tango Master movie, but it wasn't the dress or the premiere that were on my mind at that moment.

I felt a little better once I'd had some coffee and something to eat. Madeleine came back in and took Jet aside for a minute. They had a somewhat intense conversation, and I was relieved when they both came over to me, hopefully with news of a positive development.

"Madeleine has been speaking with our press officer and we have a plan that could help you," Jet announced.

"What sort of plan?"

"You've heard of Claudia Faye?"

"What? *the* Claudia Faye?" I replied, not quite believing my ears. Claudia Faye was an Australian actress who went on to become one of the biggest talk show hosts in America and indeed the world. In addition to her billion-dollar media empire she had funded a large number of cancer wellness centres across Australia and in the USA.

"Claudia's in Sydney right now and she's a good friend of mine. She called up and has offered to do an interview with you here in Sydney, so that you can tell your side of the story. They would record it later this afternoon and it will go out on-air tomorrow night," Jet said looking to Madeleine who nodded that he had got the details of the offer correct.

Madeleine spoke up.

"Claudia has also kindly offered the two of you the use of her exclusive cabin in the Blue Mountains until things settle down. It's very private so you will both be away from the prying eyes of the media," said Madeleine, much to my astonishment. I couldn't take this in. Claudia Faye was friends with royalty and presidents. She had known Michael Jackson and Whitney Houston for God's sake.

"We will need to go through the story with her this afternoon and meet with lawyers," said Jet. The thought of involving lawyers instantly filled me with fear which must have been obvious because Jet came straight over the took my hand. "It's ok Lizzie, don't worry. Lawyers are standard practice in any situation like this. I still have a lawyer present if I think an interviewer is going to ask me questions about my divorce."

For the next two hours, I never seemed to be off the phone to the UK. If it wasn't Melanie, then it was Maggie in the office who I had designated as my sole point of contact on the production team as Serena and Jeremy, the executive producers, were the last people that I wanted to talk to right now. After a number of discussions were held on all sides to clarify details, I'd agreed to do an interview with Claudia Faye and to put my side of the story across. I was angry because this was something that I had managed to keep private for the past thirteen years, yet now I was having to tell the whole world in one moment. I asked for twenty minutes of privacy while I went back through to my room to telephone my mother, as I hadn't yet spoken to anyone in my family and she had texted me earlier frantically wanting to know what was going on. Once I had calmed her down and divulged the truth to her that I hadn't had a termination behind Paolo's back, and that the end of the pregnancy was more a decision that mother nature had made on my behalf, she calmed down. I asked her to call Michael and update him as to the situation. Jayne, my best friend back home called about five minutes later so clearly news of the headlines had reached Branthwaite and beyond. Despite my apologies for never having told her about my ectopic pregnancy over the last thirteen years,

Jayne kindly reassured me that I had nothing to be sorry for and reminded me that she was there on the other end of the phone. She even went so far to give me the name and number of her husband Brian's cousin who lived in Bondi and would happily offer me refuge from the press should I need it. I thanked her and explained that Jet and his team were handling the situation admirably. I had wanted to call my brother in person but right now, time was very much of the essence. The stylist who brought me the gorgeous gowns to choose from for yesterday's premiere had arrived with a fresh selection of more demure outfits for me to choose from for the interview. I chose a simple cotton dress with a high neckline, a conservative choice but given the subject and purpose of this afternoon's interview, I felt it best not to invite any more presumptions as to my moral character. It very much annoyed me that society thinks that way, but right now I had to focus on protecting myself.

Claudia had kindly offered to conduct the entire interview from her beautiful garden overlooking Sydney Harbour and over an hour later we pulled up outside the substantial architect-designed house that topped a small mound reached by wide winding steps. I'd never been in a house quite like it, but I was sure that Jet had seen many of its kind along the beaches of Malibu and Santa Monica over the years. If he had, he was a true gentleman and paid the appropriate compliments to the owner. Claudia Faye, a slim woman in her early sixties, but looking a good fifteen years younger, greeted us inside after her assistant guided Jet, Madeleine and myself over to the large open plan living area. Our view looked out across the azure blue of Sydney Harbour and was filtered only by a wall of glass. Once we had spent an hour going through the points of the story and assessing Paolo's motivation for having sold his lies to a newspaper, we moved through onto the patio that opened from the dining room and was where the interview was to be filmed. Before the make-up artist made a start on me, Claudia took me by the hand and together we descended the steps leading onto the lawn and down to the waterside. Claudia had already had her hair and make-up done and her bright red curls fell onto her shoulder as if they belonged there. She did a magnificent job of reassuring me about the interview, but also encouraged me not to try and stifle any emotions. Under the terms of the legal agreement between us, I had been given an approval clause about the interview so if there was anything that I didn't like in the finished piece, it would need to be cut until I was happy with it. Having worked in television for several years, I was very much aware that this was not a privilege afforded to many interviewees.

Two hours later we were done and I felt as if an enormous weight had been lifted from me, despite my remaining more than a little anxious about the public reception when it goes out on the television. I felt that the interview went well and Claudia, the consummate professional, had made an excellent job of making me feel at ease but only enough that it didn't mask any of my vulnerability. Back at the hotel, I just wanted to sleep. Jet suggested that I go to my own bed for no other reason than the fact that I would get more rest in my room. We arranged to have dinner in his suite later, rather than venturing out into Sydney. We had graciously accepted Claudia's kind offer of the use of her place in the Blue Mountains and it was agreed that we would travel up there and out of the city in the morning after breakfast. I would like to say that getting my side of the story off my chest enabled me to sleep peacefully that night, but it couldn't have been further from the truth. I drifted in and out of dreams where I was holding my lost baby, seeing Paolo with that woman and his reaction to the news that the baby had died. I remember when he had been told at my hospital bedside all those years ago. It was as if a prison sentence had been lifted from him and rather than feeling any grief at the loss of our child or even remorse at his actions with our landlady, he was visibly relieved.

I think that the indifference had been in reaction to my own condition and the trauma I had been through. To wake in the middle of the night in a strange empty bed didn't help. It got to about three in the morning and there was a knocking on my door.

"Lizzie, are you ok?" Jet asked, his voice barely audible above a whispered tone. I let him in and once I was curled up in bed with his arms around me, I fell into the deepest sleep. I'd always prided myself that I didn't need a man to make me feel secure but tonight, I needed a friend not a lover and thankfully Jet was there to oblige.

As arranged with Jet's PR team and Claudia Faye, snippets from the interview were handed to a selection of the Australian and International papers and TV channels to act as a preview for tonight's exclusive interview. By nine o'clock, we had finished breakfast and Claudia's producer had arrived with a hard drive to play us the unpolished rough-cut of the interview which they had been working through the night to trim down into a half-hour programme. To see myself on the screen was surreal enough in itself, even after the high-profile events of the last week. With the setting sun shining on us in Claudia's garden, against the backdrop of Sydney harbour and my beloved Opera House, my story was told. I cried when it finished but more from a sense of relief than anything else. Jet, Madeleine, the producer and PR manager were all looking at me with kindness in their eyes. I felt so safe, a stark contrast to the time when I was alone in the hospital thirteen years ago. Now I didn't feel alone and there were people here who genuinely cared about me.

An hour later we were in the car and heading out of the city suburbs in the direction of the Blue Mountains. Streets of suburban houses eventually gave way to tree lined roads that climbed up out of the city and away from the coast. The cabin was actually most un-cabin like and more a sleek modern pied-a-terre with weathered wooden cladding finishes and walls of glass that allowed unimpeded views across the mountain range. Outside on the deck next to a large corner sofa and dining table was a modestly-sized infinity pool wrapped around on two sides by a clear glass veranda. There was a second smaller lodge about half a mile away further down the track which, also owned by Claudia, had been kindly provided for Madeleine and Kevin, Jet's Australian security manager and driver. Both properties formed part of Claudia's substantial private bushland estate. If anyone wanted to get up the road to our cabin, they would have to get past Kevin. Because of the suspected leak as to my arrival in Australia, I'd agreed with Jet that nobody back in the UK would know exactly where I was right now. I'd been in contact with Melanie my agent and Maggie at the office but told them I was going away for a few quiet days with Jet. It wasn't that I didn't trust them both with the truth, but I didn't want to put them or their teams in a position where my privacy was compromised. Within a matter of hours, Jet and I had made ourselves at home and were managing to put the tabloid nightmares out of our minds for now.

The next couple of days were spent walking on the estate, taking in the most spectacular views across the mountains. We cooked together, swam together and of course, we made love. It was perfect and Jet was wonderful. I was conscious that I might be falling for him but told myself that when the weekend came and he had to return to the States, that I too must go home. I accepted that but for now, I didn't want to worry about what was to come, but rather enjoy the magical time that I was having.

All the willpower in the world couldn't put the weekend off any longer and as Saturday morning came, Kevin and Madeleine drove up to the cabin and helped us load our luggage into the car. It didn't take too long to return to Sydney and because we had decided not to leave anything in the hotel a few days ago, we could go straight to the airport. I said my goodbyes to Jet in the car to allow ourselves a degree of privacy. Out on the concourse, I thanked Kevin and gave Madeleine the biggest hug by way of thanks for all that she had done for me.

I messaged Maggie and Melanie to let them know that I was about to board my flight home. I'd already texted James, my flatmate who thought I had forgotten about him, but he reassured me that he would let me take him for a very expensive dinner by way of apology. By the time that my plane arrived in Dubai to refuel, I checked my messages once more and saw a text from James to say that he would come to Heathrow to meet me while Maggie in the office would arrange a car to take us back to our Chiswick flat as a favour.

I was going home but having left Sydney behind for the second time, I felt happier knowing that there was no unfinished business here. Paolo was consigned to the past and I vowed that I would never allow him into my present or future ever again.

CHAPTER 20

Unexpected Visitor

As I walked through the doors of the Arrivals Hall at London Heathrow Airport, James was a sight for sore eyes, especially given the amount of paparazzi photographers and journalists that were there. I naively thought that some royalty or the likes of Beyonce must be coming through customs at the same time, but no, they weren't here for Harry, Meghan or Beyonce. They were here for Lizzie. I simply ran the gauntlet and as James hugged me and took my case, he gallantly escorted me towards the car that was waiting to take us home. I called Maggie and Melanie on the way back to Chiswick to let them know that I was back in the country and I had arranged with Melanie that I would meet with her at her office later that afternoon. I'd also confirmed with Maggie that I would appear on *UK Today* in the morning, not as showbiz reporter, but as myself and talk about everything, well, almost everything that had happened in Australia over the past week.

Once we were back in the safety of our flat above the betting shop, James made me a coffee and we cuddled up in my bed. He'd been following the events from here and despite his concerns for me when the story about my pregnancy broke, he said that he knew I was in safe hands. We gossiped for the best part of an hour, until I could fight off the tiredness no more and the moment that my head hit the pillow, I drifted off to sleep.

At lunchtime, James woke me with another cup of coffee and a sandwich and instructed me to eat up and once I'd had my lunch, I was to take advantage of the hot bubble bath that he had run for me. He'd offered to accompany me to Melanie's office in Covent Garden that afternoon, not that I needed a chaperone, but to take advantage of the opportunity to spend a little more housemate time together.

A couple of hours later, we arrived in Central London and got out of the car as near to Covent Garden as the queue of traffic would allow. James walked by my side linking my arm but rather than join me for the meeting, which I told him he was welcome to do, he informed me that he had a second date with a guy in Soho. Leaving me outside the agency's office building, he skipped off in the direction of Charing Cross Road.

Melanie and the team were so pleased to see me and as this was actually the first time that I had set foot in their offices since being signed up almost two weeks ago, it was lovely to meet the team properly. Despite the phone conversations that I had had with Melanie from Sydney, there was still plenty to tell her, and she listened intently while I fully updated her on what had happened. What I hadn't realised was that she had negotiated a six-figure sum with Claudia Faye's team and the Australian tv network for the exclusive interview last week. I was gobsmacked as to why anyone would pay that amount to hear my story.

"Lizzie, I don't think you've quite grasped that you and Jet, the red carpet, what happened in Sydney... it's the biggest showbiz story of the month, if not the year," Melanie said.

"I hadn't realised. It's different when you're in the middle of the tornado and all you can see is the blur of things and people whizzing around you," I replied.

"Lizzie, now is not the best time to talk about your future career, but this has put you on a very different trajectory and it's there for the taking if you want it. It will need to be managed carefully but you have a bright future ahead of you," Melanie told me and I thanked her for her kind words. "It's true Lizzie. The network that you're currently signed to has been talking about finding projects for you to present. There's a lot of daytime chat show type stuff, but there is one idea that I wanted to draw your attention to just now. It's a new women's lifestyle series covering the spectrum of female health matters including pregnancies that don't go full-term for whatever reason, in particular ectopic pregnancies. I know you might think it's too painful a subject matter but given the frightening statistics of this, it's happening to thousands of women out there in the UK every year. You don't have to say yes now, but promise me you will think about it."

"I will. I promise," I said, not sure that I could do such a project justice.

"The girls have some 'goodie bags' that have arrived for you from PR companies. Free perfume, shoes and God-knows-what. Get used to it, perks of the job," she told me.

Melanie kissed me on each cheek in true media style and I said goodbye to the team thanking them once again. Carrying my bags to the car, I called Maggie once I was en route to the studio.

"Hi Maggie, that's me in the car on my way to you. I'm leaving Covent Garden now so I shouldn't be long," I said, hoping that the traffic wouldn't hold us up.

"Lizzie, there's a few 'paps' hanging about with cameras outside the studio. I'm actually done for the day so I thought we could grab a bite to eat and catch up properly. Ask the driver to pull round to the steps to Waterloo station across from the Imax and I'll come round to you."

Forty-five minutes later, the driver dropped us off outside the little Thai café on Turnham Green Terrace, a short walk from my flat. I'd said to Maggie that I'd rather we just get a takeaway and take it back to the flat as we'd be able to talk properly there without anyone on a neighbouring table listening in. Once I had filled in all the gaps on my Australian adventure for Maggie, I was eager to find out what had been happening over here.

"Serena's been on top form while you have been away. When I say 'top form' I mean utterly grotesque," Maggie said, doing her best to hide a mischievous smile. "Her little boy Bertie had his fifth Birthday Party last Saturday. She had Stuey and half of the production team transforming the studio into Willy Wonka's Chocolate Factory until late on Friday, only to then drop the bombshell that she wanted everyone back in on Saturday to help with the party." The look on her face said that even she was taken aback by the demands of our somewhat unpredictable boss.

"You've got to be fucking kidding." I knew Serena's grasp on the real world was sketchy at the best of times, but with this stunt she seemed to have reached stratospheric heights of delusion. "I hope they told her to get stuffed."

"I'm afraid not. Lots of them have contracts coming up for renewal and didn't want to be binned off the programme so they complied, cancelled their weekend plans at the last minute and came into the studio.".

"That woman. Nobody ever tells her 'No'."

"It gets worse," added Maggie, as I braced myself for the next revelation. "She made Stuey and the other production runners dress up as Oompa Loompas, complete with orange faces and green wigs."

I laughed at this but not because it was funny, more so because the woman's behaviour was so ridiculous. "I have the feeling that we will still be talking about this party in twenty years' time Maggie," I said, trying to make light of it.

"Oh definitely, but for all the wrong reasons. The kids made a right mess and ran riot, the chocolate fountain tipped over and the small army of au pairs couldn't keep control of them."

"Where were their bloody parents?" I had guessed the answer before Maggie even had a chance to respond.

"They left after half an hour as Serena hosted a lunch for them all at her private members club in Soho. They left the au pairs to deal with the carnage and eventually take home two dozen kids, all of whom were high on organic artisan chocolate fountain and other crap. Apparently the studio team were in for most of the weekend, cleaning up the studio so that they could get the *UK Today* set back in place for this morning's show. The overtime bill alone has run into thousands of pounds."

"I'm not looking forward to seeing her tomorrow when I come in," I confessed.

"She won't be there. She's gone out to LA to meet with some people about a new reality show format."

"Not to choose a doorhandle?" I said, making her laugh. That was our private joke because between us, we often quoted Edina Monsoon, the character played by Jennifer Saunders in the show *Absolutely Fabulous*, who in many ways was just as ridiculous as our boss Serena.

It had been lovely to spend the evening with Maggie at the flat and I felt so relaxed and happy that we could talk privately and openly. Not being able to do so in a pub or restaurant was a downside of the fame that had been thrust upon me in recent weeks. We didn't have a late night as I was on *UK Today* in the morning, so Maggie took a cab home to Battersea and I took myself off to bed to dream of Oompa Loompas and chocolate fountains. Sorry, that should be organic artisan chocolate fountains.

I'd arrived in the studio at six the following morning just as *UK Today* was going on-air, so

I was able to slip straight into the quiet make-up room where Mandy, the make-up artist, and I caught up on my week in Sydney.

"Have I missed much here while I've been away?" I asked her, knowing full well that the make-up artists get to hear all the juicy gossip.

"Alex has been a nightmare this last week," she said, referring to one half of our presenting duo on the show.

"That's nothing new Mandy. Has he been particularly difficult?"

"Oh, much worse than usual. He's decided he wants to be controversial, but he's not clever enough to hit the right tone so he either comes across as a bit thick or painfully provocative."

"Christ, that's all we need on the show. A Pound Shop Piers Morgan," I joked. Mandy laughed.

"At least Piers is an intelligent interviewer unlike our Alex. Piers is very popular whereas Alex, he's neither intelligent or particularly popular. To be honest, I think that he's a bit paranoid."

"Why do you think that?"

Looking around to check that we wouldn't be overheard, she leaned in and whispered.

"Apparently last week there was a party in some private members club. Well, not so much of a party but Serena and Jeremy were there with other TV people and they were moaning about Alex and how the viewers were not taking to him.

They discussed the possibility of replacing him and the word is, it might not be with another male presenter. Someone must have overheard, and it got back to Alex." With that revelation, she winked at me.

"No wonder he's been so unbearable this last week."

"He's been particularly rude to Lydia and not always off-screen. It even made the papers while you were away. They're no longer speaking to each other when they're not on set. It's all very awkward and then this morning, Alex refused to come into make-up to get tidied up until Lydia had left and gone to her dressing room."

"I think that constitutes as a diva tantrum, don't you?" I said, smiling mischievously up from the make-up chair.

"There's talk of screen-testing Lydia with other presenters now."

"Any idea who?" I was now racking my brain as to who would make a suitable replacement for him.

"I've not heard anything. But I could make an educated guess. Right, that's you all camera-ready missus," she said, cheerily changing the subject with all the grace of a handbrake turn.

Stuey, our faithful production runner came pelting around the corner whilst shouting something into his radio talkback. On seeing me, he stopped dead in his tracks.

"Oh Lizzie, Hi. Listen they've just radioed down from the gallery to say they need you on set in ten minutes. Not sure why. I've left a coffee in your room."

Before I had a chance to respond in any way, he ran off again in the direction of the Green Room where we held the studio guests waiting to go on-air. I'd brought an outfit in with me and because I was being interviewed as myself rather than being there as a presenter, I thought it best to supply my own clothes this time. In my dressing room, the lights were on as was the TV which ran a live feed from the studio floor. On the screen, Alex was ranting about stuff again. I swear he was getting worse and if I had a pound for every time someone told me they had ceased watching *UK Today* because of him, I'd certainly be buying more expensive bottles of wine. This morning, his usual orange-glow had turned puce with rage while Lydia sat there looking decidedly embarrassed.

Alex was the least favourite of the on-screen talent amongst the production team, myself included. He had been a breakfast television presenter back in the late eighties before he was suddenly sacked from the station. The rumour-mill had been frothing for years with stories as to what had really happened, but nothing was ever made public. I had never bothered to ask anyone myself, for nothing more than the simple reason that I wasn't interested. As a result of the apparent fall-out, Alex had spent a few years in the television wilderness of regional news until even the local TV stations had had enough of his appalling, demanding and somewhat lecherous behaviour. Eventually consigned to the world of television shopping channels, Alex had almost managed to keep himself financially afloat despite two divorces and the thousands he paid out every year in child maintenance for his five children. I had heard one rumour going around in the industry about him. Apparently five years ago, at the memorial service for the much-loved presenter Tina Shaunessey at St Paul's church in Covent Garden, commonly known as 'The Actors' Church', Alex had gained access to the church prior to the guests arriving and placed his business cards along the pews, knowing that the building would soon be crammed with some of Britain's most notable television executives and producers. Yes, he was *that* desperate. I'd consigned the rumour to that of an urban myth until last night when Maggie had confirmed it as being true, having attended the memorial service herself. It went without saying that this little stunt of Alex's did nothing but backfire on him causing everyone in the TV industry to give him an even wider berth if that was at all possible. After lying low for a few years, all it took was one reality show as he grabbed his last chance at the limelight with both hands. Desperate to get his career back on track, Alex had readily accepted the offer of five thousand pounds, the lowest amount paid to any celebrity in the show's history and within weeks, he was back on prime-time British TV on Celebrity Desert Island. During his five weeks as a castaway in the searing heat, Alex Garner made sure that he appeared in every episode and conducted his behaviour accordingly to achieve this. He lasted the full five weeks, and in that time, despite coming across as outspoken and insincere, he won the hearts of many Brits and finished in second place. Within two months he had signed a deal to co-host the newly re-vamped breakfast show *UK Today*. Paired with Lydia Black, another new acquisition to the show, it ought to have been a match made in heaven but unfortunately for Alex, his return to breakfast TV had done little to stem the show's haemorrhaging ratings. According to Maggie and now even Mandy, the make-up artist, the channel was getting anxious and there was plenty of talk of impending change on the programme. None of this chat did anything to improve Alex's mood and we knew how desperate this made him. I even overheard him in the Green Room, saying that he couldn't go back to presenting low budget travel shows that nobody watched and staying in cheap hotels with the crew.

Once they cut to the commercial break and the regional news, the studio door swung open and I was almost knocked over as Alex barged past me, already starting to undo his flies en-route to the toilet. He stopped in his tracks as if he had had a delayed reaction at seeing me.

"Oh, it's you," he said bitterly.

"Yes Alex, it's me," I responded in a weary voice that instantly told our presenter just how tiresome I found him and his attitude to be.

"I gather you're here to talk about this so-called ectopic pregnancy," as he raised his fingers in the air to do that irritating quote marks thing. I was angry but I didn't want to let him see that.

"Don't you worry your pretty little head about it, Alex. I'll talk to Lydia if you're having difficulty understanding it," I replied in my best patronising voice. He stormed off, still fiddling about with his flies despite still being in the corridor.

I walked straight onto the studio floor after the floor manager had told me there had been a change to the running order as the Home Secretary, who was supposed to have been giving us an exclusive interview shortly, had pulled out without any explanation. Lydia, on seeing me walk in to have my radio mic attached by the crew, gave me a huge hug.

"How are you doing?" she said kindly.

"I'm OK, but I'd have been all the better for not seeing your 'on-screen husband' just now," I laughed as Lydia comically winced at the description that I'd just given of Alex.

"He's getting worse," she said, doing her best to put her hand over her radio mic, aware that colleagues in the studio gallery would be able to hear her. "To be honest Lizzie, I'm done arguing with him. Sometimes I just have to sit back and let him go for it in the hope that one day, if we give him enough rope.... Well, you know." I smiled in agreement and solidarity with her.

"Three minutes and we're back on-air," shouted the floor manager and that was our cue to take our seats.

"Lizzie, I'll do the interview. Unfortunately, there's no show without Punch but just do your best to ignore him," said Lydia.

"Thanks," I said, taking a sip of water while leaning across the back of the chair. I think I was more nervous about this interview than I was speaking to world-famous Claudia Faye last week in Sydney Harbour. Alex returned to his seat and as he unnecessarily squeezed too close to me, I could see that he had his hand in his flies and was pretending to do them up. At the same time with his back to the camera, he ran his tongue across his bottom lip.

"What the fuck?" I blurted out, not realising at

first that I'd said it down the radio mic. I didn't have the earpiece in today because I was there as an interviewee rather than a presenter. Lydia leaned over to me and asked if I was ok and in response I nodded nervously as the music kicked in around the studio telling us that we were back on-air. As promised, Lydia had conducted the bulk of the interview but rather than sitting there and remaining respectfully quiet, Alex couldn't resist jumping in at various points. It was obvious that he had little, if no sympathy for me, at first suggesting that I couldn't possibly be grieving for a baby that had been no bigger than a satsuma. His grossly insensitive approach continued and culminated in him pretty much saying that he felt sorry for Paolo, my ex for 'having to' sell his story and that it was alright for me, sitting in a plush hotel with my movie star boyfriend living the high life.

When the interview was over, and they cut to the weather, I got straight up and went out to my dressing room, thanking Lydia as I left but purposely and notably ignoring Alex. In my dressing room, I was about to get changed when there was a knock at the door. It was Jeremy, our executive producer.

"Lizzie, hi."

"Oh, hi Jeremy," I said, wondering why he appeared a tad sheepish but then I remembered that this was the first time that I'd seen him since he'd invited my flatmate James back to his flat after the Boat Race Party ten days ago.

"Lizzie, is there any chance that you can hang around until we come off-air at nine?"

"Yeah ok. I was going to go up and see the team once they were in the office anyway. Why do you need me?" I was wondering where this conversation was going.

"I'd like you to sit in the studio with Lydia and see how you two work together. Oh, and don't take your make-up off. I've texted Maggie to let her know and she's going to come in and sit in the gallery when you do it."

"Yeah, ok," I agreed.

He didn't hang around and so I went along to the kitchen where Stuey and the other runner were making toast for the Green Room guests. I poured myself another coffee from the large cafetiere that Stuey always had on the go.

"Lizzie, you shouldn't be doing that," said Stuey. "Let me do it."

"Stuey, it's me. I'm still capable of pouring myself a drink. Anyway, once you've dished them out, can you come to my dressing room please, I've got a little something for you." Two minutes later Stuey appeared at the open door to my room and I took the gift bag off the floor and handed it to him. He looked shocked.

"Is this for me?"

"No, I just thought I'd ask you to hang on to it for safe keeping."

He opened the bag and pulled out the blue Bondi Beach surfer t-shirt I'd bought him. "There's a little something else in there for you," I said. He reached into the bag and pulled out the flat parcel wrapped in orange tissue paper. His eyes widened as he realised what his gift was. "Do you like it? It's the programme from the Sydney premiere of Tango Master and Jet has signed it to you."

"To Stuey, let's have a beer next time I'm in London. Cheers! Jet Shield," said Stuey, reading out the message.

"I was talking to Jet about how you and Maggie are my best mates on the show and how you keep me sane."

"You talked to Jet Shield about *me*?" Stuey replied incredulously. "Jet Shield knows who I am?"

"Yeah, and when I saw on Instagram that you had been on a date to see the film, I showed Jet the picture and that's when he signed the programme in the hotel. That's from him. The T-shirt's from me."

Over an hour later, the show had finished, I stayed in my dressing room out of Alex Garner's way. Stuey gave me a knock when the coast was clear and I went through to the studio floor. It took the sound technician a couple of minutes to get my radio mic and earpiece sorted and then I went and took my place next to Lydia, in Alex's seat. After the last two weeks, I didn't think that my life could have any more surreal moments to offer but here was another one. Maggie came over to the desk winking at me, followed by Jenny, the head of daytime.

"Hi Lizzie. Lovely to see you and well done on the Australian interview by the way. Thanks for doing this. We're just trying out some fresh ideas for the show, is that ok?" Jenny said.

"Yeah, no problem," I said nervously, my anxiety not eased at all by the appearance of Melanie my agent, at the back of the studio set behind the cameras.

"Just relax. We're going to get you to do a few bits from the autocue and then chat to Lydia. You'll be fine and don't worry. I think we're going to have a meeting afterwards about this women's health and lifestyle series if that's ok. Break a leg," she said heading off to the gallery with Melanie and Maggie.

The screen test actually went better than I thought it would, although I was sure that was down to Lydia making me feel so comfortable and encouraged me to follow her lead. Afterwards, Jeremy came down to the studio floor to thank me with an air of familiarity that still made me feel uneasy. The meeting with Jenny, Jeremy and my agent Melanie went better than I had expected. I wasn't quite sure what to expect, but I was incredibly nervous given the personal nature of the subject matter and my recent revelations about having had an ectopic pregnancy. I had asked that Maggie hang about until after the meeting because I had an idea that I wanted to put to Jeremy and Jenny about the series. I'd agreed to do it on one condition, that Maggie be allowed to be executive producer on it as she was the one person that I emphatically trusted in the world of TV. It would also be a promotion for Maggie who had worked for many years at her producer role. Jeremy was reluctant to allow her a break from *UK Today,* but I stipulated that that was my condition and as executive producer, she wouldn't be required to work on it full-time leaving her time to continue working on the breakfast show. Maggie was delighted when I told her, and I apologised for not consulting her on the matter first before I negotiated her career move. She suggested that she reduce her hours on *UK Today* to free her up and still allowing her to have a family life with her husband and two boys.

I didn't have much time to hang around as the day job beckoned and I had to travel to a cinema in Notting Hill this afternoon to interview the stars of a new sitcom. Thankfully I had an hour in the office to watch the first two episodes and make some notes for the questions before we set off.

It was late afternoon by the time that we wrapped filming in Notting Hill and rather than travel back to the office with the crew, I took the bus home to Chiswick and looked forward to a quiet night in on my own. As the bus meandered its way along the route leaving Shepherd's Bush behind us, my phone rang and my brother Michael's name came up on the screen.

"Michael, hi. Sorry I've been meaning to call you since I got back. How are you?" I said feeling somewhat guilty.

"Not good sis. Have you got time for a chat?" he replied, sounding unusually vulnerable.

"Yeah, I'm on the bus right now but I'll call you when I get home in fifteen minutes."

"I'll see you then. I'm standing outside your flat." His voice sounded wobbly.

"Crikey. Is Elaine with you?" I asked, wondering how I would accommodate extra house guests at such short notice.

"No, she isn't with me. I've left her Lizzie," said Michael, now audibly crying. "I've left her. I've left my wife."

CHAPTER 21

Brotherly Love

By the time that I arrived home, Michael was still standing outside the betting shop situated on the ground floor below my flat. At his feet was a large canvas holdall and in his hand was a carrier bag from the off license suggesting that I was in for an evening of wine, confessions and tears. In the flat, he'd barely put his bag down in the hall before what must have been weeks or months of pent-up emotion came pouring out. We had the place to ourselves, so I took him through into the living room and sat him down. He didn't say anything, he just cried. I didn't say anything, I simply held him. We must have been sitting there for ten minutes without a word being said and it was Michael that was the first to speak.

"I need a drink," he said. I laughed but only because that wasn't what I expected him to say.

"I'll open a bottle of wine, or a beer if you prefer that," I said, remembering that his bag of drink from the off licence was sitting at my feet.

"Actually Sis, do you mind if we go to the pub?"

"Yeah of course, the pub next door has a beer garden so we can sit out in the sunshine. It's still warm out there," I suggested.

Five minutes later we had found ourselves a table in a quiet corner of the beer garden and had a couple of cold pints of lager in front of us. For a minute we sat in an uncomfortable silence. All sorts of theories were rushing through my head as to why he had suddenly left Elaine. I realised that Michael wasn't going to get the ball rolling, so I decided to speak and get straight to the point. "Michael, what's going on?"

"I've left her. I've left Elaine and the kids." More tears welled up in his eyes.

"You said that on the phone earlier. What's happened?"

"It's not working. It hasn't been for a long time. I love the kids and I'll do anything for them but staying there, staying in that marriage, I felt as if I was being strangled," Michael said.

"Does anyone know you're here?" My question was more out of concern for Elaine back in Branthwaite than it was for my brother.

"Yeah, I told Elaine that I needed some time away, so I said that I'd come down here for a week. Sorry, I didn't even think to ask you. I just got one of the lads to drop me at Durham and I got the train straight here," he explained.

"I could see there was something wrong at Dad's funeral, that week I was up there."

"Yeah, we nearly separated back then but when Dad died all of a sudden, it wasn't the right time," Michael admitted. "Elaine needs some time without me too. She said so."

"Is there any chance of you two patching things up?" I asked optimistically.

"No. To be honest, I don't want to. Since this morning, I feel as if a weight has lifted from my shoulders. Obviously I'm going to be there for the kids, but right now I need some breathing space."

"Dare I ask, have you told Mum?"

"Not yet, I'm planning on ringing her tomorrow. I just needed a day to get my head around everything. I texted Elaine from the train asking her not to tell Mum or her parents until tomorrow and she agreed." The relief on his face at this moment was clear.

"So do you have a plan?"

"Not really. I've got two weeks annual leave just now, so I have time to think. I'll need to look for somewhere to live, somewhere big enough for me and the kids."

"Are you planning on having them live with you?"

"Half of the time. I don't want to be one of those dads that just sees his kids every second weekend. I want somewhere in the village so the kids can walk round to their friends' houses and all that." I had to admit that he had clearly given this a great deal of consideration.

"Well, you can stay with us as long as you need to, but you'll have to take the sofa bed in the living room." I rubbed my hand across his in reassurance.

"Won't your flatmate mind?"

"James? No, he'll be fine with it. He's hardly in anyway."

"Where is he?"

"Oh, with this guy he's just met probably. He came to meet me at the airport yesterday morning and was full of the joys of a new relationship. We'll see how long this one lasts." The tone of my own voice made me suddenly aware how negative and cynical I sounded.

"Are you not being a bit rough on him Sis?" said Michael compassionately.

"No, he's not one for settling down when there's always a new guy around the corner."

I went to the bar and returned with a pint for my brother and a tonic water for me, conscious that I was back in the studio early the following morning. Michael took a huge gulp of his beer, closed his eyes and leaned back. It was as if you could see the weight of his troubles slowly lifting off his shoulders.

"Sorry, I haven't asked about your trip to Australia yet. How was it? I heard about you being pregnant. I'm sorry." This time it was his turn to put his hand across mine by way of comfort.

"The trip was good, despite my ex crawling out of the woodwork. I'm sorry that I never told you Michael. I've never told anyone, apart from at the time when Paolo knew about it."

"So, this guy Jet, are you and him serious?"

"I don't know. I really like him and I feel as if I'm falling for him, but we live on opposite sides of the Atlantic. Our worlds are very different."

"Everyone is talking about it back home."

"I bet they are," I said, realising I'd never given a thought as to the impact back on my family that my 'relationship' Jet would have, never mind what people in Branthwaite might say about it.

"Yeah. Mum's done an interview with the local paper and at one point there was even a news crew sniffing about the village trying to find out more about you." I shuddered at the thought.

We remained in the beer garden until we had finished that round of drinks before venturing to the All Bar One pub next door to get some food, as I hadn't had a chance to get any groceries in since my return from Australia. After dinner, we returned to the flat and I opened a bottle of wine after handing Michael a beer. He was a typical Dalesman and not a wine drinker. We were only just sitting down when the key went in the door and James trundled in, surprised to see Michael sitting on the sofa opposite me.

"Oh, hi Michael. How are you?"

"I've been better mate. Is it ok with you if I stay for a few days?"

"Stay as long as you like mate," James said, unphased by our house guest.

"Are you ok James?" I said noticing the perplexed look on his face and the two bags at his feet.

"Yeah, I just had to clear my desk before I left the office."

"Clear your desk? Why?" I asked, not understanding what was going on.

I've been offered a new job with another bigger talent agency. I had the interview last week, but they only called this morning and offered me the job. I start in four weeks." His face brightened a little.

"So why have you had to clear your desk?"

"They immediately put me on garden leave and I was escorted out of the office once I'd handed over to the boss and cleared my desk. It's standard procedure."

"Why do they do that?" Michael asked, trying to understand the nature of James's job.

"It's so you don't try to take any celebrity clients with you. It's pointless really as they all have my mobile number so if any of them wanted to come across to my new agency with me, there's nothing much to stop them," said James.

I poured my flatmate a large glass of wine and the

three of us toasted his new job. Despite Michael's circumstances, the three of us had a pleasant evening chatting away, although I made a point of only having two glasses of wine myself as I had an early start in studio the next morning. I handed Michael a pillow and a spare duvet before going to bed and left him and James drinking together.

When the car came to collect me for studio early in the morning, Michael was sound asleep on the sofa, which was no surprise given the amount of empty beer bottles that were in the kitchen in addition to an empty Jack Daniels bottle. That's one hell of a session they must have had. James had offered to show Michael around London today and I made him promise not to take my brother to any gay bars. The last thing that I needed was James going off with some guy and leaving Michael in central London alone. It wasn't that my brother wasn't capable of negotiating his own way around our capital city, but in the years that I had been living here, neither him nor Elaine had once come to visit. Admittedly, I didn't have the closest bond with my sister-in-law, but it certainly wasn't for lack of trying on my part. I'd made many attempts over the years to arrange a day out somewhere with her, but every time my invitation was met with an excuse of some sort. On realising that I was flogging a dead horse, I'd eventually conceded defeat and stopped asking.

It wasn't the easiest of shows that morning and the atmosphere in studio could be described as fraught with tension. Alex was becoming increasingly provocative on-air and as he interviewed a prominent female virologist, he constantly made reference to her looks and what she was wearing, something he never would have done had it been a man. Serena was in the studio giving the runners a hard time about the type of coffee that they were serving celebrity guests, getting her priorities skewed as usual. I'd been left an envelope with three sets of tickets for Dolly Parton's *9 to 5 The Musical* which was opening in the West End the following evening. I thought that it would be the perfect excuse to take Michael and James out into central London for an evening's entertainment.

Today, I'd arranged to meet Michael and James for an early lunch at London Bridge. We had intended to just grab some street food and wander along the Thames, but after James had noticed at least three people trying to get sly photos of me on their phones, we picked a discreet table at the back of a small café, away from prying eyes. It might have been almost two weeks since Jet twirled me on the red carpet, but I still couldn't get used to being recognised in public. After lunch, I had to meet with the *UK Today* stylist up at Bond Street so that we could go shopping for outfits for me to wear. I would need to have several 'looks' to wear in studio and out at premieres when doing interviews. I'd never been one for clothes shopping but Sharon the stylist was a pro and made the whole task thoroughly enjoyable.

A few days passed, work was busy for me as there was a glut of new films coming out for the summer. This meant that there were lots of press screenings that I needed to attend if I was to interview the stars for upcoming premieres. Also, I received the call from Melanie my agent to say that the women's health series had been given the green light. Because, like a lot of TV shows, it was going to go into production almost straight away, contracts would be drawn up and my shifts on *UK Today* would be reduced to two programmes a week in order to accommodate filming. I'd discussed the project with Jenny at the channel and with Maggie. I explained that I wanted to be fully involved with the editorial side of the series as obviously, the subject matter was deeply personal to me. It was important to me to be more than just a face of a presenter and I felt that my personal experience would give the programme more authenticity. Thankfully, everyone agreed that I would have an executive producer role on the series alongside Maggie, my trusted friend and colleague.

The weekend came and with it, the opportunity to spend some quality time with Michael. He'd been keeping in touch with his kids, Amy and Josh, every day, facetiming them before they went off to school and when they were ready for bed each night. For the time being, they'd been told that Daddy was working in London for a week and despite the fact that Michael worked in a quarry, neither of them thought to question if there was a quarry in West London. On Saturday morning, Michael and I decided to walk down to the River Thames and along to Kew to see the gardens. We'd barely turned the corner when I spied her across the street, not watching us but apparently going about her daily business. For a moment, I wasn't quite sure that it was her as I'd now stopped dead in my tracks. Slightly ahead of me, Michael had turned around to see why I had paused, and at that moment, the woman looked over. It was Carol. Dad's other woman. Whereas on previous occasions she just stared at me, this time she looked surprised at seeing me and then she clocked Michael. Putting her hand over her mouth she ran up towards Chiswick High Road away from us.

"Who was that?" Michael asked not knowing what on earth was happening.

"That's her Michael. That's her from Dad's funeral and the cemetery."

"What? The crazy stalker woman you told me about?" said Michael.

"Yes. That's the one that Dad was having an affair with." I was doing my best to remain calm.

"Are you still going on about that Lizzie?"

"Well, can you come up with a more plausible explanation?" I was a little annoyed at his suggestion that perhaps I was overreacting.

"No, but... I'm sure Dad wouldn't have cheated on Mum."

"I don't want to believe it any more than you Michael, but I'm sure of it. The text messages, the secret meetings, the scarf in the car. It doesn't add up to any other conclusion," I reasoned.

"Do you want to try and follow her?"

"No, it's fine. Something tells me I will bump into her again sooner or later."

We agreed not to discuss the mysterious Carol any longer and concentrated on enjoying our walk.

"I eventually spoke to Mum yesterday," Michael said.

"Really? You finally got through to her? Did you tell her about you and Elaine separating?"

"Yeah. She took it remarkably well and after checking that I was ok, started muttering about Elaine's family not being in the same social standing as us or something." I could see that he was also more than a little weary of our mother's incessant snobbery.

"Oh, that old chestnut. She's been making passive aggressive comments about Elaine's family for years. No surprise there. After all, our mother is the queen of passive aggressive," I said. Michael laughed.

"I told her not to call you about it as you were at your meeting about the new series. You need to tell her about the programme Sis, don't let her find out about it from reading the papers."

"I will. It's been another crazily busy week and I only found out yesterday that the series is definitely going ahead. I messaged her yesterday saying that I would facetime her on Sunday. I think she has Granny coming to visit today for the weekend."

"Yeah, she mentioned on the phone yesterday that Granny was coming. That means she will be there for a week as she never remembers to go home, does she?" Michael joked.

We both laughed thinking about how our grandmother seems to rub Mum up the wrong way with the minimum of effort.

The walk along the River Thames was just what we needed and by the time that we had reached Kew Bridge, we were in need of lunch and perhaps a beer or two. I'd started watching what I was eating as I'd only just got all those new clothes with Sharon the stylist and being aware that the camera adds at least ten pounds,

I didn't want them to be tight fitting. James then texted and asked if we wanted to join him at his friend's barbecue in her garden this afternoon. We thought that was a lovely idea, if we weren't intruding, so I offered to pick up some burgers and steaks. However, James assured us that we just needed to take some booze. As we'd already walked quite a distance along to Kew, Michael and I took the bus back to Chiswick, calling in at the supermarket to get some wine on the way. It was while we were in there that we actually bumped into James in the wine aisle so we picked up some bottles. As we were waiting to pay, my phone started ringing.

"Lizzie, it's me Maggie. Can you speak?"

"Yeah, is everything OK?"

"Not really. We've just had confirmation that Jack Sheen, the singer has been found dead at his home in Kensington."

"Jesus Christ, what's happened?" I asked, shocked at the news.

"I don't know. The details are very sketchy at the moment and there hasn't been an announcement on the news channels yet. Lizzie, I hate to ask but can you drop what you're doing and meet with the crew at West Kensington tube station? We're going to need to cover this for Monday morning's show."

"Yeah, I'm around the corner from Turnham Green station. Tell them I'll see them there in twenty minutes."

"Thanks Lizzie. Call me when you arrive, and I'll brief you down the phone as I might have more information by then." I explained to Michael and James that I needed to dash into work given that one of Britain's biggest pop stars had been found dead in his flat, aged twenty-nine. I urged them to go on to the barbeque without me and with that, I ran to the tube station.

By nine o'clock that evening, I'd been on the street outside Jack Sheen's home along with news crews from all the British news providers as well as some of the major international ones too. When I had arrived at West Kensington, I was aware that I was wearing a T-shirt and jeans so I popped into a small independent clothes shop and bought a black jumper that I could slip over my top and make myself look more appropriately dressed. As time wore on, police forensics teams arrived in large white vans and very little in way of actual factual details had been released. After two hours, officers emerged carrying Jack's body wrapped in a black body-bag on top of a stretcher and loaded him into an ambulance to take him to the hospital. Maggie called me when we were done and instructed me to go home, but asked if I could I come in tomorrow evening to record the voice over for the piece to go out on Monday morning. As this was a major news story, it was likely that it was going to dominate the headlines over the next few days and it was certainly going to be the only thing that we would be talking about on Monday's edition of *UK Today*. By the time that the taxi dropped me off outside my flat, I was exhausted. James and Michael would probably still be at the barbecue although I could imagine that they would be in some serious state of drunkenness. The flat was quiet, but I noticed that there were two wine glasses on the coffee table in the living room, both still full. That's funny, I thought. It's not like James to leave a glass of wine. I went to my room to change and then it occurred to me, where the hell was my brother? I heard giggling sounds coming from James's room.

"James, you'd better not have left my brother at some stranger's barbecue just because you have pulled some guy." More giggling was all the response that came from the other side of the door. Concerned as to Michael's whereabouts, I knocked on James's door and opened it. James was sat up in bed, naked from the waist up and under the duvet was the shape of his latest conquest covered from head to toe, too embarrassed to show his face.

"James, I can't believe you abandoned my brother at your friend's house so that you could nip back here for a shag." Now I was furious.

"I didn't," was all James said by way of reply.

"Well, if you didn't, where the hell is he?" I shouted.

Right on cue, James's bed fellow decided to come out from under the duvet and show his face. I had to do a double take.

"Michael."

"Hi Sis."

It was quiet out on Chiswick High Road on Sunday morning. I had hoped for a lie-in but I couldn't sleep following my discovery of Michael in James's bed last night. My brother. My straight married brother. My brother with two kids. My brother who works in a quarry and goes to the football. I'd boiled the kettle and discovered that we were out of fresh coffee so as I went to leave the flat, James came out of his room wearing his towelling bathrobe.

"Morning Lizzie,"

"James, I'm not sure I can speak to you right now. I'm trying to get my head around what I saw last night."

"The thing is, Lizzie, you know when you said to me the other day that you couldn't put your finger on why Michael's marriage was ending?"

"Yes, that's right."

"Well, I put my finger on it," James said, unable to suppress a smile. I didn't say anything else, but went down to the street in search of coffee, newspapers and something to eat. Twenty minutes later, on my way back to the flat, Michael crossed the road towards me.

"Lizzie, can we talk?"

"Yeah of course." I wasn't angry with him. How could I be? We walked back to a spot in the middle of the High Road where some park benches had been installed among a square of stone built raised flower beds.

"It wasn't planned. It just kinda happened."

"Michael, I don't want the gory details. So, are you gay?"

"I don't know. I think so. That's been part of the problem with me and Elaine. She discovered I'd been looking at stuff on the internet and she went mad."

"Stuff. You mean gay stuff?" I said.

"Yeah," said Michael sheepishly. I've been feeling this way for a few years and then last summer when I went on Daz's stag weekend in Benidorm, I had to share a room with his cousin who was up from Cardiff. Well, he was gay and we sort of ended up messing about a bit when we were pissed," Michael confessed.

"Messing about?"

"You know. Listen, I need to get my head around everything. That's why I came down here to get away from home."

"So, you and James, was this the first time the two of you?"

"Yeah. Don't be hard on him Lizzie."

"No, well you already did that didn't you?" I wasn't sure if I intended to crack a joke or not at this somewhat tense moment.

"What I'm trying to say is that it was me that came on to him when we got back from the barbecue, not the other way round."

"So, you like him?"

"He's not what I would call my type but…"

"You've been gay for five minutes and already you have a type?"

"What can I say? I'm partial to a farmer or some masculine type more than these city lads," he said, smiling at me. I couldn't help but smile back at him. He's my brother, my darling brother and I wanted him to be happy. He deserved to be happy.

We had a quiet morning, the three of us mooching around the flat. I had the news channel on so that I could keep up with the developments of Jack Sheen's sudden death and as predicted, no other news stories got a look in. I'd bought four different Sunday papers and absorbed what I understood to be the facts of the story and did my best to ignore the gossip and assumptions. By three o'clock, a car had arrived to take me to the studio to meet with the entertainment producer and record the voiceover for the edited story that would play out in tomorrow's programme. Before I left the flat, Michael told me that he was going to go for a couple of beers with James. I presumed that they would be heading to a gay bar, not that it really mattered.

I was back home by seven and the boys were still out. I took the opportunity to have a bath and facetime Jet as I hadn't managed to speak with him for a couple of days. I updated him on what had been happening here over the weekend and he was especially pleased to hear that my documentary had been greenlit by the channel.

The next morning on the show I found myself on-air most of the morning, discussing the death of Britain's biggest pop star. By the time that we came off-air, I was ready for a walk along the Thames for half an hour to clear my head. After getting changed in my dressing room, Maggie caught me in the corridor and she had a serious look on her face.

"Lizzie, are you heading out? Any chance you can hang about for an hour. I need to talk to you once Serena and Jeremy come in," she said, looking very serious and somewhat troubled.

"Yeah, sure. Is everything ok?" I said, concerned for my friend.

"I'm fine but something has happened in the last half an hour that affects the show. I can't say any more right now as I need to meet with Serena and Jeremy shortly. Jenny, the head of daytime is coming in too," she said, before walking away and answering her ringing mobile as she did so.

Over an hour later, Maggie called me and asked me to come up to the board room. I was incredibly nervous although I wasn't sure why. Serena and Jeremy were sat at the table opposite Jenny and Lydia, Alex's co-presenter.

"Hi Lizzie," said Jeremy smiling at me. "Take a seat."

Without waiting for me to do so, he took a deep breath and continued.

"Lizzie, a story has broken online in the last couple of hours regarding Alex."

"Alex, you mean our Alex here on the show?" I asked, purely for clarification.

"Yes, it would seem that he went to the supermarket on Saturday and there was an altercation," Jeremy said.

"Altercation? He looked fine on the show this morning. He never said anything."

"Yes," Jeremy continued. "But that isn't exactly surprising. It would seem that on Saturday, Alex parked his sports car across two disabled bays outside his local Sainsburys, causing anger from the young mother of a boy in a wheelchair. After the initial altercation spiralled, Alex uttered the line "Don't you know who I am?" before grabbing the boy's wheelchair to move him out of the way of the car. He pushed the chair so hard and let go causing the boy to fall out of the chair and cut his face on the ground."

"Christ. Did they call in and report him?" I wondered how Jeremy came to know the precise details.

"No, it gets worse. As this was happening, a bystander filmed the incident on his mobile and last night he posted a video of the entire altercation to Facebook. In the last hour it has started to go viral," he said, looking gravely at me.

"Shit," I said, not really knowing what else I could say at this moment.

"Yes. Shit exactly. Lizzie, the long and short of it is that Alex is toxic right now and we can't afford to have *UK Today* associated with him any longer. We're going to meet with him and his agent shortly, but we will be issuing a statement afterwards saying that we have suspended Alex from *UK Today* until further notice while this matter is being investigated. The police have been informed and if required, we will co-operate fully with them. Needless to say, because the video evidence is there for all to see, we can conclude that Alex will not be coming back to the show. Ever."

"Wow, how does this involve me though?" I was still somewhat confused.

Jenny leaned forward and looked me in the eyes.

"Lizzie, we had been planning a relaunch for the show in the autumn, but these events have meant that we need to bring our plans forward. Lizzie, we would like you to take Alex's place and co-anchor the show with Lydia. You're bright, you have great screen presence and after we did the screen test last week, we think that you and Lydia would make a great presenting line-up," Jenny said confidently. I was genuinely lost for words. After three weeks of living life in the crazy fast lane, my fortunes were about to take another turn. I'd gone from being the quiet northern girl on the production team to co-presenting one of Britain's biggest daily shows. Someone was definitely watching over me right now.

CHAPTER 22

A Visit From Mother

There shouldn't have been any need for me to worry, I had given her clear enough instructions and even gone to the trouble of writing them down and posting them to her. I had tried calling Mum several times that afternoon and each time it went straight to voicemail. The rational part of my brain knew full well that it was a simple case of my mother having her phone switched off, but as I paced up and down the length of the vast production office, I couldn't help but think that something had gone wrong. My concern was only natural. After all, this was the first time that she had undertaken such a long journey on her own and it was the first time that she had left County Durham since my father had died suddenly two months ago. Looking around the office, more than half of the desks were empty. The producers had gone home earlier in the afternoon and as for Serena, she hadn't even set foot in the studio or the office that day. No doubt she was off having a facial or cocktails or something.

It had been more than a month since *UK Today*'s presenter Alex Garner had disgraced himself by assaulting a disabled boy in a wheelchair and in that one moment, ended his own broadcasting career. I had reluctantly agreed to step in as co-anchor of the show alongside the talented Lydia Black, which I had been doing three days a week since then. In addition, I'd been working hard on production of the new women's health series that I was presenting. I was tired now. It had been an incredibly long week and I was getting nothing productive done sitting about the office, so I decided to head over to King's Cross to wait for my mother's arrival.

Emerging on the escalator from King's Cross tube station and onto the large shiny renovated station concourse, I looked around for the arrivals board as I tried to get my bearings. It had only been eight weeks since I was last here to return home to Durham but, even now I was disorientated. It suddenly occurred to me that, after three people almost walked smack into me as I stood gaping up towards the large screen, I was very much in the way. The station was heaving with crowds of people, most of them walking very purposefully indeed, desperate to escape the confines of the hot muggy city this June weekend. Mum's train wasn't due for another half an hour, so I took refuge in the pub that I had spied across the way next to a stand selling giant cookies. Five minutes later I was sitting at the only available table outside the entrance, nursing a large glass of cold sparkling water. At one time, I would have opted for Sauvignon Blanc, but in light of my increased public profile presenting *UK Today*, I felt safer keeping a clear head. I watched the crowds dashing backwards and forwards in front of me, something which I found quite mesmerising. It's funny spending time at a railway station when you yourself aren't travelling. I felt rather smug and chilled compared to the crowds looking up at the departures board with nervous anticipation. Across the concourse above a baguette stand, something caught my eye. A large rainbow banner had been stretched across the wall with the words "Welcome to LGBT Pride London. Network Rail are proud sponsors of Pride".

"Oh shit," I muttered out loud, drawing a look from the old lady sitting at the table next to me. Of all the weekends for my mother to visit, she was coming down on this one. I dialled James's number.

"I'm in Soho! Are you coming down?" he shouted, clearly in a busy bar.

"You could have told me it was Pride this weekend!" I said, more annoyed at myself for being so oblivious to such a major event in our city.

"What? Everyone knows it's Pride!"

"I didn't and my mother is coming down from Durham. She's due to arrive any minute," I said, sounding just a little panicky.

"Bring her here for drinks." By the sound of James's voice, I could tell that he'd started drinking several hours ago.

"I can't take her to Soho, she'll have a shit fit. I was going to take her to All Bar One in Chiswick tonight, she'll be able to cope with that."

"I need to head home as I'm meeting some friends at CeCe's later. It's karaoke tonight." CeCe's was Chiswick's only gay bar and had become an all too favourite haunt of James's in the past year since it had opened. Many an evening he would be travelling home on the bus along Chiswick High Road and the bright lights of the bar would call out to him, causing him to jump up from his seat, ring the bell and alight the bus all in one movement. Even on a weekday evening, it wouldn't be unusual for James to return home stinking of beer and sometimes accompanied by a 'friend'.

"It's fine James, I'll take her to Greenwich tomorrow. It's well out of the way of all the Pride stuff. I'll see you back at home."

"I can't wait to see her. She'll be pleased to see her potential son-in-law again," James shouted naughtily.

"James, don't you dare utter a word about Michael!" I retorted, but it was too late. Looking at the screen on my phone, I could see the call had already ended. That was the last thing that I needed this weekend, for my mother to find out about my brother and my flatmate having slept with each other a month ago. As for James's comment about being a potential son-in-law, I knew that it was nothing more than banter, as Michael had assured me, he had no intentions on striking up a relationship with James. Looking up at the clock on the arrivals board, I was reassured to see that the train was on time and would be pulling into the station in about seven minutes. That was all I had. Seven minutes of peace and quiet before three days of my mother's company with absolutely no escape route or pressure valve. At least when I was back up in Durham, I could pop up to Jayne and Brian's to get away from Mum and retain a few shreds of sanity. This weekend, there would be none of that. My mother would require entertaining and I knew that I would be pretty much the only person to listen to her wittering for the next seventy-two hours. I checked the clock again, five minutes. A chubby schoolboy in a green woollen blazer sat across from me outside the adjoining coffee shop. The waitress brought him a toasted sandwich and in turn, removed the wire stand with his order number, leaving him to enjoy his food. He must have been ravenous as he chomped his way through the steaming hot sandwich at speed, barely coming up for air, biting the next chunk off before he had even swallowed the previous mouthful. With the sandwich gone, he licked the knife and gathered up the crumbs on the plate before moving it across the table and pulling the second plate containing the supersize double chocolate muffin towards him. Taking hurried gulps of his orange juice he looked around him self-consciously, before tearing into his muffin. Aware that I had been transfixed by the boy, I looked up to the board once more. Two minutes. I drained the last of her my water and grabbed my handbag before scuttling through the crowd towards the ticket barriers at platform ten. I could see the train creeping its way along the track before coming to a standstill. Within seconds, the doors slid open with a hiss and people piled out onto the platform lugging an assortment of bags and cases as they breathed in the warm muggy London air. Initially, there was no sign of my mother on the platform but as I strained my eyes to spy her in the crowd, I didn't have to wait very long. There she was, animatedly talking to two tall guys who were each walking along on either side of her, laughing and joking. At the barriers, she rummaged through her bag for her ticket, obviously she had been too carried away chatting to her companions to have fished it out ready for the inspector at the barrier. The two men waited patiently behind her with their tickets, looking over her protectively. Once they were all through the barrier, I waved over to Mum who took a couple of seconds to catch me in her sight.

"Lizzie!" she shouted excitedly. "Lizzie, darling! How are you? I've had the most lovely... I met these two gentlemen. Let me introduce you," she said, as she spun around on her heel to see where her companions were, only to discover they were standing right behind her. The two men gave her big smiles, both of them revealing immaculately white teeth worthy of any self-respecting Californian. "Oh boys, this is Lizzie, my daughter," introducing them frantically. "Now let me get this right, you're Stephen?" she said to the taller of the two as he nodded. He had silver hair which was combed into a wavy side parting and a grey silvery beard over his chiselled jaw to match. "And this is Robin," touching the other gentleman on the arm. Robin, with his dark hair and olive skin looked Italian but with a name like Robin, I thought perhaps not. "Now Stephen and Robin are together. They are a couple! How's that for you Lizzie, they're two gays." The two guys smiled at her without any embarrassment at her forthright nature. We've had the loveliest journey down and the boys even bought me some wine!" she added with a naughty little schoolgirl giggle before hiccupping.

"Mum, are you…?"

"Drunk? Of course I'm not darling. I've only had two glasses. Well, maybe three." The boys gave me knowing guilty smiles.

"Now these two lovely boys have come down from York for the Gays Pride darling. You never told me it was Gays Pride this weekend Lizzie."

"It's Gay Pride, Mum. I actually only found out this afternoon but it's alright because I've planned for us to go to Greenwich tomorrow".

"Greenwich? What do I want to go to Greenwich for darling? Oh no! I want to go and see all the gays. What was it you said I could be?" she said turning to Stephen.

"A fag hag," he answered with another grin.

"Yes, I'm going to be a fag hag Lizzie. That's a lady who is friends with the gays."

"I know," I replied bemused at my mother's newfound knowledge of gay culture.

"Now I've swapped numbers with these two delightful boys and we are going to meet up for drinks in Hyde Park tomorrow aren't we?" I sighed a little.

"You don't have to, you know guys" I said to my mother's new acquaintances, almost apologetically.

"Oh don't be daft, we'd love to. We've had such a laugh with Kitty here…"

"Kitty?"

"After the character on Victoria Wood," Robin replied. I was momentarily taken aback by his broad Yorkshire accent, half expecting him to speak with an Italian one.

"She's been dusting her nick-nacks all day long," Stephen said quoting more Victoria Wood, as the three of them drunkenly giggled.

"Well boys, I've had such a lovely time on the train with you. The drinks are on me tomorrow. I'll send you a text in the morning." I couldn't help but stare at her.

"Text?" I said quietly. The last time I had seen my mother, she had still not really grasped the workings of a mobile phone. When the moment came to part company for the evening, Mum's hugs with the boys were worthy of old friends with twenty years friendship behind them.

"See you tomorrow," she called after them as they turned and waved at her once more, still smiling before walking off towards the escalator holding each other's hand. Turning to me, Mum said "Right young lady, I don't know about you, but I could do with another drink." I was taken aback by her newfound fondness for white wine. I had never really known her to be much of a drinker all those years but obviously, since the death of her husband, she was on her own for the first time in forty years and seemed to be embracing the freedom that came with widowhood rather than being daunted by it.

"I thought we would go back to the flat first and dump your case and head out for dinner. All Bar One on Chiswick High Road does nice food and it's just a few doors along from the flat." I suggested.

"That sounds lovely darling. Will the young man you share the flat with… Jason, is it?"

"James."

"Ah yes, James. Will he be joining us?" she asked with a hint of a twinkle in her eye.

"No Mum, he already has plans to meet friends for the Pride Weekend."

My mother's eyes widened on hearing me. "Pride.. Oh is he a gay?"

"Yes Mum, I've told you before. Several times," I said, already a little exasperated but trying not to show it after only ten minutes in my mother's company.

"Ooh, perhaps he would like to join us at Gays Pride then?"

"It's Gay Pride mother," I corrected her. "There's no 'S' in it, it's just Gay Pride."

"Well, that as may be darling, but shouldn't we ask him to join us?" Mum suggested.

"Mum, he has plans, I've told you. Let's get you an Oyster Card and get us to the flat."

"Do you travel on public transport darling? I thought now that you're all over the television you would have your own chauffeur," she said.

"No, it doesn't work like that. I still like to get the tube," I asserted.

It took almost an hour on the tube to get from King's Cross to Turnham Green and as we descended from the platform and through the barriers onto Turnham Green Terrace, I breathed a sigh of relief to be out of the clammy District Line carriage. The sun was still belting out the heat over Chiswick and everyone was wearing their sunglasses, if not over their eyes, then on their foreheads as was the West London custom. It took me every effort to get my mother straight to the flat as she was inclined to wander into every single little independent shop along the road. Eventually we crossed the road and I clicked the latch on the wooden gate next to the bookmaker's. I wasn't sure what my mother would make of the flat as this had been the first time that she had been to London since I had moved in with James. The overgrown path led us to the back of the shop and up a small set of concrete steps bordered by a black iron railing.

"Well, this is it Mum. My humble abode." I put her case down in the hallway. "You'll be sleeping in my room and I'll sleep on the sofa in the living room."

Poking her head into my room, she turned and said, "Oh darling, you have a big bed, the two of us can sleep in it no problem."

"No, it's fine," I said, nipping in the bud any ideas that my mother may have about us sharing a bed.

I had learned from past experience that sharing a bed with my mother never ever resulted in a satisfactory night's sleep, especially with her propensity for talking in her sleep and kicking the duvet off the bed. The last time we had shared had been at least fifteen years ago at my cousin's house in Galway when Mum was still in the throes of the menopause and her hot flushes during the night had resulted in me spending the several nights on the sofa.

Swiftly changing the subject, I gave her a guided tour of the flat which took all of ninety seconds. I skirted past the door of James's room and went into the kitchen to pop the kettle on, not realising that behind me, Mum had taken it upon herself to pop her head through James's door.

"He hasn't made his bed," I heard her say. Turning around suddenly, I darted along the passage where she was standing in James's bedroom at the foot of the bed.

"Mum! What are you doing in there?" I said, quickly grabbing her arm and escorting her back through into the hall, secretly hoping that she hadn't noticed the mug full of condoms and sachets of lube sitting on the bookcase by the door.

"Have a seat in the living room and I'll make some coffee," I suggested.

"Haven't you any wine darling?" she asked. "It's far too warm for coffee."

I looked in the fridge. I had bought breakfast stuff in from Marks and Spencer but not much more, thinking that we would be eating out over the weekend. I certainly hadn't banked on my mother's newly found appetite for Pinot Grigio. The lock of the flat door clicked and James bundled in almost out of breath. I only needed to take one look at him to know that he was already a little drunk.

"Honey I'm home!" James shouted loudly, in a camper than usual voice but putting on a fake American accent. Before I had even had chance to make an introduction, my mother appeared in the hallway and with a beaming smile, extended her hand to James.

"James Darling, so lovely to see you," she said in a faux posh voice that she saved for special occasions.

"Joyce, you're looking younger every time I see you. Have you had work done?" James teased. "People are going to start to think you're Lizzie's sister and not her mother." Mum giggled flirtatiously back at him.

"It's lovely to see you again James. You're my third today you know." James, still smiling gave her a puzzled look. "Gay. You're my third gay today," she said, beaming with pride as if she had begun a new hobby of collecting gay men, which actually wasn't far from the truth. "I met the loveliest couple from Yorkshire on the train, Stephen and

Robin. Do you know them?" but without waiting for a response from James she continued, "they were telling me they met in Grinder. I didn't realise that York had gay cafes." James started coughing in an attempt to suppress his laughter. He looked at me, but I had dashed into the kitchen, tears of laughter running down my face. Grinder was certainly one word that I had not planned on hearing my mother say that weekend. I couldn't wait to tell everyone at work about it and I would likely dine out on that story for years to come. James went into his room to get changed and marinate himself in more Jean Paul Gaultier aftershave. My mother wandered into the kitchen as I was pouring three glasses of wine.

"I don't think much of this essential oil Lizzie dear," she complained, holding a small glass brown bottle in one hand at arm's length. I've never smelled anything quite like it, it's like sweaty socks."

I almost dropped the wine bottle when I looked up to see my mother taking a second sniff at the glass bottle that was clearly James's amyl nitrate. Grabbing the bottle and the lid from her, I stomped through to James's room bounding in without knocking. "James!" I cried in a hushed voice, "You and your bloody poppers!"

"Where did you get that?"

"You left it in the fucking living room!" I didn't know whether to laugh or be annoyed with him.

"Language Elizabeth," said James in a mocking voice, mimicking my mother. Back in the kitchen, Mum was leaning on the Belfast sink with one hand towards the open window.

"That essential oil has made me feel a bit dizzy darling." I did my best to suppress my laughter which wasn't easy. She had been in London for less than ninety minutes and already she had used the phrases "fag hag" and "Grindr" along with taking her first sniff of poppers. Not bad going for a sixty-nine-year-old widow. James emerged from his room wearing a different shirt.

"Where are you ladies off to this evening?"

"All Bar One," I replied, causing James to pretend to yawn and dramatically placing his hand over his mouth. "We're just going for some food and a glass of wine, nothing major."

"I would come with you, but I don't think I could stand the excitement of an All Bar One on a Friday night. I mean, the place will be jumping with accountants and bankers and solicitors," James said sarcastically.

"Have you got a better idea?" Mum walked into the hall from the living room carrying her wine glass which was already almost empty.

"Why don't we nip across to Balans for some food and then go to CeCe's?" he suggested.

"What's Balans darling?" my mother asked.

"It's a restaurant across the road where the waiters are all pretty gay men, Mother," I said. "It's more expensive but the food is nice."

"Oooh let's go there. I love the gays," announced Mum, "Come on, it's my treat to you both for having me to stay."

"Sounds good to me," said James. "Do you fancy coming to CeCe's afterwards for karaoke Joyce?" I gave him a death stare.

"Is that a bar for gays James?" she asked, excited at the prospect of her first night out in a long time.

"It certainly is my dear, and if you're good, I might drag you up on stage for a Dolly Parton number." My mother giggled at the prospect while I couldn't help rolling my eyes at the thought of her doing karaoke in a gay bar.

Fifteen minutes later, the three of us were sitting at one of the tables outside Balans on Chiswick High Road catching the last of the evening sun. The restaurant was busy and as I looked around me, I was only too aware that my mother and I were the only two women sat outside. The rest of the clientele appeared to be an assortment of men dressed up for a night out, many of them wearing sunglasses and sporting bronzed tans. James had taken charge and was already flirting with one of the waiters while looking down the wine list.

"Remember this is on me," Mum said to James and I. "Why don't we have some champagne?"

"Mum! It's almost fifty quid for a bottle of champagne. I'll tell you what, I'll buy dinner now that I'm earning good money."

"No darling, I insist that this is my treat and by the way, I *can* read Lizzie. James would you like some champagne my dear?"

"That would be lovely Mrs Button," he said politely.

"Joyce, you must call me Joyce."

As the three of us sat in the evening sun, eating dinner and washing it down with champagne, I finally started to relax for the first time since my mother's arrival at King's Cross. Watching her laughing and joking with James, I was aware of the change that I had seen in her, this air of bravado that she didn't really have before. I was also amazed at her ability to hold her drink. In the thirty-three years that I had been on this earth, I'd never known her to drink this much.

Almost two hours later, we were ready to leave, Mum having paid the bill and now giggling again drunkenly when the waiter gave her a kiss on each cheek as we were going. She was certainly proving to be a hit with the gay men of London.

CeCe's was little more than a five-minute walk along Chiswick High Road in the direction of Hammersmith. The last remnants of the evening sun strained through the leafy trees that lined the road as we took our time walking. Mum, who was now linking arms with James, as much for physical support as out of affection, asked him "You must have met my son Michael when he came down." James simply smirked. "It's all such a sad sorry business," she said regretfully.

I had been dreading the subject of my brother coming up over the weekend. Michael and I had succeeded in shielding our mother from most of what had happened and although she was aware that her son's marriage had broken down and that he had now moved out of his family home, she had no idea of the real reasons behind it all. I reached my arm around behind her to give James a gentle thump in the back followed by a stare that let him know he wasn't to even think about letting the cat out of the bag.

"Oh yes Joyce, I got to know your son *very* well when he was down here," James said playfully with a cheeky smile, much to my annoyance.

"Really? He never said. Mind you, he's not saying very much these days, not since he left Elaine and the children. I think his father's death has affected him more than he is willing to admit."

Before the conversation could continue any further, we arrived at the entrance to the bar, much to my relief. Several men were sitting at the tables outside with their drinks and smoking. The vanilla smell of at least one of the e-cigarettes hit me and caught me not only in the nostrils but also in the back of my throat. I'd rather have the scent of twenty Marlboro Lights wafting through than these new things that smell like sickly sweet toilet fresheners. The bar was busy and over in the corner was a drag queen with a tower of hair piled high on her head that instantly reminded me of one or two of my mother's friends. She was singing "The Lady is a Tramp" as the sound reverberated around the room. I was conscious that, apart from the singer, my mother and I were the only two women in the bar.

"James! Lizzie!" a voice hollered from the bar. It was Dan, James's best gay friend and Soho drinking buddy. "I'm getting served, what are you having?"

On seeing that Mum was now appearing rather drunk and recalling that she'd already had the wine on the train, another glass back at the flat and a bottle of champagne at the restaurant.

"Do you want an orange juice?" I said to her, in an effort to coax her away from the alcohol.

"Orange juice? It isn't breakfast Elizabeth." Mum opened her handbag and handed Dan two twenty-pound notes. "Hello young man, I'm Joyce, Elizabeth's mother," her posh voice returning. "Take this for the drinks, I'll have whatever you're having." She turned back to see my astonished face. "When in Rome and all that Elizabeth..." she said, her voice tailing off as she already started walking over to a table of men in front of the stage. I took a deep breath as I tried to take in this newfound bravado that she seemed to have acquired. She had introduced herself to the drinkers at the table who had already asked her to join them.

"Right, we'll have one drink here then I'm taking her home," I said to James. I knew that my intentions would be worthless the minute she saw Dan step back from the bar with a tray containing six Jaeger-Bombs. At the table, holding a Jaeger-Bomb in her hand, my mother stood up and shouted across the bar as the karaoke song had finished.

"I love the gays!" she yelled. "Here's to Gays Pride!" The entire bar cheered and burst into applause. Looking around the room, several guys had their mobiles out and were filming my mother who downed the Jaeger-Bomb in one and proceeded to step up onto the stage, taking the microphone from the drag queen. As the opening bars of Big Spender played out of the speaker, I wanted the ground to open at that moment and swallow me up. Mum however saw the opportunity for a moment in the limelight and she grabbed it with both hands.

CHAPTER 23

Pride Comes Before A Fall

Consuming a number of shots and Jaeger-Bombs was always going to ensure that I woke up with a fuzzy head. If a headache wasn't enough, I had a stiff back from sleeping on the sofa. James came in with a cup of black coffee for me and plonked it down on the coffee table.

"Remind me never to go drinking with drag queens," I said to my flatmate. "Did you sleep ok?"

"Yeah, but I woke up over an hour ago as I could hear your Mum on the phone in your room."

I looked at my watch and saw that it was only eight o'clock.

"I wonder who she was calling at seven in the morning?"

"I don't know but she's on the phone right now. I heard her talking when I came past the door," James said, sitting himself down on the sofa opposite me. A few minutes later, I heard my bedroom door click open and she appeared at the living room doorway with a puzzled look on her face.

"Good morning, James darling. Lizzie, do you know anyone called Carol?" she asked. I suddenly had that sickly lurching feeling in my stomach when I saw that she was holding Dad's mobile phone in her hand.

"Shit," I said, unable to think quickly or take my eyes off the mobile that she was holding. "Carol?" I replied, attempting to feign innocence.

"Yes, Carol," she said, looking more serious now. "I was in bed on the phone to Marjorie about the buffet for the church fete next week and ten minutes later, I heard your father's mobile phone ringing on your bookcase. I knew it was his phone as he had the theme for the *Antiques Roadshow* set as his ringing music. I saw the name Carol come up on the screen and so I answered it."

"It must have been a supplier to do with his work," I said, immediately regretting my feeble attempt at an excuse. "Someone who obviously didn't know that he had died." That last comment I added in an effort to give the excuse a bit more credence.

"Well, whoever she is, she asked for you and she said that she was sorry for everything that she had done. I couldn't get a word in and eventually I said that I was David's wife and enquired why she was ringing my late husband's phone and not yours." I had to think on my feet now.

"Oh, *that* Carol. She's my ex-boyfriend's mother.

I've been using Dad's mobile since the incident on the red carpet as the number that I give out to people that I don't want calling on my personal mobile. I should have asked you first. I'm sorry." I was now secretly hoping that this time she would buy my tall story.

"No that's fine," said Mum passing me the mobile and sitting down next to James who immediately got up and went to make her a coffee. "Lizzie, you said ex-boyfriend? Not the awful boy that got you into trouble out in Australia?"

"You mean the one who got me pregnant? You *can* say it Mum. Yes, it was his mother," I said, regretting another lie. I was also conscious that this was the first time that my mother had mentioned the news of my historical ectopic pregnancy since arriving in London. Her visit was the first time that we had seen each other in person since the story broke.

"Why is she calling you?" My poor mother was trying to piece together a jigsaw puzzle that didn't actually exist.

"It was over that bother I had with him in Sydney, because I wouldn't give him any money," I said, now determined to change the topic of conversation. "So Mum, what would you like to do today?"

"I thought we were going to the Gays Pride. I've texted the boys that I met on the train and they are going for brunch before the parade starts."

"Are you seriously wanting to go to Pride and see the march?"

"Of course I do darling, you know how I love the gays. Is it a march darling? I thought it was a parade with them wearing all their fancy outrageous costumes?"

James came back into the living room and handed my mother a cup of coffee.

"Well, it's a bit of both Joyce," James said. "It's still a political march with an element of a Mardi Gras parade."

"Oh, that sounds lovely. The boys on the train asked if we wanted to meet them outside The Ritz and watch the parade from there and then we can all go to Hyde Park together for the carnival."

Having ensured that Dad's mobile phone was switched off and hidden in the back of my wardrobe, I got ready and the three of us took the tube to Green Park which was the nearest station to meet Mum's new friends from the train. Having made fairly good time, Stephen and Robin were waiting for us outside The Ritz. Despite them not saying anything yesterday at King's Cross station, today they admitted that they recognised me as Jet Shield's girlfriend and before we got settled by our spot on the street for the parade, they asked if they could have a selfie with me, to which I obliged and pulled in Mum and James for the picture too. Minutes later a lady came up to me wearing a high-vis vest and rainbow colours painted onto her face. She introduced herself as one of the organisers of Pride and recognised me from the TV and papers. Out of the blue she asked if I was going to Pride and I told her yes and that we needed to go and buy tickets. I confirmed that there were five of us in our party not wanting to leave out Stephen and Robin and with that, she handed me five VIP wristbands which afforded us not only free entry but backstage passes. We all thanked her energetically and she went off waving, after having a selfie with me. That then set the tone for the day as I was stopped for selfies constantly, each time I smiled and willingly obliged. It took no effort for me to have my picture taken with strangers and judging from the reactions of those who took the selfies, they couldn't believe their luck at meeting someone famous. For today, I managed to put my feelings of imposter syndrome aside and go with the flow.

The Pride March was wonderfully exhilarating and moving in equal measure. Groups of people from all walks of life marching together with one common goal of equality, acceptance and love. I had selfies taken with an assortment of marchers including firefighters, nurses, two gay rugby teams and of course, the obligatory drag queens. By the time that the last of the marchers passed us and the Westminster Council clean up team followed in their wake, it was time for us to walk down Piccadilly and onto Park Lane into Hyde Park. We made a beeline for the VIP area first so that we could make use of the toilet facilities and get our bearings. Out on the field we slowly wandered around the stalls with my mother stopping anyone in any kind of costume and asking them if she could have a photo taken with them. Mum wasn't a fan of selfies as she always said that she preferred photos of herself to be taken full-length whereby she would put her hands on her hips and stick her leg at an angle as if modelling in a 1980s catalogue. It was while we were backstage that I bumped into Melanie my agent who was there with two of her clients that were appearing on the mainstage. After insisting that I come and meet them, she brought over a bottle of champagne and glasses to toast us working together. After twenty minutes of chatting, I was conscious of having abandoned Mum and James, so I politely made my excuses and walked over to the bar where James was chatting animatedly with Stephen and Robin, the boys from the train.

"Sorry about that," I said to them, looking around for sign of my mother. "Has my Mum gone to the loo?" I asked James.

"No, she said that she was going over to the stalls to have a wander around."

"James, please tell me that you are kidding me. You let her go out there alone?" I was now starting to panic as to the whereabouts of my mother.

"Calm down Lizzie, she's a grown woman and perfectly capable of going for a walk around the park on her own. Anyway, she said to call her on her mobile if you needed to find her."

I left the VIP backstage area and made for the stalls that we had seen on our entry into Hyde Park. It took another thirty minutes to find her and finally I heard her voice before I actually saw her. As I entered the Moet & Chandon champagne tent, there she was sitting at a table with a glass of fizz surrounded by three drag queens.

"Lizzie! Darling," my mother shouted when she saw me at the entrance to the tent. "Lizzie come and meet the girls." As I approached the table, the drag queens took one look at me in astonishment. "Bloody hell! You're Lizzie Button from *UK Today*," said the most beautiful drag queen I'd ever clapped eyes on. She must have been at least six foot tall, actually closer to six foot six once you allowed for the height of her hair and wearing an all-in-one glittery body stocking and bodice, she had the most flawless complexion and make-up.

"Lizzie this is my new friend Tess." Mum made an introduction to her new drag queen friends.

"Hi, I'm Tess, Miss Tess Tickle and this one over there is Miss Cara O'Hara and that one is Emma

Royd, thick as shit she is," Tess said, joking about her friend. The other queens reached over to give me more air kisses and before long, we were sharing a second bottle of champagne together. The queens were actually from my neck of the woods up in County Durham, but they were down in London as they were performing in a number of venues across the Pride weekend, most notably the main stage there in Hyde Park. As Mum got herself a little tipsy, she became even bolder and pulled her compact digital camera out of her bag and got the queens to pose for photos with her in the middle of the tent.

"Lizzie, my new friend Emma says that I should get myself one of these Instamatic accounts on the internet," she said.

"You mean an Instagram account," I corrected her.

"Yes, one of them. I feel sorry for that poor girl Lizzie. Do you know her name is actually Emma Royd?" She had a concerned expression on her face.

"Yes Mum, Tess introduced us," I reminded her.

"Well dear, I didn't like to say anything to the poor girl, but her name sounds like haemorrhoid, like what old people get on their bottom. I didn't like to say anything when she's having a nice day out, but you would think that one of her friends would tell her." The play on words had clearly gone way over her head.

"Mum, the name is meant to be funny. You do realise that those are not their real names, don't you?"

"Really? Oh, silly me," she said giggling, which I suspected was as much from the champagne as from the joke.

As Tess, Emma and Cara had backstage passes too, we headed back there so that they could prepare for their first appearance of the afternoon. I caught up with James and we went to get some food from the catering van. It was while we were in the queue that I could hear Miss Tess Tickle over the speaker as she was now on stage.

"Ladies and Gentlemen and everyone else, we have a very special guest joining us on stage this afternoon. We met her an hour ago in the champagne bar and it turns out she is a celebrity mum with a very famous daughter."

"Oh shit," I said to James. "She hasn't."

"Pride London, please can you put your hands together for the mother of *UK Today's* Lizzie Button, Mrs Joyce Button," said Tess, as cheers rang out across the front of the stage along with lots of whistling.

My mother walked onto the stage flanked on either side by Emma Royd and Cara O'Hara, waving to the crowd. Tess handed Mum the mike who shouted.

"I love the gays! Thank you for having me to Gays Pride!" and now the crowd went wild.

"Now Ladies and Gentlemen. Joyce is going to go off with our Emma and they will be back in fifteen minutes with a special surprise for you all."

It was at least another ten minutes before we got our food so at James's suggestion, we joined the crowd watching the main stage and as promised a short time later, Tess was back on stage.

"Well, you met our Joyce a short time ago. Now she's back and our Emma has worked her magic. Ladies and Gentlemen, please give a huge Pride London cheer for our latest drag sister. She's tasty, she's hot and she's finger licking good. Please welcome on stage, Miss Kay EffCee!"

Walking on stage were Cara, Emma and in the middle, my mother wearing a bright yellow wig, glittery dress and a feather boa draped around her neck, the look now complete with her own drag name. After following the other queens to the middle of the stage, the three of them proceeded to mime their way through "Sisters", a drag version of the Beverley Sisters. My mother looked as if she knew all the words and rather than be embarrassed, she was having the time of her life and who could deny her that after her recent troubles? Gays Pride was certainly a day that I'll never forget, for all the right reasons.

CHAPTER 24

Gotcha!

After the fun and frolics of the Gay Pride weekend and Mum returning back up north, I was straight back to work finishing the women's health series. The channel had decided to call it *All Woman* and I rather liked the nod towards the Lisa Stansfield song of the same name. We had two more days of filming that week and then it was a case of Maggie working her magic with the editor to turn the first programme into the finished article. The channel wanted to air the first episode the following week while my story was still in recent memory so once we had finalized the script, I went into the edit to record the voice-over. That evening, after several retakes, I bought pizza in for Maggie and Rob the editor to thank them for working late and then I accepted the offer of a taxi home.

Despite being so tired, I found it difficult to get to sleep and my mind drifted back to the call from Carol to Dad's mobile when my mother was staying here at the weekend. Thankfully I'd successfully managed to steer Mum off the scent with a white lie. In bed, I switched on my bedside lamp and removed Dad's phone from the back of the wardrobe, turning it on in the process. I hadn't expected there to be any notifications but there it was, a small banner across the screen telling me that I had one new message. The common sense in me said not to open the message when I was trying to get to sleep but I never was good at listening to reason. I pressed on the notification and in an instant, the message appeared.

Lizzie, I'm sorry. I need to talk to you, Carol.

Fuck, what does she want? I was annoyed and as much as I wanted to confront this woman, I had no time for any half-baked explanations. Her very existence had interfered with my grieving process enough as it is without her popping up here and there around London. I had accepted that my father had been having an affair. I didn't like it, but I accepted it so I didn't see any point in dragging this out. I wanted to get on with my life and pretend that she didn't exist. I wasn't going to respond right now because to be honest, I didn't know exactly what to say. I picked up my own phone and texted Clive, Dad's boss asking when he was next going to be in London and could we meet as a matter of urgency. Clive immediately texted back asking if I was ok and that he would be arriving at King's Cross at lunchtime tomorrow and that he had an hour free before needing to travel on to his first meeting.

I wasn't on *UK Today* this week due to my commitments publicising *All Woman* as the first episode was going to air across the UK on Wednesday night. Between now and then, I had a busy couple of days touring TV studios, radio stations and a series of press interviews at a central London hotel. Despite all this, I needed to see Clive and check if he knew anything about what Dad had been up to. Not wanting to spend the morning in a taxi stuck in traffic, I took the tube to King's Cross to meet him on his arrival in London. By the time that I boarded the District Line at Turnham Green, the Monday morning rush hour had passed and I easily found myself a seat on the tube. A lady in her sixties was sitting opposite me at the quiet end of the carriage and by the time that we reached Hammersmith, I noticed that she was staring at me.

"Excuse me, I'm sorry to bother you but are you that Lizzie off the telly?" she said.

"Yes," I replied smiling but feeling a little cornered. The last thing that I wanted was to talk about Jet or *UK Today* all the way to Embankment when I planned to change trains.

"I just wanted to say thank you." I could see that her eyes were welling up with tears.

"What for?"

"For talking about it. I went through it in 1975 and nobody helped me. I was just left to get on with it."

"You mean, you had.."

"An ectopic pregnancy. I went through hell and nobody understood what I was going through." She was crying now and so I moved over to sit next to her, taking her hand in mine. "We didn't talk about.... you know, those things back then. We just called them 'women's troubles.' You don't realise it, but you making these television programmes, you're going to make a difference to a lot of women."

"The first episode is going to be on Wednesday night."

"Yes," I read a thing in the Sunday paper about it." The train slowed down as we pulled into Victoria station. "This is my stop darling."

"I'll get off with you, I can change here just as well as Embankment." We walked to the escalator together and stopped. "I'll need to go up here to get the Victoria Line." I pointed in the opposite direction.

"Thank you, Lizzie. Thank you for making a difference. God Bless," she said, hugging me and then turning to the escalator, grabbing the handrail with one hand and using the other to wipe her eyes with a tissue.

I continued my journey on the Victoria Line, up to King's Cross and rather than worrying about meeting Clive to discuss Dad's extramarital affair, I found myself thinking about the woman on the tube. What she had said to me had left me thinking about the potential impact of sharing my story. Throughout the production of this new series, I was fully aware that the story was so much bigger than me and that it could have far-reaching implications, but to have this complete stranger tell me that I had made a difference, that had a profound effect on me.

I'd arranged to meet Clive in a coffee shop on the station concourse as he would then need to get the Piccadilly Line to Holborn for his first meeting. I was relieved to see him as he embraced me in a hug, his large frame enveloping me.

"Lizzie, good to see you. I say that, but I have been watching your career progress on the television. Your father would have been very proud."

I smiled back at him, not quite sure what to say.

"Lizzie, your message last night did concern me. What's wrong?"

I took a deep breath and went straight for it.

"When Michael collected Dad's car from the hotel after he died, we found a woman's scarf in the glove compartment, and it didn't belong to our mother. His mobile had messages from a woman called Carol and there were diary entries noting when he had arranged to meet her."

Clive looked at me with no sign of surprise.

"Did you know that Dad was having an affair?" I asked, now suspecting that Clive did actually know what was going on.

"I knew something wasn't right. He was very secretive. He would go to a house in Yorkshire on his way to meetings or to the hotel. The night before he died, we had a drink in the bar and he said that he had got himself into a tricky situation, that he felt as if he had backed himself into a corner."

"Did he say what about?" I asked, wondering where the hell this conversation was going.

"No, he was rather cagey about it, but he said that he planned to sit down and tell your mother something monumental once we had come back from the conference in Lisbon."

I then proceeded to tell Clive about this Carol woman turning up at the cemetery and at various places in London.

"I feel as if she is stalking me."

"Lizzie, if it is her, do you think she could be trying to reach out to you rather than having any malicious intent towards you?" he said, showing more compassion for her than I was prepared to exert.

"I don't understand what she wants from me. I don't want any pathetic explanations from her.

Reading the messages that she sent him, she knew fine well that he was married. She knows he's dead. Why can't she leave it in the past?" My voice was now full of frustration. Frustration and resentment. Clive reached across and took my hand by way of offering comfort.

"That's something only she can answer, Lizzie."

"What should I do?" I said, looking at him for some much-needed paternal advice.

"I would message her back on your father's phone and suggest that you meet her. Arrange to see her during the day and in a wide, open space such as a park. That way, if it all becomes too much, then you have an exit route." He looked at his watch and announced that he needed to get to his meeting. As we both stood up, we hugged each other.

"Tread carefully Lizzie. I wouldn't want to see you getting hurt, but I understand that you do need answers. Lizzie, your father was a good man. Remember that." His parting words hung in the air as he walked away.

I reached into my bag and retrieved Dad's mobile that I had brought with me, my heart racing as I typed in the reply to Carol's message.

"We need to talk, face to face. Saturday 11am. Outside the Boat House on the Serpentine, Hyde Park."

I'd chosen the location knowing that it would be

busy enough should the meeting not go to plan. I was aware that given my current high profile, it might not be the most private of places to meet but I was more concerned about being alone than having people recognise me. I found myself a little café just off Tottenham Court Road for lunch and while I was enjoying some falafel and salad, Maggie texted to ask if I was anywhere near Soho. I confirmed that I was, and she asked me to pop down to the edit house on Poland Street as she had finished the final cut of the first episode of the new series and Jenny from the channel was on her way to view it.

Two hours later, sitting in the edit viewing room, I was speechless. Maggie and Rob, the editor had worked their magic, as had the production team and the finished article was a powerful piece of television. I was relieved to have been able to watch the finished first episode in such a private setting where I felt comfortable. The first episode of any new series needs to have an impact, and this certainly did that. I couldn't wait to see the remaining two episodes when they were finished. I immediately phoned Jet, not giving a thought to the time difference and that it was only six in the morning in LA. I had managed to wake him but he wasn't bothered one bit. He said that he would be looking forward to watching it over in California and that he wished he could be in London right now. I was really missing him and hoped that it wouldn't be too long before we could meet up and again and carry on where we left off in Australia. Maggie informed me that Jeremy and Serena had arranged a Wrap Party for Thursday night in Soho and had booked out a dining room at Soho House for the occasion. I wasn't a frequent visitor to the famous private members club that had long been the meeting place for the higher echelons of the tv industry, but I was happy to just go with the flow.

The programme aired on Wednesday evening, and I'd chosen to watch it at home with James. No sooner had the credits gone across the screen at the end, did my phone start going mental. Text message after text message fired through and after two minutes of beeping, I found myself having to turn the phone's volume off. My mother phoned, crying her eyes out and apologising for not having been out there in Australia all those years ago when I lost the baby. Meanwhile, James was sitting on the sofa next to me rapidly scrolling through his phone.

"Twitter has gone crazy, Lizzie. The programme is the number one trending subject in the UK right now."

Such an immediate response was incredible to see and for the first time since stepping onto the red carpet, I felt truly validated and no longer like an imposter. Maggie messaged and asked if I could come onto *UK Today* in the morning to talk about it. Because there was already such an astounding and positive reaction across the country, they wanted to maximise the exposure for the subject (and the channel, I thought cynically). I agreed and Maggie said they would send a car round for me at the usual time in the morning. An early start required me to get straight to bed although when I saw that Jet was calling me from LA, I allowed myself a little time to talk to him. He had watched it from the US and told me how immensely proud he was and was sorry that he couldn't have been with me to watch it. I told him that there was a party arranged for the following evening at Soho House to celebrate the hard work put in by all the team to get the programme made and turned around in such a short space of time. He wished me a good night and I fell asleep thinking of him and the short precious moments that we spent together in the Blue Mountains.

The next day proved to be just as busy as the run up to the first episode going out on-air. After doing two spots on *UK Today*, I was booked in for three more tv shows including one at the BBC. By three in the afternoon, I was heading home in a chauffeur driven car and planning a much-needed afternoon nap. By seven o'clock that same evening, I'd arrived at Soho House in central

London and was met outside by several paparazzi photographers. I wasn't sure as to how they had found out I was going to be here, but I assumed that someone must have leaked the details of the party. I said to them that if I posed for photos now, would they go away and leave us for the rest of the night? They conceded and two minutes later, having got their desired images, they left. Maggie had come out to see what was happening and escorted me into the private dining room. I hadn't known that everyone was already going to be there and as I walked in, the room erupted into cheers and applause. Everyone in the production team including Rob the editor and the runners, they were all there and as my eyes scanned around the room, they stopped when I saw a familiar face at the back of the group almost in the shadows and at that moment, my jaw dropped in astonishment.

"Jet!" I shouted. There he was, smiling and his beautiful blue eyes sparkling. He stepped forward and wrapped his arms around me as everyone in the room cheered again.

"I talked to you last night and you were in LA," I said, trying to get my head around him being there with me.

"I was but I was packed and ready to go to the airport. I wanted to surprise you, so Madeleine gave your Maggie a call and together we hatched a plan."

I kissed him.

"You did this for me?"

"Of course, I did. I love you." Those three words. Nothing could have prepared me for them, but I didn't have long to give them a second thought as the production team swept us both through into the adjoining room and onto the dance floor.

It was the party to end all parties and despite my trying not to get drunk, I did have a few too many glasses of champagne and got rather caught up in the moment. I'd ignored my phone all evening but decided to check it and saw that I had three missed calls from James in the last half an hour. Fearing that something was wrong, I decided to step outside and call him.

"I'm just going to get a breath of fresh air," I said to Jet before going downstairs and out onto Old Compton Street. It was a warm muggy night in Soho and the air was far from fresh. I used this moment of peace to take in the enormity, not only of the programme and its reception, but that Jet Shield had told me that he loves me. I called James who answered immediately.

"Hi James, are you ok?" I asked concerned.

"I'm fine but I have something to tell you. I've been out for drinks with a friend whose boyfriend works on one of the big tabloids. Your name came into conversation and this guy divulged who had been calling the papers to let them know your whereabouts." He was doing his best to be heard above the din in the background. I was stunned.

"Who is it?" I asked, unable to wait a second longer to find out who had been telling paparazzi photographers where I was going to be each time I went to an event or a hotel.

"It's Bianca Harding, the girl who was sick at the Boat Race Party. She's been giving away your location in exchange for money. It's proved to be quite a lucrative little scheme for her these last two months."

I'd say that I couldn't believe it but actually it was the most logical explanation. Bianca had held a grudge against me since long before my incident with Jet on the red carpet and it had been amplified tenfold since then. That would explain the photographers outside Claridges, Sydney Airport and a whole host of other places. She must have been listening in to Maggie's conversations with me while she was in the office. I took a moment to think how I was going to handle this, but I didn't want to spoil my special night. I'd have to deal with her later. Despite that, my head began to spin. It was all too much. I looked at the people coming out of the theatre across the road until something caught my eye.

Carol. She was right there across the street staring straight at me. Five seconds must have passed before she turned and started to walk away. "Oh no you don't lady," I said, as I ran across the road after her. She wasn't going to get away this time but because at that moment, I only had Carol in my sights, I didn't see the taxi that rounded the corner. The horn blared and I felt my legs giving way under me and as I flew for a split second into the air, the last thing I saw was the neon lights of the café across the road and Dad's face appeared in my vision. Suddenly the noise and the images disappeared.

CHAPTER 25

The Truth Will Out

I could hear people moving around me long before I was able to open my eyes and see them. I remember the nurses. Lots of nurses. I remember people talking to me. James, Maggie, Jet and my old flatmates Moira and Rhona. At least I think that it was them. I was sure that I heard Jet's voice but then I would fall asleep again.

Awake. I'm awake and there's a nurse looking after me. He's a handsome looking guy with a shaved head, olive skin and the most sparkly eyes. I tried to speak but no words came straight away. I fell asleep again and when I woke, he was still there, the handsome nurse.

"Hi Lizzie, I'm Martin and I'm a nurse. You're in the University College London Hospital," he said in a soft Scottish accent.

"My head feels fuzzy." My entire body was suffering from the hangover from hell.

"Well, you will go picking fights with moving

taxis," he said in jest, his mouth smiling along with his eyes. The taxi. It was coming back to me now. Carol, she was there on Old Compton Street. She was staring at me and I ran after her. I was aching from head to toe but I wasn't in real pain. They must have had me pretty doped up on pain killers.

"So Lizzie, it would appear that you have had some mild concussion, bruising and a fractured leg. You've been lucky."

"Fractured leg? You mean my leg is broken?" I asked, trying to move it.

"Yes, it's broken and it's going to need to be pinned. Now that you're awake I'll get the surgeon to come and talk to you about the operation."

"Operation? Do I need surgery?" I asked. I was worried at the thought of going into an operating theatre, the last time being when I lost the baby in Sydney all those years ago.

"Yes, you will need surgery to pin the bone back together. The doctor will explain everything. We moved you into a side room because a journalist tried to get into the ward," he said sympathetically.

"Thank you, Martin," I said gratefully, hoping that my being here wasn't causing the staff any trouble.

"You're lucky. It's not often that the there's a side room free otherwise you'd be slumming it in the main ward with other patients trying to get selfies with you while you're using your bed pan," he joked. I laughed at his hospital humour and presumed it to be a pre-requisite for working here.

"Oh, by the way, you've had a few people call in to the unit to check on how you're doing. Your mother has been on the phone regularly and there's a lady that has called about six times already. Goes by the name of Carol." I felt quite sick at that moment. Not content with stalking me on the street, she's calling the hospital ward. It didn't take long for the doctor to come into the side room. She was a pretty woman with blonde hair tied up neatly.

"Well Miss Button. You're a lucky girl. It's a good job that the taxi wasn't travelling too fast otherwise your injuries would have been a lot more significant. We did a brain scan and everything appears to be fine but you did suffer some mild concussion. Your x-ray shows a fairly clean break so now that you are awake, we will take you down to surgery in about an hour. The anaesthetist will be along to see you shortly," she said as she smiled and left.

There was a knock at the door.

"Hey you," said Jet walking in. "How are you feeling?"

"I've been better," I replied.

"You gave us quite a fright."

"*You* got a fright?" I laughed. "How did you know that I'd been knocked over?"

"We heard a crash and a woman who had been smoking outside the entrance came rushing in to say you had run out into the road into the path of a cab."

"She was there, Jet. Dad's other woman, Carol. The one he was having an affair with. She was down there on the street staring across at me. She walked away so I went after her."

"Are you sure that it was her?"

"It was definitely her. The nurse just said that a woman called Carol has called half a dozen times asking how I'm doing. That's her. She knows I'm here," I said. I wasn't scared as there was nothing to be fearful of. All I knew was that I couldn't face talking to her while I was lying in my hospital bed. I was still quite groggy and I was uncomfortable.

"Lizzie, you can't worry about that now." Now he was leaning over me, brushing the hair back off my forehead.

"Jet, last night you said something to me in the restaurant."

"I said lots of things Lizzie but if you're asking me to confirm that I told you that I love you then yes, I did. For the record, I'll say it again with no alcohol involved. I love you Lizzie Button." At that moment, he kissed me on the lips.

Before I had chance to reply to him, the

anaesthetist and Martin appeared behind Jet.

"Sir, if we could ask you to step outside for a moment," said the anaesthetist, a handsome South Asian man in his early fifties.

"No problem, I'll go away," said Jet, not wanting to be in the way.

I'll only be two minutes Mr Shield and when we are done here, perhaps my colleague Martin and I could trouble you for a selfie?" he said, breaking into a huge grin.

"For you guys? Anything."

Five minutes later Jet came back in the room and to show his gratitude, not only did he take selfies with the medical team but recorded a series of Happy Birthday video messages for their relatives and friends. Since meeting him all those weeks ago, I was still taken aback at how humble he was. Considering that he was Hollywood's biggest star, he knew that taking the time to speak to someone or give them a selfie would make not just their day, but for years to come, they would talk excitedly about the moment that they met Jet Shield.

By four o'clock that afternoon I was back in my side room, feeling sore having had the surgery to pin my leg back together. Jet was the only visitor that afternoon because he had to fly straight back to the States to resume filming on his movie. By the time that the following morning came,

I was starting to feel much better and amongst the medical staff there was talk of me being discharged. James called in to visit with a bag containing a change of clothes for me. The dress that I had been wearing on the night of the accident had been consigned to the bin. In his hand he had my suitcase and a second one that looked suspiciously like his own.

"Why the suitcases James? We're not going on holiday, are we?"

"No, not quite a holiday. Your boyfriend thought it would be a good idea to book us a two-bedroom suite at Claridges Hotel until you're back on your feet again."

"Claridges? Are you kidding? We don't have that kind of money James."

"Don't worry, Jet said that it's on him and we are to get room service for every meal."

"How did this happen?" I said, still somewhat confused.

"He said that he remembered that you told him our flat was on the second floor with stairs being the only access. I tell you what Lizzie, even discounting the fact that the guy is a millionaire movie star and sexy to boot, he's a keeper."

Two hours later I was dressed and ready to leave. Maggie and Stuey had arrived from the studio and had a car waiting outside to whisk me off to my luxury hotel. Maggie mentioned that she had received a phone call from James to inform her that Bianca had been the person who had been leaking my locations to the press. She had been obliged to inform Serena and Jeremy who readily agreed that it was time that Bianca's tenure at *UK Today* should come to an end.

After saying goodbye to the amazing staff who had looked after me, I happily posed for the selfies that they asked for. After I hobbled into the wheelchair with my crutches, Maggie pushed me along the corridor while James and Stuey went ahead with the cases. Maggie had given me the heads up that there were press outside the hospital, so I thought it best to get the photos over and done with. As I was wheeled through the large door at the entrance, a small crowd of photographers were waiting, a few of them I now recognized as familiar faces on the paparazzi and media circuit. I eased myself out of the chair and used the crutches to steady myself. After a minute of photos, I spoke into the group of microphones and thanked the brilliant hospital staff and paramedics for their impeccable care and treatment before asking for privacy to recover from the ordeal. James spoke up and said to the press that now they had got their photos, please could they disperse and leave us in peace. With that, the photographers moved off and the tv crews quickly packed back into their vans. I spent another couple of minutes accepting the requests for selfies with the group of well-wishers who had been waiting outside, some of whom generously gave me cards and flowers.

With Maggie's assistance, I limped towards the waiting car. At that moment, across the road the sight of a woman stopped me in my tracks. It was her. It was Carol. She was standing as if transfixed. I asked Maggie to wait by the car as I slowly hobbled across the road, taking care not to get knocked down this time. I had no need to hurry because she didn't move an inch from her spot. A minute later I was face to face with her and I was burning with anger.

"No more chasing. What the fuck do you want from me?" I screamed at her, not caring who might still be outside the hospital. I took a breath and a moment to steady myself on the crutches. "So, are you Carol? You came to my dad's funeral and left flowers on his grave?" I said, challenging her. She nodded. "Carol, let's get this straight. I don't care if you were having an affair with my dad. He's dead. You said goodbye at the funeral and you couldn't leave it at that could you?" I screeched, tears running down my cheeks. "You've been stalking me for weeks now. Don't you think it's been hard enough for me, coping with losing him and then me having to get my head around you having an affair with him?"

"Will you just shut up!" she screeched. After seeing my startled reaction, she paused and took a deep breath. "Lizzie, I love him, I'll always love him but I wasn't having an affair with him," she said ever so calmly. Carol was now also crying but I wasn't about to let her squirm out of this one. I was still fuming with rage.

"He was your lover. I'm not stupid Carol, I can put two and two together. Did you know that he was married with a family?" I shouted at her.

"Yes," she said.

"But that didn't stop you, did it?"

"Stop it! Stop this," she shouted back at me. We were both crying as much as the other and I thought I was going to lose my balance on my crutches at any moment. "Lizzie, I wasn't his mistress. We weren't having an affair. David..... David was my father."

I thought I was going to fall and my ability to remain upright on my crutches waned. As I felt myself beginning to fall over, Carol caught me in her arms, steadying me for a moment.

I shouted over to James. "Can you bring that wheelchair across please?" He readily complied and wheeled the chair across the road to where Carol and I were standing. "You guys go ahead to the hotel. I'm just going to have a coffee," I said, nodding my head to the small café that we were standing outside. "I'll get a cab shortly."

"What's happening Lizzie?" James asked, not wanting to leave me.

"James, I'll see you in a hour and I'll explain everything then. Just go, please."

Carol and I found a table in the café and the owner kindly moved a chair out of the way to allow access for my wheelchair which Carol maneuvered into place. It felt so strange to have her behind me pushing me in a chair. After having my guard up for months, the woman who had been tormenting me was now, at this very moment, the only person who was helping me. I propped my crutches against the window next to me as Carol ordered a couple of coffees at the counter. The situation was so uncomfortable between us that she couldn't bring herself to ask me what I wanted to drink. Such a question would have classed as small talk and now was certainly not the moment for that.

Carol placed two cappuccinos on the table in front of me and before she had even had chance to pull out a chair and sit down, I blurted out my first question that could wait no longer.

"How can you be my sister?" I asked, trying to make sense of her revelation.

"I was born about two years before your dad met your mum. I say *your* dad but obviously he is *my* dad too," she said tentatively as if walking on eggshells.

"Obviously," I replied, aware that my tone came across as more than a little sarcastic. I sipped my coffee in silence, allowing her to continue.

"Years before your parents met," Carol continued, clearly taking great care with her choice of words. "My mother, Valerie, she was at college with your dad and they had a fling for a couple of weeks when they went interrailing around Europe. By the time that they had reached Rome, they had split up and gone on to travel with separate groups of people. After that, they lost touch but by that time, my mum was pregnant with me. She didn't discover until a couple of months later and by that time your dad, my dad had gone to France to start an engineering job. They lost touch and never saw each other again. Mum would never tell me who my dad was. She finally had a change of heart when she was on her death bed about three years ago. She had cancer..." She couldn't go on talking, the painful memories must have come flooding back and stopped her in her tracks.

I could see that this was hard for her now that I'd had the opportunity to calm down.

"I'm sorry to hear that." I was already regretting having shouted at her.

"After Mum died, I managed to track him down and we arranged to meet up. It took me a few years to find him and once I did, I didn't want to let him go. We met for the first time in a motorway services café. It wasn't awkward and it felt so natural. We both cried and I remember him saying that he felt guilty that he hadn't been there for me all those years. How could have been? He didn't even know that I existed. We met up a couple more times in the months following that first meeting. Not frequently at first because my kids were still at school and my husband was working."

"You've got kids?" I asked, thinking that this was new information but immediately remembered the text messages on Dad's phone where Carol had referred to her children.

"Yes, two girls. Rebecca and Sarah. They're twins and in the middle of their A levels at the moment. They're staying with their dad," said Carol.

"Are you divorced?" I asked, unsure if the enquiry was too intrusive.

"Separated. It's all very amicable and the girls are fine with it."

"So, in your text conversations with Dad, you said that you wanted him to tell my mother about you." I was trying my best to be compassionate.

"Yes. I could see that it was weighing heavily on his mind and he was uncomfortable keeping my existence a secret from Joyce. Not just Joyce, but from you and Michael too." It felt strange to hear her say the names of my mum and brother.

"Carol, I understand that this has been difficult

for you but how come you saw me so many times and never said anything? I thought you were stalking me," I said, still trying to understand her behaviour. Those occasions when she was staring at me from the crowd next to the red carpet, the times that I saw her around London.

"I kept bottling it to be honest. I wanted to speak to you Lizzie, desperately and then when you suddenly became famous, it seemed to make it so much more difficult for me to approach you," Carol confessed.

"But it's still the same me, the same Lizzie. So, if you were living in Yorkshire, how come you have been in London so much and that time my brother and I saw you in Chiswick?" I said, trying to make sense of the last few months.

"I've just been promoted. I'm now working in London two days a week and the other three days I work from home in York. I'm considering moving to London as the girls both have offers from London universities if they get the grades in their exams."

"What is it you do?" I asked, wondering if such a trivial conversation topic was appropriate for such a momentous occasion as this, meeting my half-sister properly for the first time.

"I'm a media lawyer," Carol replied. "I've been renting a spare room from a friend who actually lives around the corner from you. That's why I was in Chiswick all those times. I'd been to the theatre last night and afterwards when we came out, I saw you outside on the street. I wasn't stalking you and I didn't want you to think that I was following you," she explained. Slowly, minute by minute, the pieces of the puzzle began to fit together. "I'm sorry that I've caused you so much distress Lizzie. I never meant for you to be hurt by this. Your dad, our dad, he loved your mum dearly and was making all sorts of plans for his retirement," Carol said, now reaching into her pocket for a tissue to wipe her eyes.

"I'm sorry that I was so suspicious in thinking that you were actually his mistress."

"You have nothing to apologise for Lizzie. I can see how you arrived at that conclusion," Carol said kindly. I felt foolish at my judgements, or rather misjudgements. I was so full of regret at that moment, not just for the way that I had spoken to Carol when I saw her earlier, but more so for the way that I had judged Dad. How could I have thought that he would be cheating on Mum?

"I feel like an idiot Carol, I'm sorry." I took her hand, hoping that the simple gesture of reconciliation would be accepted. It was and Carol generously reciprocated it by placing her other hand over mine. The both of us were trembling, able to feel each other's nerves.

"There's no need to be sorry Lizzie. That's all by-the-by now. We're together, we're talking and that's a start."

I took a deep breath and smiled at her.
"It certainly is a start," I replied.

We spent the next two hours talking, not moving from the spot in the café. Carol gave me a rundown of her life so far and we were soon more than comfortable in each other's presence. I had received a message from Michael to say that he and Mum were coming down to London the next day and had booked themselves into a hotel near Claridges where I would be staying. I'd decided that when they came to see me on this visit, I would tell them both about Carol and the truth about her being Dad's long-lost daughter. I couldn't be sure how Mum would take the news but I had decided to put an end to the secrecy here and now.

As it was, two days later when we were sitting in my hotel suite, Mum took the news rather well. Admittedly she shed a few tears and decided that on this occasion, she might not be quite ready to meet Carol but she graciously encouraged Michael to do so. Plans were made for us all to meet up in London. Once the summer holidays started, we had arranged that Michael would bring Josh and Amy down to stay and we would meet up with Carol and her daughters, Rebecca and Sarah.

Six weeks later, the sun was shining on High

Street Kensington as we walked along carrying two bags that contained a lazy picnic. Four bottles of champagne, a dozen paper cups and an assortment of Marks and Spencer sandwiches. I pointed out as we passed the entrance gates of Kensington Palace that my mother had made many a pilgrimage there since Diana had died. As we crossed over the Broad Walk that ran down towards the Albert Memorial, we dodged an array of skateboarders and roller skaters, some doing tricks and others simply doing their best to remain upright. Over on the south side of the Round Pond, a group of people were sitting on picnic blankets and sarongs spread out on the grass, basking themselves in what was the hottest day of the year so far.

Stuey, Maggie and James were sitting amongst the group as they looked up smiling at our arrival.

Hi guys, I'd like you to meet Carol, my sister."

I looked around at my friends and thought to myself, life doesn't get any better. Maggie stood up.

"Everyone, I'd like you to raise a toast to the birthday girl, Lizzie Button who got a new sister for her birthday."

Everyone cheered and shouted, "Happy Birthday Lizzie."

"It's a shame we forgot your birthday cake," said Maggie.

"Don't be silly, I've got everything I want right

here."

"Everything?" said the voice behind me which I recognized immediately. Standing there holding a caterpillar birthday cake was Jet, smiling at me. I lunged at him not having seen him for four weeks and after planting the biggest kiss on his lips I turned to my friends and said, "*Now* I have everything I want."

THANK YOU

I would like to thank Fee Clark for sharing your own story with me and sowing the initial seed of inspiration for this book.

Sandi Toksvig – I owe you a debt of gratitude for all your encouragement and support. If it hadn't been for you, I may never have believed in myself as a writer. You are a remarkable woman whom I adore.

Trisha Ashley – You have been there for me every day that I have been writing this book. Thank you for believing in me, for your generosity of spirit and invaluable advice. You are the most incredible author and you inspire me each day.

Kaye Adams, Diane-Louise Jordan, Lorraine Kelly, Debbie McGee, Jon Marsh, Mark Robert Petty, Carol Vorderman, Kirsty Wark & Owain Wyn Evans – all of you gave me such an incredible boost by standing up and shouting about *Orphan Boys* and this is the first chance I have had to publicly thank you all.

To my army of advisors Sue Andrews, Viv Hall, Julie Hanson, Vicky Heales, Anne Hodgson, Chantell Hodgson, Lucy Pearson, Jo Rodger & Elaine Williams-Jones. Thank you for your unfailing support, your patience and above all your honesty.

To Bill Holden. A wonderful friend and mentor. You and your Masonic brethren gave me the gift of an education that ensured the security of our family unit all those years ago. I will never forget your kindness, wisdom and compassion. I shall miss you greatly. Rest in peace x

Elizabeth Gill, Avril Joy and Louise Marley – each of you a brilliant author and you have been kind enough to offer me advice and support during the writing of this book. Thank you from the bottom of my heart.

To Chris Powell and everyone involved with Weardale Word Fest. Thank you for supporting me as a writer and for creating such a lovely unique festival, one that I'm very much proud to be a part of.

To Diane Wright at Woodhalls in Stanhope, Sue Curry at Poplar Garden Centre in Shincliffe Village, Cogito Books in Hexham, Forum Books in Corbridge and everyone at Amazon, WHSmith, Waterstones, The Works, Barnes & Noble and all the wonderful shops around the world who have sold my books. I really do appreciate everything that you have done to support me and sell my work.

To all the amazing librarians out there – the unsung heroes. Libraries are one of our most precious resources and must be protected at all costs (along with the NHS!). Please do visit and support your local library – use it or lose it.

To Tess Tickle, Emma Royd and Cara O'Hara. Thank you for allowing me to feature you in my story, for all the amazing work that you do for the LGBT+ community and for looking after Joyce at Pride.

John R – I can never thank you enough for that simple message you sent me in March 2020 and as a result I'm here to tell more stories. Thank you for reaching out in my darkest hour.

Jayne Williams – for inviting that shy, scared 22-year-old lad out to Sydney thirty years ago. Thank you to you and Paul for your lasting friendship and for changing my life.

Stephen Bennett – you are the most wonderful friend and most incredible film maker. To have had your support since I first put pen to paper has meant the world to me. I love you my friend and value your friendship dearly.

Maggie K, Sarah Marie and others who chimed in with their own brilliant telly making anecdotes. Between us we have enough for Lizzie to have many more adventures.

The late Barbara Windsor. Working with you during those early years of my TV career was a pleasure and an inspiration. Thank you for all that you taught me and as promised, I put it into practice every day.

To all the lovely telly folk out there who I have worked with over the years. Thank you for making it such a wonderfully creative industry to be a part of. Special love to all those working in Breakfast TV – you are all brilliant and working hard while the rest of us are sleeping. Breakfast telly is still the hardest genre I've ever worked on.

The Film & TV Charity. Thank you for helping so many of my colleagues including myself during our darkest hour. Our industry was decimated during the Covid pandemic and so many freelancers fell between the cracks with no government assistance. Your kindness made such a difference to so many of us when we needed it most.

Sean Stembridge and the team at Creative Chameleon for the fantastic book cover and artwork designs. Collaborating with you has been a pleasure and I look forward to us working together on my future books.

To my wonderful family and friends for your love and nurturing, especially Jackie Mews for throwing me a lifeline when the Covid pandemic left me without a way to earn a living. I was proud to be a parcel ninja alongside you. Thank you x

My husband Martin. Thank you for your love, patience and for keeping me going when the hours were long, the contract gaps looming and all the drama in between. I love you dearly and I'm proud to shout it across the world.

Finally, thank you to all my readers. Without you, I wouldn't be on this exciting ride, doing what I love. Your support, feedback and loyalty mean the world to me and I hope that you have enjoyed Lizzie's adventures just as much as the Orphan Boys.

ABOUT THE AUTHOR

Phil Mews

Born in Bishop Auckland, Phil grew up on his family farm with his parents and two brothers. Following the death of his parents in the late 1970s, Phil was sent away to boarding school  at the age of eight with the help of a grant from a Masonic charity. After graduating from university, he spent time working in India, Israel and Hong Kong before returning to the UK.

He has spent the last twenty-four years in television production working alongside Barbara Windsor, Liza Minelli and Graham Norton on some of Britain's biggest productions, one of which led to him and his team being nominated for a BAFTA award. Phil has also reported from the red carpet at the BAFTAs and numerous film premieres for Channel 4, interviewing a host of Hollywood A-List stars. In 2015 whilst working together, writer and broadcaster Sandi Toksvig encouraged him to write his childhood memoir, Orphan Boys which was published in July 2018 by John Blake and has sold thousands of copies around the world propelling the book into Amazon's Bestseller lists.

The Girl On The Red Carpet was inspired by Phil's time working in breakfast television. Phil is currently writing his third book and is still working in television production. He lives in County Durham with his husband and their Jack Russell terrier.

BOOKS BY THIS AUTHOR

Orphan Boys

Orphan Boys

"Them poor bairns, it's heartbreaking," she said as she wiped a tear from her face with her duster. "Poor little orphans." "For a second I wondered who she was talking about and then it hit me. Orphans? We were orphans. I felt as if I'd been punched."

1976 – the hottest summer for a generation and life was perfect for the two young brothers, Philip and Roger. They lived an idyllic life on a farm in the picturesque dales of the north of England.

Their days were spent on the farm, playing on Tarzan swings, building dens and swimming outdoors, until their perfect existence was plunged into darkness when tragedy struck the family. Within a ten-week period, the boys had lost both their parents and were left as orphans.

This is the story of how Philip and his brother Roger found the courage to live as orphans, of how their grandparents and aunt stepped in to bring them up and how a community came together to deal with the consequences that the devastation of death had left behind.

Orphan Boys is a story full of love, strength and hope – an uplifting tale of one family's survival and of how they faced down the huge challenges that life – and death – can inflict on us.

Praise for Orphan Boys:

"A charming, heartfelt, heart-breaking memoir" – Sandi Toksvig, Broadcaster and Writer

"A wonderful, affecting, moving and powerful story" – Kirsty Wark, Broadcaster, Journalist and Writer

"Highly recommended" – Diane Louise Jordan, Presenter: Songs of Praise, Blue Peter

"An uplifting, heart-warming and life-affirming memoir" – Trisha Ashley, Sunday Times

Bestselling Author

"The captivating and tragic story of a family who, within ten weeks, lost their mother and father. Written by their son with loving tenderness, it uniquely captures the confusion and sense of time and place whilst allowing the emotion to play out. With powerful, visual testimony, this is highly recommended" - Stephen Bennett, BAFTA winning Director

AFTERWORD

If you have enjoyed this book, please do take the time to leave a review on Amazon and Goodreads. These reviews help us authors enormously and spur us on to write more books for you to enjoy. Thank you.

Printed in Great Britain
by Amazon

25535777R00245